PRAISE FOR *THE FIRST WOMAN*

A S..., ..., OBSERVER, *DAILY MAIL*, *BBC CULTURE*,
OPRAH MAGAZINE, *TIME MAGAZINE*, *WASHINGTON POST* &
IRISH INDEPENDENT BOOK OF THE YEAR, 2020

A *GUARDIAN*, *TELEGRAPH MAGAZINE*, *TIMES*, *I*, *STYLIST* &
IRISH TIMES BEST BOOK OF THE AUTUMN

A *WATERSTONES*, *EVENING STANDARD*, APPLE BOOKS &
BOOKSELLER BEST BOOK OF THE MONTH

'Jennifer Makumbi is a ...   ...ddo-Lodge

'A novel bursting with ...   ...mythic and
the modern, happily i...   ...ss Uganda's
miscellaneousness, it'...

...*unday Times*

'Kirabo's odyssey makes for a riveting, exuberant novel, a coming-of-age
like no other… A mesmerizing feminist epic.'   *O, the Oprah Magazine*

'All around, Nansubuga Makumbi opens up vistas of oppression: Idi
Amin's reign of terror and the patriarchal despotism against which
women have to struggle. Bursting with resilient humour, the novel is as
engaging as it is informative.'   *The Times* (Best Books of 2020)

'[Makumbi] does for Ugandan literature what Chinua Achebe did for
Nigerian writing.'   *Guardian*

'Fantastic… Packed with passion and drama – and in possession of
sharp political elbows – *The First Woman* finally becomes a moving
and resonant celebration of sisterhood.'   *Daily Mail*

'Makumbi's prose is irresistible and poignant, with remarkable wit,
heart and charm – poetic and nuanced, brilliant and sly, openhearted
and cunning, balancing discordant truths in wise ruminations. *The First
Woman* rewards the reader with one of the most outstanding heroines
and the incredible honor of journeying by her side.'   *New York Times*

'The genius of this novel is in its subtlety: home truths about the treatment of women throughout history are hidden like gems within the utterly engaging tale of a single girl... So, I'm calling it now: *The First Woman* will soon be considered a coming-of-age classic. And rightly so.'

Stylist

'*The First Woman* by Jennifer Nansubuga Makumbi is the feminist coming-of-age story we've been waiting for. With the timeless quality of a story shared from lips to ears, this novel is a page-turner and a mind-blower.'

Tayari Jones, author of *An American Marriage*, winner of the Women's Prize for Fiction, 2019

'Bewitching... Jennifer Nansubuga Makumbi is a mesmerising storyteller, slowly pulling readers in with a captivating cast of multifaceted characters and a soupçon of magical realism guaranteed to appeal to fans of Isabel Allende, Julia Alvarez, or Yaa Gyasi's *Homegoing*.'

Library Journal (starred review)

'*The First Woman* is captivating, wise, humorous and tender: Makumbi has come back stronger than ever. This is a tale about Kirabo and her family, and her place in the world as she searches for her mother and a true sense of belonging. But most of all, this is a book about the stories that define us, and those we tell to redefine ourselves. A riveting read.'

Maaza Mengiste, author of *The Shadow King*

'A beautiful coming-of-age story, *The First Woman* by Jennifer Nansubuga Makumbi is set to the backdrop of a small Ugandan village. Surrounded by strong women, protagonist Kirabo starts to miss the mother she never knew and the book follows her journey growing up and finding her place in the world. It's a tale steeped in folklore and feminism, rebellion and longing.' *Evening Standard*

'Makumbi balances heartbreak with humour... The novel is also a discourse on power (whether political, social or sexual), but executed with a beautifully light touch.' *Daily Telegraph*

'A standout coming-of-age novel about parents, friendship and story-telling.'
Mail on Sunday

'In lyrical prose, Jennifer Nansubuga Makumbi renders Kirabo's coming-of-age tale as a tender depiction of evolving womanhood, self-awareness in a tight-knit community and the path back to family and history.'
Time

'In *The First Woman*, Jennifer Nansubuga Makumbi takes the classic male quest for identity and turns it spectacularly on its head. Kirabo's journey toward self-possession is a beautiful, wise, and exhilarating read.'
Lily King, author of *Writers & Lovers*

'An intoxicating coming-of-age tale set amidst the brutality of Idi Amin's Uganda, *The First Woman* is a hymn to survival, rebellion and the enduring power of the female spirit.'
Waterstones (October's Best Books)

'Kirabo, the protagonist of Jennifer Nansubuga Makumbi's *The First Woman*, is a wonderful, daring character who is growing up in the patriarchal society of 1970s Uganda. Intricately woven with themes of feminism, mythology and tradition, this exquisitely written and compelling story delivers a thoroughly satisfying ending.'
Abi Daré, author of *The Girl With the Louding Voice*

'A feminist coming-of-age epic... Her intimate prose is charming and compulsively readable. With equal parts wisdom and wry humour, [Makumbi] casts Kirabo as a character you care about... *The First Woman* is a refreshing bildungsroman that offers both a formidable heroine and an ornate snapshot of 20th-century Uganda.'
Literary Review

'A powerful coming-of-age tale... Kirabo is a fantastic character – headstrong and curious – and the way Ugandan myths are woven through the story is mesmerising.'
Good Housekeeping

THE FIRST WOMAN

Jennifer Nansubuga Makumbi

ONEWORLD

A Oneworld Book

First published in Great Britain and Australia by Oneworld Publications, 2020
This paperback edition published 2021
Reprinted twice in 2021

ISBN 978-1-78607-858-2
eBook ISBN 978-1-78607-789-9

Set in Monotype Dante by Tetragon, London
Printed and bound in Great Britain by Clays Ltd, Elcograf S.p.A.

Oneworld Publications
10 Bloomsbury Street
London WC1B 3SR
England

MIX
Paper from
responsible sources
FSC® C018072

CONTENTS

THE WITCH

1

May 1975

Until that night, Kirabo had not cared about her. She was curious on occasion (*Where is she? What does she look like? How does it feel to have a mother?*, that sort of thing), but whenever she asked about her, and family said *No one knows about her*, in that never-mind way of large families, she dropped it. After all, she was with family and she was loved. But then recently her second self, the one who did mad things, had started to fly out of her body and she had linked the two.

On this occasion, when she asked about her mother, and family fobbed her off again with *Don't think about her; think about your grandparents and your father*, something tore. It must have been the new suspicion (*Maybe she does not want me because I am…*) that cut like razors.

A mosquito came zwinging. It must have gorged itself on someone because its song was slow and deep, unlike the skinny, high-pitched hungry ones that flew as if crazed. Kirabo's eyes found it and followed it, followed it, and, rising to her knees, she clapped it so hard her palms burned. She brought her hands to the candle to check her prize. Black blood: yesterday's. There is no satisfaction like clapping a bloated mosquito out of existence mid-air. She wiped mosquito mash on a stray piece of paper and sat back and waited again.

Kirabo wanted storytelling, but the teenagers were engrossed in gossip. They lounged on three bunk beds in the girls' bedroom. Some lay, some sat, legs dangling, others cross-legged, squeezed cosily, two or three to a bed. They had gathered as usual, after supper, to chatter before going off to sleep. Kirabo was not welcome.

For a while she had watched them, waiting to catch a pause, a breath, a tick of silence in their babble, to wedge in her call to storytelling – nothing. Finally, she gritted her teeth and called 'Once, a day came…' but her voice carried too far above the teenagers' heads and rang impatient in the rafters.

The hush that fell could have brought down trees. Teenagers' heads turned, eyes glaring (*But who does this child think she is?*), some seething (*What makes you think we want to hear your stories?*). None answered her call.

Another twelve-year-old would have been intimidated – there were ten teenagers in the room – but not Kirabo. Not visibly, anyway. She stared straight ahead, lips pouting. She was the kabejja of her grandparents, which meant that all the love in the house belonged to her, and whether they liked it or not, the teenagers, her aunts and uncles, would sit quietly and suffer her story. But Kirabo's eyes – the first thing you saw on her skinny frame, with eyelids darker than shadows and lashes as long as brush bristles – betrayed her. They blinked rapidly, a sign that she was not immune to the angry silence.

Unfortunately, tradition was that she could not start her story until the audience granted her permission, but she had begun by annoying them.

On the floor in front of Kirabo was a kerosene candle. The tadooba only partially lit the room, throwing her shadow, elongated like a mural and twitchy like a spectre, against the wall. She looked down at the candle's flame. A slender column of smoke rose off it and streamed up to the beams. A savage thought occurred to her: she could blow the flame out and turn the room blind dark. And to annoy the teenagers properly, she would scamper off to Grandfather's bedroom with the matchbox. Instead, Kirabo cradled the fragile flame between her palms to protect it from her breath. Her evil self, the one who quickened her breath and brought vengeful thoughts, retreated.

Still no response to her call. The teenagers' rejection of her story gripped the room like a sly fart. Why were there so many of them in her home, anyway? They came uninvited, usually at the beginning of the year, and crowded the place as if it was a hostel. The sheer number of them made her feel like a calf in a herd.

Kirabo blinked the spite away. Most of the teenagers were Grand-mother's relatives. They came because her grandfather was good at keeping children in school. Also, Great-Grand Luutu had built the schools and churches, and Grandfather was on the board of governors for all schools – Catholic and Protestant, primary and secondary – in the area. When he asked for a place in any of the schools, he got it. His house was so close by they did not have to walk a long way to school. Grandfather's mantra was 'A girl uneducated is an oppressed wife in the making.' Grandmother was renowned for keeping girls safe from pregnancy. All the girls that passed through her hands finished their studies. Still, Kirabo wanted to tell the teenagers to go back where they came from if they didn't want to hear her stories, but some were her father's siblings. Unfortunately, she didn't know who was who, since everyone seemed to come and go during school breaks and they all called Grandmother 'Maama' and Grandfather 'Taata'. To ask *By the way, who are my grandparents'* real *children?* would earn her a smacking.

'Kin, you were our eyes.' Grandfather's voice leapt over the wall from the room next door, granting her permission to tell her story.

Kirabo perked up, her face a beam of triumph. She glanced side-ways at the teenagers; their eyes were slaughter. She bit back a smirk. She had worked hard at this story. Told it to Giibwa – her best friend when they were not fighting – and Giibwa was awed. Grandmother, not disposed to wasting words on empty compliments, had said, 'Your skill is growing.' The day before, when Kirabo took the goats to graze, she stood on top of an anthill and told it to the plain. The story came out so perfectly the goats stood in awe.

'Once, a day came when a man – his name was Luzze – married his woman—'

'Would he marry *your* woman instead?' a boy sneered under his breath. Kirabo ignored him.

'They had many children, but they were all girls—'

A girl snorted as if Kirabo's story was already predictable.

'Luzze became sad, as every time the woman had another girl. At first, he thought it was bad luck that girl babies kept coming. But then the woman made it a habit; every time, girl-girl, girl-girl, eh. One day, Luzze called her: "I have been patient," he said, puffing on his pipe, "but I have decided to bring someone else to help you."'

Kirabo took a breath to gauge her audience's attention; the teenagers were silent, but their ire was still stiff in the air.

'That year, Luzze married another woman. Through time they had many children, but they were all girls. Luzze despaired. Why were girl-bearing women not labelled, so he could avoid them? Still, he married a third woman. She bore him many children, but they too were girls. One day, Luzze called his three wives into the house and gave them an ultimatum. "From today onwards, if you, or you or you" – he jabbed a finger at each woman – "bear me another girl, don't bring her home."

'That year, the women worked harder. They fell pregnant. The first one to deliver had a daughter. One look at the baby and she was packing. The second delivered. It was a girl. She too left. When the third delivered, it was a boy. She lifted her breasts to the sky. But wait; there was something left in her stomach. She pushed, and out came a girl. The woman despaired. She looked first at her son and then at the daughter, at the son again and then the daughter. She made up her mind.

'Next to her was an anthill. You know, in those days babies were delivered in matooke plantations. The anthill had a big hole that opened into the ground. The woman picked up the baby girl and stuffed her inside the hole. Then, she carried the baby boy home and presented him to Luzze.

'The celebration! The jubilation!'

Kirabo was so lost in her story, waving her arms about, making faces, making Luzze's voice, that she did not care whether her audience was engrossed.

'Luzze named the boy Mulinde because he had waited a long time for him to be born. Meanwhile, every day, the woman crept back to the plantation and nursed her daughter. As she stuffed her back into the hole, she would shush, "Stay quiet." But as the daughter grew, she devised songs to keep herself company and to make the darkness bearable. Meanwhile, Mulinde explored the villages, fields, hills, swamps, until one day he walked past the anthill and heard a sweet but sad song:

'"We were born multiple like twins – Wasswa.
   But Father had dropped a weighty word – Wasswa.
   You bear a girl, don't bother bringing her home – Wasswa.
   But a boy, bring the boy home – Wasswa.
   I keep my own company with song – Wasswa.
   Oh, Wasswa, you are a lie – Wasswa.
   Oh, Wasswa, you are a lie – Wasswa."

'The song tugged at Mulinde's heart. When he went home, the song followed him. The following day it hauled him back to the anthill. And the day after. And every day. At mealtimes, he kept some of his food, and when he got a chance, he crept to the anthill and threw the food down the hole. Still the song came.

'Luzze noticed that Mulinde was growing cheerless. When he asked what was wrong, Mulinde had no words. Luzze was so troubled he kept an eye on his son. In time, he noted that Mulinde kept some of his food and after lunch disappeared into the plantation. One day he followed him.

'What he saw almost blinded him. The anthill in the plantation started to sing, but instead of fleeing, Mulinde trotted, *titi-titi, titi-titi*, up to it and fed it his food. Luzze grabbed his son, ran home and sounded the alarm drums – *gwanga mujje, gwanga mujje, gwanga mujje*.

'All men, wherever they were, whatever they were doing, picked up their weapons and converged in Luzze's courtyard. Luzze addressed them:

'"Brothers, this is not for shivering cowards. Something beyond words is in my plantation, inside an anthill. We must approach with caution. If you are liquid-hearted, stay here with the women and children."

'Real men – warriors, hunters, trackers, smiths and medicine men – tightened their girdles and surrounded the plantation. Then they proceeded, muscles straining as they crouched, palms sweating around weapons. They trod softly, as if the earth would crumble, hardly breathing. Finally, they had the anthill surrounded. It started to sing. Luzze put his spear down and carefully dug the anthill. After a while, a girl child emerged. She was fully formed, totally human, only crumpled. The men threw their weapons down and wiped away their sweat.

'Even though the sun blinded her and she had to shield her eyes with her hand to look up at the huge men, even though she was as pale as a queen termite from the lack of sunshine, even though she was surrounded by a vast world she did not understand, the girl sang:

> '"We were born multiple like twins – Wasswa,
> But father had dropped a heavy word – Wasswa.
> You bear a girl don't bother bringing her home – Wasswa,
> But a boy, bring the boy home – Wasswa.
> Oh, Wasswa, you are a lie – Wasswa…"

'Luzze looked at his son, then at the girl, at the son again, then the girl. Finally, it dawned. He lodged his spear so forcefully into the earth it quivered. "Where is she? Today she will—" He did not complete the threat. The misnaming of his family – a Wasswa called Mulinde? And poor Nnakato denied sunshine? Then there was himself, Ssalongo, ultra-virile, called plain Luzze, like ordinary men.

'For some time, nothing stirred. Just this long hush that fell over the gallants and over the matooke plantation and stretched to where the women and the cowards stood. Now and again, the real men shook their heads and sucked their teeth, but no words. Their spears lay useless on the ground. You see, in the face of a singing child, the weapons accused them.

'"Women," one of the heroes finally sighed, "the way they seem so weak and helpless and you feel sorry for them. But I am telling you, beneath that helplessness they are deep; a dangerous depth without a bottom." He nailed the words into a fist with an open palm. "You live with them, love them and have children with them, thinking they are fellow humans, but I am telling you, you know nothing."

'"Kdto. Even then" – another shook his head – "this one is a woman and a half."

'"Me, I gave up on women a long time ago," another said. "You expect them to do this, they do that. You think they are here but they are there. Today they are this, tomorrow they are that. A woman will kill you with your eyes open like this" – he opened his eyes wide – "but you will not see it coming."

'But it was the women who were most enraged. You know what they say: no wrath like moral women against a wicked one. At the sight of the child, the good women of the community lacerated themselves with fury.

'"A whole woman – hmm? With breasts – hmm? To bury her own child in an anthill?"

'"She is no woman, that one – she is an animal."

'"It is such women who make us all look bad."

'"And you wonder why the world thinks we are all evil."

'"Where is she? Let her come and explain."

'The women so incensed themselves that had they got their hands on Luzze's woman, they would have ripped her to shreds. As for me, Kirabo Nnamiiro, I could not wait for retribution. I hurried home to Nattetta on these feet' – Kirabo pointed to her feet – 'to tell the tale of a woman who buried her daughter in an anthill to remain in marriage.'

For a moment, the house was silent. Kirabo had begun to revel in the success of her storytelling when she sensed an anxiety in the air. As if she had stumbled on to something she should not know. But then Grandfather broke out: 'Oh, ho ho ho. Is this child a griot or is she something else? Ah, ah, this I have never seen. Just like my grand-mother. When my grandmother raised her voice in a tale, even the mice fell silent.'

'Dala dala,' Grandmother agreed.

But the teenagers did not congratulate her. Girls stood up and threw the boys off their beds. The boys slid down, yawned and ambled towards their bedroom. The teenagers' rejection of her story stung. Kirabo's head dropped, her eyes welling up. That was when she whis-pered, 'Where is my mother?', making sure her grandparents did not hear.

The teenagers stopped, exchanged looks.

'I want to go to my mother,' Kirabo mumbled. She was sure her mother would love her story.

'Ha,' a boy clapped in belated awe. 'Did you hear Kirabo's story?'

'Me, I told you a long time ago – that child is gifted.'

'Too gifted. I couldn't tell stories at her age.'

'I still couldn't, even if you paid me.' That was Gayi, one of the big girls.

The teenagers were working hard at their awe because if Grandfather found out Kirabo had been made to long for her mother, someone was going to cry. Kirabo had to be consoled before she went to bed.

'Oh, Kirabo' – Gayi's crooning would melt a stone – 'is sleep troubling you? Let me take you outside to relieve yourself.' She held

Kirabo's hand and led her into the diiro, the living and dining room, picked up the hurricane lamp on the coffee table and stepped outside. Normally, Kirabo enjoyed their mawkish attention after she threatened the teenagers, but not this time. No one had answered her question about her mother. She slumped into self-pity.

'My mother does not want me.'

The teenagers stiffened.

'Because I am a witch.'

Kirabo did not see them relax. She had never confessed about her two selves, let alone flying, but that day the pain was intense.

'That is silly, Kirabo.' Gayi rubbed the back of her neck. 'How can you be a witch?'

'Then where is she?'

'We don't know. No one does.'

The other teenagers, who had also come out to use the toilet, remained quiet; a desperate quiet, as if Kirabo had opened the doorway to where a monster was chained.

'Don't think about her.' Gayi pulled Kirabo close to herself. 'Think about Tom and how he loves you.'

'Indeed,' the teenagers agreed.

'And you know your grandparents would give the world for you.'

'Too true,' a boy said. 'I tell you, Kirabo, if you died today, those two would offer to be buried instead.'

Kirabo smiled despite her pain. It was true, although Grandmother loved her carefully because loving her too much could be tragic. But Grandfather was brazen. He did not care that she might get spoilt. And Kirabo wielded his love ruthlessly over the teenagers and the villages. As for Tom, her father, his love was in a hurry. He came briefly from the city and wrapped it around her for an hour or two. Nonetheless, that night, Kirabo felt that once again the family had avoided telling her about her mother. Yet to ask her grandparents would be to say their love was not enough.

As she waited for the teenagers taking turns to use the toilet, she looked around. The night was solid. The moon was mean and remote, the stars thin and scanty. A shooting star fell out of the sky, but as Kirabo gasped, it vanished. *My mother is somewhere under that sky. Perhaps she found out her baby had a split self and abandoned me. Perhaps I started flying out of my body as soon as I was born.* Perhaps and perhaps swirled, stirring a pain she could not take to Grandfather or Grandmother and say *Jjajja, it hurts here.*

This is when Kirabo decided to consult Nsuuta, the blind witch down the road. Though Nsuuta was practically blind, behind her blindness she could see. But Nsuuta was not just a witch – she was Grandmother's foe. Their feud was Mount Kilimanjaro. Apparently, Nsuuta had stolen love from the family. Tom, Kirabo's father, loved Nsuuta as much as Grandmother, his own mother. Some said he loved Nsuuta more. If that is not witchery, then there is no witchery in the world. Thus Kirabo consulting Nsuuta meant betraying Grandmother in the most despicable way. But that night, with none of her family offering to help find her mother, Kirabo saw no other option.

2

'Sit properly!'

Kirabo snapped her legs closed.

'Hffm.' A boy turned his head away, fanning his scrunched-up nose as if the smell from between her legs was killing him.

'Thu,' another dry-spat. 'She is twelve, but we still remind her.'

Kirabo tightened her legs.

'Kirabo' – Gayi's voice was soft – 'you cannot sit like men. Always kneel. You will not offend anyone that way.'

Kirabo got down on her knees and sat back on her heels in a feminine posture. But inside she was tremulous with palpitations. Revulsion, self-disgust and anger tore at her; she never chose to be born with that *thing*.

'That is better,' Gayi was saying. 'When you sit on a chair, cross your legs at the ankles to—'

Kirabo did not see it happen. She blinked once and next her evil self was out of her body and into the room. She flitted from wall to wall, like a newborn ghost lost. She flew with eyes closed because the emotion was too intense. For a long time, she swooped and darted, her mind raging over this foul body that made people spit. She swooped and darted, swooped and darted, a bat spooked in daytime.

But then, outside the house, it started to rain. The din on the iron roof was so harsh it muted everything. She stopped flying, hovered and listened to the rain. There was something magical about rain pummelling iron sheets. It soothed, lulled. Her breathing slowed. Calm descended. She opened her eyes. The beams, big and black, were so close she could touch them. The walls seemed to have hemmed them in. The rain stopped. It stopped suddenly. As if it too was listening. *Matalisi*, a radio programme, wafted like a whisper. When the voices of the teenagers drifted to her, Kirabo looked below.

In a corner, her body was fidgeting in the feminine posture. Kirabo had not learnt to sit like other women. Her legs hurt easily. Guilt set in about leaving her good self down there under the bullying eyes of the teenagers. The thought set her heart racing, emotion rising again. Luckily, the rain came back, this time wild, as if a giant in the sky was pouring pebbles on the roof. It drowned her racing heart and it slowed. Yet she could not find rest. She decided to fly out of the room.

On the right was Grandfather's bedroom. If she flew in there, he was probably dyeing his hair with Kanta using a blackened toothbrush. Or he was screwing the segments of his Gillette razor together, readying himself to brush the soapy lather across his jaw and shave, making faces as he went. Grandfather's bedroom smelt of Barbasol.

To the left was Grandmother's bedroom. No chance of flying in there. It was the darkest and stuffiest room in the house. Its small window, which Grandmother opened grudgingly, never refreshed the room.

She flew through the third door into the diiro. She ignored the pictures on the walls – a blue-eyed Christ with peculiarly feminine hands on a calendar, Sir Edward Muteesa, whose handsomeness made women swoon, then her favourite picture, Grandmother and Grandfather on their wedding day. Instead, she soared to her favourite place, the ceiling. She turned, lay flat on her back and stared at the ceiling. She counted the patterns of squares, deepening her solitude. There were smaller squares within the squares; she counted those too. But there were even littler ones in those, and then littler ones within them, until the ceiling was nothing but a swarm of squares. Tranquillity unfurled like a blanket of clouds. Her seclusion was complete. The rain was background noise. The anger, the revulsion, even the disgust at the foulness between her legs, drained from her body and dripped to the floor. Lull.

She did not know how long she had been up on the ceiling when she heard someone calling.

'Kirabo?'

She plummeted…

'Your grandmother's calling you.'

…and fell back into her body. A trembling feverishness gripped her. The walls of the back room were unsteady. She lifted her bottom off her heels. The left leg was dead, the right one hurt desperately. She closed her eyes to stop the dizziness and stretched out her legs to allow blood to flow into them.

'Kirabo, did I say your grandmother's calling you?'

She opened her eyes. The world was steady now.

'Kirabo!'

'What? My legs are numb!'

'Don't you snap at me.'

'Are you sure that child is not hard of hearing?'

'No, just selective; she hears what she wants to hear.'

'I swear she fell asleep.'

'Did I hear someone picking on kabejja?' Grandfather's voice came from his bedroom. 'Is it possible she is tired?'

The teenagers fell silent, but their eyes made threats. Kirabo hid her smile as she stood up. She was relieved. The teenagers hadn't seen her flight – they were irritated, not worried.

Outside, darkness was total. A residual drizzle from the downpour persisted. Kirabo sidled along the verandah until it ran out. For a moment, she stood on the edge, dreading the mud. Then she plunged. The cold of the rain stung. She tried to sprint, but the mud held back her slippers, sucking them away from the soles of her feet.

'Where were you?' Grandmother asked when Kirabo got to the kitchen. 'I have been calling and calling.'

Kirabo shivered.

'Are you all right?'

She nodded.

Grandmother looked in her face, then felt Kirabo's forehead with the back of her hand. Reassured, she said, 'Take that basket of food to the house.'

It was two days since Kirabo had made up her mind to consult Nsuuta, the blind witch. Two days during which she had not found a moment to slip away. But after this flight to the ceiling, right in front of the teenagers, she had to create an opportunity. What next: flying in class during lessons?

3

The moment presented itself at dusk the following day. Grandfather was in his bedroom listening to *Omulimi*, a farmers' programme on the radio. Grandmother was getting supper ready. The teenagers had gone to fetch water. Kirabo was not welcome at the well in the evening because that was when the big boys were sweet on village girls and the big girls lowered their guard around village boys. Apparently, Kirabo had a nasty habit of dropping these things into conversation with her grandparents. Whenever she tried to join the teenagers, they hissed threats. There was still daylight, so Kirabo decided to go and sit with Grandmother in the kitchen and wait for the dark.

She paused at the door. Grandmother looked up, a lusansa straw pinched between her lips. A huge roll of the mat she was weaving sat coiled beside her feet. She moved up on the mat to make room for Kirabo. She added the lusansa to the edge of the mat and wove again, criss-crossing the straws above and beneath, sometimes skipping two or even three at a time, to make patterns. Kirabo remained at the door, held back by guilt that she was about to betray her grandmother.

'Are you going to stand there all evening like an electricity pole?'

Kirabo stepped inside. When she sat down, she leaned her back against Grandmother and closed her eyes. She listened to Grandmother's heart. Her body expanded and fell, expanded and fell with each breath. *I am not betraying you, Jjajja: I love you too much.* Kirabo was sure Grandmother's heart could feel hers.

She opened her eyes. Ganda chickens were strutting in. Apart from the one with chicks, they made a fuss as they flew up to the rafters. The mother hen went to the nest in a corner where she hatched her chicks and made roosting noises. The chicks ran and collected around her legs. Slowly, they disappeared into her rump as she sat on them and closed her eyes. Something caught in Kirabo's throat about Mother Hen's kind of love.

Grandmother nudged Kirabo to sit up and leaned forward to stoke the fire. When she sat back down, Kirabo did not lean against her again. She turned and looked at her. She stared for so long Grandmother asked, 'Have I grown horns?'

Kirabo wondered whether to tell Grandmother that age spots had appeared under her eyes. God must have sprinkled them while Grandmother slept, because they were not there the other day. On her chin were two hairs, thick and curled. Kirabo reached to touch them. Grandmother looked up sharply. Kirabo's hand fell. 'There is a hair on your chin.'

'It means I am going to be rich someday.'

'Giibwa said a hair is coming on my chin too.' Kirabo rubbed her chin.

Grandmother lips twitched. 'Let me see.' She tilted Kirabo's chin. 'You are going to be very rich: my wealth and yours combined.'

'Why do you smile small, Jjajja?'

Grandmother picked up another straw, tore it with her teeth and sighed. 'You are growing up, not down.'

'Hmm?'

'Now don't go hurrying to grow up to find out.'

Kirabo laughed.

'Mosquitoes have started. Go and check in the water barrels. If there is water, take a bath and stay in the house with your grandfather.'

Kirabo jumped up. Darkness was complete. She ran to the barrels but did not check them. Instead, she ran around the kitchen to the back path that went to Batte's house. There was no chance of meeting anyone that way. Batte, the village drunk, lived alone. He had already gone to Modani Baara, the local bar, to drink. She reached the rear of Batte's kitchen and crossed his front yard. The house was in total darkness. When she got to the main road, she heard the teenagers returning from the well. She stepped behind a shrub. Nothing to worry about; there would be an hour of taking baths before they noticed her absence.

When the teenagers turned into the walkway, Kirabo jumped from behind the shrub and sprinted down the road, past the Coffee Growers' Co-operative Store, known as *koparativu stowa* by everyone in the village. It was so dark that bushes, shrubs, coffee shambas and matooke plantations were one solid mass of blackness, a shield rather than a threat. Kirabo couldn't even see her hands. When she got to Nsuuta's, she ran across her courtyard, but stopped before she got to the door and tiptoed the rest of the way.

Nsuuta had not closed her front door, but a lantern was lit. *An invitation to mosquitoes*, Kirabo tsked. But then again, Nsuuta could be one of those witches even a mosquito would not dare bite. She peered through the door: Nsuuta was nowhere to be seen.

The witch's diiro was small. The lantern sat on top of a packed bookshelf with glass shutters. On the wall a huge portrait of Kabaka Muteesa II – this time in royal garb, sitting on his throne – took up most of the space. On the other wall was a calendar: December 1968. On it was the familiar image of Sir Apollo Kaggwa with Ham Mukasa that every household had on its walls, as if attempting to turn back time and wish Idi Amin away. In a basket placed next to the lantern was a heap of spectacles, some plastic, some metallic.

'Koodi?' Kirabo called.

'Karibu; we are in. Who is there?' The voice came from the inner rooms.

'Kirabo.'

'Eh?' Disbelief. 'You mean Kirabo, Miiro's morning sunshine?'

'Yes.' Kirabo had no qualms about that description.

'My grandmother, Naigaga,' Nsuuta swore. 'Is everything all right?' She appeared from the inner room, frowning. She stood in the doorway, too tall and erect for an old woman and too dignified for a witch, as far as Kirabo was concerned. Nsuuta stared at Kirabo with glassy blue eyes. 'Come, come in.'

Kirabo was transfixed. She had no idea old people could be beautiful. She had seen Nsuuta up close five years ago at Aunt YA's wedding, but all she saw then was a witch. In her own home, Nsuuta had the light skin of a gourd. Unlike Grandmother, who plaited her hair in small tucked-in knots, Nsuuta cut hers short and brushed it backwards. And her house? Too tidy. She must have trapped a newly hatched ghost, on its way to the ancestors, to do her chores.

'Everyone is fine.' Kirabo whispered to indicate that she had come on the stealth. She took a breath as she kicked off her slippers at the door. When she stepped inside, she felt Grandmother's trust evaporate with a shiver.

'Something big must be chasing Miiro's favourite.' Nsuuta sat down on a mat. 'Come, tell me what it is. But first, how is your grandfather?'

'He is there. Very well.'

Now inside Nsuuta's house, Kirabo didn't know how to start.

'Come close, let me see how you have grown.'

Kirabo shuffled forward on her knees. Perhaps Nsuuta would sense her problems through touch. Nsuuta felt Kirabo's hands, then her arms, measuring them at the joints. She touched Kirabo's face with both hands, feeling her cheekbones, eyebrows, forehead and chin.

'Hmm.' She seemed worried. 'Your features are well arranged.' Nsuuta felt Kirabo's neck. 'Oh, your grandmother's neck. Now we have a problem.'

'Ah?'

'You might turn out good-looking and dumb.'

'Ah?'

'You didn't know? Once the world stares at beauty, the brain stops growing.'

'Why?'

'Beauty brings all the fine things in life, but a plain girl needs her wits about her.'

'But I am so dark-skinned they call me Kagongolo.'

'That might help. By the time people realise a dark woman is beautiful she has walked past. But light-skinned women, *mya*' – she made a flash with her hands – 'they dazzle and blind.'

Kirabo wanted to laugh; did Nsuuta have any idea how light-skinned she was?

'People say my legs are "embarrassed".'

'Who cares about skinny legs? You are going to bury them in a busuuti.'

Kirabo had never thought of that.

'However, you might get too tall if you don't stop growing now.' Nsuuta cupped Kirabo's face in her hands. Unlike Grandmother's coarse ones, Nsuuta's hands were as soft as a baby's. *She does not do chores*, Kirabo thought.

'How old are you?'

'Started walking my thirteenth this month.'

'Just made twelve? Wo! You are already too tall. Listen, if people ever say to you, *Oh, Kirabo, you are good-looking, you are beautiful* – ignore it. You have not earned it. Otherwise, beauty can get in your way.'

'Already they call me Longie, for longido or lusolobyo.'

Nsuuta laughed relief. 'We Ganda cannot stand tall women.'

'I will never get married, anyway.'

'Good. I mean…why?'

'I am a witch.'

Nsuuta sat back and batted her eyelids. 'A witch?'

'Yes.'

'What kind of witch?'

'A real one.'

'Oh.' Pause. 'Have you talked to your grandmother?'

'How? She would not understand.'

'And I would?'

'You are the only witch I know.'

Nsuuta's face shone as if it was a compliment.

'Everyone says that despite your blindness you can see. And you make men do things for you.'

'I do.' Nsuuta was shameless. 'Tell me, how do you know you are a witch?'

'There are two of me.'

'Oh? That *is* serious. Where is the other one?'

'Right now? Inside me, both. But recently, the bad one keeps flying out. Are there two of you too? Does one of you fly out, does she make you do bad things?'

Nsuuta sighed. 'Yes, there are two of me, but we are looking at you, not at me. When did you find out there are two of you?'

'They have always been there, but then the bad one has started to fly.'

'Hmm.' Nsuuta sighed. Tell me, Kirabo. Of your two selves, who are you now, who is talking to me?'

Kirabo looked blank.

'I mean, when the bad self flies out, do you stay with the good self or do you fly with the evil one?'

Kirabo wanted to lie that she stayed with the good self, but Nsuuta already knew.

'It is a crisis, it is it not, Kirabo,' Nsuuta asked, 'when you realise you prefer your evil self?'

'I don't. In truth I don't. She takes me with her all the time.'

Nsuuta sighed. 'Your two selves are different from mine.'

'How?'

'Yours seem special… I think you are a special girl, Kirabo.'

'But I want to stop the dreadful things.'

'What dreadful things?'

'Oh—'

'You can trust me, I am a witch too.'

'Ah…it is not good…'

'If you don't tell me, how can I help you?'

'You know when people say *Don't do that, you are a girl*?' Kirabo picked at Nsuuta's mat, not meeting her eyes.

'Yes?'

'I wait until no one is around and do it,' she said. 'Just to see what happens,' she added quickly. 'Like the other time—'

'What did you do the other time?'

'You know the jackfruit tree behind our kitchen?'

Nsuuta nodded.

'I pulled down my knickers and flashed my...erm to see whether it would die or stop bearing fruit.'

'Oh, Kirabo.' Nsuuta clapped shock.

'I fight with the boys – they don't pass the ball to me and I throw them off my grandfather's pitch. I hate chores, I hate kneeling and I cannot stand babies. Sometimes I feel squeezed inside this body as if there is no space. That is when one of me flies out.'

'Kirabo.' Nsuuta held Kirabo's shoulders with both her hands and looked into her eyes. 'Maybe everyone, even your grandmother, feels squeezed sometimes.'

'Nooo.'

'Maybe occasionally she hates being a woman. Did you know she loved to run naked in the rain when we were young?'

'That grandmother of mine?' It was impossible to imagine Grandmother young, let alone running naked in the rain.

'It is our whisper; don't ever tell anyone.'

Kirabo looked into Nsuuta's glassy blue eyes. They looked back at her. Nothing in her manner suggested she was blind.

'As for your two selves, you will have to come back. I need to consult my powers.'

Something warned Kirabo against coming back. *That is how addiction to witching starts – with multiple consultations.* But what was the alternative? She had to stop the flights before they got out of hand.

'Okay, but I only want to stop flying, that is all. I don't want to do anything horrible.'

'Don't worry, I will take care of it. When you find time, come back and I will tell you what my powers saw. Now run home before you get in trouble. And remember, not a word to anyone about this.'

'I promise.'

As Kirabo stepped outside she remembered the other thing that had been troubling her.

'Nsuuta, can you find my mother for me?'

Nsuuta started. Kirabo did not wait for her to recover. She ran across the courtyard and back into the road. Behind her, Nsuuta smiled. A huge, fat smile. Twelve years ago, when Tom arrived with a six-month-old baby without a mother, Nsuuta had predicted this moment. What did her grandparents expect? That they could love the mother out of the child? Through the years Alikisa, Miiro's wife, had turned Kirabo and the rest of the family against Nsuuta. Then her blindness had grown worse, making it impossible for her to lure Kirabo over to herself. Yet, out of nowhere, Alikisa's spite had delivered the child right into her hands. With a bonus – the idea of flying out of her body. It was as if Kirabo was biologically Nsuuta's own. This notion of flying would give her the perfect angle to start. Nsuuta clapped wonderment. Sometimes God loved her as if he would never kill her. She stood up and closed her door. She was ready.

4

Since there was not a grain of sleep in sight, Kirabo opened her eyes. She raised her head off the pillow and listened. Across the room, Grandfather breathed evenly. She put her head down again, yawned, turned on her left side, then on to her back. She pushed the covers below her waist, then kicked them to the foot of her bed.

When she had returned from Nsuuta's house, her absence had not been noticed. But during supper, seeing Grandmother's trusting face, the way she fussed over her ('Why are you toying with your food, Kirabo?'), made her feel like a hyena. A chill came over her. She pulled the covers back up, yawned again and turned on her right side. She tucked in her knees and when she started to warm up, she eased on to her back. Her head fell to one side. Her hands became so weak she could not lift them.

She was outside the house, floating above the doorstep. It was as dark outside as it was in the bedroom. The wind was strong. Banana leaves flapped so close it sounded as if she stood in the middle of Grandmother's plantation. She flew across the front yard, on to the road. She started up the hill, counting the houses as she went. All the homes were asleep, the road empty, the silence blissful. Even malice appeared to be taking a rest. She came to the last home before the hilltop, the reverend's house, where Grandmother grew up when her father was reverending the villages. Closer to the hilltop, the dispensary stunk of disinfectant even at night. Nsuuta was its first nurse before she lost her sight.

Kirabo reached the top of the hill. The road cut between the twin peaks of Nattetta Hill. On the right peak was the Protestant church and its schools. On the left peak was the Catholic parish and its schools. She turned to the right, the Protestant side and her church. She flew to the roof and climbed the steeple. She stood on top of the spire holding on to the cross, the highest point in Nattetta. She held the other hand out and leaned away from the cross. She started to swing round the cross, round and round, picking up speed until she spun so fast the village below disappeared and heaven was a vortex. Then, like a cannon, she launched into the sky, up, up, until she couldn't go higher. She stayed. The world below was nothing, pitch-black. She waited, waited. Then a light began to germinate, sprouting out of the ground below like a bean planted in a tin. It grew to the size of a candle flame. When it became the size of a bulb, Kirabo's heart expanded; that was the place where her mother liv—

Bo, I am calling.

She fell back into bed. Batte was returning from Modani Baara. As drunk as a frog. Kirabo buried her head in the pillow. Somehow he only started singing when he reached Miiro's house.

> 'I am a smile-thrift, you know, Mother ran out of smiles.
> Mother gave me a voice so huge I cannot help singing.
> It was so heavy, God held it with both hands.
> But humans are such, they would bear the sky a grudge.
> Hmm-hmm, let me sing: I am a son of beauty.
> Hmm-hmm, let me dance: life is a thief.
> Hmm-hmm, let me drink: the dead were hasty.
> Where is my mother, the most beautiful…
> Who has seen her, I will reward—'

Batte's voice staggered under a high note and collapsed. The problem with Batte, Kirabo thought, was that he was shrouded in mystery. On the one hand you had Batte the village drunk, who sang the residents awake every night; and on the other there was Batte the shy recluse.

There was the rare one, Tom's best friend, whom you glimpsed when Tom came to visit. What Kirabo knew about him, she had gleaned from whispers and careless remarks.

Apparently, as a boy, Batte lived with his mother, Nnante, an unfortunate second wife in whom the husband quickly lost interest. Batte was her only child. He was a hard-working boy – always at home helping with chores, then doing homework. In school, he was so clever Miiro got him into Kololo High, an Asian secondary school in the city. However, when the time came to go out with his friends like teenage boys do, Batte remained the same good boy. Nnante started to hint that she would manage the chores, that he could put away his homework and go with Tom to look for fun, but Batte refused. She shoved him outside, saying, 'The kitchen is for women.'

'Poor Nnante,' Widow Diba once sighed, 'how she haunted the bushes.' According to Widow Diba, Nnante found every leaf, root, seed, sap and stem of a plant recommended to cure Batte's lack of adventure. It did not matter where – deep in the jungle, in the swamps, on riverbanks or on hilltops – Nnante made the journey. And she administered the herbs in all forms: smoked, sniffed, chewed, tied around Batte's waist, mixed with food or mixed in his bath. Nnante tried everything. She even took him to the River Nile and immersed him in water – but wa, nothing. Until a snake put an end to her quest.

Nnante was found stiff and dry in the bush with herbs gripped in her dead hands. Widow Diba pried them out. And when Batte was collected from the city where he worked, Diba said to him, 'You see these herbs, young man, you see them, hmm? I had to break your mother's fingers to prise them out. Take them. If they don't heal you of whatever is wrong, then I don't know.'

The herbs did worse. Batte did not go back to his city job. He stayed in his mother's little house and cried and degenerated into the village drunk – reticent and reclusive by day, singing his mother out of the grave by night.

Kirabo's mind grew incoherent. She was at Batte's house, but the church steeple floated by, followed by Nsuuta's book cabin, then her grandparents' wedding picture. Footsteps were coming, faint. They crunched loose gravel, getting louder. The shoes appeared, then the legs. She would recognise her mother's skinny legs anywhere. But before the rest of her body appeared, the legs were whipped away.

Why does rain make pee painful? Kirabo crossed her legs and made rhythmless wiggles. She peered outside; there was no one about. The toilet was too far and the rain would not stop. *You can pee on the verandah; the rain will wash it away.* She edged along the verandah. By the time she got to the furthest end, the pee was unstoppable. She fumbled with her knickers and barely managed to squat in time. Glorious relief. Columns of rainwater, formed by the corrugated iron roof, fell like lines of colourless strings. On the ground, puddles receiving them danced in rippling waves. Her own rivulet snaked from between her legs, hesitant at first, then certain, hurtling across the verandah until it fell over the edge into the puddles. The waves in the puddle grew outwards. Too bad she had run out of pee. Funny, though: it was getting warm, cosy even despite the rain.

Kirabo woke up. A wet patch under her hip was starting to get cold. She sat up. It was not even raining outside. For a while, she sat in her pee trying to come to terms with what she had done. If only she could sew her peeing hole closed. She could already hear the teenagers jeering *What map did the cartographer draw last night?* as she took her bedding out for washing. She eased her bottom on to the patch – it would be dry by morning – and lay back. But after a while, the wet patch started to make her skin itch. She sat up again.

'Jjajja?'

Miiro caught his breath and lifted his head. 'Has it rained in your bed, kabejja?'

'Yes.'

'Hop into mine then.' And he moved towards the wall.

Kirabo pulled off her wet nightdress, felt for a dress in the dark and pulled it on. She jumped into her grandfather's bed, curled into his back and smelt Barbasol on his skin. By the time he pulled the blanket up to her neck, she was asleep.

5

She almost danced when she arrived at Nsuuta's house and the front door was open. It had been two days since the first consultation, and between family and chores she had not found a single gap in which to slip away. But yesterday old Teefe had died; all the grown-ups were at her funeral. Nonetheless, Kirabo looked cautiously up and down the road, then peered into the gardens close by before sprinting across the front yard. She had also carried a satchel with her playthings, as if she was on her way to Giibwa's to play. As she got to the front door, Nsuuta appeared from the inner room, dishevelled.

'Eh, I woke you up? Forgive me. I saw the door open and thought *What luck – Nsuuta is at home.*'

'Yes, I was—'

'Did you not go to Teefe's funeral?' Kirabo stepped into the diiro. Nsuuta grabbed the door frame on both sides as if Kirabo was pushing to go into her inner rooms.

'I returned in the morning to doze a bit. I must have overslept. What is the time?'

'Towards six hours of day. The sun is almost in the middle of the sky...' Kirabo's nose caught something in the air; she sniffed, and a puzzled look came over her face.

'What is it? Does my house smell?'

'Is my grandfather here?'

'Who, Miiro? What would Miiro be doing here?'

'I smell him.'

'Smell him, child, how can you smell a person?'

'I know my grandfather: he has been here.'

Nsuuta's eyes moved left and right, left and right, without focus. 'I've been sleeping all morning: Miiro has not been here.'

'Then he is coming.'

'Really?'

'I told you, I am a wit—'

'You have to go, Kirabo.' Nsuuta crossed the diiro, grabbed Kirabo's arm and led her out of the house and across the courtyard. When they got to the road, Nsuuta let go of her hand and whispered, 'Tell me, how does your grandfather smell?'

'Like love. Love smells like flowers.'

Nsuuta threw back her head and laughed.

'But Grandmother smells like vegetables – aubergine, garden eggs, jobyo spinach.'

Nsuuta stopped laughing. A shadow floated across her blue eyes.

'I know my grandfather; he—'

'You know nothing.'

Kirabo was startled.

'How can you know anyone when you don't even know yourself?'

Kirabo wanted to protest – *I know myself* – but she was smarting from Nsuuta's rebuke. Then Nsuuta touched her shoulder as if she had snapped at the wrong person.

'What I meant, child, is that we are our circumstances. And until we have experienced all the circumstances the world can throw at us, seen all the versions we can be, we cannot claim to know ourselves. How, then, do we start to know someone else?'

Kirabo was perplexed. All she had said was that she knew her grandfather. Why all this grown-up talk?

'I have to return to Teefe's funeral,' Nsuuta said. 'Come back soon; I have got news for you.'

'You have? Did you see my flight the other night?'

Nsuuta nodded.

'I swung on the church steeple again.'

'And I saw your mother.'

Kirabo gasped. 'You too saw the light grow at her house?'

'Hmm, now go.' Nsuuta turned away.

As she watched Nsuuta walk away, Kirabo covered her mouth as if it was too much happiness and she needed to hold it back. Then she ran up the road, the satchel of playthings bobbing on her back. Finally, she was going to see her, she would know what it felt like to have a mother. Then she made promises to herself: *I will never take her for granted, no rolling my eyes the way Giibwa does at her mother.* She skipped up the road. *I will be cured of flying.*

There was still time to go and play with Giibwa before the grown-ups came back from Teefe's burial. Kirabo crossed the road and took the trail to Kisoga, Giibwa's village. The path was overgrown on both sides with bamboo thickets. Kirabo skipped along. The day was perfect – no chores, and thanks to Teefe's timely death, no grown-up in sight. Everywhere was a lightness in the air, one that came only when grown-ups were away. All that loving, that making sure you are okay and behaving, got heavy sometimes. Everywhere children played tappo, nobbo, gogolo, seven stones. The only sad thing was that Kirabo had made a promise to Nsuuta to keep quiet about her mother, which meant she couldn't share the good news with Giibwa.

She came to the Nnankya, a stream which formed the border between Nattetta and Kisoga. Because Nnankya, the spirit who owned the stream, was a clanswoman, Kirabo walked to the bank to say hello. The stream was silent, as if still. Yet tiny fish wriggled against the flow. They were so transparent she could see their spines. Kirabo shut out the rest of the world to hear the Nnankya flow. Water made irate noises where stones or plants stood in its way; it sucked its teeth when there was a dip in the gradient. Something hidden under the silt blew bubbles to the surface, tadpoles probably. For a while Kirabo listened to the stream. Then she jumped in and made a splash. Fish vanished, water muddied. Her feet sang at the cooling effect. After a while she stepped out on to the stones and skipped from one to another until she reached the other side. She said 'See you' to Nnankya and carried on.

A stench of cow dung and urine whipped her face, and Miiro's kraal came into view. It was empty; the herdsman had taken the cows to graze. She walked past the kraal, past the herdsman's house, past four other dwellings until she came to Giibwa's home. Only the labourers who worked in Miiro's coffee, cotton and matooke shambas lived here in Kisoga. Their wives grew food on the land Grandfather allocated to them while the husbands laboured. At the end of the month the men came to the house and Miiro counted out their money, which they signed for in a book.

Giibwa's mother was using her bare hands to level cow dung for mulching and manure. Kirabo knelt and greeted her. She replied in Lusoga, even though Giibwa and her father were Ganda. Apparently, Giibwa's mother had said, 'Why speak Luganda, which is lame Lusoga?' The audacity. All the grown-ups said it. Because of this, residents called her Gyamera Gyene behind her back. Some bullies called Giibwa the same to her face. But the phrase did not make sense to Kirabo. Gyamera gyene is of trees; it means they grow by themselves rather than being planted.

Kirabo asked if she and Giibwa could go out to play.

Giibwa and Kirabo could not have been more different. Giibwa was cherubic, whereas Kirabo was trouble. Giibwa was shorter, a little chubby where Kirabo was a reed. Giibwa smiled like a sunflower, Kirabo frowned and blinked. Giibwa was meek, while Kirabo was in charge, all-knowing, her views thrust on friends. Giibwa was so light-skinned, people called her Brown – 'You mean Bulawuni?' – and marvelled how God gave Mwesigwa, Giibwa's father, a beautiful daughter, and a pang of jealousy would stab Kirabo. But it would not last, because she was Miiro's kabejja and Giibwa was the daughter of his labourer.

'Some food, Kirabo?' Giibwa asked.

Kirabo shook her head: no way was she eating anything there, not after seeing Giibwa's mother roll dung with her bare hands. Giibwa served some beans and a few planks of cassava. Watching her eat, hunger started to scrape Kirabo's stomach. But it was too late now. She could not change her mind. She watched Giibwa wipe away thick gravy with the plank until the plate was clean. Before they set off, Giibwa dropped two clusters of ndiizi bananas into Kirabo's satchel.

'Today, we will go to my house,' Kirabo said.

'What do you mean, "your house"?'

'You mean I have never told you? I have a house. It is big, huge, with a lot of land. My grandfather gave it to me. Come, I will show you.'

Giibwa followed Kirabo reluctantly. 'Why would he give you a house?'

'To belong to me.'

'But you are just a girl.'

'My grandfather says I am special. It belonged to Great-Grand Luutu.'

Giibwa kept quiet. They turned into a trail going southward, which avoided the crossing at the Nnankya. They walked between sweet potato gardens, cassava, beans and maize. And when they reached the swamp it was gardens of sugar cane and yams. Finally, they joined the main road and walked towards the border between Nattetta and Bugiri, where Kirabo's great-grandfather Luutu's house was located.

The house was huge. Bigger than Miiro's. A mansion compared to Giibwa's home. It had a large stoep surrounded by mosquito mesh, which must have been the fashion back in Great-Grand Luutu's time. The rest of the house was skirted by a wide, elevated veran-dah. A shell of a car, a Zephyr, perfect greenish skin, sat on the ground overgrown with weeds. A woman vaguely related to Miiro lived there.

Kirabo, hands on hips, shook her head at the unkempt state of the property. 'This is unacceptable. Look at the state of the compound.' She waved a hand like a seasoned landlady. 'I am going to have a word with Grandfather; these are breeding grounds for snakes.'

'Why can't we play at our usual place?'

'You don't like my house: are you jealous?'
Giibwa did not reply.

Their playhouse was a space under a canopy of three young trees. The girls started by sweeping out the dry leaves. Then they tied the flowers they had picked on to the tree trunks, spread a sackcloth on the floor and laid down their babies to sleep. Kirabo had made her baby out of banana fibre, while Giibwa had moulded hers out of mud. Kirabo also laid out her white plastic doll, although she rarely played with it. She was outside peeling 'food' when Giibwa gasped, 'Kirabo, Kirabo, my cores have come.' Kirabo placed the matooke in a Blue Band tin on the fire and hurried 'inside' to Giibwa.

Giibwa had been attempting to nurse her clay baby when she made the discovery. She pulled down the neckline of her dress, but because of the buttons at the back, it came down only a fraction. As she tried to lay the baby back on the sackcloth, its head rolled off. Giibwa put the rest of her baby down and poured water in the dust to make mud, which she used to reinforce the baby's neck and reattach the head. She laid her baby out for the neck to heal. Then she turned around and asked Kirabo to undo the buttons at the back of her dress. She pulled it down and revealed a paler chest. Both Giibwa's breasts pouted. She felt the areola of her right breast. 'This one.' She shoved it at Kirabo. 'Feel it.'

Kirabo pinched and felt a lump the size of a lozenge. She gasped. 'It is real.' Then she felt the one on the left. 'This one is lagging behind: it is a pea.'

'First, the one on the right comes' – Giibwa had the impatience of a breast specialist – 'and then the one on the left.'

Kirabo pulled down her own neckline and pinched her areolas, from one to another. Wa, just empty skin which gathered as she pinched but on release spread flat across her chest. She was reaching to feel Giibwa's miracle again when Giibwa snapped her chest out of reach.

'Don't.'

'Eh?'

'Young breasts are shy: they could go back.'

Kirabo was alarmed.

'If you tamper with them, touch-touching, when they have just arrived, they disappear.' But her face said *You have a house, I have breasts; who is happier?*

'Okay.' Kirabo swallowed the snub. 'Squeeze them yourself; squeeze and see if there is milk.'

Giibwa pressed the areola hard. A tear peered from the teat and Kirabo shrieked 'Maama!' and held both cheeks in frozen awe. Giibwa sighed and stretched out her legs like a grown-up preparing to breast-feed. Kirabo sat back, dejected. To lift her spirits, she took her banana fibre doll and tried to nurse it, but without a face the doll was not appealing to nurse. Giibwa lifted her baby to breastfeed. The neck had not healed and the head rolled off again.

Kirabo laughed. 'Someone's baby has lost its head.'

'At least it has a face, but someone's – you cannot tell the face from the back of the head.'

'At least I have a proper doll.'

Kirabo lifted her plastic doll, a present from Aunt Abi who lived in the city. The doll rolled its eyes up-down, up-down, like a bulb flickering. When she turned it, a cry emanated from the back, under a lid labelled MADE IN CHINA. Kirabo caressed the long yellow hair.

'Put it on your breast then,' Giibwa challenged. 'Why don't you ever nurse it if it is your child?'

Kirabo rose to the challenge. She pulled down the top of her dress and put the doll on an indifferent nipple. The contrast between the white doll and Kirabo's black chest was so stark Giibwa burst out laughing. She hooted, pointing, unable to speak, until she paused to catch her breath. 'That charcoally breast feeding that Zungu baby. Talk about baby snatchers.' She convulsed again.

For a moment, Kirabo could not find words. Giibwa snubbing her house was one thing, the arrival of Giibwa's cores before hers was another, but this 'charcoally' jibe was more than Kirabo could take in a day. She grabbed Giibwa's baby and flung the torso outside. It shattered and the pieces scattered across the ground.

Giibwa stared at her, stunned. Then she screamed, 'You evil goat!' and grabbed Kirabo's Zungu doll. She skipped outside with it. There, she plucked off a chubby hand and threw it on the ground. Kirabo ran out and chased after her. Off came the second hand, and Kirabo stopped to pick up the doll's limbs.

Kirabo gave chase again. 'If I catch you—'

'What will you do, Charcoally? Oh-oh, there goes a leg.'

Kirabo picked up a clod and hurled it at Giibwa. Giibwa, knowing Kirabo would not dare hit her with a clod, made a show of dodging it.

'Don't ever come back to play with me, cow-udder.'

Giibwa laughed. She did not mind being cow-udder light-skinned. And that was the problem. While Giibwa had an arsenal of names emanating from Kirabo's apparent physical defects, Kirabo had none. Giibwa went for Kirabo's eyes.

'Panda eyes has no breasts, so she tells lies – *I have a house. My grand-father gave me land.*' She tossed her tail this way and that.

'It *is* my house; my grandfather gave it to me.'

'Women do not own land, jacana legs.'

'In my family we do.'

'That is because you stole us.'

'*Stole* you?' This was a new insult.

'You Baganda raided us and brought us here from our homes. My mother says you stole women and property. You stole women to improve your looks. Everywhere you went, devastation.'

'What are you bleating about, stinky goat?' Kirabo was confused. Apart from her mother, Giibwa was Ganda too.

'Now you are rich from selling us, you show off. My mother says Ganda women were so ugly your men turned to abducting women from other tribes.'

'All your mother knows is rolling dung. Who buys humans? Firstly, did your mother go to school? No. So, she does not know what she is talking about. Secondly, you stink of dung: who would buy a stinker? You are just dumb because you don't go to school.'

Giibwa lost confidence in the abduction jibe. Not going to school was her sore point. She revisited Kirabo's dark skin.

'Kagongolo, your skin is so scorched, you will bite both the upper and lower lip to bleach it with that Ambi cream.' Giibwa sucked both her lower and upper lip between her teeth and pretended to scour her face with effort.

This time, Kirabo ran after her resolutely. Giibwa was not lissom where Kirabo was wind. Giibwa kept glancing over her shoulders. As Kirabo caught up, Giibwa threw the torso of the doll at her and Kirabo stopped to pick it up.

At a safe distance, Giibwa taunted, 'All your aunts are sluts.'

'What did you say?'

'That is why your grandfather gives you property.'

'WHAT DID YOU SAY?'

'Guy, public bus; your aunt Gayi, village coach. Fancy a ride?'

Kirabo stopped chasing and pulled out her trump card. 'You know what, Giibwa? It is time my grandfather had a word with your father. You have gone beyond.'

Giibwa's face collapsed. The consequences were dire. She turned and ran out of sight. Kirabo did not chase her. When she returned to their 'house', smoke was everywhere. The matooke and mushrooms, which had been cooking, were burning. Fire had travelled to their 'house'. The sackcloth and all of their playthings on the floor were on fire. Kirabo knew she could call Giibwa back, could forget their fight and ask her friend to help her put out the flames, but she did not. Giibwa had gone too far this time. Instead, she broke leafy branches off the trees and beat the fire on the ground until it died. Everything in their 'house' was lost.

6

Nsuuta sat against the wall batting her ointment-covered eyelids. She stared through the doorway into the road as if watching the world go up and down. It was still morning, five hours of day. And because the heat had not yet escalated, a sweetness in nature persisted. Kirabo was a few metres away from the door when Nsuuta called, 'On whom do I see?'

'On me.'

'Ah, Kirabo. Come in, come in.'

Kirabo stepped in, trying to control her excitement. Even though Grandmother had travelled, Kirabo made sure to sit a little distance away from the doorway. Widow Diba might see her. Diba was that kind of resident who, if you saw her coming while you peed by the roadside, you sat down in your pee and smiled.

'Grandmother has gone to Timiina.'

'To see her relations?'

'She left this morning.'

'Wonderful. It is good for a woman to take a break from marriage and mothering. Let her clan pamper her. She will come back refreshed.'

Kirabo frowned. Was Nsuuta being old, or just being a hypocrite? Old people say pleasant things for the sake of it. Every time Widow Diba came around, Grandmother said *Happy to see you*, but under her breath she groaned *She has come*. Kirabo searched Nsuuta's face, but there was no trace of sarcasm.

'How is your grandfather?'

'He is there like that. You have news for me?'

'Oh, she is impatient,' Nsuuta clapped. 'She has not even asked how I have been.'

Kirabo greeted Nsuuta, wondering why a witch would care about good manners.

'I have considered the matters you brought to me.' Nsuuta batted her eyes as if the ointment stung. 'But I will only tell you more on condition you will not tell anyone.'

'Not a word; in God's truth.'

'Well then, firstly, look no further: I found your mother.'

'You did?' Kirabo's eyes almost popped out.

'She is alive.'

Kirabo clapped and held her mouth.

'She finished studying at Kyambogo Technical College and got married.'

There was silence. Kirabo was not interested in her mother's intellectual or marital life: where was she, when would she see her?

Nsuuta must have read her mind, for she continued, 'But she cannot see you yet.'

A knife ripped through Kirabo's chest.

'It is not safe for her to see you.'

'Not safe?'

'She has not told her husband about you.'

'About me?' Kirabo did not understand why she would be a secret.

'She was very young when she had you. And you know what the world is like to girls who get pregnant in school.'

Kirabo did not speak.

'But I saw her heart crying.' Nsuuta held both Kirabo's shoulders. She was so close Kirabo could see an outer ring, whitish, around Nsuuta's faded irises. 'As soon as you can see her, my powers will let me know. But you must promise to be patient.'

Kirabo blinked rapidly, her long lashes exaggerating the act. All the anticipation about seeing her mother, the first words she would say to her, the way she would hold her, the beautiful things her mother would say, the mountains and mountains of gifts her mother would give her.

'When will it be safe?'

'I will keep checking.'

'Can you not make her sneak to see me? I will never tell, will not even call her "Mother". Once I clap my eyes on her, *ba ppa*! I am done. Never to contact her again.'

'I don't make people do things. Only evil witches do that.'

Anger started to harden Kirabo's forehead. A witch was a witch, no such thing as a good one.

'Don't worry, you will see her. If you promise to wait until her marriage is gulu-gulu strong, I will take you to her. You don't want to destroy her life, do you?'

Kirabo did not shake her head. A marriage built on deception was already dead. The reverend said so in church.

'Keep coming to check on me so I can tell you the latest news about her. Now, the other problem—'

'What is her name?'

'Whose name?'

'My mother's.'

'The name did not come to me.' Nsuuta wiped her lips. 'The other problem was flying, yes?'

When the tears reached her eyes, Kirabo ground her teeth. You cry for the living, you give death permission. The tears remained there, not spilling, not going back.

'There are two of you and one flies out, yes?'

'Hmm.'

'Then be happy.' Nsuuta shook Kirabo's shoulders as if to loosen her pain. 'Look at me, Kirabo. You are not a witch. You are just special, eh?'

'Grandfather says I am special.' But it came out as a wail.

'He has discernment, that man, but I don't think he sees the whole picture. Listen.' Nsuuta leaned forward. 'You fly out of your body because *our original state* is in you.' She poked Kirabo in a *Lucky you* way.

'Our original state?'

'Yes, the way women were in the beginning.'

'We were not like this?'

'Of course not.' Nsuuta was indignant as if this current state were contemptible. 'We changed when the original state was bred out of us.'

Kirabo looked at her hands as if to see the change. 'Was it bad what we were? Is it what makes me do bad things?'

'No, it was not bad at all. In fact, it was wonderful for us. We were not squeezed inside, we were huge, strong, bold, loud, proud, brave, independent. But it was too much for the world and they got rid of it. However, occasionally that state is reborn in a girl like you. But in all cases it is suppressed. In your case the first woman flies out of your body because it does not relate to the way this society is.'

'Oh.' Kirabo thought for a moment. 'Does my mother know about it?'

Nsuuta was confused.

'I mean, is it the reason my mother does not want me?'

'Who told you your mother does not want you?' There was panic in Nsuuta's face.

Kirabo scratched her ear.

'Has anyone ever told you that?'

'No.'

'This has nothing to do with your mother. Your mother does not know anything about it. I am the only one who does, unless you have told someone else.'

'No! But how do we get rid of it?'

'Get rid of it? Child, it is a gift. Let it grow, let us see what we were like, what we are capable of.'

'How do you know all of this?'

'I am a witch.'

'Does it mean I am possessed?'

'No. Nothing like that. It is here.' Nsuuta put her hand on Kirabo's heart. 'It is our story.'

'Our story?'

'It is an untold story.'

'Untold?' Her eyes lit up.

'It got buried a long time ago until it was forgotten.'

'But you know it?'

'I dug it up.'

In Kirabo's experience, there was nothing like telling a story no one else knew. It guaranteed you the undivided attention of the audience, no one questioning the 'facts', no judgement of how you told it, no one smirking like they had told it better.

'Then how was it bred out?'

'In a lot of ways.' Nsuuta stood up, arms last. 'Let me go outside for a moment. There is no catching a breath with you, is there?'

Kirabo watched Nsuuta step outside towards her kitchen and wondered whether 'There is no catching a breath with you' was a rebuke. She decided she was reading too much into it.

While she waited for Nsuuta to return, Kirabo skipped through Nsuuta's back corridor to find the latrine. At the back door she was arrested by the sight of a tiny grave. It lay at the edge of the back yard, in the middle of a flower garden like a shrine. Kirabo's pee stopped pressing and she ran back to the diiro.

Nsuuta came back with two glasses of water on a wooden tray. Kirabo drank hers at once. She gave Nsuuta a moment to finish hers. After a polite interval, she prompted, 'You were saying how our original state was bred out?'

'Maybe you should come back another day—'

'That is fine, but *why* was it bred out?'

Nsuuta sighed. 'It had been perverted, made ugly.'

'That is frightening; I do not want it.'

'Probably it chose you because you are strong.'

Kirabo stopped. The idea that the original state had trusted her was confounding. Then her frustration exploded. 'Was it Adam who persecuted Eve? Was it Kintu doing it to Nnambi?'

'Kintu ne Nnambi, Adam and Eve, Mundu and Sera, they are the same people. Every tribe gave them different names. And no, it was not them. This was a state of being.'

'And you will tell the story to me?'

'On condition you will not get rid of our original state until you know all the facts.'

'All right, I will keep it. But tell me some.'

'I am tired.'

'Just a little, to help me decide whether I want to hear the rest of it.'

Nsuuta shook her head the way grown-ups surrender to a manipulative child. 'How does one start the story of our original state?'

'From the beginning.'

Nsuuta reached for Kirabo's hand and entwined it with hers. 'In the beginning—'

'Kin, you were our eyes.' For Kirabo, storytelling etiquette had to be observed.

'— humans were mere residents of the earth. We did not own it, we did not rule it; we shared it equally with plants, insects, birds and animals. But then one day, our ancients realised they could be more – they could own the earth and reign over it. Do you know what they did?'

'No.'

'They made up stories.'

'Stories?' Kirabo had imagined war.

'Yes, stories that justified our dominion. First, they came up with Kintu and made him the first human on earth. And what does being the first mean?'

'Winner and leader. Oh, and owner.'

'Exactly. The first son is heir. The firstborn has power. Even the first wife wields power. Here in Buganda we created Kintu, who married Nnambi, and they brought all plants and creatures to earth from heaven. Europeans created Adam and Eve, then claimed that their god, apparently, created everything and then gave them the earth to name, and to rule. There are similar stories around the world that justify human dominion. Through these stories humans gave themselves so much power they could destroy the world if they wished.'

'Destroy the earth how?'

'When I was young, there were wild fruits, vegetables, yams and other plants all over this place. But they no longer exist because people cleared miles and miles of the land to make way for shambas of cash crops brought over by the Europeans. Thousands and thousands of plant species replaced by two: coffee and cotton. Soon, little animals and insects that live in the soil will disappear too.'

'Kdto,' Kirabo clicked. Put like that, humans were despicable.

'As a result of these stories, humans grabbed territory – *this hill is mine...that plain is ours*. Creatures which could not fight back were tamed and locked up; those that resisted were hunted down.' Nsuuta sighed catastrophe. 'But then one day male ancients said, "Women, stop. You cannot join in."'

'Why?'

Nsuuta stood up. '*Why* is where we will start next time.'

'You cannot stop there, Nsuuta; it is going to kill me. It is like giving water to a thirsty person but taking it away when they have only had a tiny sip.'

'Go home; I am exhausted.'

'I come back tomorrow?'

'Tomorrow is too soon. I need to rest.'

'When, then?'

'In three, four days. Now go or I will forget the rest of the story.'

Kirabo used the back door. First, she went to Nsuuta's jackfruit tree, which bulged with fruit. She spat in both her palms and rubbed them together to get a good grip. As she climbed, the fact that she was not going to see her mother soon turned the knife. She got to the fruit, tapped on each along the way up, listening. None had that deep-belly sound of ripeness. She came down. Nsuuta had found her mother. It was a start. She walked to the passion fruit thicket under Nsuuta's musambya tree and shook the shrub. Fruit fell like hailstones. Kirabo shook it until nothing more fell. She collected the fruit into a heap, tied a fibre string tight around her waist and dropped the passion fruit inside her dress until she bulged. She made her way to Giibwa's home, cracking the shells between her teeth, sucking the sweetness. No, consulting Nsuuta had not been fruitless; her mother had been located. And soon this old state of being would be out of her.

Kirabo was about to turn into the trail that led to Kisoga to visit Giibwa – she had forgotten about the fight – when Kabuye's black Morris Minor came down the road. She stopped. Why were they coming home at midday? Then she remembered. It was Friday; they came home early on Fridays. Kabuye lived two villages away in Kamuli. He, his mixed-blood wife and their son, Sio, were Zungus – they kept themselves to themselves and spoke English everywhere.

Kirabo stepped off the road and stood on the ramp. She prepared her rudest face. Sio, Kabuye's son, was the recipient. The car came down. As expected, Sio sat in the back as if he was the car battery. He too was ready.

Kirabo glared.

Sio frowned.

She scowled.

He glowered.

The car went past. Sio turned and stared through the rear window. The dust raised by the car formed a cloud in the air. Kirabo stepped back on to the road, fanning the dust out of her face. Mortification burned under her skin as she recalled her first encounter with Sio many years ago.

She was seven, Sio was ten or eleven. It was at Sunday school. Kirabo's Busy Bees class was merged with Sio's Pathfinders because it was raining. The Busy Bee classroom windows had no shutters; the gusty rain blew right in.

Kirabo found herself sitting next to Sio. She had never seen him up close, and now she stared at him. At first, he stared back, and Kirabo did not look away. Sio, uncomfortable, pursed his lips and started to frown, but Kirabo kept staring. Then he smiled. Kirabo giggled. Before she could admonish herself for giggling at a boy, he reached into his pocket and gave her a red lollipop. Kirabo grabbed it. A lollipop was a lollipop, even when given to you by a boy. She unwrapped it and stuck it into her mouth. The sweetness was so intense on her rural tongue that her legs swung beneath the bench and her head tossed from side to side.

She glanced at him and asked, 'When do your feet ever breathe? You wear shoes and socks all the time.'

Sio did not reply.

'Are you dying? The way your parents never let you out of their sight.'

Sio smiled.

'Do you eat sweets and cakes and ice cream all the time in your house?'

When he did not reply, Kirabo became suspicious. She looked at him from the head downwards, taking in his pale skin, his T-shirt striped with all the colours in the world, his blue shorts, his chubby legs, his pretty socks and shoes. Along the way, she became conscious of her dry, dark, scrawny self. *He thinks he is better than us*, she thought. There was a time when her grandfather was the richest and her family the most educated in the three villages – Nattetta, Bugiri and Kamuli. Kisoga, Giibwa's village, did not count. Only labourers lived there. There was a priest in the family – Faaza Dewo, Miiro's oldest brother. There was a doctor in the family – Levi, Miiro's youngest brother, though he preferred to be called Dokita. Miiro had a diploma in agriculture from Bukalasa. All his children were educated. But then Kabuye arrived from Bungeleza with all his cars, haughty mixed-blood wife and their spoilt son, and Kirabo's family started to fade.

'You are so delicate I would beat you at football.'

Sio smiled.

'I would wrestle you to the ground, sit on your stomach, cross my legs and you would scream *walalala*.'

Sio gave her another lollipop, a yellow one this time.

It tasted like pineapple. Kirabo had two lollipops in her mouth; talking was difficult. She caught her breath and took them out of her mouth. She looked at them; they were still big. Before sticking them back in she said, 'My father speaks English properly like *pshaypshay, pshay.*' She mimicked her idea of English.

Sio said nothing.

Kirabo licked the sweets from yellow to red, concentrating on the flavours. 'Unlike your father, mine lives in the city. He drives a car bigger than your father's Mercedes. He works for the Coffee Marketing Board, but I don't show off.'

Sio burst out laughing. Then he choked and coughed. The Sunday school teacher came and tapped him on the back until he stopped.

'*I am sorry,*' Sio said in English.

'Ha,' Kirabo could not believe it. Sio spoke real Zungu English. Then it dawned on her. He did not know any Luganda. All along he had not understood a word she had said. No doubt he looked down on her because he was born in Bungeleza and his father was a surgeon and his mixed-blood mother was a nurse and they had cars and a multi-storeyed house and Sio studied in the city in a posh school and he was driven everywhere as if he had no legs and they spoke woopshywoop English. She scowled at him for the rest of the class while she ate his sweets.

At the end of the class, Sio gave her three more sweets. If it was not for the fact that she rarely saw sweets, Kirabo would have declined them, but she said '*Thank you very much*' to let Sio know she spoke English when necessary.

Sio's smile broadened and he ran to his mother, who had come to collect him. After the service, Kabuye's family never lingered. They snapped elastic smiles – which residents called *lying smiles* under their breath – and walked on to their car. But Sio came back running, with a bag. He put it down and pulled out a contraption that looked like a cross between a camera and binoculars. It had the word VIEW-MASTER between the eyepieces. All this time he spoke, but his words sounded like *schpshpsh*. He held the contraption against Kirabo's eyes.

She looked in and gasped. Inside, it was like a motionless film. It was so lifelike Kirabo did not realise she had reached to touch it until she felt Sio bring her hands down.

'It is London.'

She understood that.

He lifted Kirabo's hands and showed her how to hold the contraption. He put her forefinger on a lever and pulled it down, his finger on hers. A new picture came. Kirabo made noises. She let the lever go and it snapped loudly. She jumped. They laughed. Kirabo looked in again. London was still there. As she pulled the lever again, Sio said, *'Tower Bridge... Buckingham Palace... Westminster Abbey... Change of Guards... Crown Jewels...'* Even though Kirabo did not catch a word he said, it did not matter; the world was crisp.

She was so lost in London she did not hear Sio's mother calling. She dialled, a new picture emerged and she *ahh*ed. She dialled, dialled, while Sio gave her a commentary. When the picture she first saw returned, Sio grabbed his contraption, removed a cardboard disc, put it in a paper wallet with so many other discs, put the contraption in its leather skin, waved and dashed to his mother, leaving Kirabo in mouth-open wonderment.

When she recovered, she ran to Giibwa's to tell her about that Sio, Kabuye's son, his sweets, the *sinema* in his camera and how he did not speak an ounce of Luganda.

'Not at all?'

'Not one tiny bit like this' – Kirabo indicated a segment of her tiny finger and the girls felt so superior. 'Oh, by the way, he is so left-handed he chews with the left side of his mouth.'

'You lie. But there are no blessings on the left hand.'

'Does he need blessings? His parents are wheezing with wealth.'

Soon after that, Sio joined his parents in church for the adult service and Kirabo never saw the contraption again. He went to boarding school and grew tall and his Zungu airs grew higher. In the holidays, when he came to church his eyes looked above people's heads. He scowled all the time and Kirabo glared at him.

*

Kabuye's car had disappeared in the valley below when Kirabo realised she was inflated with passion fruit inside her dress. Ha! She stopped. Sio had seen her looking like that? She looked down at herself in dismay. Now that boy was going to imagine only his family was civilised.

7

Despite Nsuuta's instructions, by midday the following day Kirabo was running across Nsuuta's courtyard. Her excuse? *Grandmother might return from Timiina sooner. Then I will not know the story. Then I will have to get rid of our original state.* The truth was that she had thought about nothing but her mother. By morning she had convinced herself that her mother had made contact with Nsuuta in the night.

Nsuuta was not sitting in her usual place. Kirabo walked up to the door without Nsuuta's usual greeting, 'On whom do I see?' She peered inside. Nsuuta was nowhere. Then she heard the radio in the kitchen. She turned and walked to the kitchen, which was set a few yards from the house. Like all old people, Nsuuta was listening to the bilango – for the dead and their burials, last funeral rites and where they will be held, those who are in hospital dying and the mentally ill who have been lost or found.

Kirabo crept to the kitchen to test Nsuuta's fabled lumanyo, the ability to see behind her blindness. She hoped the radio would mask her footsteps. When she got to the doorstep, Nsuuta was lifting a pan of food from the fire. Kirabo stopped and stood still. Nsuuta placed the pan on the floor, threw off the thick outer layer of banana leaves and steam blew everywhere. Then she cooled her hand in cold water and removed a satchel of steamed katunkuma vegetables. She mashed them, then added them to the groundnut stew, sprinkled in salt and stirred. Kirabo remained still. Nsuuta placed the kneaded mound of matooke in a basket and on top she added pieces of sweet potatoes and cassava. Then she looked up and said, 'Kirabo, take the radio to the house first, then come back for the food basket.'

Kirabo's knees went soft; she almost suffocated on her mortification. She knelt down and greeted Nsuuta. The look on Nsuuta's face said *Don't you ever try that again.*

Nsuuta's radio was exactly like Grandmother's Sanyo. Apart from the handle and a gap where she turned the knobs on and off, it was wrapped in a kitambaala, a home-made tablecloth with crocheted floral patterns, to keep it looking new. Kirabo put the radio on the coffee table in the diiro and returned to carry the basket of food while Nsuuta took the stew to the house. Because of her rudeness, it became difficult to ask about her mother immediately.

'Get the plates from the cupboard.' Nsuuta pointed to a high cupboard in the back room. 'Today, I am not eating on my own. Even a witch gets tired of humming to herself. Then I will tell you some of the story.'

Kirabo panicked. It was rude to say no to food, but eating in Nsuuta's house was to take familiarity with a witch too far. How would she explain missing lunch at home, anyway?

Nsuuta answered Kirabo's thoughts. 'I have been thinking. Now that you come every day, we will eat early, just a little, I will tell you bits of the story and you will run home for lunch at two o'clock. How do you see that?'

'That is okay, but last night I had a feeling my mother made contact.'

'You did? That is because I saw her again, and this time she revealed more of herself. You have her eyes.'

'I do?'

'You took Tom's colour, facial structure and height, but you have your mother's eyes, nose and lips.'

Kirabo was on her knees, drinking in every word.

'For those who have never seen your mother, you look like Tom, but I tell you, if your mother had not been so light-skinned, you would look like her exactly.'

'She is light-skinned?'

'Very.'

'Yii?' Kirabo sat back wondering how that could be. Everyone said that her dark skin had been soaked in Kanta hair dye for nine months. How could her mother not be dark? 'Did she say how soon I can see her?'

'She cannot escape her husband. He is watching her too much. She does not even visit her parents. But I saw her pain.' Nsuuta held her heart. 'It is killing her, poor woman. So, whenever your hurt becomes unbearable, remember she hurts more.'

Kirabo absorbed that quietly, because her tears were not listening. Nsuuta must have felt her struggle for she rubbed Kirabo's back, round and round, the way Grandmother used to do when she struggled with constipation.

'Tell me, is your grandfather back from the city?'

'Who lied you? Grandfather has not been to Kampala at all.'

'Not even to Kayunga or Jinja?'

'Not once.'

'So how does he spend his day?'

'As usual. In the morning, he is in his coffee or cotton shambas, afternoon, if he is not at the *koparativu stowa* or those school board meetings, he goes to Nazigo.'

After eating, Nsuuta put away the food wraps while Kirabo washed the plates behind the kitchen. Then Kirabo sat down and waited.

'Where did we stop yesterday?' Nsuuta asked.

'When women were prohibited from grabbing land and animals.'

'Oh yes, that was because the ancients had told another story – that women were not of land.'

'Women not of land, how?'

'Ancients saw the universe as divided into four realms. Bring me the pencil on top of the bookshelf' – Nsuuta pointed above Kirabo's head towards the bookshelf – 'and the blue exercise book. I will show you.'

She opened the exercise book to a fresh page, placed it on the floor and drew a cross compass. 'The first realm was heaven.' She wrote HEAVEN where North would be. 'Then underworld.' She placed it on the South point. 'Then sea.' She placed it on the West point. 'And finally, land.' She placed it on the East point. 'That is the ancient compass.'

Kirabo stared at the compass. It made better sense than the one pinned on the wall of her classroom. She was tempted to say *You are not really blind, Nsuuta*, but she swallowed it.

'Heaven was the world of the gods, yes?'

'Yes.'

'The underworld is where the dead begin a new life – yes?'

'Yes.'

'If land belonged to man, what is left?'

'The sea.'

'Ah haa. The sea, the ancients claimed, was woman's realm. '

'Whaat? Women belonged in water?'

'And if they did, they could not share in land wealth, could they? "If you want property," they told women ancients, "go back to your sea and grab to your heart's content."'

'Yii yii, even when they saw baby girls born the same as boys?'

'They claimed that the very first woman rose out of the sea while the first man emerged from earth.'

'But that is not true. Nnambi was Gulu's daughter. She came from heaven.'

'Gulu was her father, but who was her mother?'

'She did not have a mother, only a father and brothers.'

'See? They had found a hole in their first story of Kintu ne Nnambi and now filled it. Nnambi got a mother. A woman who, apparently, rose from the sea. Her name was Nnamazzi. In fact, Nnamazzi was said to have brought all water bodies on land.'

'I have never heard of her.'

'Because this story was buried.' When Kirabo did not respond, Nsuuta carried on. 'Apparently, Nnamazzi was so magnificent that when Gulu saw her he was mesmerised. She gave him a lot of sons, including Walumbe, the bringer of death, and Kayikuuzi, the burrower, but only one daughter, Nnambi. Then one day, after years and years of being together, Nnamazzi, without provocation, without explanation, got up and went back to the sea. She never came back. Gulu was so heartbroken, he never remarried. He brought up his children on his own. So, if the first woman came from the sea and returned to it, women belonged there.'

'I like Nnamazzi. I like that I came out of her.'

'Focus, Kirabo; she is a story. A story which aggravated our situation. They used her to link our original state to the sea. You do not realise, but ancients had such an irrational fear of the nature of women that they would try anything to keep them under control. They supported this story by pointing to the sea. Apparently, both women and the sea were baffling, changeful: today they are this, tomorrow they are that.'

'How was the sea changeful?'

'Water has no shape, it can be this, it can be that, depending on where it flows. The sea is inconstant, it cannot be tamed, it does not yield to human cultivation, it cannot be owned; you cannot draw borders on the ocean. To the ancients, women belonged with the sea like in marriage.'

Kirabo gnashed her teeth because ancients, especially Ganda males, were just too dumb for life. 'And to them land belonged with men?'

'Land was tame. It did as it was told. They tilled it, dropped seeds into it and a few months later they harvested. They divided and owned it.'

'Like in marriage?'

'Exactly.'

'And that is how women were stopped from owning land wealth?'

'Stories have such power you cannot imagine. That one turned women into migrants on land. Since then, women have been root-less – moved not just across places but clans, tribes, nations, even races. Here in Buganda, they sold mainly girls and women into slavery to the Arabs. They were considered rootless.'

Kirabo's chest rose and fell, rose and fell. She imagined women cast into the sea – swimming, drowning, fighting sharks, building houses under the sea, being swallowed by whales – then women being sold to Arabs, being brutalised in Buwarab, and her complaints paled. She burst out, 'But could they not see that women had no gills or fins?'

'Do not make me say the obvious, Kirabo.' Nsuuta was getting impatient. 'Besides, the world is blind. Life is too rich for the eye to see everything we look at. You think you can see, but right now you are blind.'

Kirabo looked at Nsuuta's eyes.

'Yes, Kirabo,' Nsuuta answered the question in her mind. 'I only started to see what I had looked at all my life after I lost my sight.'

Kirabo closed her eyes as if it would stop Nsuuta from listening to her thoughts.

'When our ancients looked at women,' Nsuuta continued, 'they saw something else.'

'What did they see?'

'Water *in* women. Women *in* water. Think, Kirabo: how many of our stories link women to water?'

'Hmm…' Kirabo hummed her memory into action. She had been paralysed by the idea of women learning to live in water. An idea occurred to her and she snapped her fingers. 'Like River Mayanja? A woman gave birth to it. Oh, and those twin rivers, what are they called?'

'Ssezibwa and Bwanda?'

'Yes. A pregnant woman was travelling when birth pains started. She squatted on the roadside but instead of a child, water came out. It split in two. One half flowed to the east, the other to the west, and two rivers were formed. Oh' – Kirabo's memory had woken up – 'most bodies of water – wells, spas, streams – belong to women spirits. Goddess Nnalubaale owns Lake Victoria. Goddess Nnankya owns that stream on Grandfather's land. Goddess Nnambaale owns our well.'

'Because, as ancients claimed, Nnamazzi brought all the water on land.'

'Eh,' Kirabo marvelled.

'So, your grandfather's family owns most of the land in Nattetta, but does it claim Stream Nnankya or Nnambaale, the well where we collect water?'

'No.'

'Because they can't contain it.'

'Oh, I've just remembered a big one.' Kirabo was on her knees. 'This is big, Nsuuta, huge.' She held her hands above her head to show its hugeness. 'I swear ancients used this story to make women belong in water.'

'Tell me.'

'Mijinni.'

'Mijinni?'

'Don't you know mijinni, Nsuuta?'

Nsuuta shook her head.

'Tsk, mijinni are female spirits that live in rivers, wells, lakes or seas. In daytime, they stay in water. But at night they creep out. And when they come out, they turn into real women to tempt men. There are a lot of them in Jinja, they creep out of the Nile. They are beautiful, I mean, killer beautiful. When men see them, they cannot help falling in love because they seem quiet, gentle and restful. A man says *Yii maama, your beauty is going to kill me right now if I cannot be with you.* But once he takes her to his home, *ba ppa*, what happens?'

'Tell me.'

'She turns into a terrifying creature and tortures him.'

'Really?' Nsuuta's face shone.

'One time, a man took a mujinni home like that. She kept saying, "My friend, maybe this is too rushed; maybe we should get to know each other first," but did the man listen?'

'No.'

'That night, when the man got up to turn the light out, she said, "I will do it," and stretched her arm across the room and snuffed out the flame. Then, in the dark, she started to torture the man, non-stop, throughout the night. She had arms like an octopus. They were everywhere. In the morning, the man woke up on a crag in the middle of Lake Victoria, bruised and broken.'

Nsuuta gasped happily.

'Don't ever go to Mombasa, I have warned you; it is crawling with mijinni.'

'Oh?'

'You can tell a mujinni from a real woman.'

'How?'

'A mujinni has icy hands and feet.'

'Thank you for the warning. Wait there.' Nsuuta stood up and retrieved a book from the top shelf. It bulged with paper cuttings stuffed between the pages. She removed the cuttings and gave them to Kirabo. Some were images of mermaids; some were pictures of ancient ships with a woman's bust as a figurehead. The figureheads had their breasts exposed to the sea.

'Eh.' Kirabo realised something. 'But these white people: their ancients thought the sea loved women's breasts?'

'Ancient sailors thought they were trespassing on water because it was not their realm. So they used images of women to pacify the sea.'

'But what model of foolishness is this?'

'At first, they tied real women to the bow.'

'You lie, Nsuuta,' Kirabo gasped, and thanked the gods she was not white, not born in those dark days. She came to another image and exclaimed, 'Ayayayaya!'

'What?'

'This one is serious, Nsuuta.'

'What is written on the picture?'

'Ah, The Sirens and Uliesis? I cannot say the word...by William E-t-t-y.'

'What is in the picture?'

'Three naked women...are those dead humans behind them? Nsuuta, there are bones and skulls all over the place: I think the women have killed and eaten them.'

'Killed what?'

'Men. Now, a storm is bringing another ship full of men. The women are singing and dancing, glorying in the terror of the men.' She giggled. 'Oh, my father, this is mad. On the ship, the sailors are struggling with the storm to steer the boat away from the women. But this huge idiot wants to reach out for the women's breasts. The sailors are struggling with him too.' She looked at Nsuuta. 'Poor Zungu women ancients. Their men thought they were man-eaters?'

'You have no idea, Kirabo. Some claimed the women turned into seals.'

'Tsk.' She riffled through other images, then stopped. 'This one is a photograph. She is in only a bra and knickers, at a seaside holding seashells. Her name is Usula.'

'Ursula. That is James Bond.'

'He is dumb like that too?'

'Don't even ask.'

'Now look at these stupid ones.'

'Who?'

'Five men are kneeling before a woman. I think she has just emerged out of the sea because her hair is dripping and the men are pleading, or are they worshipping her?'

'They still do.'

'Oh, this one looks like us.'

'That is Yemaya. She protected slaves as they were trafficked across the seas.'

'Oh.' Kirabo paused as she imagined being trafficked across the seas. 'At least she was not an evil story if she protected our people.' Nsuuta did not respond. 'I wonder what ancients saw when they looked at women.'

'I think that in their buziba mind, the unconscious one, women were two things at once – aquatic and terrestrial. Human but fish, beautiful but grotesque, exciting but frightening, nurturing but malevolent. Today they are this shape; tomorrow they have shifted into something quite different – dubious, slippery, secretive and mysterious. What do you do with that?'

Kirabo shook her head.

'Either you tame them, or you drive them back into the sea.'

'Tame them? Like animals?'

'Indeed. Like with animals, men started to raid other societies for women. I am sure animals were laughing; look how humans are treating each other over property.'

'So it is true?'

'What is true?'

'Giibwa said our men raided Ssoga women because Ganda women were ugly.'

Nsuuta's eyes darted sightlessly, as if she had not meant her story to get too close to recent history.

'Forget Giibwa. Your family never raided anyone. Put the cuttings back in the book and return it to the shelf, exactly where it was.' When Kirabo was done, Nsuuta said, 'Now go home. I need to rest. Tomorrow, I will tell you how they got rid of our original state and shrank women.'

Kirabo ran out of Nsuuta's house, forgetting to use the back door.

8

Nsuuta was in her garden picking doodo, bbugga and nakati spinach. She did not lift her head when Kirabo announced herself, not even when she knelt to greet her. Kirabo stood up and started to help picking the vegetables, but Nsuuta stopped her. Apparently, Kirabo would pick the wild leaves. Kirabo looked at Nsuuta's faded eyes and stifled a click. There was anger in Nsuuta's silence. Someone had been and upset her. That, or Nsuuta was full of moods. Kirabo waited uneasily. Obviously her mother had not made contact; Nsuuta would be eager to tell. The realisation still had power to twist the knife in her chest. She watched Nsuuta's fingers feeling the leaves before plucking them, shaking off the soil, and putting them in the basket. *With these moods, it is no wonder she lives alone*, Kirabo thought. Nsuuta looked up as if she had heard her think.

'Let's go to the kitchen,' she said.

For a while Nsuuta worked quietly, washing the vegetables, sprinkling salt before wrapping them in banana leaves. Kirabo sat on the ramp where all Nsuuta's stoves were built into the concrete, feeling like a burden. Then Nsuuta asked, 'Is your grandmother back?'

'No; would I be here?'

'And your grandfather?'

'He is fine.'

Nsuuta sighed. She wrapped matooke in banana leaves, put the mound into a large pan and the vegetables on top for steaming. For a long time, she worked in silence. When everything was finally covered with layers of banana leaves, she stood up, arms akimbo.

'Have you been on any new flights since the last?'

'No.'

'Have you wet your bed?'

'Not since.'

'Maybe your flights are not a problem.' Nsuuta paused as if waiting for Kirabo's response. Kirabo remained quiet. 'Maybe our original state is trying to soothe you. From what I have *seen*, you are at peace when you fly. Why would you want to stop that?'

'Because it is evil.'

'Of course it is.' Nsuuta did not bother to mask her sarcasm. 'After all, everything we cannot control feels evil to us. Now, what did I say we would talk about today?'

'How our original state was bred out.'

'That is easy; if something about you is perceived as ugly, what do you do?'

'Hide it.'

'Women in our original state were rejected.'

Kirabo kept quiet. Normally Nsuuta would have built up and dramatised the rejection to give context. 'But I thought you said they were worshipped as well.'

'Worship, persecution, where is the difference?' she snapped.

When Nsuuta was off, she was really off. How could worship and persecution be the same? Her foul mood was killing the story. Kirabo cursed whoever had made her grumpy that morning.

Nsuuta knelt before a hearth and burrowed under the ash with a stick until she reached the embers. She seemed lost in her own world, as if Kirabo was not around. She removed all the ash and blew on the embers until they glowed. Next, she covered them with hay, then put a crumpled piece of paper on top. When smoke began to drift upwards, Nsuuta added thin twigs and blew on them. The fire caught easily, eating the straws and paper, licking the twigs tentatively. She waited until the flames were burning confidently before adding firewood and sitting back on her heels. Then she raised her head and smiled, as if Kirabo had just arrived. Kirabo began to suspect that she had been in the presence of the evil Nsuuta.

'You know that one person's mother is another's bad luck, kisirani.'

Kirabo nodded, but inside she was doubtful. Women being kisirani was petty persecution. Besides, it was not just men; there were women who believed they carried bad luck on their bodies. She decided to prompt Nsuuta into talking about real persecution. 'I heard that in those dark days if you got pregnant before marriage, they hung you up a tree and set a fire below.'

'When *your* grandfather opens the door in the morning and sees a woman first, what does he do?'

'Closes it and goes back to bed.'

'Why?'

'Some women are such bad omens they will foul your day, or week, or even a whole year.'

'Aha.'

Kirabo realised what Nsuuta meant and jumped to Miiro's defence. 'But it is not just Grandfather. Ssozi is the worst. If you are the first person at his shop in the morning, he tells you to wait until a man buys something from him first, or you go home and bring your little boy, even if he was born yesterday, so that he takes the money from him. A lot of women don't wait to be told; they take their baby boys with them in the morning just in case.'

Nsuuta shrugged. 'Shadows of the past.'

'Shadows?' Kirabo decided that as far as storytelling was concerned, the day was dead. Nsuuta was not trying to make it interesting at all.

'One day a man will throw himself at your feet: *I don't know what you have done to me, Kirabo. Only you can save me.*'

Kirabo laughed.

'And you,' Nsuuta said, pointing an accusing finger at Kirabo, 'feeling the little power he has given you in that moment, will forget that women were once burned alive for bewitching men.' Nsuuta sucked her teeth in disgust.

'Kdto.' Kirabo smiled. Real Nsuuta was back.

'Look, a woman worshipped here as a mother goes over there and fouls someone else's day. Or she fouls nature. Have you not heard of grown men who will flee if a woman strips naked in public?'

'Yes, Nsuuta! Oh my God, Nsuuta.' Kirabo was on her knees, gesturing everywhere because the foulness of her nakedness was the one thing that made her want to tear herself out of her body and bury it. It vexed, revolted and sickened her. At home, she had to hide her knickers after washing them so boys would not see them, even though they could display their underwear in the open to dry in broad daylight. She had never seen Grandmother's knickers; in fact, the idea of them felt vulgar. Kirabo had to sit with her legs closed, even before the hearth, because her whatnot would put the fire out.

'Do you know why I flashed that jackfruit tree?'

Nsuuta shook her head.

'Grandmother found me up the tree with the boys and said, "And you, Kirabo, climbing trees like a boy? From now on the fruit on this tree will go sour."'

'She did not!'

'The boys turned on me. That Ntaate spat and climbed down. The following day, when no one could see, I said, "Let me go back and flash that tree right and lavish."'

Nsuuta's silence was livid.

'The problem is down there.' Kirabo snapped her legs open and closed.

Nsuuta threw back her head and laughed. 'Oh, Kirabo, I love the way you don't bite your words; down where?'

'There. All the ugliness, all the rot, all the wickedness and the witchery are packed in there. When Grandmother still bathed me, she would say, "Squat and I wash your ruins."'

'You lie!'

'God in heaven.' Now Kirabo whispered, 'People call it all sorts.'

'They do? Sometimes I forget how humorous your grandmother can be – *ruins*, oh, oh.'

'Giibwa says her mother calls it "the burden" – "Did you wash your burden properly?"'

Still laughing, Nsuuta picked up the pan with the food and placed it on the fire. She asked Kirabo to take out the pan filled with dirty water and pour it outside. When Kirabo returned, she whispered to Nsuuta, 'Did you hear about the woman on the radio?'

'Which one?'

'The young widow. The one whose husband died and whose father-in-law came to her house to throw her out?'

'No.'

'Where have you been, Nsuuta? She is the only topic anyone can talk about.'

'Tell me.'

'Her husband died suddenly. He was young and rich – the only one with wealth in the family. He left her with several little ones who could not protect her. After the burial, she went home with her children. A week later, who arrives?'

'Who?'

'Father-in-law, with his clan. He says, "Eh, Muka Mwana? I have come for our children and our property. Eh, pack your bags and go back where you came from." Muka Mwana says, "As you say, Taata, I will go and pack." She goes to the bedroom. Guess what she does?'

'What?'

'Comes out naked.'

'You lie: which naked?'

'Starkers. Like a plucked chicken. She sits before her father-in-law, opens her legs wide like this' – Kirabo opened her hands wide – 'and places the whole of her foulness right there, like *bwaaa*. Then she asks, "Taata, before I go: where do I place this one? It was your son's favourite property."'

'You lie, Kirabo.'

'Father-in-law scrambles out of the chair, screaming, "Walalala, help, I have been killed." Sprints out of the house like a youth. "Muka Mwana has killed me today." Last I heard, he had to do all sorts of rituals to cleanse himself. You know what Grandfather said?'

Nsuuta shook her head.

'He said, "If the old man had become a ŋwaŋwuli that is empty of decency and has washed shame out of his eyes, let him go blind." But Grandmother said, "No amount of property is worth your essence. Once a woman has revealed herself to the world like that, that is it: her whole self is gone.'''

'Haa, but...'

'But Gayi said that what little power women have is found there. She said the widow used hers very well.'

'Aha, Miiro's sunshine. Today, you came to kill me with laughter.'

'I told you Grandfather is easy. Tom, I mean my father, is the same: they don't put barriers against me. It is Grandmother, it is always other women, apart from you, who put up barriers against girls and on themselves. I know men can be tyrants, but a lot of women are nasty to women – everybody says it, unless you have not met Jjajja Nsangi, Grandfather's sister.'

'Kirabo, have you seen God come down from heaven to make humans behave?'

'No.'

'That is because some people have appointed themselves his police. And I tell you, child, the police are far worse than God himself. That is why the day you catch your man with another woman, you will go for the woman and not him. My grandmothers called it kweluma. That is when oppressed people turn on each other or on themselves and bite. It is as a form of relief. If you cannot bite your oppressor, you bite yourself.'

For a while Kirabo was silent. Then she blurted out, 'But Grandmother does not police herself; she—'

'Did you know Alikisa has a beautiful voice?'

'Who is Alikisa?'

'Your grandmother; you did not know her name?'

Kirabo twisted her lips. All she knew was Muka Miiro.

'Alikisa Lozi Nnanono. Those were her names before she married.'

'Grandmother's voice is gruff.'

'No, child, Alikisa has the most beautiful voice in this world. Deep like the humming drum, yet soft. When we were young, I wanted a voice like hers. Unfortunately, since we have grown up, she tries to make it thin and it comes out gruff.'

'And did all the women shrink?' Kirabo steered Nsuuta away from Grandmother.

'With that kind of perversion, who would not shrink? Who would want to be huge, or loud, or brave, or any of the other characteristics men claim to be *male*? We hunched, lowered our eyes, voices, acted feeble, helpless. Even being clever became unattractive. Soon, being shrunken became feminine. Then it became beautiful and women aspired to it. That was when we began to persecute our original state out of ourselves. Once we shrunk, men had to look after us, and it was not long before they started to own us. Fathers sold daughters; husbands bought wives. Once we became a commodity, men could do whatever they wished with us. Even now our bodies do not belong to us. That is why when they need it, they will grab it. Things were so bad in some cultures, women had to be hidden away to protect them, in separate spaces where no men were allowed. Soon, they had to be spoken for by men.'

Kirabo kept quiet. An air, heavy like a warning, had sucked the light-heartedness of storytelling out of the room.

'And no one has seen our original state since?'

'I suspect Kabaka Muteesa Mukaabya did. His Amazons were in our original state. He must have put out a search for them before they were crippled. He nurtured their original state for his army. That is the last I heard.'

Kirabo went silent. For a while she blinked. It was a gross injustice Nsuuta had told her. But she was not sure she wanted to nurture a state which had been erased out of women.

'But the Bible says that God created Adam and Eve in his own image.'

'If he created them in his own image,' Nsuuta snapped, 'then afterwards Adam re-created Eve in his own image, one that suited him.'

'But which image is that, Nsuuta? You will burn in hell for saying things like that.'

'The state we are now, the shrunken one.' Nsuuta sighed dramatically. 'Kirabo, all this time I have been telling you the stories ancients used to change women. Did you hear me at all?'

Kirabo scratched her head. This was the problem with Nsuuta. Sometimes, when you challenged her, she became ruthless. Sometimes, it seemed she did not care that Kirabo was twelve.

'Look, Kirabo. Creatures belong to their creators, not so?'

Kirabo nodded.

'In this shrunken image we are in right now, we are the creatures of men. And creatures worship their creator. But the original state in you gives us hope.'

Kirabo kept quiet but thought *Who wants to be an ancient woman who everyone has rejected?* But she could not argue with Nsuuta, not when she still hoped to use her to take her to her mother.

Hearing Kirabo's silence, Nsuuta sighed as if she had overestimated Kirabo's intelligence. 'Okay, Kirabo,' she said. 'Forget everything else. Remember one thing – when it comes to persecuting women, we are most vicious to ourselves.'

Kirabo rolled her eyes. *As if I need to be reminded.*

'By the way, how often do you visit your grandmother's people in Timiina?'

Kirabo stretched her legs and yawned. 'I have never been. Maybe Grandmother took me when I was young, I don't know.' She was not particularly curious. 'I will ask Grandfather for permission.'

Nsuuta's blue eyes looked at Kirabo for a long time. Then she said, 'It is time for you to go home – now.'

'What, already?'

'Go, now!'

Kirabo jumped up and out of Nsuuta's house. Once outside, she turned and looked towards the darkened doorway, wondering if Nsuuta's evil self was back.

There was little improvement the next time Kirabo visited. Nsuuta was in another one of her foul moods. She sat deep inside her diiro, listening to the radio. When Kirabo announced herself, she waved for her to sit down and keep quiet. Nsuuta sat as if coiled into herself.

It was a live broadcast. There was a lot of static. Nsuuta kept touching the antenna, bending it, turning, straightening it, pulling out all the segments, but the static persisted, and the voices that echoed out of the radio sounded distant. From what Kirabo could gather, a big conference was going on in Mexico. It was in English. But it was for women only.

Kirabo gave up on the radio; the static was too much. 'Can I look at your magazines, Nsuuta?' Nsuuta nodded briefly.

From the dates on the issues on top of the pile, the magazines were very old, some dating back to 1942. Yet they looked almost brand new, no film of dust. Kirabo imagined the hapless ghost, Nsuuta's slave, dusting, doing the chores. She flicked through the pile looking for *DRUM* magazine, specifically for *The Adventures of Spearman*, a pull-out comic that came with it. Its hero, Lance the Spear, kicked crooks better than James Bond, better even than Bruce Lee, all the while swigging whisky or smoking a cigar. When she got to the bottom of the pile and there was no *DRUM*, she put them away.

Kirabo turned to the radio again. But this time, two men were talking over the conference in Luganda. Their voices were crisp and clear. Apparently, the women at the conference were getting greedy:

'Have they seen us go into their kitchens or their maternity wards?'

'Have you not heard of mwenkanonkano?'

'My sister started to talk about that nonsense and I told her that the day children will start to belong to their mothers is the day men and women shall become equal.'

Nsuuta sucked her teeth long and loud. When the men finally stopped talking, it was possible to make out the voice of one of the conference delegates. Nsuuta increased the volume. She seemed to hang on every word out of the radio. There was a round of applause, but it was soon overpowered once more by static. The Luganda speaker interrupted again and *Munnamasaka*, the programme for the Masaka region, came on. Kirabo held her breath. Nsuuta stared at the radio as if she wanted to hit it. Then she snapped it off.

Kirabo apologised for the rude men. 'It is terrible those men spoke over your programme.'

Nsuuta made a gesture that said the men could not help themselves. As if to blame them was to blame a child for being childish. 'But the women too were—'

'The women on the radio?' Kirabo was baffled.

'They think that we all think the same.'

'Was it wrong what they said?'

'Not wrong. But this is the wrong start. If your roof leaks, what do you do?'

'Find the hole, plug it and then mop.'

'Those women' – Nsuuta pointed towards the radio – 'have started with mopping. I don't even know whether there was a Ugandan who took our voice there. And if there was, I don't know whose voice she took.'

Kirabo sucked her teeth at the women's brand of blindness. Even she who was only walking her thirteenth year knew better.

'Even though we are all women, we stand in different positions and see things differently. The first thing should have been for our representative to rally us and say *You know, people, aren't you tired of this leaking roof*, to make certain everyone – young, old, servant, mistress, educated or not, willing, unwilling – is aware. Humans are funny; some may claim not to see the leak. Some may say *Don't disturb us, we don't mind a little bit of damp*, or *a roof leaking is normal; that is the nature of roofs*. Other women, who sell mops, might even encourage the leak. There would be some who would be afraid that once you start repairs you will open up new holes. There are all sorts of people in this world. But when you have involved everyone and heard their reactions, then you know how to proceed.' She made to walk away but then turned around. 'Soon, and I am telling you it will be soon, those women will find out that the women they are trying to save are an obstacle.'

'What about my story?'

'What story, child?'

'Our original state.'

'Not today, Kirabo. Come back another day.'

9

It would be Kirabo's last day of consultation with Nsuuta. Grandmother had returned from Timiina two days earlier. Kirabo went early to Nsuuta's, so that by midday she would be home again.

After the previous meeting, when Kirabo told her that Grandmother had returned, Nsuuta told Kirabo to go in search for stories about men. Nsuuta on the other hand would collect stories about women. Then they would declare whoever had more stories the winner. Afterwards, if Kirabo still wished, Nsuuta would get rid of the original state. Then they would devise ways to keep in touch in case Nsuuta had to pass on news about Kirabo's mother.

Kirabo arrived worried. She had chosen stories about men because this would give her an advantage. During storytelling Kirabo would nominate a story about a man and Nsuuta would tell it. If Nsuuta failed, Kirabo would tell it to get ten points. If Nsuuta told it, they would both get five points. The way she saw it, all she had to do was collect as many titles about men as possible. After all, Nsuuta would tell them. And since she knew most of the stories about women, she would snatch away points from Nsuuta.

But after scouring the villages, including asking grown-ups, Kirabo had found only two stories about men, the one about Luzze whose wife buried their daughter in an anthill and another about Tamusuza, a widower. No one had stories about evil stepfathers, horrible stepsons, conceited handsome men or ugly spoilt sons to share. Her chance of winning lay in snatching every five points Nsuuta presented to her. If

Nsuuta did not know either of Kirabo's two stories, she had a chance at winning.

Nsuuta went first. She challenged Kirabo to tell the story of the lukokobe. Kirabo snapped her fingers and danced. She knew it.

'The lukokobe was an old, old woman who lived alone—'

'She was a widow,' Nsuuta interrupted.

'Was she?' Kirabo was not bothered because it did not affect the story. 'At dusk, the lukokobe crept out of her lair and sat by the roadside. Along came a young man. She asked, "Yii Grandson, will you carry an old woman home?" Every young man would hurry to help a broken old person: they are a well of blessings. But the moment he put her on his back, *ba ppa*, her ropy legs locked around his waist and her wiry arms around his chest. Then talons drew out and sunk into his flesh. The lukokobe ordered him to start walking. "Faster," the lukokobe demanded. The young man kept going round and round in circles. At dawn, she vanished off his back. People found him passed out by the roadside, bleeding.'

Nsuuta grinned like she had won.

'What?' Kirabo was alarmed. 'Did I not tell it properly?'

'Oh, you did; take your five points. I was thinking that if you insist on marrying young virgins when you are old, don't be resentful if they outlive you.'

'Hmm, hmm.' Kirabo did not fully understand what Nsuuta meant, nor did she care about the young virgins who lived too long. 'My turn now, Nsuuta. Tell the story of Tamusuza.'

'I beg to tell you, Kirabo, that the story of Tamusuza is about the evil stepmother who abused his little girl—'

'Nsuuta, you will try to take a story from me even when I could find only two folk tales about men?'

'Maybe it is because your precious folk tales were used to persecute our original state.'

'How?' Kirabo did not wait for Nsuuta to respond. 'It is wrong to mistreat stepchildren.'

'Who makes women stepmothers...?'

At that moment, Grandmother stepped through Nsuuta's door. Kirabo held her breath for so long that she felt herself breathe through her skin. Grandmother standing inside Nsuuta's house was like the cardinal standing in the middle of your traditional shrine. You know he has come to burn down your gods.

When she started to breathe again, Kirabo gulped such large chunks of air she could not speak. Meanwhile, Nsuuta knew exactly who had walked in. But instead of shock, she clapped in happy surprise, 'Ha, finally, Alikisa drops in on us.'

Kirabo's 'Ha' escaped involuntarily. Otherwise she would have choked on Nsuuta's lack of remorse.

'Look here, Nsuuta,' Grandmother said unkindly. 'Stay away from her. You will not fill her head with nonsense. Did you warn her that you say this but do that?'

Nsuuta's eyes looked at Grandmother calmly. As if she loved her. 'How was Timiina?'

Grandmother faltered. She had not anticipated this. 'I said, stay away from her.'

'I would like to visit. I am sure Timiina asked about me.'

'Timiina does not like witches.'

Nsuuta turned on her pretty smile. 'Tsk, my witchery. Our Kirabo here has been trying to turn me away from my wickedness, have you not, Kirabo?'

Kirabo nodded vigorously.

'*God will burn you in hell, Nsuuta*, that sort of thing. You have brought her up well, *our* grandchild. I hope you will not turn her head into a battleground.'

'Let's go, Kirabo.' Grandmother held her shoulder. At Nsuuta she spat, 'If my father was not a reverend, I would have asked you to share the craft you use on my family.'

Nsuuta's hand shot out faster than a chameleon's tongue catching a bug. She gripped Grandmother's wrist. Grandmother, taken by surprise, stood still, startled. Kirabo held her breath.

'What happened to you, Alikisa? Why all this poison?'

Grandmother must have been too shocked to react. Her head turned slowly, slowly and she looked outside through the window – maybe to regain self-control. She looked down at Nsuuta's hand grasping her wrist. The wrist shook. She turned to Kirabo. 'Step outside, Kirabo.' It was a whisper, but Kirabo ran. When Grandmother whispered like that, you did not wait for her to repeat herself. 'Let go of my hand,' she heard Grandmother's voice choke. Kirabo wanted to shout *Let go of her hand, Nsuuta*, but Grandmother's voice came again. 'Kirabo?' She knew Kirabo would eavesdrop. Kirabo ran to the road and called back, 'I am over here by the road, Jjajja.'

At first, no noise came out of Nsuuta's house. But then voices, harsh whispers, rose and fell. Then Grandmother tore out of Nsuuta's door. Nsuuta appeared after her with the satisfied look of a family cat which had hissed the nosy dog out of the house.

'That heart of yours, wrapped in hate, is taking you to hell, Alikisa.'

'It is Muka Miiro to you.'

'Ha,' Nsuuta laughed scornfully. 'You have turned that name into a song – Muka Miiro, Muka Miiro, Muka Miiro. As if you were the first bride ever. Go *Muka Miiro* yourself somewhere they don't know the truth.'

'What did you say, Nsuuta?' Grandmother's voice caught. Nsuuta kept quiet. Grandmother grabbed Kirabo's hand; her grasp was hand-cuffs. When they stepped on to the road, Grandmother looked back. 'I am going to send this child away to the city.'

'Oh, go swallow a lake.' Nsuuta said, dismissing her.

Nsuuta's verbal flourishes confounded Grandmother, who was not quick with words. Nsuuta concluded with 'I recommend ash, *Alikisa*. It is good for selfishness. Go lick some ash.'

Grandmother walked hard, her steps pummelling the ground, her busuuti flapping. She said nothing to Kirabo. No rebuke, no *How could you do this to me, your real grandmother?* Kirabo wanted to bite and flog herself for the pain she had caused. She did not deserve her grandparents, or her mother. Nsuuta's audacity had reached the beyond.

She was thanking God for the empty road when the ugly nose of Kabuye's Morris Minor came around the corner. Kirabo deserved any punishment, but not Sio. *Let that boy not be in the car, please God, not today*, she prayed. But she could see his head, like a shadow, in the back. She felt her feet go cold. Then the coldness climbed up her legs. The car came down. Slowly. Sio saw Grandmother drag her as if she was about to flog her and his jaw dropped. The car crawled. Sio turned and stared through the back window. Kirabo expected him to make the praying mantis sign – *You deserve what is coming to you* – but his mouth remained open until their car disappeared.

Grandfather was standing by the poultry barn of the Zungu chickens when they arrived. Instead of asking what was going on, his face fell as if he had been part of Kirabo's plot to visit Nsuuta all along. Grandmother dragged Kirabo into the kitchen, but instead of getting a stick to whip her bottom, she let go of her hand. Kneeling before the hearth, even though the fire cooking supper burned steadily, Grandmother blew and blew, and the fire roared and roared until she ran out of breath. Then she stood up, stormed out of the kitchen, across the yard, past Grandfather. She picked a pan off the dish-draining katandalo constructed on the side of the kitchen. As she whizzed past Grandfather, she said, 'Kirabo's going to the city.'

Grandfather did not respond, but his eyes said *No one is going anywhere*.

When Grandmother returned to the kitchen, she threw the pan on the floor. It rolled on its bottom edge in loops, round, round, round, until it was so fast it was just a vibrating blur. Then it fell silent. Grandmother sat down and buried her head in her hands. She pulled up the flaps of her busuuti and covered her face. For a moment, she was silent as if she were not breathing. Then she gasped and sucked in air long and deep. A sob escaped. Kirabo stiffened. Grandmother blew her nose, stood up again, fetched her coiled mat from the wall hammock, sat down and started to weave. Kirabo rolled her eyes skyward to stop the tears because she had no right to cry. She remained still for some time, staring into the tongues of fire licking the sides of the pan. Kirabo wanted to pick up a stick, give it to Grandmother and say *You really need to whip me this time.* Grandmother said nothing; she didn't even look at her. After a while, Kirabo stole a step backwards, then another and stopped. She carried on like that until she finally reached the doorstep and ran.

The house was silent all evening and throughout supper. The teenagers looked at Kirabo as if they had never realised the evil she was capable of. No one taunted her; it was as if she was beneath bullying. After eating, Grandfather tried to lead them in prayer, but he lacked enthusiasm. Afterwards, everyone went straight to bed.

Kirabo lay in the dark, sleepless. She started to consider that perhaps she should go to the city and live with Tom as Grandmother wanted. She might run into her mother on the street: *You look familiar, are you my daughter?* Someone might recognise her: *You must be so and so's child.* One day Tom might come home and say *Guess who I bumped into?* She lifted her head and listened for Grandfather's breathing – silence. No gentle rhythmic breathing. Grandfather was sleepless too? 'Jjajja,' she called softly. 'Can I come to your bed?'

'Come on; don't cry, kabejja. No one will send you away unless I say so.'

Kirabo clambered into her grandfather's bed, curved herself into his back and breathed in the familiar smell of his skin. It was not long before she was deeply asleep.

This time, there was no wee pressing and no rain falling in the place where sleep took her. Just the talking bull. For some reason she was early to school, alone. She arrived at the thicket where the bull lived, and stopped to peek. The bull was tethered to a post, grazing. Kirabo wondered how she would get past it without being seen. It stumped a hind hoof and swung its head towards the stomach to shake off flies, but they stayed put. The skin on the stomach twitched and when the tail whisked, the flies lifted but they soon settled back as if it was a game. Kirabo waited until the bull bent its head and blew loudly on the grass. When its tongue snaked out and wrapped itself around a sheaf, she sprinted. The bull lifted its head, saw her and narrowed its eyes – *You, I am going to kill you today.* As it rushed to untether itself, Kirabo ran. When she got to the end of the thicket she looked back, but the bull was not yet in sight. She kept running because it always caught up. She rounded the corner and this time decided to turn off the road. There was a tree behind the bushes. She climbed it.

She heard the hooves galloping. They stopped where she had turned off the road and the bull's head appeared. It sniffed the air for her scent, then looked around for her. She prayed that it would carry on. It turned off the road into the bush, coming towards the tree. The noise of its hooves was loud, as if the ground was of concrete. It stopped and sniffed the air: *Where are you?* Kirabo gripped the tree. It took a few more steps, coming closer, closer; it stopped right under the tree. Kirabo was busting to breathe. *I know you are here somewhere.* Then it looked up.

1 0

By afternoon the following day, the house had not recovered. All day, Kirabo had been by Grandmother's side, helping her with chores. She had neatened up the kitchen – scooped out all the ash from the hearths, swept the floor, arranged the firewood into a pile in one corner and put fruit, ripe ndiizi bananas and avocados, in another, but Grandmother had not said a word to her. Nothing in her demeanour said she was still hurting, but Kirabo hoped she would say *You did me wrong going to that woman, Kirabo*.

Kirabo was helping Grandmother prepare Sunday supper. Grandmother had finished barbecuing a piece of beef over the embers to flavour it, put it in the bokisi pan and added onions and tomatoes. When she reached for the salt, the tin was empty. She reached into the sash fastening her busuuti and gave Kirabo two simoni coins. Kirabo ran across the road to Ssozi's shop. All preparation to wrap the food and steam the meat was put on hold.

As Kirabo approached Ssozi's, she heard voices. She stepped up the ramp, held on to the bars and looked inside. There was no one behind the counter. Open sacks of dried beans, rice, cassava flour, soya flour and maize flour would not let her further into the shop. On the counter, large jars of Nubian kabalagala pancakes, honeyed sesame balls and green pea samosas obscured the view. On the wall was President Idi Amin Dada's picture. He was dressed in an army uniform like Muteesa II, but he had very many kyeppe and medallions all over his chest and stomach. It was the only picture of him in the entire village. Recently, women had stopped cursing it when they came to buy things, because walls had grown ears. Ssozi had put it on the wall so he and his shop would look patriotic.

Kirabo was stepping away to go to the back of the house and call when she heard Ssozi's voice.

'You two are new to this village. You do not understand this feud.' From the way they sounded, Ssozi and his family were having lunch. 'All of you women will take Muka Miiro's side because she is the ringed wife, but—'

Kirabo's heart jumped; the whole village knew?

'It is not taking sides,' Ssozi's first wife said. 'Nsuuta is trespassing on her marriage.'

'Nsuuta was the first with Miiro. Muka Miiro snatched him right out of Nsuuta's fingers.'

'But he did not marry her, did he?' the first wife insisted.

'Where is the difference? She has always been his woman.'

The second wife was impatient. 'If Nsuuta is Miiro's woman, why are they sneaking around?'

'The church. Tsk, you joke with these Christians. Their hypocrisy is old and greyed. Miiro cannot take Holy Communion and sit between two wives.'

Kirabo eased away from the door. Her heart pumped so hard she was almost blinded.

'To anyone who does not know the origin of this feud, Muka Miiro is the docile wife trying to hold a marriage together while Nsuuta sits in her house plotting to bring it down. But I am telling you, Muka Miiro is not blameless.'

One of the wives muttered something Kirabo could not hear. Ssozi replied, 'Do you know she nearly killed Nsuuta back in '46?'

'How?'

'You ask, kdto.' Ssozi lowered his voice. 'We don't talk about it, but Muka Miiro found out Nsuuta was expecting Miiro's child and her head swelled with wrath. Me, I have never seen that kind of possessiveness. I accept Muka Miiro was a reverend's daughter. There was no second wife in her home as a child. But even then, most women, when they find out they are sharing their marriage with another woman, step back and concentrate on their children. Not Muka Miiro. That morning we woke up to the news that Nsuuta had been rushed to hospital. She did not only lose the pregnancy; she could never have a child.'

'Oh? That is terrible.'

'I don't care what people say,' Ssozi continued. 'That was murder.'

Ssozi's second wife sucked her teeth. 'These Christian wives, they take the idea literally of husband and wife becoming one on the wedding day.'

'That skinny Muka Miiro hit someone?' Ssozi's first wife scoffed.

'Ho. You joke. That woman is a buffalo. At the time, a Lundi woman who had run away from her marriage was taking a break in Nsuuta's house. Muka Miiro beat her up too, for trying to save Nsuuta. In fact, there was a man in the house – could have been the Lundi's husband who had come to beg his wife to return to him. He is the one who saved Nsuuta.'

'You lie.'

'Not only that. Muka Miiro was pregnant with Tom. Ask Widow Diba.'

The first wife was not going to blame Muka Miiro. 'Still, two women hating each other all this time? Muka Miiro has had children, the children have had children, Nsuuta has lost her sight, her head has bloomed white, but they still hate each other over a man?'

'Christians are dumb—'

'Ask yourself,' Ssozi interrupted, 'why did Miiro hand Tom over to Nsuu—'

'Kirabo, where is the salt?'

Kirabo jumped. Grandmother had crossed the road and was coming towards her.

Ssozi, hearing Grandmother's voice, appeared behind the counter. 'Oh, how is everything, Muka Miiro? You sent Kirabo a while ago?'

Grandmother shook her head as if Kirabo was a lost cause.

'I went to the toilet first.'

Ssozi stole worried glances at Kirabo as he scooped salt from a sack into a brown paper bag. He picked up an imperial weight and placed it on the smaller part of the scales. The salt flew up. He added tiny bits into the paper bag, measuring it out to the last grain. When he was satisfied with the amount, he threw the scoop back into the sack, folded the paper bag and gave it to Kirabo. As she walked towards Grandmother, Kirabo told herself *She is my grandmother, she is my grandmother; she does not hit people.* But she could not shake the image of the tiny grave behind Nsuuta's house. Grandmother grabbed the bag and they crossed the road together. As they came to the mango tree in the courtyard, Grandmother said, 'Next time you have a problem, Kirabo, bring it to me.'

Kirabo stopped and looked down. 'Forgive me, Jjajja.' She was barely audible.

'I am trying to bring you up in the real world. Nsuuta lives in the clouds with her stories and ideas. If we all allowed her stories to guide us, the world would grind to a stop.' Grandmother paused, as if considering her words. 'We don't know where your mother's love is. If we did, do you think we would keep you away from her?'

Kirabo shook her head.

Grandmother carried on to the kitchen. Kirabo remained where she stood, finally overcome by tears. All she had wanted was to get rid of the flying, to be a good girl and find her mother. But look what she had found out instead. Grandmother had killed Nsuuta's baby. Grandfather was cavorting with Nsuuta. She was a secret child. And the original state was in her.

That night, as she got into bed, she whispered to Grandfather, 'Is it true Grandmother killed Nsuuta's child?'

Grandfather almost jumped. He frowned so hard a huge vertical vein appeared down the middle of his forehead. 'Where did you hear that, Kirabo?'

'It was Ssozi at his shop. He was laughing with his wives.'

'Kirabo, Ssozi hauls gossip from here to there and by the time it returns, it has neither head nor legs.'

'So Grandmother never hit Nsuuta or a Lundi woman?'

'Of course not. Kirabo, she is your grandmother. She cannot even bring herself to punish you. How could she hit someone who was pregnant?'

'I know.' She dropped her head in shame.

'Ssozi keeps two wives in the same house. Do any of them look like they have common sense?'

'But he told his wives Nsuuta is your woman.'

Grandfather stopped getting into his bed. 'That is it, hm-hm, Ssozi has gone too far.' Grandfather came to Kirabo's bed and wiped her tears. 'Baasi-baasi, baasi-baasi, stop crying. I am going to have a word with Ssozi tomorrow.'

Kirabo nodded.

'Now go to sleep, kabejja. Leave everything to me.'

Kirabo had hoped to ask why Tom was Nsuuta's son too, but at the sight of her grandfather's pursed lips, she swallowed her question and got into bed.

'Sleep well, Jjajja.'

'And you, kabejja.' He pulled her blanket up to her neck.

But long after the lanterns and tadooba candles in the village had been blown out, long after all creatures, guilty and innocent, had gone to sleep, Kirabo blinked in the dark.

11

You would think that after Kirabo had hurt Grandmother so spectacularly, the teenagers would behave. Not Gayi. She must have thought
You think Kirabo is wicked? Let me show you.

Gayi was born Nnaggayi. The daily bus service from Kampala
was a Guy model, the unfortunate pun for Giibwa's insinuation.
Gayi was eighteen or nineteen, but she was only just taking her O
levels because she kept repeating classes. She was kind and gentle
with Kirabo, but Gayi was getting spoilt. Not spoilt like an indulged
child; spoilt like milk going off. A girl going bad was so total, so
irreversible, so disgusting, she became rubbish on the roadside. And
people treated her as such. Men touched her anywhere, even in public.
Any man – drunks, riff-raff, sweat-stinking labourers – would ask
her for sex as if they were entitled to it. 'Eh, Gayi?' they would call.
'When will you give me some?' because she had turned herself
into a communal plate. There was no salvation for Gayi whether
she dropped out of school or got pregnant, both of which seemed
inevitable.

But Gayi was indifferent. She carried on with her man like a bug
had burrowed into her brain. For Kirabo, no matter what people said,
Gayi was not responsible for her actions. Not with her floaty eyes
that made her look like she was half asleep. Not with men calling her
shapely backside 'sakabuzoba spesulo', shock-absorbers special. Not
with her aubergine skin. When she fastened her school uniform belt,
she looked like a black wasp. Ugly girls were good girls; they worked

hard in school. But for Gayi, the world had stared and admired. She had noticed and her brain had stopped growing.

Once, Widow Diba came to talk to Gayi the way elderly women do when trying to save a wayward girl from self-destruction. Grandmother had talked and talked until she ran out of words. Diba said, 'I am telling you, Gayi: that body of yours which makes you float above all of us will one day abandon you like a bad friend. Three births and that waistline will fill out and thicken. Then you will see your own stomach step out in front of you as if showing you the way. And that backside – *chwe.*' She made a wiping gesture across her mouth. 'Worn away. And that man will discard you like a used toilet wipe. All of us here were beautiful once, but where is that beauty now? Stay in school, add value to your looks and men will die to marry you.'

When Miiro found out Gayi had a man, he did not bother with that nonsense cajoling of *Let us talk, let us reason.* He pulled out a cane and flogged Gayi. Then he threatened to withdraw her from school and marry her off to an old man like they did in the past. But did Gayi learn? No. When her older brothers from the city, Tom and Uncle Ndiira, came to visit, Miiro told them about Gayi's interest in 'men'. Tom, being the eldest son, was so angry he flogged Gayi for wasting Grandfather's money in school fees. But did the madness in Gayi budge? No. Instead, she mumbled between her tears, 'What have I done that Tom did not do?' and went back to seeing her man. Eventually Grandfather threw her out of the main house. 'There is room for one *woman* in this house – your mother,' he said. 'Everyone else is a child.'

Gayi started to sleep in the biggest boys' house, built separately for them so they could do whatever they wished in privacy. She no longer used the same bath basins as Grandmother and Grandfather because, as she had 'started men', her parents might catch that shaking condition, Parkinson's. Another father would have withdrawn Gayi from school altogether. Some fathers threw such shameful girls out of the home entirely so as not to infect the younger ones. In the village, people laughed: 'God gave Miiro bright children, but he gave him Gayi too, kdto. Not a flicker of light in that head of hers…' 'She repeats classes like a child returning to leftovers…' 'She has a mighty itch down there: Miiro can flog all he wants but it will not scratch an itch like that.' But Grandfather kept Gayi in school, insisting he would rather she dropped out of school with at least an O-level certificate than abandon her to a gloomy future.

For a while, after Gayi was evicted from the main house, Grandfather and Grandmother thought she had stopped seeing her man. But Kirabo knew better. One moonlit night, when she went outside to toilet before bed, she heard whispering near the road. She sidled along the wall until she got to the front of the house. On the road, a man wheeled a motorbike silently. Gayi slunk from behind. They wheeled the motorbike up the road further away from the house. Kirabo followed. When they thought they were far enough away, the man swung a leg over the bike and kicked a pedal once, twice; the third time the bike burst into life and growled. The man sat astride it. Gayi swung a leg over, sat, pushed her pelvis into the man, wrapped her arms around his waist, laid her head against him and they set off. From that night onwards, Kirabo listened out for the motorcycle and when she heard it, she looked at Grandfather and felt guilty.

But this time someone with twitchy lips must have seen Gayi sneak out with her man the previous night and tipped Grandfather off as they held a meeting of coffee growers at the *koparativu stowa*. Grandfather came home sparking like a faulty plug. He rode his bicycle to the house at speed. Normally, he dismounted at the road, wheeled it up the walkway, then pulled back the stand with a foot and leaned the bicycle against it. This time he asked, 'Where is Nnaggayi?' as he dismounted and let the bicycle fall to the ground.

No one answered.

'Did she escape last night?'

Silence.

Grandfather marched to the coffee shrub near the kitchen and broke off a switch. While he plucked the twigs and leaves off, the teenagers vanished. In moments like that, you did not hang around. Grandfather might tell you to catch Gayi and hold her down while she was flogged. Despite her rebellious ways, Gayi was one of those girls who, at the sight of a cane, ran screaming.

As Grandfather prepared the whip, a window on the bigger boys' block flew open. Gayi's head popped up. She looked around and then climbed on to the sill. She paused for a moment and then plunged. She ran to the road and disappeared. Grandfather, cane in hand, walked to the road and looked it up and down – no sign of Gayi. He walked back to the house, threw the cane on to the rubbish heap outside the kitchen and went to his bedroom. In the kitchen, Grandmother's eyes were red. Kirabo did the only thing she knew in moments like this. She sat with Grandmother and leaned against her in the quiet hope that it would soothe her. The teenagers did their homework and chores quickly. Grandfather did not come out to supper. Grandmother was quiet all through eating, all through clearing up and taking the wraps back to the kitchen. There were no prayers. No after-dinner blather for the teenagers. Soon after, all the tadooba candles and lanterns were blown out and the house fell silent. Gayi did not come home that night.

The following day Grandmother wept openly. The teenagers' eyes were dark with worry. They whispered a lot. Grandfather was sullen. Kirabo, excluded from all conversation about Gayi, imagined the worst. At night, the murderous bull returned to torment her.

It was then that she found out Gayi was Grandmother and Grandfather's real child, their youngest of five. People kept coming to commiserate. Grandmother did not say much, only wept. Grandfather would shake his head and sigh, 'Children. They don't belong to us. We only bring them into the world.' No child brought up in that house – and there had been many – had ever rebelled, least of all a girl.

Three days later, Miiro's older children, Aunts Abi and YA, Tom and quiet Uncle Ndiira, came and there was a family meeting in the diiro. Afterwards, they put announcements on the radio asking Gayi to come home because everyone was worried. Some of these notices said she could go to her siblings in the city, but so far, no Gayi. Then they put out other announcements threatening whoever was keeping her with kidnapping and child defilement – still nothing. Not even to say *Stop worrying, I am fine.*

Miiro's brothers, Faaza Dewo, the priest and Jjajja Dokita, the doctor, came and they hugged, whispered and sighed. But horrible Jjajja Nsangi, Miiro's only sister, stayed for a week. Nsangi was one of those women who were men in their brothers' houses. She called Grandmother 'Wife'. Grandmother knelt as she waited on her. Jjajja Nsangi claimed that in her brothers' houses there was room to raise her voice and to stretch her legs. Miiro loved his sister too much to say anything. Grandmother was on her best behaviour whenever Nsangi visited. She reinforced her maleness by asking the teenagers, 'Who am I?'

'Ssenga,' they replied.

'And what does ssenga mean?'

'It means *if*.'

'Let me hear the whole saying.'

'If you were not a woman,' the teenagers would chorus, 'you would be our father too.'

'Don't you ever forget it.'

After commiserating, Nsangi asked Miiro to buy her kangaali, her words for alcohol. 'I need to engage the gears,' she said as if she was a car. And Miiro bought her beer even though Nsangi had been diagnosed with rich people's afflictions – high blood pressure and ulcers. She also suffered from sugars and had been told to eat small-small meals frequently, and to skip the rope. When Grandmother heard, she whispered, 'By the time doctors tell you to skip a rope your laziness is so middle-aged it has grandchildren.'

After Nsangi left, no one talked about Gayi again. When Kirabo tried to, the teenagers elbowed her – *Shut up* – as if Gayi were worse than dead. But every time the bus went past, it flashed the word GUY and Kirabo's heart turned.

THE BITCH

1

4 January 1977

Kirabo walked back to the house, deflated. Running back and forth to the road to check whether Tom was coming was juvenile, but she could not help herself. With Tom she became a child again – running, screaming, throwing herself at him whenever he arrived. Besides, there is nothing like telling the villages you are leaving for the city – grown-ups giving you their blessings, friends saying they will miss you, some giving you envious looks because you are wearing city airs already – only for them to wake up the following morning and find you breathing rural Nattetta air.

Tom was expected at ten hours of day. At twelve hours in the evening, Kirabo felt compromised. Her smartest dress had lost its going-away effect. It was an 'already-made' dress with a MADE IN GHANA label, unlike the 'made in Nattetta' sack-like things, run off the local tailor's sewing machine without imagination. Tom had bought it for her last Christmas. Kirabo wore it to church, and even Sio stole guarded glances as he hurried to his parents' car. You don't wear that kind of dress to go away and then linger like unsold fish.

Grandfather had let Kirabo go. Instead of Grandmother, it was Tom who asked to take her to the city, though Kirabo suspected that after the Nsuuta affair, Grandmother had been pushing Tom to take her with him. One day, he arrived on one of his hurried visits and announced, 'Kirabo will start to live with me when her results come back.'

It was casual. As if he were humming to himself. He stood under the mustani tree in the western courtyard between the house and the kitchen. Grandfather stood by the window of his bedroom, which opened out into the courtyard, while Grandmother sat by the kitchen door. As he spoke, Tom picked up a green stone seed that the mustani had dropped and threw it high in the air. It whistled as it soared, then dropped somewhere in the coffee shamba.

'Ah haa.' Grandmother smiled so widely Kirabo saw all her teeth. But not Miiro. He asked, 'Why now?'

Tom walked towards Grandfather's window to avoid raising his voice. 'I want to keep an eye on her education.'

'And what have *we* been doing all this time?'

'You have been helping me.'

'Listen to that: we have been "helping" him. As if the child is his alone.'

Tom did not respond. He stood by Miiro's window, as if anticipating further protests. But when none were forthcoming, Tom walked over to Grandmother and squatted near her. Unlike other males in the family, Tom never stood when speaking to Grandmother unless she was standing too. As he settled down, Miiro's voice came again: 'Have you chewed this decision over properly?'

A look of exasperation clouded Tom's face. He returned to Grandfather's window, folded his arms and replied in a low voice, 'Of course.'

'Hmm, because we don't want to hear choking later.' Grandfather came to his window. His silhouette was distorted by the thick anti-burglar bars, but Kirabo could make out his forefinger wagging furiously as he whispered something to Tom. Then he went back to tidying his bedroom. Tom replied under his breath, making sharp cutting gestures with his hands. Grandfather *hmm*ed. Kirabo, who was washing dishes by the katandalo, strained to hear what was being said.

On his visit the following weekend, Tom had changed his mind. At the time, he had been visiting every week because Kirabo's primary leaving exams were coming up. He talked her through exam etiquette, bringing her pencils, pens and the Oxford Mathematical Set. He also brought PLE past papers for revision, which they would work through together. He visited her teachers and paid them for Kirabo's coaching. On this occasion, Tom had decided he would come for Kirabo not when her results came back in March, but in early December, soon after the exams. She needed to get used to her new home before she started secondary school.

Miiro was not amused. 'Forget that,' he had said. 'She will eat Ssekukkulu with us. And after we have held the first day of the year together, you can take her.'

Tom said he would collect Kirabo on the fourth of January.

Kirabo had never been curious about Tom. She had never been interested in who he was beyond Tom, her father, who visited late in the evening and was always in a hurry. Tom, who would throw her up in the air when she was still small, catching her and tickling her cheeks with his stubble as she squealed, 'Stop, please, Tom, stop!' No sooner would he put her down than she would throw her arms in the air, squealing, 'Again, Tom, please, again!' Beyond that she had never given him much thought as long as he visited and brought her gifts.

The prospect of living in Kampala had given Kirabo hopes of seeing her mother sooner. Away from Nattetta, the promise she had made to Nsuuta not to look for her mother would become void. Ever since Nsuuta told her not to go looking, Kirabo's obsession with her mother had become all-consuming. But she had made adjustments. Living with her mother was out of the question. All she wanted now was to look at her, hear her voice, see her smile, feel a little of her love, so she could finally say to herself: *This is where I come from.* Still she imagined her mother's life. She lived in a flat in Kampala. Her husband, a horrible man, was bald, had a beard and never smiled.

Despite what Nsuuta had told her, in her mind her mother was still millipede-dark, tall with long skinny legs. She wore a yellow maxi circle skirt and a blouse of indeterminate colour and platform shoes. She had a huge round Afro like Diana Ross on Grandfather's gramophone disc. The only thing Kirabo could not see clearly was her face. It was always in the dark.

The house was at supper when Tom arrived. A short knock, and there he was – tall, very dark, white long-sleeved shirt, tie, jacket in his hands, impatient. Kirabo glared at him – none of the usual running and throwing herself at him. She had lost all credibility when she took off her going-away dress. Her friends, who had hovered all evening to see her off, had slunk away in embarrassment.

Tom did not step in. He stood on the doorstep looking at Kirabo. 'You mean you are not dressed yet?'

'Kdto,' Miiro clicked. 'Tell me you are not travelling with a child at this time of night.'

'I left the office late.' Tom spoke as if Miiro did not understand the demands of city life. But this time he had gone too far.

'Office this, office that, always in a hurry; it has to stop. If there is no time to come, then there is no time to come. But don't ever come here at night again.'

Tom kept quiet; his frustration deflated like slow air out of a tyre. Kirabo rose to go and change.

'Will you come in and eat something?' Grandmother asked.

'I'll roll down the road to see Maama Muto for a bit.' Tom called Nsuuta 'Maama Muto', younger mother, and Grandmother 'Maama Mukulu', senior mother.

He disappeared so fast he did not see his mother's face fold. He did not take long. By the time Kirabo came back from getting changed, Tom was turning into the walkway. She had thought he would not go 'down the road', as he called his dashes to see Nsuuta, because it was late. When he was in a lesser hurry, he disappeared to Nsuuta's for long hours and when he returned, he said, 'I have already eaten,' despite Grandmother's pain. On one occasion, at Aunt YA's pre-wedding party, Tom spent the whole night at Nsuuta's, blaming the noise and revellers. He barely made it in time to receive the pre-wedding kasuze katya gifts from the groom's family and to hand over the bride.

Grandmother, who had left the room as Tom arrived from Nsuuta's, returned with a pair of her best white linen bed sheets. All Kirabo's life, those sheets had been washed in water with Blue-loo to keep the whiteness sharp. They were always ironed and ready for hospital emergencies. Grandmother also gave her a red oval tin of Cussons scented petroleum jelly, a cake of Sunlight toilet soap and a tin of Vicks VapoRub. Then she sat Kirabo on her lap and said, 'Don't worry about Miiro; I will look after him for you.' She pulled her into her bosom and Kirabo smelled firewood smoke on Grandmother's busuuti. 'Just get the best out of those city schools and be like your aunts. My job is to show off that my eldest grand-child is in secondary school; now she is at university. *Do you see me boasting myself?*' Kirabo laughed because she had never heard Grandmother speak English.

Miiro went to his bedroom too. When he returned, he sat Kirabo on his lap and said, 'Yesterday you arrived a baby and I was showing off that I had a brand-new wife. Now, the village is going to laugh. But I am going to be strong. This is for both of us.'

Tom sighed impatiently.

Grandfather gave her two hundred shillings. Everyone gasped. 'Keep it safe,' he said, but he looked at Tom as he added, 'You might need it.'

Tom turned away, tapping the door frame lightly. 'There is food in my house.'

'Then make sure she gets it.' Miiro turned to Kirabo. 'A heifer and nduusi goat for your O levels and again for A levels. And if you bring me a degree, two heifers, two nduusi goats.' Kirabo felt the tears. She cared for neither cows nor goats. What mattered was that she had been too excited about leaving to realise it would hurt.

Tom extricated her from the arms of her grandfather. 'Come, come, we are running late.'

Grandmother and Grandfather stood in the doorway and waved. The rest of the family walked Tom and Kirabo the mile to Nazigo, where the taxis to the city stopped.

Word must have gone around that Tom had arrived because when they came to the Nazigo Trading Centre, all youths, Kirabo's friends, even those from further-away villages, were hanging around the shops.

Kirabo saw Wafula first and her heart leapt: *He is here!* Wafula and Sio were inseparable. Soon, Sio's silhouette flickered across the corner of her vision and her eyes stopped searching. She would recognise that shadow anywhere. He leaned against the wall of Posta, his back against the metallic postboxes. He looked away from her as if he had not seen her, but she could sense that his body was in turmoil.

As Tom waited for a taxi, Kirabo went around hugging everyone, including Ntaate, the village creep she would never touch under normal circumstances. Indeed, Ntaate stretched himself like a cat being stroked. He stole a glance at Sio while whispering in Kirabo's ear, 'So these are the luxurious hugs Sio enjoys!' Kirabo sucked her teeth in disgust. Ntaate was Ntaate – a creep to the marrow.

After a nervous delay, she tottered over to Giibwa, who stood next to Sio. She looked at Giibwa as if Sio was not there. Then she sighed, 'I am going.' Giibwa shrugged as if she did not care, but even as she did so, her face collapsed. Sio shifted and stood on one leg. The other, folded at the knee, stepped on the Posta's wall as he leaned back. He said nothing. Giibwa chewed her upper lip. Kirabo kept her eyes on Giibwa.

'So, you are really going.' Sio looked at her as if she was being unreasonable.

Kirabo sighed.

'It is a waste of time to think you will remember us.'

'I will write.' She sneaked a glance at him.

'That is what you say.'

'I mean it.' She looked at him properly now.

Sio sucked his teeth and walked away.

Kirabo was stunned. Was that it? That was goodbye? She had planned to hug him. That was the only reason she had hugged all the other boys. After a brief hesitation, Wafula left too, even though everyone knew he would rather stay and watch Giibwa toss his heart in the air and catch it. When at the end of the Posta block the night swallowed Sio, Kirabo grabbed Giibwa and hugged her.

Giibwa said, 'Don't worry; I am coming to the city too. My aunt in Kampala asked me to go and live with her. This Nattetta is limited.' She wrinkled her nose. 'No possibilities at all.'

'Then we shall be together again,' Kirabo enthused, though her eyes were at the end of the block, 'and bring our Nattetta along?'

'Yes.' Giibwa jumped up and down. She hugged Kirabo again. This time Kirabo hugged Giibwa for Giibwa, and for the promise of getting together again.

The taxi, a Land Rover Defender, had two bench seats in the back facing each other. Kirabo, sitting with her back to the window, had to turn to wave. Her friends made a racket pretending to speak English: '*We will missioooo... Seeoo soon...*'

Kirabo glanced at Tom and then glared at her friends but the boys doubled over, clutching their bellies as if in pain. Even Ntaate, who did not like Sio, held his stomach.

'*Seeoo soon.*'

As her friends, and then the shops, and finally the whole of Nazigo disappeared, Kirabo closed her eyes. She felt her life merge with the motion of the car until everything became fluid. Fluidity became loss. She opened her eyes and looked through the window again. Tiny pale lights, like drops randomly scattered across the vast darkness, were suspended all around her. The dark seemed to have neither beginning nor end; there was no ground, no sky. And yet those tiny lights were homes, full of life, full of the people she had always known, people like Sio, like Giibwa, like her grandparents. But the night had reduced them to teardrop flames, tossed aside as the car sped forward.

For a while, Kirabo's mind hung on to Giibwa. She could not remember a time without her. She could not remember when, where or how they met. They just were. Like life – you don't remember when you were born. Or the sky – sometimes dark clouds came, sometimes it rained, but the next moment the sun burst through and the sky was limitless. In the last year, when Kirabo's study for her exams intensified, Giibwa would come as Kirabo studied and sit quietly with her. Giibwa could be quiet, unobtrusive and patient. Sometimes, as they played, she would ask Kirabo, 'Have you done your homework?' because Kirabo was the kind to do homework at the last minute. Everyone knew that about Giibwa. She was the kind of girl to say, 'Let's go and help this new mother with her baby.' Kirabo only went along so people did not find out she had no heart. Sometimes, Giibwa spent days at Kirabo's home. She melded into the household seamlessly, doing chores like she knew the rhythms of the house and everyone said, 'If only Kirabo were half as a good!' The memory made Kirabo's eyes sting. She imagined this was how it felt to have a sister.

It was Giibwa who made the appointment with Nsuuta to bury the original state. Yet she did not ask questions. If it had been the other way around, Kirabo would have demanded *Why are you sneaking about with a blind old woman?* Kirabo never told Giibwa about her two selves. It was not a decision. She just did not. Giibwa seemed contented with life, with herself, with everything. Being two entities, one of which flew out of your body, was like hairs creeping on your privates. You see them for the first time, you secretly choke on disgust. Guilt stabbed her, but she told herself that Giibwa would have been uncomfortable if she had told her. Besides, the original state was dead and gone, buried under the passion fruit thicket which roped itself around Nsuuta's musambya tree. The day before it was buried, Kirabo had sent Giibwa to Nsuuta to say, 'Kirabo is coming about that issue: she still does not want it.' Giibwa had run back with, 'Nsuuta says it is fine. Tomorrow take an item of clothing to her that you love but don't use any more.'

The following day after lunch, Giibwa came to Kirabo's home and as soon as Grandmother went to harvest food for supper, Kirabo took a pair of white socks, the ones with pink diamond patterns on the sides, and ran to Nsuuta's. Giibwa stayed by the road to keep watch.

After greeting one another, Nsuuta informed Kirabo that her mother had had a second child but was not yet free to see her. For Kirabo, it was painful to confirm what she had suspected for the last one and a half years. But she consoled herself; after all, it was going to be easier to find her mother in the city. Although Nsuuta was disappointed that Kirabo was getting rid of the original state, she was quick. She led Kirabo to the musambya in her back garden, dug a hole under the passion fruit thicket and asked for the item. She explained that since the original state had chosen her, the least Kirabo could do was to bury it with an item she once treasured. Nsuuta muttered an apology into the socks, something about not being courageous enough – which left Kirabo feeling like a sell-out – and buried them. Then she turned to Kirabo. 'No more flying. You will be a good girl from now on,' she said with sarcasm. Kirabo looked down, because being a good girl had never sounded so wicked. God must have been hanging upside down when he created Nsuuta.

Kirabo was about to sprint away when Nsuuta grabbed her hand. 'I hear Tom's taking you to the city.'

'Yes, to live with him.' Kirabo felt guilt for not mentioning it, for not saying goodbye.

'Let us pray that the city treats you well.'

Was that worry creasing Nsuuta's brows? Kirabo rolled her eyes. *Grown-ups. Step out of their little rural world and you are in danger of being gobbled up by the big, bad city.*

'Study hard, you hear me?'

'I will.'

'And, Kirabo, I don't know when I will talk to you again. Life is unpredictable. Do you remember what I told you?' Kirabo shook her head. Nsuuta held both her hands. 'Don't judge the women you meet too harshly.'

'I won't.'

'Often, what women do is a reaction. We react like powerless people. Remember kweluma?'

'When women bite themselves because they are powerless.'

'Tell me that whatever happens, you will not make another woman's life worse.'

'I won't, Nsuuta!' Kirabo was miffed that Nsuuta would ask.

'Remember, be a good person, not a good girl. Good girls suffer a lot in this life.'

It was stupid to keep pretending that she did not know Nsuuta just wanted to love her. She was Tom's daughter, after all, and all poor Nsuuta wanted was a grandchild. She looked up and realised that Nsuuta was waiting for a response.

'I will be a good person,' Kirabo said, not really paying attention to the words she was saying.

Nsuuta did not look convinced but said, 'Good, very good.'

Most women in Nattetta, when they heard that Kirabo was leaving, had dispensed some wisdom or advice as a ntanda for her to carry to the city and to see her through life. 'The only wealth I have is my experience,' they would say. 'Books are a woman's friend…they don't know prejudice…' 'Don't look left, don't look right, look straight – at the blackboard…knowledge will set you free…' 'Love like you have been loved in Nattetta; hate hurts the hater more intimately…' 'Kampala is a prostitute; it loves money only…' That kind of thing. Yet the profound ntanda Nsuuta had packed for her was not to be a good girl and never to treat another woman badly.

'Thank you for caring all this time,' Kirabo said, throwing herself at Nsuuta, and Nsuuta had to steady herself to avoid falling backwards.

'Now, look at this child thanking me for caring.' She hugged Kirabo tightly.

'But don't say unkind things to Grandmother, Nsuuta. She cried last time.'

Nsuuta took a deep breath and said, 'I will not, Kirabo. If you say I should not, then I will not.'

'Thank you. Now I am gone.' Kirabo extricated herself and dashed through the garden to where Nsuuta's land bordered the trail to the well. Behind her, Nsuuta listened to the receding footsteps with apprehension. She feared that Kirabo was too young for the world awaiting her outside Nattetta. She doubted that she had prepared her adequately. She prayed that where Kirabo was not prepared, she would be mentally tough enough to carve out her own tools to thrive. But for Kirabo, running towards Giibwa, the guilt at seeing Nsuuta looking old and lonely and blind and worried, knowing that she cared a lot for her but pretending not to, chased after her. The guilt at betraying Grandmother had thinned in the last one and a half years. It had thinned because Tom loved Nsuuta. How could he love her if Grandfather was cheating with her? Without facts, Kirabo relied on instinct. In her gut, Nsuuta felt harmless. Just like Grandmother felt perfect in her gut. Just like Grandfather belonged to her. They were all truths.

Kirabo's neck began to hurt and she turned from the window. It was silent in the car. She looked across at the passengers on the other bench but did not see them. She took a deep breath. It was time to shake Nattetta out of her head. Life was moving on. The world was spreading out. It was futile to keep looking back. Her mother was getting closer. Life was young. Sio was hers. It was wonderful to be Kirabo.

She looked ahead through the windscreen at where the headlights merged. Though there were no teardrop lights in the dark any more, she could hear, even smell the landscape outside the car through the gap in her window. When they drove into a valley, the sound was whirly. The sound in wooded areas was muffled, as if she was inside a packed suitcase. In open spaces, the sound was distant, as if the echoes couldn't be bothered to return. Sometimes the smell of swamp clay came along, or a fragrance from a tree, but sometimes a hostile tree gave off a foul smell as if urging them to move on. She recognised some places – Mu Ntooke, Nakifuma – and soon they were in Mukono. It grew cold. She tugged at the window to close it, but it was stuck. Tom yanked it closed and the noise from outside was muted. Kirabo took a deep breath and leaned back in her seat. But Nattetta was not ready to let go of her yet.

2

Sio. The day she felt him for the first time.

In a way it was like finding out that you have beautiful eyes. You have carried those eyes on your face all your life; you should have known.

It happened towards the end of the previous year, during Wafula's kadodi carnival. It was a day of surprises. First, Kirabo heard Sio speak Luganda. A Luganda as faultless as if he was born and bred in Bugerere. Then she saw him do the kadodi dance as if he was a Mumasaaba about to be circumcised. But what amazed her was that no one stared. As if a London-born dancing kadodi was an everyday sight in Nattetta.

Kirabo nudged Giibwa and pointed with her lips. 'When did he become one of us?'

'Sio? He has been around for some time now. When he comes home for holidays he mixes with us. You have been buried in books.'

'Now he even speaks Luganda?'

'Learnt it in boarding school.'

'And how does he know how to dance kadodi?'

'He is too much, isn't he?'

Kirabo glared at Giibwa.

'Okay, he might have practised with Wafula. See how he does it on one leg.'

But Kirabo did not look. She was not about to be seen admiring a London-born rotating on one leg as if he had been walking on his own legs all his life. She decided not to ask where the flab on his legs had gone.

According to Giibwa, Sio was on the long holidays after his O levels and roamed the villages looking for adventure, like other boys. He was tight with Wafula, who went to the same boarding school. Kirabo had not seen him much. The few times they met at church, she pouted and looked away. As far as she could see, he still had airs. But whether they were rich airs or British airs she could not tell.

Unlike Giibwa's parents, who did not monitor her, Grandmother had kept Kirabo close to her elbow for the past year. Whenever Kirabo left the house to go anywhere, she had to be in the company of other family members. She was at that perilous age where if a girl talked to a boy, grown-ups panicked: 'Eh, eeeh, that girl does not fear men.' Thus, girls performed outrage when a boy spoke to them. Every youth knew Kirabo was destined for a great education. Apart from Giibwa and other girls still at school, youths avoided her except when they mocked: 'Profesa, what are the books saying?' During childhood, the burden of communal vigilance was occasional; now as a teenager, it was constant. This was a society gripped not just by the fear of teenage pregnancies but by a certain nature in men. Boys and men were wolves – they had this overwhelming desire which, if stirred, made them animals. It fell on girls not to awaken the animal in men. Thus, as soon as traces of stretch marks behind Kirabo's knees and hints of rounding out were visible, Grandmother kept her close, rarely out of sight. Until she sat her exams, Kirabo was cut off from the youths' daily commune entirely. The day Kirabo felt Sio, she and Giibwa danced so far from home with Wafula's kadodi carnival that when they came to their senses, they did not recognise their surroundings.

The villages had been waiting for this day for two years. Everyone said that Wafula's carnival would break all records. On the day, by ten hours in the afternoon when the sun had started to tire, every girl and boy in Nattetta was feverish. Girls from all over the villages had collected at Miiro's house, waiting.

When they first heard the echoes of the drums, Kirabo and Giibwa ran to the house, tied sweaters around their waists and tried out their dancing strokes – swinging hips, twisting the waist, shaking the shoulders, jutting out their breasts. As the drums drew closer, girls and boys crowded the roadside, showing off their dancing. When the carnival came down the hill, the drummers saw the throng near Miiro's house, and the drums became acute. Wafula, his hands held out at his sides, danced like *I know I am a dream*. The high-pitched drums were insistent, like an itch in the ear, impossible to ignore. The flute suggested things and the bass drum agreed. But it was the jingle, the rattles of Wafula's rhythm that set the girls on fire. His fly whisks must have flicked Giibwa's inhibitions to hell because she shrieked and leapt into the road to show why Wafula was dying for her. Not to be outdone, Kirabo joined her, tossing her tail this way, that way, kicking and jumping. Girls swung their hips at Wafula, goading, challenging. His smile said, *You have no idea*. All girls from villages far and wide were in the carnival. Even young wives without common sense were dancing on the road. The boys pulsed their torsos, showing off their chests, twisting as if their pelvises were boneless. Soon the carnival was dance-jogging down the road, taking Kirabo and Giibwa with it. By the time they realised, Nattetta was more than four miles away and it was getting dark. The only person they knew in the crowd was Sio. Kirabo glanced at him; he did not look like he was about to stop.

'What do we do?' she panicked at Giibwa.

'Ask him.'

'Who?' Kirabo pretended not to know who Giibwa was talking about.

'Sio.'

Kirabo looked over. Bit her nails. 'You go and ask him.' She pushed Giibwa in Sio's direction.

'Why me?'

'He is Wafula's friend, and Wafula thinks you are sugar.'

'Ah, you do it.'

'Okay, we will go together, come on.' Kirabo led the way to where Sio dance-jogged. When she got to him, she shouted above the drums, 'Are you going home yet?'

Sio frowned *What is it to you?* but then realised she was asking and stopped dancing. He scanned the crowd. Everything about him said he wanted to carry on. Kirabo looked back to garner Giibwa's support; Giibwa had stayed behind. The duplicitous hare! Kirabo stood her ground. She had already poured all her dignity at Sio's feet; she might as well swallow the humiliation of begging.

'Okay,' he said at last, 'let's go.'

Kirabo almost danced, but seeing his regret, she apologised. Then she beckoned to Giibwa, who skipped over to join them.

'This time she is going to kill me,' Kirabo mused.

'Who?'

'My grandmother. To her, only girls gone bad run on with the kadodi.'

'Cannot blame her: apparently there is a spike in teenage pregnancies after an imbalu year.'

'If you are stupid.'

Conversation stalled. Giibwa had not contributed a word. They walked and ran, walked and ran. When they ran past Sio's home in Kamuli, Kirabo nudged Giibwa to say *He is walking us all the way*. Giibwa walked slower than them and kept falling behind. Kirabo would look back, beckon for her and Giibwa would run to catch up.

As they came to the fringes of Nattetta, Sio became a problem. They were coming to the houses of residents who looked out for Kirabo. It was bad enough to be seen in Sio's company without her family in daytime, but at night, alone with him, would be monstrous. Giibwa did not count: she had no future to lose. Kirabo could already hear Widow Diba hurrying to Grandmother clapping, *Muka Miiro, Muka Miiro? I don't like what I saw last night. That Kabuye's son? Hmm-hmm.*

Kirabo tried to get rid of Sio. 'I think we will be safe now.'

'I think I should see you home.'

By the time they came to the trail that led to Giibwa's home in Kisoga, Kirabo was desperate. 'You know, Sio,' she said, 'I will be all right from this point on, but Giibwa's home is further up there. It is dark and bush all the way to Kisoga.'

Sio stopped and looked at Giibwa for the first time. Giibwa squirmed. Kirabo felt that this was the moment for Giibwa to flash her dimples, but she just stood there like a tree stump. Kirabo added, 'She crosses the stream, Nnankya. Some nights the spirit comes out and sits on the bridge.'

'Okay, hurry up,' he said to Giibwa like a man who has no patience with spirit nonsense.

As they walked away, Kirabo called in English, *'Thank you very much for escorting us, Sio.'*

He turned, threw a curt 'Kale' at her and carried on walking.

That was the moment Kirabo felt Sio. He hurt. His 'Kale', flung at her when she had attempted to speak his language, cut deep. What would it have cost him to say the English equivalent, *Okay*, or *You are welcome*. She glanced back. Sio and Giibwa were shadows. Suddenly, Sio seemed too close to Giibwa. And they were on their own. As if he preferred Giibwa. It hurt. As if he could not wait to be alone with her, even though it was she, Kirabo, who had asked him to walk them home while Giibwa pretended modesty. The pain was outrageous, absurd even. Especially as she had asked Sio to walk Giibwa home, especially as Sio had been reluctant. But the ache did not listen. That was the moment Kirabo stopped making sense to herself.

From that day on, Sio was everywhere – at the shops, on the road, even at the *koparativu stowa*. Now he lingered at church. Some Sundays his parents drove away without him. All the girls talked about him, Sio this, Sio that...and Kirabo sucked her teeth at their crooning. Then Giibwa began to say things like 'Your Sio was at the shops today' and 'That Sio of yours is really funny.'

Finally, Kirabo exploded. 'Why do you call him mine, hmm? Have I called Wafula yours?'

'Hmm hmm.' Giibwa shrugged as if she had never considered this before.

3

In Nattetta, a thing between a boy and a girl started with Boy saying to Girl, *Can I talk to you?* and Girl shrugging, which was the most positive response a boy in love could hope for in Nattetta. Then Boy whispered, *I feel like you are my twin; can we be twins?* At this, Girl sucked her teeth contemptuously – *Do I look like a slut?* – while the rest of her body screamed *Yes, yes, yes.*

The thing between Kirabo and Sio did not start the normal way. Sio did not say a word to Kirabo. He did not give her a chance to perform outrage. Thus, Kirabo did not see herself change. Besides, this thing came with such force it overwhelmed her common sense, overran her instincts and bungled her sense of judgement.

Sio started coming to Nattetta's well even though there was running water in his home. There were wells in Kamuli in case Kabuye's tap water had been turned off. And if God turned the springs off in Kamuli, there were a few wells in Bugiri, the village closest to Kamuli. Yet Sio came to Nattetta's springs, three miles away from his village.

In the evenings, the well was crowded with bigger boys and girls. For some reason, rather than line up their debbe containers the way they did early in the day, the big boys preferred to push and shove. Girls stood on the elevated sides of the well clicking their tongues and shaking their heads at the madness. When this testosterone-fuelled shoving started, Sio took Kirabo's debbe and drew water for her. He did not ask her. He just motioned with his hand and she handed over the tin container. The first time he motioned his hand, Giibwa, who stood close to Kirabo, held her breath. When Kirabo handed him her debbe, Giibwa looked away, pouting: *Why did you deny he is yours?* Kirabo pulled a *Why don't you ask him yourself?* pout. For a moment the girls did not speak. Then the moment passed. When Wafula came and tried to help Giibwa draw water, she rolled her eyes in a *Don't be silly* way. Wafula did not try it again.

Because Sio was bigger than most of the boys, and his parents were rich and Zungu and he spoke English so British Nattetta folk did not catch a word, no one challenged him. But Ntaate, the village creep, was not happy. On one occasion, when he realised that Kirabo was close by, he said to his friends, 'But these Bazungu really crumpled us the way God crumpled lady parts between their legs. Now, look at this Sio: he is not even white but we don't challenge him at all.'

Sometimes, Sio lugged Kirabo's twenty-litre debbe of water from the well to the top of the hill, where he helped put it on her head. But he never said a word. Kirabo accepted his silent attention with a pride that pretended to be indifferent. If Sio chose to draw water and carry it for her, that was his problem. All she said was *'Thank you'* in English. But that did not stop girls from sighing at her, 'Aah, but, Kirabo, you are sweetening yourself for Sio,' and Kirabo would snap, 'How?'

Fetching water was a sweaty, unglamorous chore. It was impossible to look beautiful while balancing a tin debbe vertically on your head. Sometimes, a leaking debbe dripped down your head, drenching your dress. But Kirabo started to take baths, to moisturise her skin and comb her hair before she went to the well. Grandmother watched her with half-closed eyes. But Kirabo had done nothing wrong. All Sio did was draw water for her when the boys fought. In fact, Kirabo always came home earlier than everyone else. As for Giibwa, she carried on pretending not to see. She would tense whenever she caught Sio and Kirabo exchanging looks. Kirabo was aware of a kind of disappointment or hurt in Giibwa about the whole thing, but Giibwa never raised the issue.

When Kirabo came to the well with her family, Sio ignored her. It made sense, but it made her desperate. Then she stole relentless glances at him until she caught his eye. When his lips lifted in the suggestion of a smile and a spark reached his eyes and they curved upwards, half closing, the tingling in Kirabo stood on its toes. And that would be it until the following day.

Four weeks after the kadodi incident, when this thing she felt for Sio could not get any more intense, Kirabo told him that she was going away to Kampala to live with her father.

'Huh,' was all Sio said as he lifted the debbe on to her head.

'Tom, I mean my father, is coming on the Wednesday after the first day of the year to collect me.' She looked at him to see his eyes. She hoped to see dismay, hurt even. But Sio adjusted the debbe on the nkata cushioning her head and looked past her.

'I see.'

'I am not coming back.'

'Hmm.'

She stormed past him. She had attempted to talk to him and all he could manage was 'I see.'

'You call your father Tom?' he called after her.

Kirabo stopped and gave him a stare that said *That is what you picked out of what I just told you?* She walked away, shaking her head.

That week, Sio started to visit Kirabo's uncles in the evening. God knows when they had become friends. Now there was an anxiety in his glance. Kirabo wished he could say that it was terrible she was going away so she could say it too. Nonetheless, she enjoyed his anxious glance and basked in his worry.

Two days before Tom collected her, Sio did not draw water for her until very late. Then he carried her debbe all the way home, right to the walkway. All the way from the well, Kirabo walked behind him swinging her arms like *Look at me, I am a princess*. People shook their heads at the brazen display. Girls rolled their eyes. Women clicked, 'Miiro is in trouble; she has gone bad too.' To make matters worse, Kirabo and Sio walked slowly on the thin trail from the well, holding everyone up. In the end, people pushed past them, sucking their teeth, some huffing.

'Ever seen a calf flirting with a bull?'

'What did you expect – to pick tangerines off a lime tree?'

Stung by the reference to her parents, Kirabo wanted to shout *A boy carrying water for you does not make you pregnant, idiots*. But she kept quiet because people in Nattetta were incredibly dumb. By the time she and Sio joined the main road, darkness had fallen. A sensible voice in her head warned that she was being reckless, but she already felt out of reach of Nattetta gossip.

When they got to the walkway, instead of putting the debbe on her head, Sio rested it on the ground. Then he turned and looked at her with eyes so intense she looked lower, focusing on the baby hairs on his upper lip. They had started to crawl. His lower lip was so pale it was red. She could make out the whisper of a goatee on his chin. She looked away at the ramp by the roadside. But he stared at her until she looked at him again. His eyes said *This is me, that is you, we are*.

Kirabo looked away again.

'Aren't you going to say goodbye?' Sio asked softly.

The night tightened. Kirabo stood first on one leg, then on the other, but no words came, just her breathing.

'Okay, if you are not going to speak to me…' He folded his arms.

Her chest rose and fell, rose and fell.

She felt his breath on her face before she realised he had leaned in. He whispered, as if Widow Diba was nearby, 'Tomorrow, I will be waiting behind the Co-operative Store; come after lunch when it has closed.' He paused, then leaned further in and added, 'Bring some words.' As he withdrew, his lips brushed somewhere. Might have been her ear or her lip; it was hard to tell because a bolt shot into Kirabo's pants. It bleeped there like a car indicator, *bleep-bleep, bleep-bleep*. For some time, she stayed on the spot, her insides quivering. She attempted to lift the debbe on to her head but failed. She lugged it by the handle up the walkway, limping around the house via the back so as not to be seen by her grandparents. When she got to the bath cubicle, she emptied some water into a basin and bathed. At least then she trembled from the cold.

The following day, as if women had not warned her that men were all after one thing, Kirabo gave Grandmother the slip and ran to behind the *koparativu stowa*. Sio was sitting on the huge log behind the building. When he looked up and she saw the little scar on his Adam's apple her heart exploded. She smiled, but he did not. She stopped, and almost came to her senses and ran back home when he burst out, 'You don't even care what people suffer.'

'But I have come!' She had expected smiles and hugs and holding hands and looking at each other properly because Nattetta was too mean to give them the space and time. Even language in Nattetta was so limited it could not articulate their thing.

'*My father is taking me, I am not coming back,*' Sio mimicked. 'You just don't care all this time.'

'What can I do?'

'Let me show you.'

He walked towards her, unbuttoning his shirt. The heartbeat in Kirabo's knickers started again. The skin beneath Sio's shirt was even paler than his face. His chest was wider than she had imagined. Narrow waist. As if he had been gutted. He stood in front of her and raised his hands. 'Feel it.'

The bleeping in Kirabo's pants threatened to perforate her knickers.

'Go on; feel it.'

She put her hand on his heart and he caught his breath. His heart jabbed slightly away from her hand. He put his hand on hers and adjusted it to the left, on top of his heart. 'Do you feel it now?'

It jabbed into her palm, double time. Kirabo pulled her hand away.

'You have nothing to say to that: do you?' Sio challenged. 'You have nothing to say to the fact that even way back to when I saw your grandmother drag you on the road as if she was going to kill you, I could not sleep.' He walked back to the log, buttoning up his shirt.

'Forgive me.'

'What good is that? You are happy to go away and proud not to come back.'

'I am not. It is my father taking me away.'

'Do you suffer?'

'I do.' But what else could she say; that she suffered more, especially when he did not come to the well, when doubt accosted her? That it was rapture when the following day he looked at her, that his stare made her feel as if the world was scorched but she was the only plant sprouting? These were things you felt, but words in Nattetta were inadequate.

'Then I will come to your house tonight, behind your kitchen.'

'Don't,' Kirabo pleaded. 'Grandmother is extra tight on me at the moment. It was hard to steal myself away just now.' Then an idea occurred to her. 'Do you want to touch my heart?'

Sio looked at her.

'It beats like yours.'

Sio's eyes fell to her breasts. Then he looked away. He thought for a moment, but then he shook his head.

'It will only hurt more.'

He got up and walked away. Kirabo stared in dismay. She had never risked so much for a boy. All he had to do was feel her heart. What was she thinking, coming to meet him like this in the first place? She bolted. *Never again. I will go to Kampala and leave him in stupid Kamuli.*

Yet she was restless for the remainder of the day, anticipating, dreading, hoping, waiting. When it got dark, she wanted to check behind the kitchen, but Grandmother's eyes were glued to her, telling her to do this chore and that, not letting her out of her sight. As if she knew what Kirabo had in mind. When supper was readied in the diiro and everyone started walking to the house, Kirabo fell behind. Grandmother noticed and came back.

'Why are you hovering in the dark?' Her voice was gravel. 'This way.' She pointed to the house.

Throughout supper Kirabo imagined Sio behind the kitchen, in the cold, mosquitoes revelling. After eating, she rushed to help clear up the banana leaf wraps. As she carried the baskets to the kitchen, Grandmother said, 'You stay here,' and told the boys to help. When she made to go outside to the toilet, Grandmother said, 'Wait.' She grabbed a lantern, walked her outside and waited by the side of the toilet as Kirabo peed. When she could not pretend to pee any longer, Grandmother reached for her arm. 'Come and wash your hands.' They stopped at the water tank. Kirabo washed her hands as if scrubbing at glue, glancing towards the kitchen, hoping that Sio had realised they had no chance that night. When Grandmother closed the door, it caught Kirabo's heart and crushed it, but Grandmother locked it anyway.

Tom must have heard her sigh because he reached for her shoulders, lay her head on his lap and said, 'Sleep; I will wake you when we get there.'

4

When Kirabo and Tom arrived in Kampala, they alighted at The Yield, locally called ku Yaadi, on Jinja Road. Kirabo staggered when she stepped out of the taxi. The city's bright streetlights, after the natural nights in Nattetta, stunned her. She shivered and Tom draped his jacket, heavy like a blanket, around her shoulders. He held out his hand. Kirabo took it and they walked along a wall towards a roundabout. The tarmac was yellowish. She looked at her feet: they were yellow. She let go of Tom's hand and pushed her own through the coat's sleeves: they too were yellow. The tall eucalyptus trees on the left were yellow; so was the long wall on the right, the passing cars, the pedestrians. Kirabo looked up. It was the street lights. They made everything yellow. She wanted to skip, jump and bask in the yellowness of the night but Tom was hurrying ahead. She wondered who turned on the lights. It had to be a huge switch. They walked a short way past the roundabout, crossed the road and stood on Old Port Bell Road, where they caught another taxi to Bugoloobi.

All the way through the industrial area, past the abattoir, across the railway line, into the swamp with yams, Kirabo stared through the window. After a while they came upon the most beautiful building in the world, the Coffee Marketing Board, with its multicoloured glass panels of yellow, blue and green. It was surrounded by bright lights. She tugged at Tom's sleeves. 'Your office.' Tom looked up and smiled.

They got out of the second taxi in Bugoloobi Town. The shops on either side of the road were imposing. On a high wall was a large advert:

OMO THE BIG ONE, BLUE BAND, COLGATE, KIMBO, JIK, VIM. A man held his wife's hand and she held her daughter's hand who, in turn, held her little brother's. They were happy because they used these products. Another advert in a lightning bolt screamed CHIBUKU FOR WINNERS.

Now the shops were behind them. Kirabo, walking behind Tom, noticed how his body moved, the way his head nodded with his gait, his Afro thick and round. This being close to Tom, this being his daughter, was new. Her mother too was drawing nearer: she could feel her. Nattetta had been too far from the truth.

They turned into a murram road with a Nattetta kind of darkness and Tom became a shadow. Kirabo hurried to his side and slipped her hand into his. He slowed his pace and she tried to fall into his rhythm, but her strides would not fit into his: she had to hurry and hop.

When she could not bear the silence any longer, she said, 'Taata.'

'Daddy; you call me Daddy from now on.'

'Dadi?'

'Daddy.'

'Daddie?'

'Yes.'

'How come you visit Nsuuta when you come home?'

'Because she is my mother.'

'But how? Grandmother is your mother.'

'Grandmother gave birth to me, but Nsuuta brought me up.'

'Oh?' She contemplated for a while. 'Grandmother does not like her.'

'That is their problem.'

'Grandmother does not like me to visit Nsuuta.'

'Then don't visit her.'

Kirabo dropped Nsuuta, but soon the silence became too much again. She wished Tom would say something. She cast around for something to talk about. She was shocked to hear herself say, 'Where is my mother?' It just came out.

'What?' Tom's head turned to look at her. Kirabo could not see his expression. 'Are you unhappy?'

'No.'

'Then why do you want her?'

'To see what she looks like; so she can start to be my mother.'

'I don't know where she is.'

'Why?' Kirabo was not deterred by his clipped answer.

'No one knows where she is.'

'Because people will find out she had me while in school?'

Tom stopped walking. 'Who told you that?'

'Nsuuta.'

'Did she?' He started to walk again.

'All she said was that my mother finished studying and is married.' Because Kirabo had to run to keep up with Tom, now her voice vibrated as she explained, 'I was pestering her when she told me.'

Tom did not respond, but Kirabo felt his anger. She could not believe she had betrayed Nsuuta so quickly, only to hit a wall.

'Why did you not marry her?' The reckless streak in her decided that if Tom was going to be angry with her for asking, then she might as well deserve his anger. She thought back to the advert she had just seen, imagining Tom holding her mother's hand, her mother holding Kirabo's own. Perhaps they would have a baby boy and Kirabo would hold his hand and they would all be happy.

'You do not ask me such questions, Kirabo. I am your father. Clearly Miiro has spoilt you so much I don't even know where to start correcting you.'

It was no use. Tom did not understand that she did not have to be unhappy to want her mother. Yet she felt her. With every step she took, Kirabo felt her mother coming closer. If there is a bond between a mother and her child, as people say, this was it. A sense. It was all around.

A huge block of flats came into view, then another and another. It would be awesome to live in the famous Bugoloobi flats. She asked, 'Dadi, is it true these flats were being built by Israelis when Amin stop—'

Tom elbowed her and she swallowed the rest of the question.

They walked in silence until they turned into a tarmacked road. The air here turned from Ugandan to European. Like the air of those colonial residential neighbourhoods, Kololo or Nakasero. All the bungalows on this road were similar. Dark, tall hedges, security lights, large compounds, paved walkways, tall gates. Tom stopped at the fourth house, picked up a stone and knocked on the gate. A plaque on the wall with a light above said PROPERTY OF COFFEE MARKETING BOARD. Footsteps came hurrying over. The inset gate opened. Tom bent low and stepped in. Kirabo followed.

A dark figure greeted them. 'Welcome back, sir.'

'Thank you.'

The figure replaced the heavy chain.

Why did Tom need such a huge house? Security lights, on the front porch and on the side, failed to dispel the immense shadow thrown in front of the building.

They climbed three steps and stood on the porch. A girl, about fifteen, opened the door. Kirabo wondered if she was a maid or relative. The girl's eyes lingered on Kirabo. The diiro was European, the furnishing and the layout very spacious, like in magazines. Nattetta was a pigsty compared to this. Kirabo started to feel the dust on her feet. Even her dress, which she had thought so pretty, now felt drab. For the first time in her life, she felt impoverished.

'Sit down, Kirabo,' Tom said.

She went to the couch and sat on the edge. The partition between the dining area and the sitting room was a huge piece of furniture. At the bottom it was a chest of drawers; at the top, a wall unit. The top two shelves were filled with books. Below, on a wider shelf, a Philips TV, a JVC radio cassette player and two large jars, one filled with roast groundnuts, the other with biscuits. Two doors led out of the dining area – one to the right, the other straight on. A heavy, metallic hum led her eyes to a wide fridge with the word FRIGIDAIRE on the door. The TV flickered a static-filled screen. As Tom removed his shoes to step on the carpet he said, 'Can you switch that TV off?' Then, 'Why are you having supper so late, Nnaki?'

'Madam said it is okay since tomorrow is weekend.' The girl, Nnaki, was a maid, then.

Madam? Kirabo was perplexed. Which madam? She was getting up to switch the TV off when a little girl of about six peeled off a sofa and padded across the room. Her patterned pyjamas had so blended into the settee that Kirabo had not seen her. She turned a knob and it clicked like Grandmother's tongue. She returned and threw herself back on the sofa, feet and all. Something rigid about the girl said to Kirabo *I don't want to know you.*

'Are you not going to greet me, Mwagale?'

The girl ran across the room and threw herself at Tom. 'Welcome back, Daddy.'

The insides of Kirabo's stomach dissolved. *My sister?* She looked down because she felt emotions she never knew she had. Her feet, coated with dust, were dirtying the carpet. She tucked them out of sight. *First a madam, now a sister?* She withdrew her feet, wiped the dust with her hankie, and then regretted it. The hankie was now filthy. *Why did I not know?* She crossed her ankles, raised her eyes and looked at the little girl. Resentment, blindingly intense, came in waves. The fact that Mwagale's name meant Beloved, while Kirabo's only meant Gift, did not help.

Nnaki now fed a child of eight or nine months sitting in a high chair. He dribbled his food. The girl crooned, 'Please eat, Junior, have some.' She scooped up the dribble around the child's lips and sunk it back into his mouth, only for it to be dribbled out again. *Only a maid would put up with that nonsense,* Kirabo thought. If she fed the little monkey, she would have stopped a long time ago. You don't drag a person with chills to the fire. God, she wanted to pinch the little thing and slap the little girl and throw them out of her father's house.

The door on the right opened and a woman in a blue satin night-dress and a matching gown floated in. Her hair was done in the latest Zairois plaits – chunks wrapped tightly in black thread until they stood like spikes. When she reached the partitioning shelf-cupboard, she saw Kirabo and stopped.

'Who is this?'

Kirabo was too shocked to reply. She noticed that the hairdresser had pulled the woman's hair so tight it had formed ebisuko bumps along the hairline.

'That is Kirabo,' Tom said without looking up.

'Which Kirabo?'

'How many Kirabos do you know?'

The woman slumped on to the sofa. For a while, she held her head in both hands as though it was too heavy for her neck. She looked vaguely familiar but Kirabo could not place where she had seen her before. The woman lifted her head and asked, 'Why was I not told?'

'This is her home.'

The woman seemed to deflate. 'How long is she staying?'

Tom turned away, his body saying *Don't be tedious*. But then he said, 'I thought I said this is her home, or was I munching myself?' He got into some house slippers and walked through the door on the right. The woman was momentarily speechless. Then, gripping her nightie, she stormed after Tom. Nnaki, who had stopped feeding the child, stared as if she was paid for it. The little girl scrambled off the sofa and marched through the door her parents had passed through just moments before. Nnaki lifted the baby out of his high chair and they too went through the same door.

Kirabo's isolation was complete. Her head buzzed. She looked up and saw, on a pelmet above a window, a long black-and-white wedding portrait. Tom, in a dark suit, his body slightly angled towards his bride. He looked straight at the camera, his lips pulled back in a wry smile. Kirabo felt so betrayed she could not bring herself to look at the bride.

She stood up and went to the window, noticing as she parted the curtains that her hand shook. Outside, she could not see beyond the light on the porch. She needed to step outside the house and breathe.

'What are you doing?'

Kirabo jumped. Tom had returned.

'It is not polite to peek through windows.'

She moved away. Nnaki came back without the child. She retrieved a bundle of table mats from a chest of drawers and set the table, then disappeared through the other door and came back with food in dishes and then on wide plates. When she finished, Tom asked Kirabo to join him for supper. She shook her head. Even if Tom's wife had been welcoming, the idea of cutlery was off-putting.

'Looks like only Nnaki and I have an appetite tonight.' He turned to Kirabo. 'Your mother is not feeling well.'

He ate a forkful, chewed at leisure, swallowed. Forked again, chewed, oblivious to the riot within Kirabo compounded by the statement he had just tossed at her so insouciantly, 'Your mother is not feeling well.' Kirabo's head swelled as anger piled on top of the shock and hurt and confusion. This was not what she had expected when she felt her mother draw closer. Had Nsuuta not cured her of flying, she would be raging in the winds up and down Nattetta's road. Of course, if the witch was Tom's wife then she was, by tradition, her 'mother'. But this was too sudden, too insensitive; so unlike the way she had imagined the first moment with her mother. If the woman had been human, Kirabo would have thought maybe in time she could consider her as a mother, but not this witch of a stepmother straight out of a folk tale.

After eating, Tom thanked Nnaki and said, 'Come with me, Kirabo.'

Kirabo stood up. She could not bear to look at him. His betrayal – marrying that woman and having two children with her behind Kirabo's back – was too raw. All this time she had thought Tom was hers.

The door on the right opened into a corridor. Tom pointed to the left. 'That is the toilet, that is the bathroom. The water heater is behind that door. Further down the corridor, the door on the left is our bedroom.' He turned to the right and opened the first door. 'This is your bedroom. The one opposite our bedroom is Mwagale and Nnaki's. Now, go to bed.' And with that, he disappeared down the corridor.

Kirabo stood there uncertainly. She would have preferred to sleep in the same room as Nnaki. Somehow, even though they had not spoken much, Kirabo related to the maid. Not just in age; Nnaki seemed like she too came from a village like Nattetta.

She opened the door. The bedroom was twice as large as her grandfather's, and the bed was made like one in a hotel. On the right was a chest. She walked to it and pulled out the drawers for no reason. They were empty. She went to the wardrobe in the wall and opened the double doors. Naked hangers.

Someone knocked on her door. It was Nnaki with Kirabo's bag. She had left it in the sitting room. Nnaki gave it to her with a 'Sleep well.'

Kirabo looked at her belongings inside the bag and wrinkled her nose. The white linen Grandmother had given her, her dresses and knickers wrapped up in a green cotton kitambaala crocheted with flowers, were so rural she flung them into the wardrobe and closed the doors. Tom appeared at the door and gave her his T-shirt: 'You will have to use this as a nightdress tonight.'

When he had gone, she took off her dress and put on his T-shirt. Then she stopped. What if she dreamt and wet the bed? She opened the door and ran to the toilet. For a long time, she sat on the toilet, squeezing out every last drop. Finally, when noises in the house had ceased, she tiptoed across the corridor to her bedroom and turned out the lights. But the security light on the porch would not let proper darkness into her room. She lay on top of the bed and stared at the ceiling. In one evening, she had acquired a daddy, an evil stepmother and two brats, Mwagale and Junior, for a sister and a brother? She began to understand Miiro's warning, 'We don't want to hear choking later.' She thought back to his abrupt manner when he bade her goodbye, thought back to Nsuuta's worry.

The money! Kirabo jumped out of bed. She turned on the light, pulled her bag out of the wardrobe and searched it. She could not find it anywhere. She removed the tablecloth, undid the knots, picked out the items and shook them one by one. No money. She opened the door and tiptoed to the dining area. The light was on but there was no one about. She went to the couch where she had sat. There, in the tight space between the cushions, was the money, folded. She prised it out and opened it. It was all there in twenties and fifties. She turned to leave and there, on the settee, was Tom's wife, staring at her. Her eyes were huge and red and puffy. Kirabo ran out of the room, jumped into her bed, covered her head and shivered.

5

'Slept well?'

Kirabo woke up to Tom standing in the doorway, his collar up, knotting his tie. She squinted: *Does he work on Saturdays?* The world was too bright to be waking up. It had to be at least two hours of day. Everything was wrong. Too much space in the bedroom, the paint on the walls too bright, the silence in the house. Outside, no weaver birds, no cockerels calling or animals bleating, not even a warble from the Zungu chicken barn. Just too many cars going too fast, too close to the house. In Nattetta you heard one car every two hours. And you did not have to see it to know which car, whose it was, unless it was a stranger.

'At around midday, your Aunt Abi will collect you to go shopping.' He adjusted his coat.

Kirabo rolled out of bed and knelt on the floor to bid him good morning, but when she looked up he was gone. She got up and sat on the bed to reorient herself. She was in Kampala. She was in Tom's house. There was an evil stepmother outside her door with a couple of spoilt brats. And Tom, who had brought her to this place, had just abandoned her to them. For a moment she felt weak, as if she might fall asleep, but she snapped out of it. Still, she wanted to jump out of the window and run down the road to Nsuuta's house and scream *Real evil stepmothers exist; I have one*. She sighed. What now? Venturing outside her door was scary. Going back to bed was lazy. Sunlight, through the window, had spilled beneath the curtains, down the wall.

She made the bed. Then lay on top of it. Then sat up. The air in her room was tired and limp. Had Tom said Aunt Abi was coming? She looked to the window in anticipation. Aunt Abi was her favourite. She was Miiro's second-born. Tom came after her. Aunt YA was the eldest. Uncle Ndiira was fourth and Gayi was last. In the past, whenever Kirabo had come to the city for school holidays, she had stayed with Abi in her flat in Old Kampala. Tom and Aunt Abi were very close. As close as Miiro and his horrible sister, Nsangi.

Kirabo walked to the window and peered between the curtains. The compound looked less daunting in daytime. The lawn was level; dew glistened like tears. *Are those kuule shrubs?* she thought, peering. Someone had just planted the tiny shrubs – some reddish, some yellow, some green – to edge the lawn and perhaps camouflage the grey kerb. Kirabo clicked. In Nattetta kuule shrubs were such a bad omen it was reckless to bring them into your home.

Eggs were frying. Kirabo's stomach stretched noisily. She walked across the room and listened at the door. Silence. She opened the door a little. Listened again. Nothing. She opened it further, put a foot outside and waited. Silence. As she walked towards the toilet, a woman's voice exclaimed, 'He sprung her on you without telling you?'

Kirabo held her breath.

'Like a car accident.' Tom's wife's voice. 'I made it clear right from the start; I'm not bringing up children who are not mine, *full stop*. Look at Mother. Every time Father took a walk, he came back with a child. Mother reared them all. But what has she gained beside ingratitude? Me, I'm not. Besides, you accept one child today, tomorrow he brings another. Not me. It is me, my children, *full stop*.'

'But this one was born before—'

'It does not matter. If I had had a child, would Tom have married me?'

'It is not the same; he is a man.'

'It is the same to me.'

'The child belongs to him, this is his house, it is the clan system, you will get in trouble—'

'Is his clan running this house? I said I am not bringing her up, *full stop.*'

'But it is not the child's fault.'

Kirabo edged to the door and peered into the room. A woman sat on one of the dining chairs. They must be sisters: they looked ridiculously alike. As if their parents were too lazy to make new faces. Life had not been as generous to the visitor though. She had bleached her face, but since Amin had outlawed bleaching the sun had reclaimed it. The new black was like a scar. Now Kirabo remembered where she had seen Tom's wife: at Aunt YA's wedding. She had been pregnant then. Must have been with Mwagale. Why had her grandparents not mentioned that she was Tom's wife? Normally, they would introduce her: 'Kirabo, look at this person carefully. She is your...' Why had the woman not visited Nattetta all this time? Or brought the children to see their grandparents? But then again, if Tom's wife had made it clear that it was her and her children alone, she would not be welcome in Nattetta.

'By the way, does Nnakku visit?'

Tom's wife snorted. 'People say I have a stone for a heart, but compared to Nnakku I am an angel.'

Kirabo smiled. This Nnakku had to be ultra-wicked to make Tom's wife an angel in comparison.

'Nnakku's heart is the same as her mother's.' The sister's voice was high-pitched. 'That Jjali; everybody says it. By the way, where is she?'

'Who, Nnakku or her mother Jjali?'

'Kirabo.'

'Still in bed. Probably she is used to being woken up by Miiro. Nnaki?' Tom's wife called. 'Can you wake that girl up? We don't want her dying in bed.'

Kirabo ran back to the bedroom, jumped into bed and closed her eyes. The door opened. Nnaki hurried in and shook her. 'Kirabo, Kirabo, breakfast is ready.'

'Oh.' Kirabo sat up. 'I am sorry I overslept. What time is it?'

'Coming to four hours of morning.'

Kirabo gasped shame.

'You went to bed late.' Nnaki drew back the curtains and opened the shutters. The morning air was cool and fresh. Kirabo rushed to the bathroom to wash her face, then changed. When she could not put it off any longer, she opened the door to the dining room. The women turned towards her. Tom's wife looked away, as if her husband's mistress had just walked in. Kirabo knelt to bid them good morning.

'Oh, Kirabo,' the visitor gushed, 'how you have grown.' She turned to her sister. 'She has taken after Tom's height: has she not?'

Tom's wife ignored her. Kirabo's smile started to hurt.

'I see happy times in the future.' The woman winked. 'That is all we old women think of. Happiness that our children are married.'

Kirabo's smile vanished. As she stepped into the kitchen, she heard the visitor whisper, 'She got the eyes?'

'She has everything – the heart too, I suspect.'

'Maama, they are grown-up eyes. If they could kill, I would be lifeless on the floor right now.'

'See what I will have to put up with?'

'I was going to take your breakfast to the table,' Nnaki said, bringing Kirabo's mind back to the kitchen.

'Like I don't have hands?' Kirabo smiled. She was eager to show Nnaki that she had rural etiquette.

As Nnaki put her breakfast on a tray, Kirabo looked around the kitchen. Everything sparkled so clean and white you could eat off the floor. Forget smoke, soot and ash in Grandmother's kitchen. There was no going to the well in this home, no firewood. Life in Tom's house seemed so lazy; Kirabo imagined a people who woke up, laid their hands on their laps and yawned *I think I am hungry*. Grandmother would have a fit.

Breakfast was maize-meal porridge with milk and sugar. Then TipTop bread with Blue Band margarine. Sugar so thrilled Kirabo's tongue that had she been in Nattetta she would have asked for more porridge. She could not remember when they had last tasted sugar or bread or margarine in Nattetta. It was as if the disappearance of necessities from the shops had not affected people in the city. In Nattetta you ate sweet potatoes with tea to render it sweet. Soap and cooking oil had to be rationed. Now, it seemed as if European embargoes on Uganda had not affected everyone equally. Breakfast was so lovely Kirabo dismissed not having the fried eggs which she saw Mwagale eating.

From the vantage of the dining table, Kirabo studied Tom's wife. She was probably beautiful if you liked chiselled features – chin, nose and cheekbones – and pale skin. But tiny beads of sweat had formed on the bridge of her nose: a sign of a quarrelsome disposition. She and her sister had large eyes, but Muka Tom's were slanted like a snake's.

After eating, Kirabo took her tray to the kitchen and began to wash the dishes. Mwagale brought her cup and plate. Kirabo smiled. Whatever their mother's faults, the children were blood. And Kirabo being the eldest, had to act it. But as she reached for the cup, Mwagale threw it into the sink and ran. Then she came back to the door and shouted, 'You are not my sister. Go back where you come from.'

Kirabo stood still, then bit into her lower lip.

Nnaki clicked in disgust. Then she drew close to Kirabo and whispered, 'She may deny all she wants, but the two of you are like two ten-cent coins.'

Kirabo was too vexed to pay attention to Nnaki's comment. In Nattetta, she would have gone after the imp and put her in her proper place with a wagging finger and few sharp words.

'Mwagale,' Muka Tom called. 'What are you provoking that girl for? Do we not have enough trouble as it is? If she hits you, don't come crying to me.'

That settled it. After the dishes, Kirabo went back to her bedroom.

When Kirabo saw Aunt Abi's yellow Fiat drive in, she ran out of the house screaming, the way she used to in Nattetta. For the first time, she noticed that Aunt Abi looked like Grandmother did in her wedding picture. Apart from her big Afro, she was as skinny with the same skin tone. Only her voice, so much higher than Grandmother's, was different. She wore an *Amin, leave me alone* maxi dress, the fashion after the president had banned short skirts. After hugging Kirabo, Aunt Abi asked, 'Where is your mother?'

'Which one?'

'You know who I mean – Nnambi.'

'Nnambi?' Kirabo looked at Aunt Abi incredulously. 'That is Muka Tom's name? What blasphemy.'

'I tell you, child.' Aunt Abi humoured her.

'Maybe,' Kirabo laughed, 'she missed the class about Kintu ne Nnambi in primary school…'

'Maybe she is rebelling against the name.' Aunt Abi talked to Kirabo as if they were the same age.

'She went to town with her sister.'

'Thank God. Get in the car.' As she drove away Aunt Abi asked, 'So, how did Muka Tom take your arrival?'

'Like swallowing live soldier ants.'

'Good. Let her see the sun. She is possessive, that woman. Finally, Tom is being a man—'

'But, you people,' Kirabo interrupted heatedly, 'where is my mother? I ask this one – *I don't know*; I ask that one – *I don't know*. Who knows?'

'You are asking the wrong person, Kirabo. Me, I saw nothing. I was in boarding school when Tom arrived home with a baby. When I came home and saw you, I said, "This one is mine." I bathed you, washed your clothes, fed you, everything. Until Mother insisted that YA and I take turns. But you have always been mine – everyone knows it.'

Kirabo leaned over and put her head on Aunt Abi's hand to say *I love you too*. But she realised she would never ask Aunt Abi again.

'Tell me,' Aunt Abi asked, 'how was Nattetta when you left; is Widow Diba still Widow Diba?'

'That woman has an axe for a tongue.'

'What about Nsuuta?'

'She and Grandmother are still at it.'

'As for those two…' Aunt Abi performed fatigue.

'But what I don't understand is why Tom, I mean Dadi, visits her without Grandmother stopping him.'

'Can Tom be told off?'

'He said Nsuuta brought him up.'

'True, but if your mother hates her you need to keep a distance.'

'Is Nsuuta Grandfather's woman?'

'Aaah haa, child…' Aunt Abi hesitated. 'Will you manage?'

'Manage what?'

'Oh well, you have grown; you might as well know.' She sighed. 'Nsuuta was Father's woman too when we were young. I don't know what is going on now. Perhaps they still are at it.'

Kirabo's heart ripped. 'Why did he not make her his wife then?' It was hard to suppress the pain in her chest. Ssozi the slanderer was right after all? Grandfather was—

'He tried to make Nsuuta's status in the family public, and Mother seemed okay with it. The way I saw it, Mother had no chance against Nsuuta anyway. Certain things you accept. I mean, God gave Nsuuta everything: beauty, brains, money. Legend has it that she is the woman who ate Father's heart. In her day, Nsuuta was something. She would wear her nurse's uniform and walk down that road and Nattetta would say *Ha, but God can sculpt*. But Mother? She did not care about things like that. It was as if she had dug a hole, jumped in and piled soil on top of herself. I mean, if your man is carrying on with another woman who looks like an angel, you get up and panel-beat yourself; see what I mean?'

Kirabo nodded without seeing what she meant.

'Not Mother.'

'So what stopped him?'

'Family and church, especially his older brother. Because he is a priest, Faaza Dewo would not allow it. To this day he still hates Nsuuta. Listen, by the time I started to understand the world, Tom lived with Nsuuta. Father spent some nights at her house openly. I did not even know Tom was Mother's. I thought Mother had me, YA and Ndiira, who was a baby at the time. Gayi was not yet born.'

'But could you not see Dadi resembles Grandmother?'

'As a child, you don't see such things.'

'Hmm.'

'On Saturday afternoons when Father bought meat for Sunday meals, there were always two bundles. One for us at the first home and a small one for the second house. He would hand both to Mother. I swear Mother barbecued it for them because Nsuuta worked weekends as well. It seemed to me that Mother was happy to share Father.' Abi paused. 'Maybe she was taking care of Tom's interests, I don't know. Whenever Nsuuta came around the house she and Mother whispered all the time. After the church and Faaza Dewo intervened, their relationship went underground.' She sucked her teeth. 'When Mother yanked Tom away from Nsuuta, her reason was that Nsuuta was spoiling him, giving him things we did not have.' Aunt Abi shook her head. 'I tell you, Kirabo, Mother brought me into the world and I so love her the earth is not enough, but how could we be jealous when Nsuuta did shopping, especially around Christmas, for all of us? Even for Mother. Nsuuta had only Tom to look after and her father was rich. We were not happy with what Mother did. Tom almost never forgave her, but she is our mother, you let go. I guess Tom decided to love them both.'

'But why did Grandfather give Tom to Nsuuta in the first place?'

'I was a child, remember. All I am telling you is what I saw or heard as a child. You know Nsuuta is barren?'

Kirabo nodded uncomfortably.

'Mother had two children already. Traditionally, wives share children. You could not leave your co-wife to live a childless life while you hoard all your progeny to yourself.'

Kirabo muted the image of the little graveyard behind Nsuuta's house.

Aunt Abi turned from Namirembe Road into Rashid Khamis Road. She lived on a row of semi-detached houses that had belonged to Asians before they were expelled. The architecture was Indian. The buildings were white with curved parapet roofs. Everything was concrete – the front yard and the wall fencing. Aunt Abi's house was closest to the former Gurdwara Temple, which was now a mosque.

As they walked towards the alleyway on the side of the building, the pain of Nsuuta and Grandfather returned. Kirabo was reminded of Ntaate, the village creep. Ntaate was the kind of boy who saw you happy in your ignorance and decided to shatter your bliss. Like that time when Kirabo was six. Ntaate saw her kick Miiro's ram. That ram mounted anything on four legs – dogs, goats and ewes. It was riding a lamb. When Kirabo kicked it off, Ntaate told her to leave it alone.

'Where do you think lambs come from?'

Kirabo knew, of course. She had grown up with insects, chickens, dogs, everything mating around her. But it was the way that ram smelt the ewes' backsides and then bared all his teeth to the sky that disgusted her most.

'Where do you think you came from?' Ntaate was relentless.

'From my mother's stomach.'

'And who put you there?'

Kirabo shrugged.

'Tom.'

She fell on to him and hit him everywhere, screaming, 'You are disgusting, pumpkin-head, stinky billy goat. My father is not like that.'

Ntaate extricated himself and ran, laughing. When he was at a distance he called, 'Tom and your mother, *ghi, ghi, ghi,*' grinding his pelvis. 'Miiro and Muka Miiro, *ghi, ghi, ghi.*' Kirabo, incensed, screamed that she slept in Grandfather's bedroom, that Grandmother slept in the room across the corridor, that if such a thing happened, she would know.

But Ntaate was not having it. 'Where do you think Tom came from?'

That was the first time in her life when her perfect grandparents were not perfect. It had hurt for a long time. But along life's way, she accepted that human beings also behaved that way. Now, in the same way, she had to accept that perhaps Grandfather was hurting Grandmother by being with Nsuuta. She sighed. This is what Grandmother had warned: 'Don't go hurrying to grow up.'

Kirabo and Abi entered through the back gate into an enclosed concrete yard. They ducked beneath laundry on clothes lines and into the shared foyer. Aunt Abi fumbled for the keys in her bag. When she could not find them, she went to the window where there was sunlight and emptied the contents of her handbag on to the windowsill. Aunt Abi's bag was a kikapu – it hauled everything but the charcoal stove. When she found them, she sighed and returned to the door.

'The house is a mess,' she warned as she opened it.

Family whispered that when it came to tidiness, Aunt Abi took after Grandmother. Apart from the worn-out furniture, you would think she had six toddlers the way everything was strewn about. Paper bags, books, coffee-stained cups, shoes and clothes on the floor. 'You are welcome,' she said as she cleared the sofa and picked things off the floor. Apparently this was why she never kept a relationship for a decent period. Aunt Abi was Jjajja Nsangi's headache. Specifically, her boyfriends who had failed to evolve into a husband. Nsangi, because she was Miiro's only sister, was Abi's formal aunt and had prepared her for everything feminine in life. Every time Nsangi saw Aunt Abi she asked, 'Abisaagi, what are you up to in the marriage department? Time is running. Let me know if you need help,' and Aunt Abi scowled.

'By the way, there is nothing to eat in the house.'

'I am all right.' Kirabo opened the front door to the balcony. In the corner were all the potted plants Kirabo had planted the last time she came. They were dead, the soil in the pots compact and cracked. That meant one thing. Uncle Nsibambi, the botanist, was no more. When Aunt Abi had been dating him, she had been hot on plants.

Kirabo was savouring the vista that opened out below her. First, Nakivubo, the valley and canal between Old Kampala Hill and the Nakasero Hills. Then, Sawuliyaako, the largest market for traditional ware and medicines, notorious for not catering for customer comfort;

the Equatorial Hotel as Nakasero Hill started to rise; the Norman Cinema, and then the hill disappeared behind buildings and trees.

'Here are the clothes I have bought so far,' Aunt Abi called, and Kirabo ran back into the house. Aunt Abi dropped a bundle of clothes on the sofa. 'I hope I got your size right: you are growing too fast.' Then she exclaimed, 'You need a bra already: when did this happen?' Before Kirabo responded, Aunt Abi frowned. 'Have you started your MPs?'

Kirabo nodded.

'Bannange!' Aunt Abi sank herself into a sofa. 'Then you know that a moment with a man, even tiny like this, will take away your childhood. I did not know you had started! Look at me when I am talking to you, Kirabo. I am your aunt; this is what we do.'

Kirabo glanced at her. She had had this talk with Grandmother, who made it seem as if Armageddon had arrived between her legs and quickly moved her out of Grandfather's bedroom as if Kirabo had become unclean. Then Aunt YA, being Tom's eldest sister, arrived from the city in a big way, laden with a huge roll of cotton wool, rolls of toilet paper, aspirin and black knickers like a formal aunt ready to start the aunt sessions. Aunt YA had treated the whole thing like a lesson – 'You must wash properly, be discreet, change your pad three to four times a day depending on how heavy your flow is.' How to roll a pad out of cotton wool and toilet paper. How to dispose of it – 'It must be thrown in the pit latrine or buried, because if rain falls on it and your blood runs off with rainwater your MPs will flow non-stop for the rest of your life.' How easily babies are made – 'One moment you are with a man, the next, wu, you are a mother. Use aspirin only when the pain is unbearable. Let me see your armpits. Pluck them using ash: razors make the hair grow back fast and all over the place.' Kirabo had felt her carefree childhood screech to an end. Nsuuta was right, too many liquids in women.

'Have you been with a man already?'

'What?' Kirabo shouted. 'Aunt Abi!'

'All right, all right, just asking. Me, unlike YA, I am Aunt Liberal. I don't say you should never get a boyfriend. Look what happened to

Gayi. Besides, virginity is overrated. Me, I would not take a bulb home if I had not tried it out: what if it did not light?'

Kirabo thought Aunt Abi should have been Nsuuta's child instead of Tom.

'Besides, you know the goat given to your aunt if you are a virgin on your wedding night?'

'Yes?'

'It is cooked without salt.'

Kirabo laughed.

'What I am saying is that when you get a boyfriend, don't sneak around like a thief. Bring him to me, let me meet him and he will treat you with respect. Stolen love is dangerous. It takes you to bushes and what-what.' She looked at Kirabo as if waiting for a response.

'Okay, Auntie,' she said, but inside, Kirabo was thinking *No way I am mentioning Sio*. You couldn't trust grown-ups, not even Aunt Abi.

'Your eyes are shifty, Kirabo. Is there something you wish to tell me?'

'No.'

'But you promise to tell me when you meet someone?'

'I will.' But Kirabo knew a trap when she saw one. What grown-up would not drop in fits when told by a girl, not quite fourteen, that she had a boyfriend?

'Has YA told you about labia elongation?'

'Yes.'

'Of course she has! She must be your formal aunt, must she not?' Kirabo now began to see a conflict between Aunt Abi, who had said, 'This one is mine,' when she first arrived, and Aunt YA, who was Tom's oldest sister, 'But I will help too.' Aunt Abi was saying, 'Don't do too long. Long is old-fashioned, before men discovered women.' She wrinkled her nose. 'Just a little, like this.' She indicated the upper two segments of her tiny finger. 'Doors to keep things closed.' She pressed her hands together. 'And don't pinch them at the top. Otherwise, you will get strings. Hold them right at the base with the thumb on one side and both the fore and middle fingers on the other. That will keep them wide.' Kirabo nodded. This was the kind of Aunt Talk which never seemed to end. 'You will have to show me how far you have gone. Don't worry; I will show you mine.'

The idea of looking at Aunt Abi's bits. Kirabo must have pulled a face, for Aunt Abi asked, 'Did YA explain why we elongate?'

'She said I will not have children if I don't.'

'Kdto!' Aunt Abi was outraged. 'Trust YA to use scare tactics. Kirabo, elongation is the one thing we women do for ourselves. It is for when you start having sex. A man is supposed to touch them before, you know, to know you are ready. By the time the entire length of them is wet, you are ready.'

'We do it for ourselves?' Kirabo wrinkled her nose in disgust.

Aunt Abi shuffled to the edge of her sofa in earnest. 'Look, Kirabo, don't delude yourself. Everything about us, our entire world, is built on how men react to us. So yes, in that respect we elongate because men can be inept. They are also supposed to guide them to the bean if you are still dry. Child, never let a man rush you. Tell him *I am not ready*, show him how to use his member to whip the labia, slow and gentle at first, then fast. Within a minute, you are ready. If you land on the kind of husband who does not know what to do, pack your bags and come home – hmm, hmm. An inept husband is a life sentence.'

Kirabo smiled. Nsuuta would have stated that elongation was evidence of selfish lovemaking our foremothers had to put up with.

Aunt Abi must have misread her thoughts, for she looked at her with a worried face. 'Have you ever looked at yourself down there, Kirabo?'

'No.'

'No?' The incredulity. 'Could you not find a mirror? You must look at yourself properly. It is the most magical part of you. You know a flower that is beginning to unfold?'

'Yes.'

'That is your flower. Explore it, love it, find out what it is capable of before you hand it over to a man.'

Though Kirabo had no intention of looking down there, it was inspiring to see Aunt Abi's attitude towards it. Now it was a flower, not ruins.

'All right, enough of the Aunt Talk. Me, I don't hold sessions, but I am not going to wait for your bridal session to talk about sex: what if you never marry? Now you are in the city with us, I will teach you things spontaneously, as I remember them. However, YA might sit you down with a pen and paper.'

It was true. Aunt YA took the whole thing of being a woman too seriously. She was extremely married. Her whole being revolved around pleasing her husband so he did not cheat on her. She distrusted maids. They came to work and to steal husbands. She made hers wear ugly uniforms, no jewellery or make-up on the job and certainly no sitting on her sofa. If Aunt YA sat with her husband in their car and they gave a lift to a man, she left the passenger seat for the man so not to emasculate him, while she sat in the back. Everyone at Miiro's knew the car belonged to her. They knew she paid her children's school fees but made them thank her husband. He behaved like a petty chief. You dared not sit on his sofa, not even visitors, when he was not around. It would stay empty like a throne. It was placed strategically towards the TV, commanding the sitting room. He sat at the head; his plate was special. Aunt YA enforced these rules fanatically. Kirabo did not like going to her house for holiday breaks because the one time she had, Aunt YA kept reminding her, 'You are a girl, Kirabo,' as if the world could forget. 'A woman breaks, my child. Don't stiffen yourself. I see hardness in your eyes, Kirabo. Don't be like your Aunt Abi. A woman's knees bend. Even when your man is wrong you allow him to be right. The women you see without marriages are the stiff ones.' Yet when she came home to Nattetta, when the whole family got together, Aunt YA did not break. She took the whole notion of being Miiro's eldest child seriously, especially when she wanted to assert herself over Tom, who wielded real power as the eldest son. She always reinforced her arguments with 'As the eldest child in this house, I am saying…' Grown-ups kept telling her that she took after her aunt, Nsangi – they were obedient wives but strong women outside their homes. Poor Aunt Abi, as the second daughter, had no power in the family whatsoever except over her brothers' wives.

Most clothes fit except a few skirts, which were loose around the waist yet too short. Kirabo looked at herself in the full-length mirror. Her bottom was narrow and modest. Not rounded out like Giibwa's. Her legs were still skinny and long. Not fleshy and soft like Giibwa's. The tiny waist rescued her from total boyishness.

Aunt Abi saw her frustration and said, 'You are still a bit of a reed, but you will curve out eventually.'

'But the legs…' Kirabo sighed as she surveyed her calves.

'You are a beautiful girl; you have no idea how many people would kill for your eyes. I do not want to hear buts.'

Aunt Abi had included a pair of jeans. Kirabo picked them up and gave her aunt a look that said *Where will I wear trousers?*

'Try them on,' Aunt Abi said. 'We are indoors, no one will see.' When Kirabo pulled them on, curves emerged from nowhere. The skinny legs were gone.

'I knew it; you were built for trousers; may Idi Amin die a horrible death for banning them.'

Kirabo looked at herself again. Sio would pass out, she decided. She did not take them off. When Tom came to pick her up in the company car, he laughed. 'Is this the same Miiro's sunshine I fetched from Nattetta yesterday? Now take off the trousers.'

'We must go out for a meal to celebrate Kirabo's arrival.' Aunt Abi was looking for a way out of cooking. They ended up at the Officers' Mess in Kololo. Aunt Abi ordered Irish chips and liver for Kirabo – 'You will like them; all children love chips' – but the grown-ups ate traditional dishes.

After eating, Tom and Aunt Abi retired to the high stools around the bar and started to drink. Kirabo settled on the comfy sofas and watched TV. First came *Daktari*, a series about a white man and his daughter who had a monkey, Judy, for a partner. They were tracking African poachers again. They soon caught the idiots, who were a waste of muscles as far as Kirabo was concerned. Kirabo was engrossed. TV was far better than calling family to storytelling. Then *I Love Lucy* came on. It was laugh, laugh, laugh, but often Kirabo missed the cue to laugh. *Kyeswa* was the only comedy in Luganda. Finally, *Bud Spencer*, a western comedy, came on before TV closed down. To Kirabo, she had arrived in the city – eating chips with tomato sauce instead of the boring steamed food of Nattetta, drinking soda instead of banana juice, sugar, food fried with Kimbo.

It was approaching midnight when they got home. Muka Tom was waiting in the sitting room. 'Where have you been?' was her greeting. Tom walked past her. But Kirabo floundered. In Nattetta, you had to greet grown-ups when you returned home. Muka Tom looked her up and down. 'Where are you coming from?'

'Aunt Abi's.'

'What have you been doing all this time?'

Kirabo looked at the bag of clothes she carried. Should she mention the restaurant? In Nattetta, it was rude to eat out if supper would be kept for you at home. 'Nothing.'

'Was anyone else with you?'

Tom's head popped through the door. 'Kirabo, go to bed.'

Kirabo skipped out of the room. The sight of Nnambi's miserable face! God pays back in cash with interest. For Nnambi's gloomy face, Tom's mistakes – marrying and having children behind Kirabo's back – were forgiven.

6

From that day on, Tom and wife became Dog and Leopard – they could not bear the sight of each other. They did not quarrel; rather they existed in a fog of silence that wafted in and wrapped itself around the house. Locked away behind the heavy metal gates there were no noisy children, not even nosy neighbours coming and going to dispel the hostile gloom. The silence became predatory. Everyone was consumed. Even little Tommy's whinging was low. In the evening when Tom came home, he brought false cheer with him and spoke to Kirabo as if his voice alone could fill the void.

However, Nnaki the maid thrived. She took pleasure in the couple's woes. In the month Kirabo had been living with the family, she had gleaned a lot of information about Tom and Nnambi from Nnaki. But Nnaki's friendship was accessible only when Muka Tom was not around. Nnaki resented Kirabo rather dramatically in her mistress's presence. Because of this, Kirabo guarded what she said to her.

Nnaki, whose full name was Nnakitto, had been with the family since before little Tommy was born. She came from Mityana, the same village as Nnambi's family. Apparently, when Kirabo arrived, Nnaki had been confused. 'I thought Nnambi was your aunt.'

'What?'

'I swear, you look so alike – eyes, nose, lips – but I know the truth.'

Kirabo rolled her eyes because people will allege the most tenuous resemblance.

Nnaki's father was an alcoholic. Her mother got cancer of the womb but instead of helping, her father took to drinking. For a long time Nnaki looked after her mother and her little brother.

'Cancer took its time eating her and I got fed up.'

Kirabo could not believe anyone could get fed up with their mother.

'If someone is going to die, then they should get on with it.'

'You wanted your mother to die?'

'She was not my mother any more. She was a child. The minute she died, *ba ppa*, I told people I was looking for a domestic job. I was recommended to Nnambi by her mother. When she agreed to take me, I said to my brother, "Let's go." I left my father crying into his alcohol and took my brother to my aunt in Busega while I worked.'

'What about your father?'

'Hmm-hmm.' Nnaki shrugged with that ruthless air of hers. 'He is his problem if he is going to waste his life crying for his wife. One day he will wake up and realise he had children too.'

This was Nnaki's first job. She planned to do it for another three years, then to take a course in cookery and start a bakery. Her brother was in school. She paid his fees. 'He has the chance to go to school. I lost mine,' she said. 'If he squanders it, he is on his own too. I have told him, I did not birth him.' That was how Nnaki spoke. With hardness. But she delighted in the troubles of 'Husband and Wife', as she referred to Tom and Nnambi.

'Husband has changed since you came.'

'Really, how?'

'Before you came, he snubbed Wife because she would not allow you to live with us.'

'Hmm.'

'He only brought home sleep and change of clothes. No appetite, no curiosity about anything. We cooked food, served it; he walked past it. Wife did things – changed the house, curtains and things – but did Husband see?'

'And what did Wife do?'

'She cried. But Husband is a wall.'

'Ha.'

'The rich, kdto,' Nnaki clicked. 'You see them cruising around in their fancy cars, living in their fancy houses, speaking their fancy English, *bikoozi-bikoozi, yesh-yesh,* and you envy them. But get close – the stench.'

Kirabo felt implicated and exonerated by Nnaki's indictment. She was Tom's child, but she did not belong with the rich people who cruised around in their fancy lives. The Europeanness of Tom's wealth had alienated her, especially the way it reduced Grandfather's wealth to nothing. As if she had lived a deprived life. At Tom's house, she had all these attractive things around her and they showed on her body in the way she dressed, walked, spoke and carried herself. But Tom's European wealth was in house gadgets, a car and in speaking English. Grandfather's wealth was Ganda. His biggest wealth was his children and their education. Of course, he had land and land and land: you would have had to cycle for days to see it all. Not to mention livestock – cows, goats, sheep and Zungu poultry – then coffee, cotton and matooke shambas. But there was no glamour in that kind of wealth. Not in harvesting coffee beans or digging in the shambas or collecting firewood. Cows stunk. Milking them was disgusting. Goats' droppings strewn everywhere. Mucking out chicken poo in the Zungu poultry barn. But here in the city, Tom wore a suit and tie to work. A car collected him. No mud, no dust, no debbe leaking down your head. Blue Band margarine, Kimbo cooking fat, Tree Top orange squash, a maid, Mateus, Cinzano, a cassette player rather than a gramophone which Grandfather played on special days. In this way, European wealth trounced Ganda wealth so thoroughly that no amount of land or farms could beat having electricity in your house. When you have grown up putting embers into the belly of a thick heavy iron, waiting for it to heat up, not being able to regulate it apart from putting it in water to cool down or swinging it to fire it up, and then one day you pick up this paper-light Philips flat iron, plug it into a wall, turn the dial to suit your garment and *ssssss,* it slides effortlessly across your garment, no amount of loyalty to Ganda wealth would pull you back.

Kirabo was not of Tom's world yet, but she knew she was on her way there.

The sun barely touched her skin because she rarely stepped outdoors. She had not sweated since she arrived. Her feet had not touched dust. She showered in the morning and in the evening with warm water. She dressed like she was going out all the time. She did not do chores any more in fear of running into her stepmother. Her clothes were washed, ironed and stored in the cupboard or hung in the wardrobe. Every day about mid-morning, Nnaki came to her bedroom and asked, 'Do you have any clothes for washing?' Kirabo had lost the rural anxiety over Nnaki cleaning up after her. Even when she heard Nnaki in the kitchen doing chores long after everyone had gone to bed and then so early in the morning before anyone got up, she no longer felt guilty because Nnaki was Tom's wife's friend. Besides, she was paid to do it. But she knew that if Grandmother found out she lay in her bedroom doing nothing while a girl slaved away on her own all day, that after eating she left dishes unwashed in the sink, she would whip her backside raw.

Kirabo had even learnt to balance her mind at that precarious edge where she saw time in its natural, Ugandan mode but articulated it in the upside-down English mode. At first, it had felt schizophrenic as her mind computed ten hours of day but she said *four in the afternoon*.

The situation between Tom and Wife got so bad Nnambi's mother came to deal with it. Kirabo was in her bedroom when Nnaki opened the door and gasped, 'Time has turned on itself. Mother-in-law has arrived to intervene.' The door closed and Nnaki ran back to the kitchen.

Kirabo's heart sank. Tom's wife was going to complain the whole day long about Tom and his daughter born on the side! Kirabo had found out that Nnambi, having married in church, gave Mwagale and Junior the central position in the family. Apparently, Kirabo was born on the edges of the family unit, and was therefore peripheral, regardless of her position as the eldest child. Of course, you would not hear such a thing in Nattetta, where a child was a child. But in the city, among the educated, the family had been restructured.

Nnambi's mother was a typical rural woman – middling height, skinny, age spots, a nylon busuuti, a head wrap. She looked nothing like her daughters (Kirabo had by this time met two other sisters). Nnambi's mother did not have their trademark large eyes, wide lips or sharp nose. She arrived carrying a load on her head. Inside it was a live chicken whose head peered through a hole in the fold; yams; an array of rural fruit for her grandchildren – apiculata, jackfruit, soursop, ginger lily, custard apple, guava and cape gooseberries – and a small gallon of banana juice, which was put in the fridge to chill. Mwagale squealed as her grandmother unpacked the rural delights and Kirabo rolled her eyes.

The old woman was not resentful. Her attitude was *You are not my grandchild, but you are a child*. After lunch, mother and daughter sat outside on the porch to talk men. From where the world starts to where it ends, when women start to lament men the sun could drop from the sky and they would not realise. Nnambi and her mother must have forgotten that Kirabo's window opened right above the steps to the porch. Or they meant for her to hear them. Nnambi started by enumerating an arm's length of Tom's marital crimes. She concluded with, 'I had borne all of that, Mother, but then he brought the girl without telling me and my children ceased to be. Kirabo is a princess, the whole house is about Kirabo!'

There was silence. As if the old woman was too shocked to speak. Then she sighed exactly the way Grandmother would at a petty city wife.

'Me, the way I see, it looks like love in your marriage is growing old. But what is special about that? Love grows old. And like all things ageing, complications have started to appear. In your case, he has brought his child. Show me the problem in that.'

Kirabo smiled.

'Mother, I swore I would not bring up a man's child. Men will not marry you if you have had a child – why would I bring up his? Look at all Father's children you brought up. You encouraged him by accepting them. On top of that, none of them has been grateful to you.'

'I chose to bring them up. You have no right to get angry for me.'

Kirabo was liking this woman.

'But this too is my decision, Mother. I want to bring up my own children, *full stop.*'

'So why did you send for me?'

Nnambi's mother was as soft as nails. Even Grandmother would have put it a bit gently.

Nnambi started to cry. 'I *hic* just *hic* wanted *hic* to *hic* talk *hic* to *hic* you.'

'Okay, okay, stop crying.' Her mother mellowed a little. 'No man is worth your tears; you hear me? Keep them for your children.' Kirabo lay still. The air was so electric she could feel the static. 'I begin to suspect you married for fickle reasons. We knew about the child. Maybe she is a difficult child – I don't know – but she is not the problem here.'

'But—'

'Listen, Nnambi,' she interrupted harshly, 'getting married is not going to heaven. Maybe the first two, three, even five years it is heaven, but you must drop back to earth some time. Sooner or later the storm strikes. You are busy with the children; he is bored with the routine. The marriage is tossed this way and that. Mostly, he is tossing it, but the world belongs to him. He can get another woman on the side for relief. So, what do you do – pick up your breasts and throw them in the hearth?' There was a pause. Nnambi blew her nose. 'Now is the time to decide whether you came into this marriage for a visit, in which case I suggest you pack your bags and come home with me, or if it is about those two little ones, in which case I suggest you tighten your girdle because this is just the beginning. From what I see, you have made him the centre of your life and armed him with arrows to hurt you. We sat you down for the bridal sessions and told you the hard facts of marriage, but did you listen? No. Because you were in love, love, love. Now love is rusting, you are crying.'

'But yii, Mother—'

'Let me put things into perspective. Do you know what your father was really like?'

'I know he had children all over the place.'

'That is nothing. Most men do that.' She paused. 'When it came to contemptuous men your father was the flagbearer. He so slept with everything with a wiggle in that village they named him Mutayisa. Put a banana tree stump in a dress and that man would stop to check again. One day, before you were born – who was the baby at the time? It was around 1947; it must have been your brother Mpiima – your father came home with Jjali.'

'This Jjali, Nnakku's mother?'

'The very one.'

'Jjali was this city girl who called herself Solome. Your father had Zungucised too, he called himself Franco. Jjali was bleached ripe like I don't know what. She had a huge luggage for a backside, which she put in those minidresses called kokoonyo. Yii, that day, I stole looks at Jjali while cowering in my ruralness because the god who gave her everything had just served her my man and my marriage too. They arrived at night. Your father brought beef because Jjali felt like eating meat. I cooked it even though it was late. Because we had no extra bed, your father told me to leave my bed for their use.'

'What?!'

'I slept in the diiro that night with Mpiima, who was still on the breast.'

'What?'

'Perhaps he did it to get rid of me because he was too cowardly to throw me out. Meanwhile, in the morning, Jjali needed a hot bath and breakfast.'

'Mother!'

'Fried eggs!'

'Don't tell me, Mother, you waited on them.'

'Kdto.'

'Me, no.' Nnambi's voice huffed very close to Kirabo's window. 'How could you let them?'

'Sit down and tell me what I should have done; gone back to my parents with eight children? Or become a nekyeyombekedde and sold alcohol in the city like Jjali did after your father left her? What if he did not look after my children? Had I taken you away from your father or abandoned you to another woman, I doubt we would be sitting here, you talking to me like this. Remember he has been a good father to you all. And when he returned to us, our family was intact. Yes, I suffered, but you all share the same father. In any case, even if I had left him, what were the chances the next man would be different?' She paused and took a breath. Then she gave a cynical laugh. 'God knows what that woman, Jjali, did to your father, because when he left her, he never looked back, not even to toss a coin towards your sister Nnakku's upkeep. Sometimes I want to go to Jjali and say *Whatever you did to our man, thank you.*'

'Hmm-hmm, Mother, me? *No way.* Forget him loving his children. He is supposed to! *No way. No. Way.*' Nnambi said *no way* the same way she said *full stop* in English.

'Hmm.' Her mother laughed sarcastically. 'Suddenly your Tom is a novice compared to your father.' She sighed. 'And, child, you would bear everything if you had eight children. You would leave your bed so he could lie with his harlot.'

'I knew about Nnakku and her mother, but I never thought it was so blatant as that. These days Father is always at home taking care of you, so active in church… Why did he do it?'

'Because there were no consequences for him.'

Silence.

'You both look settled, so contented with each other I envied you.'

'Hmm!'

'Did you forgive him?'

'Forgive him?' The mother laughed. 'Child, how do you forgive something not apologised? Instead, I forgave myself of him as we say. My heart let him go and I stopped hurting. Maybe I am contemptuous sometimes. Once upon a time, he sailed up there in the sky. But now he is so old, a hyena would not eat him spiced. His being a good husband now is perhaps his idea of an apology.' A sigh. 'However, your brothers, because they saw it all, will not forgive him. They have even offered to build a house for me so I can leave him. It is your brothers who buy my clothes, it is your brothers who bring me money, it is I who give him some sometimes…'

'True, the boys worship you, Mother.'

'That is what I am trying to say, Nnambi. Think about it: for all your brothers' worship of me, are you sure they are not cheating on their wives?'

'Kdto!'

'Here is another thing. Can you believe I wake up in the middle of the night and your father is wide awake with worry?'

'Why?'

'He says you should leave if you are unhappy.'

'He does?'

'You are his princess. No man should make you cry. But I was my father's princess too.' The woman's voice caught. She must have contained the emotion because her voice came back strong. 'That is why women of old used to say to their men, "What you do unto me, some bastard will do unto your precious little girl." It is like a law.'

There was a pause, as if Nnambi had accepted her mother's perspective, but then she exploded. '*No way*, Mother, *no way*. I am not you. The world is changing…'

Kirabo was indignant. *My father is not a tyrant, Miiro is not a bastard, Sio is not a dog.* She considered warning Tom. But what would she say? That your mother-in-law was here and said you are bored with marriage and are wrecking it?

7

The silence in Tom's house tightened, despite Nnambi's mother's intervention. Until Friday night the following week, when the boil burst.

Tom came home early, at around three. One car door banged, which meant he was driving. Perhaps he had come to pick something up, Kirabo thought. She heard him get into the corridor.

'Nnambi?' he called cheerily.

Kirabo realised that Tom was calling for a truce and she was disappointed. Tom should have held out; truth was on his side. Now Nnambi was going to make her life unbearable.

Ten minutes later, Kirabo's door opened and Nnaki's head popped in with feverish excitement. 'It is hotting up in the master bedroom.' And her head popped out again. Kirabo sat up, readying herself. She knew she would end up at the centre of it. She did not wait long.

'Kirabo?' Tom called.

'Yes, Dadi?'

'Hurry up here.'

She rapped, then opened their door and leaned in.

'Take a wash and get dressed: we are going out.'

She looked from Husband to Wife, thinking *Why go out with me?* Wife lay on the bed facing the wall. Husband shone his shoes. The tension was solid. Wife had rejected Husband's compromise, Kirabo realised. She stayed standing at the door until Tom asked, 'Did you not hear me? Wear something formal.'

She closed the door, took a bath and pulled on a frock. She rubbed a little talcum powder on her face as she had seen Nnambi do. It gave the skin a smooth, even texture and got rid of the greasy shine of petroleum jelly. Then she fashioned her hair, combing some of it into her forehead to get a mini Afro. She glossed her lips with Vaseline and looked at herself in the bathroom mirror. She wished Sio was at the end of the journey. As she got into the car, Kirabo glanced back. Nnambi was peering through a window. Kirabo smiled – *Your cheap tricks will not work* – and got into the car.

It was a Coffee Marketing Board staff party at the International Hotel. Tom kept apologising for his wife's absence. 'Nnambi is unwell, but she asked to bring our daughter in her stead.' Kirabo endured curious glances, especially from the women, until Tom explained, 'She is an early one,' with a wink. Male colleagues smiled knowingly, as if Tom had been the lovable rogue in school. As for the women, they were dumb. They kept saying, 'She looks a bit like Nnambi.' Kirabo barely held back a sneer.

She had never seen such a beautiful display of food. Some of it was nonsensical. Who eats fried pieces of pineapple with avocado on a toothpick? Someone malicious had mixed raw onions in with what looked like raw eggs. Ntaate once said that expensive hotels in Kampala caught frogs and snails and snakes and put them on the menu. Everyone had shut him up because Ntaate could say some freaky stuff. Seeing dead milk, bongo, labelled yoghurt and fried pineapple, Kirabo wondered whether Ntaate knew what he was talking about. She kept close to Tom and only ate what he ate.

When dancing started, Kirabo took a walk. Jubilee Park rolled down the hill around her. It was dotted with flower beds, fountains, statues and monuments. The park was littered with people, especially young couples, lying on the ground or sitting and reading or strolling. She lingered around the swimming pool to watch the swimmers, then walked to the bottom of the park to see the independence monument. On the way, first, was a mouldy bust labelled KING GEORGE VI, then a metallic statue of a drummer, a rattle man and a woman dancing like a whirlwind. She walked through the ivy-clad archway to where the independence monument stood. It was lofty but lifeless. The old woman had fallen asleep behind her child, and the child's delight at being free was frozen. Kirabo walked down the steps and looked out at the Bank of Uganda, the roundabout, then the Standard Chartered Bank. Rich army men and wealthy mafuta mingi sat outside the Speke Hotel, smoking. When a chill came, she walked back to the party. She piled a plate with cakes and biscuits, grabbed a bottle of Mirinda and went to the lounge to watch TV. From time to time, she went to the hall to check on Tom.

Nnambi was not waiting in the sitting room this time. Kirabo hurried to her bedroom. She switched on the light and there, lying on her bed, was Nnambi. Her father's wife sat up as if disturbed by the light.

'I'm sorry I borrowed your bed. I have a headache; could you sleep with your father tonight? I would like to sleep on my own.'

Kirabo stared, unconvinced.

'I hope you don't mind.' Nnambi winced.

Kirabo grabbed her nightdress and went to the toilet to change. Then she walked to the main bedroom and knocked on the door. No answer. She pushed the door open. The light was turned off but the beam from the corridor flooded the bed. Tom was sprawled on his back, already snoring. Though his lower half was obscured by a thin blanket, Kirabo could see that his chest was covered in thick fur. She stood and stared, unsure. Grandfather did not look like that. She hesitated, hoping that the beam would wake him up. It did not. She went to the bed and nudged him to move over. 'Dadi, Dadi?'

He opened his eyes.

'Could you move over, please?'

He lifted his head.

'I am sleeping here tonight.' Kirabo started to slip under the covers.

Tom sat up and then jumped out of the bed, taking a sheet and the blanket with him. The blanket fell. He clutched the sheet around himself.

'Dad, it is me, Kirabo.'

'Why?' Tom gasped. 'Do you not have your own bed?'

'Mum is sleeping in my room. She told me to sleep with you.'

As soon as the words were out, she realised Nnambi's request '… sleep with your father…' was sexual. To make matters worse, she became aware that Tom was naked underneath the sheet.

'Step outside so I can get dressed,' her father said.

Kirabo ran out. She went to the sitting room feeling sick. She gave in to tears. The idea that she had almost got into bed with her naked father brought on a new wave of nausea. She wept for everything that had happened to her since her arrival in Kampala. She was returning to Nattetta first thing in the morning. She would tell everyone what a witch Tom had married. She was not living this disgusting life a minute longer.

A door banged. 'Let go of me,' Nnambi screamed. Kirabo ran to see what was happening. Tom dragged her out of Kirabo's bedroom and dumped her in the corridor.

'She might as well share your bed. After all, she is your wife now.'

'I begged you to come.'

Nnaki and Mwagale stood at their door, staring.

'Tomorrow, pack your bags and go back to your parents. You hear me?' Tom panted. 'I should not find you in my house when I come home. Take whatever property you wish, but don't touch my children. You two' – he pointed at Nnaki and Mwagale – 'back to bed.' He turned to Kirabo. 'Come on, let's go to bed.' He led her back to his bedroom and helped her into bed. He covered her and rushed out. 'You heard me, Nnambi? Pack your bags tonight-tonight.' He clapped his hands rapidly to denote the urgency. 'Now-now. Back to where you came from first thing in the morning. Then we shall see who is who in this house.' He returned to the bedroom, breathing hard. Then he stormed out again. 'And do not touch my children. You go back to your home exactly as you came.'

Nnambi was silent. The minute Tom threw her out of their marriage her tongue froze into ice.

Tom appeared at the door and got into bed fully clothed.

'Go to sleep, Kirabo.'

Kirabo lay at the edge, even though it was a double bed. But she was soon overcome by exhaustion, and woke up to the sound of Tom's alarm. He got up and told her to go back to sleep. Kirabo covered her head, but the events of the previous night came back with such force she moved to the edge of the bed again. Tom got dressed in the bathroom. When he came back to the bedroom, he guzzled tea like water.

'Can I go back home?'

'This is your home, Kirabo.' He wrapped a tie around the raised collar of his shirt.

The sound of the chain on the gate clinked. A car drove in. Tom grabbed his coat and said, 'Come, Kirabo.' She jumped out of bed and followed him back to her bedroom. Her bed was made. The witch had not slept in it after all. 'Stay in here. Don't go out until Nnambi has left.' As he hurried out, he called, 'Nnambi, I don't want to come home and find you here.' The house went silent again. Kirabo closed her eyes. *Where is my mother?*

UTOPIA

1

Kirabo put the last piece of her luggage into the car boot and closed it. She wore the uniform of her new school – a brown wrapper, beige short-sleeved shirt tucked in, brown back-to-school shoes from Bata and grey scholar's socks with three yellow bands. The uniform felt stiff with newness. The shirt was a tent, the skirt too long, her head newly shaven.

Two days earlier, Aunt Abi had sat her down on the floor, held Kirabo's shoulders between her knees and, with a razor mounted on a soft comb, shaved her hair according to the new school's regulations. At first, Kirabo felt the hair fall over her shoulders soft and light, but as Aunt Abi got to the back and her head was bent low, she saw her hopes of growing a decent Afro drop around her like black soap suds. She had picked up the thicker tufts and rolled them into a tight ball. For a while, she hung on to that ball until it became unhygienic to mourn hair like that. Touching her head now, she felt a growth of prickly stubble.

Before she got in the car, Kirabo looked back at her new home. Who would have known when she was showing off about leaving Nattetta that the city would trounce all the truths she knew? She looked at the mosque that had once been the Gurdwara Temple, the semi-detached houses formerly belonging to the expelled Asians, and realised Kampala was such that she could be dead, carried out of that house like a log, and this place would look exactly the same: indifferent. In Nattetta, if she was going away to boarding school for the first time, the whole village would have wished her well, old people saying *Let your ancestors' blessings walk with you*, grown-ups sneaking pocket money into her hands, relatives sitting her down to talk about 'hard work' and 'good behaviour' and warning her to stay away from men. Who knew she would miss Nattetta's aggressive *Your-business-is-our-business* attitude?

She opened the back door, stepped into the car and slammed the door behind her. Tom started to mess with the gears. 'We go?'

She nodded.

'Got everything?'

'Hmm.'

Aunt Abi, in the passenger seat, turned and scrutinised Kirabo's face with a happy smile. She touched a finger on her tongue and scrubbed something crusty out of Kirabo's eye. 'There,' she sighed. 'Big girl going to secondary school.' The car reversed into the road. Then Aunt Abi's house started to recede. When it disappeared, Kirabo leaned back in her seat and contemplated the fluidity of her life, the constant departures and arrivals, the packing and unpacking. It was beginning to make her feel rootless. *It is because you don't have a mother...* She stifled the thought and stared out of the window.

Nnambi won. She did not go back to her parents as Tom had ordered her; instead it was Kirabo who left. At around two that day, Grandmother came with Aunt Abi to collect her. When Nnambi saw Grandmother arrive, she jumped out of the chair to humble herself as if she were human. As she knelt, Grandmother cut her off. 'I have come for my grandchild.'

Imagine your husband's mother talking to you like that. Grandmother did not sit down, she did not even ask about her grandchildren, or say *Can I have a glass of water?* as you do in a house you are visiting for the first time. Nnambi remained on the floor, kneeling. Grandmother told Kirabo to pack her bags. Then she turned to Nnambi. 'I understand you have been told to go back to your parents.'

Nnambi wept into the armrest. 'I was about to leave when you arrived.'

'Ha,' Kirabo started to protest, but Grandmother raised a finger.

'I suggest that you stay and bring up our children. I will talk to Tomusange.'

The shock of seeing her grandmother intervene on the side of Nnambi halted Kirabo's tears. Her injured air vanished. Nnambi was not only walking free after the abomination of her behaviour, she was keeping Tom too. Aunt Abi, who would have made Grandmother see sense, had stayed in the car once she found out that Nnambi was still in the house. Aunt Abi and Nnambi did not occupy the same space. If Nnambi was in a place, Aunt Abi stayed away, and vice versa. Apparently, Nnambi once told Aunt Abi that she clung on to her brother too much. 'Get your own man,' she had said.

An urge to push Nnambi over gripped Kirabo, but she held herself back. *You had your moment*, she told herself. *Small, but a moment nonetheless.*

'Have you finished packing?' Grandmother's voice was gravelly.

Kirabo ran to her bedroom. By then, defeat hung everywhere. That house and everything in it had rejected her. So when Nnaki came to help her pack, Kirabo ignored her. After she had packed, she walked out without a word to her.

Kirabo's moment arrived around noon, just before Grandmother arrived. She had been in her bedroom all morning as Tom had instructed, waiting for Nnambi to leave. She had not had breakfast. Desperate with hunger and buoyed by Tom's decisive eviction of his wife, Kirabo decided it was time to assert herself, Jjajja Nsangi-style, to raise her voice and stretch her legs in her father's house. She was blood; Nnambi, on the other hand, was a chance meeting on a street. A marriage certificate could be ripped up, but blood was indelible. She went in search of her.

Nnambi was in Tom's bedroom tidying up; she had absolutely no intention of going back where she came from. 'This woman is a lukokobe proper. She has got her talons dug too deep into Tom's back to retract,' Kirabo muttered under her breath. Because the bedroom was in semi-darkness, Kirabo walked past Nnambi to the window and drew back the curtains. Nnambi spun around.

'Don't you knock?'

Kirabo turned, raised her eyebrows as if to say *Who are you?* and went back to opening the shutters. When she finished, she asked, 'Why should I?'

Nnambi floundered.

Kirabo walked away from the window, the question ringing in the air.

But Nnambi was a fighter. 'Do you call my bedroom a market?'

'No.' Kirabo stopped, crossed her arms and looked down at Nnambi's head to emphasise that she was taller. 'This is my bedroom now. I slept here last night. I don't have to knock any more.'

'What do you want?'

'Did I say it is my bedroom or was I munching myself?'

When Nnambi's eyes flickered uncertainly, Kirabo seized the moment. She sat down on the bed and crossed her legs, knowing very well that to sit on Nnambi's marital bed as though it was a public bench was the rudest thing she could do to her. She had not planned this. She had come to ask Nnambi when she hoped to leave so she could come out and have something to eat, but this was so much better.

'When you were young' – Kirabo looked up at Nnambi – 'did anyone ever tell you the story of Tamusuza, whose wife died and left him with a little girl?'

Nnambi stood like a tree. She stared as if she could not believe the world.

'Oh.' Kirabo clapped to emphasise the oversight, as if it fell to her to rectify it. 'See, Tamusuza married another woman to help him bring up the orphaned child, but this woman, the new wife, hated her stepchild because the little girl was so beautiful and everyone loved her, and' – Kirabo leaned in and whispered – 'the woman had given birth to an ugly daughter who was also spoilt.'

Nnambi's eyes dilated.

'Every time people walked by, they asked about the orphan and picked her up and tried to make her smile because she was always sad. Do you know what the stepmother did? She stopped giving the orphan baths and did not feed her properly. She would wash and oil her ugly child and then put both out to play. People came by, but still they pointed at the orphan – *That filthy child over there, how pretty she is.* The stepmother, maddened, smeared the orphan with chicken poo, can you imagine? Chicken poo. But wa! People came, people saw, people said *Is that scrawny child crying over there…is that chicken poo?*'

'So what are you saying?'

'Nothing. Just saying.' Kirabo stood up and stepped out of the room.

As they drove away from Tom's home that day, Aunt Abi sighed, 'Mother, Nnambi is a demon. My brother is under torture. As soon as he comes home, she descends on him. I am telling you, the minute Tom put that ring on her finger, *ba ppa*, Nnambi said, *I have got you*. What could Tom do? He was in chains.' Kirabo sensed an accusation at the edge of Aunt Abi's voice: that Nnambi was as bad as she was because Grandmother and Grandfather had not intervened. But Grandmother only said, 'Hmm', and looked through the window. 'This is exactly what she wanted,' Aunt Abi was saying. 'To drive Kirabo out of Tom's life entirely, so she and her children could occupy it exclusively. She must be celebrating.' Still Grandmother did not volunteer an opinion. When they got to Aunt Abi's house, Grandmother talked about Nattetta: 'Rain is late. All the maize we planted died; termites cut the stalks… groundnuts were eaten by insects before germinating…weaver birds are back, all my banana leaves shredded…' and Kirabo felt herself melt into the familiarity of her grandmother's words.

That evening after work, Tom came straight to Aunt Abi's house. Before Kirabo and Aunt Abi could say to him *Welcome back, how was your day?* Grandmother pounced on him. 'So, you threw out your wife, hmm?'

She took everyone by surprise: there had been no indication that she was waiting to chastise Tom. 'How many women do you intend to bring into the family, hmm? This one enters, that one exits, this one arrives, that one departs, in-out, in-out.'

'But, Mother—'

'You are talking back now, hmm? You have become an important man, a ssenkulu, hmm?'

Tom kept quiet. You could see bewilderment rattling in his head.

'That child' – Grandmother pointed at Kirabo – 'is without a mother. Are you going to make those two motherless as well?'

Tom could not take it any longer. 'Mother, Nnambi is not a woman: she is a mujinni…'

'Wangi?' Grandmother almost choked. 'What did you call her? Let me hear you say it again, Tom.'

Tom shot Aunt Abi a desperate glance, but Abi just stared at the floor. He plopped into a chair and kept quiet, but Grandmother was not yet finished.

'Let me hear that you have thrown your wife out of her home like rubbish, when her children are watching, and Tomusange, I promise you will see a side of me I have been hiding. Now' – she stood up – 'I am going to find my way back to Nattetta. But do not make me come back here, Tom. And you, Abisaagi.'

'Yes, Mother?'

'Look after my grandchild. And you, Kirabo.'

'Yes, Jjajja?'

'Stay here with your aunt, child. You will not manage to live among these educated marriages of nowadays. As for you, Tom, this is free advice. Never let your Maama Muto find out you called your wife a mujinni. She might pull your cheeks.'

Both Aunt Abi and Tom stood up, then looked at each other. 'I will drive Mother home,' Aunt Abi offered.

'Did you bring me? I will find my own way.'

Tom threw his arms up in defeat. Grandmother stormed out, her black plastic sandals slap-slapping her feet. Aunt Abi, then Kirabo, ran after her and opened the back yard gate. They walked behind her through the alleyway, but when they got to the front yard, Aunt Abi realised it was no use walking with Grandmother. She said, 'See everyone for us, Mother, especially Father.'

Grandmother relented. 'I will see them for you.' She paused. 'Don't worry, Abisaagi. I don't see why you should drive me to Nattetta and then drive back, wasting fuel, when the Baganda buses are down the road. Be well, Kirabo.' She walked away.

When Aunt Abi and Kirabo got back into the house, Tom exploded. 'What is wrong with Mother?'

'Old people,' Aunt Abi sighed. 'They are incomprehensible.'

'What did I do wrong? Nnambi left me no choice.'

Aunt Abi shrugged.

'I don't know what to do. Really, I don't.'

'Maybe Mother feels guilty that she has loved you too much.' Aunt Abi tried to lighten the mood. But Tom had lost his sense of humour.

'So you set her on me?'

'Look, Tom, all I did was send a message home that your marriage is dying. The next thing I see, Mother is at my office. She says, "Take me to Tom's house, right away." I thought she was going to tune Nnambi straight. If I kept quiet and she had heard it in rumours she would have said, *And you, Abi – to keep quiet while your brother's marriage died?*'

'Did you tell her what *actually* happened?'

'I did, but she didn't say a word. I thought, hmm, that is old people for you. When something is too much, they keep quiet.'

'Nnambi is going to grow tentacles all over the place.'

'No one is going to step into your house again.'

'Kirabo,' Tom said, turning to her. 'You will stay here for the time being, while we sort things out.'

Kirabo did not look at him. There was no 'for the time being' about the situation. She would never return to his house.

'My house is your home. You know that.'

'I know,' she lied. She could not help feeling sorry for him. His home was Mwagale's, little Tommy's and their mummy's. Even Nnaki belonged there more than she did. Life in the city was upside down. In Nattetta, a woman daring to throw a man's child out of his house? How? It made Tom look weak. In her childhood bragging contests, Kirabo would claim that Tom would knock out Lance the Spearman with his hands tied behind his back. And if Ntaate insisted his father would lick James Bond, she would say Tom would take Bruce Lee, James Bond and Lance the Spear at once while lying on the ground. But now, looking at him so defeated he could not protect his child from a mere wife, Kirabo felt her heart twist.

'If I were you, Tom, I would write my will right now.'

'That is morbid, Abi. To write a will is to invite death.' He turned to Kirabo. 'Home is a funny thing, is it not? I might call that place in Bugoloobi home, but when people ask me where my home is I say, "Nattetta with Miiro." All these are places we live at, but Nattetta, where our kin alive and asleep are, is our true home.'

Kirabo wondered what he was talking about. In Kampala, a child belonged in her parents' home. The way she saw things, she could never have a home in that sense. She had no mother, and Tom was a part-time dad.

That night Tom drove back to his house to collect the clothes he would wear to work during the week. He came back to Old Kampala to spend the rest of the week with Kirabo and Aunt Abi. He would drop in at Bugoloobi to check on Tommy and Mwagale and then drive back to Old Kampala. As the weeks passed, and the wider family found out what had happened, there was such anger that Kirabo wondered whether Nnambi slept at night. Relatives, however distant, cousins who had once lived in Miiro's house, came to Aunt Abi's, asking, 'Is it true? I came to hear it for myself.' Aunt YA said, 'For me, it will take something huge to drag me to Tom's house again.' Even quiet Uncle Ndiira shook his head: 'Of all the women in the world, Tom married a mujinni.'

Even before this incident, the wider family had nursed a grudge against Nnambi. Apparently, before their wedding, Nnambi was a nice, sociable girlfriend:

'So beautiful you looked at her and agreed that Tom had made the right choice.'

'Kdto, what you didn't know was that something sinister lurked underneath that beauty.'

'Indeed. Then Tom married her and brought her home. In that instant, Nnambi changed.'

'That woman came with an agenda, to isolate Tom from his family.'

'She commenced torturing him immediately.'

Apparently, no sooner had Nnambi's aunt led her out of the honeymoon bedroom than she grabbed a broom and swept out all the *I am Tom's brother, sister, cousin-sister, cousin-brother, village-mate and I live with him because he is paying my school fees and he has a big empty house* hangers-on. 'Bugoloobi is not Nattetta,' Nnambi told them. 'We don't have a matooke plantation in the back garden. Food costs money.'

When reports about Nnambi's behaviour reached Nattetta, Miiro told them, 'Get out of there; leave them alone.'

But for the young generation, a grudge brewed. Beneath the smiles, they kept a hostile eye on Nnambi. Now the whole clan was simmering.

Soon after she left Tom's house, Kirabo's PLE results came out. Two weeks later, a letter of admission to St Theresa's Girls' School arrived. From that point on, Kirabo's mind was focused on St Theresa's. Everyone said she was lucky to go to a girls' boarding school. St Theresa's, run by women, was renowned as a haven for girls. It was a ticket to success. Her future was secured.

The list of things to take was ridiculous. St Theresa's had apologised for the amount of provisions they asked students to bring, but they were afraid in the current economic conditions the school was no longer able to supply necessities like soap for the laundry or the bath, toilet paper, mattresses and other bedding, flat irons, peeling knives, forks, spoons, plates and the like. Luckily, Tom's sense of guilt indulged Kirabo. Every day, Aunt Abi came home with more items. Kirabo's bedroom looked as if she was moving house. Tom spent most of his evenings with them. Some nights as well. For Kirabo, whenever they went out together for a meal, she imagined they looked a bit like that family in the OMO-Kimbo-Blue Band-Colgate-Jik-Vim advert.

After twenty minutes of driving, they came to the Busega roundabout and Tom took the road to Mityana. The world outside the car, the towns of Bulenga and Buloba, looked like Nazigo – a few shops half asleep on either side of the road; tiny market stalls selling jackfruit, sugar cane, mangoes and spinach varieties; children walking barefoot; goats tethered at the roadside. Then stretches and stretches of bush. Once in a while there were swamps covered in papyrus and yams. Like most routes, the drive was a careful negotiation between potholes. On the car radio, Prince Nico Mbarga crooned about his sweet mother and how she suffered for him. Tom and Abi chatted about a cousin involved in magendo, the black market. It was from him that they got things like sugar, margarine and biscuits. They were worried he was getting too rich too quickly, too visibly. But Kirabo was restless. One moment she contemplated the kind of life waiting for her at St Theresa's, the next she was thinking about Sio. She had immunised herself against the pain of him but sometimes it still broke through. Had he returned to St Mary's for his A levels? How was he? Did he miss her? She was sure Nattetta missed her. She imagined how proud her mother would have been when she found out Kirabo had made it to St Theresa's, but the next minute her outrage at Nnambi's wickedness came flooding back. Oh, her heart stopped. Her mother could be a teacher at St Theresa's. Or her mother might have a younger sister studying at St Theresa's. One day the younger sister would say, *You look familiar; are you Kirabo, my sister's daughter? You look just like her.*

2

After two hours of driving they arrived at Zigoti. It was a tiny trading centre, but St Theresa's signpost, towering over even the buildings, promised that the school was anything but rural. Mangled local signposts squatted around it. They attempted English: GOD REMEMBERED ME CLINIC. ZIGOTI TRUSTFUL TAILOR. DDEMBE RELIABLE DOBBI. EVEN COCKERELS WERE ONCE EGGS COBBLER.

They turned into a murram-covered feeder road. Cars to and from the school had maddened the dust into a cloud. Kirabo rolled up the window. Five minutes on the feeder road and traffic came to a standstill. Kirabo became restless.

'Why is the school in such a remote area?'

'To minimise escaping.'

'Missionaries believed cities were corrupt...morally.'

The car crawled up a steep hillside until they finally came to the school gate, which sat at the very top of the peak. A hedge of old fir trees. The school motto welded above the gate claimed YOU EDUCATE A WOMAN, A NATION IS EDUCATED. Now Kirabo realised. The fir hedge was a facade; behind it was a high wall, topped with jagged glass shards, then barbed wire.

They drew up to the gate and a guard waved them in.

Kirabo tried to look excited, but her heart was tremulous. The school rolled down the hill, vast and strange, all around her. It was mostly old buildings, no-nonsense and ugly. The few modern ones seemed frivolous. Aunt Abi was turning her handbag inside out looking for Kirabo's admission letter, pass slip and fee payslips: 'I had them in my hand, now-now.' Tom shook his head at her and lifted Kirabo's wooden trunk out of the boot. Then her cardboard suitcase. Kirabo still gawked at the school. Aunt Abi found the forms. They were in the glove compartment. She smiled: *I knew I had them.* They started towards the queue, past an ancient building labelled SANATORIUM. A plaque on the wall said:

THIS SCHOOL WAS OPENED BY SISTER SUPERIOR STE FOI
(MISSIONARY SISTERS OF OUR LADY OF AFRICA)
ON THIS DAY, THE 16TH FEBRUARY 1909 ANNO DOMINE.
'MENDING BUGANDA'S BROKEN ARM'

At the top of the registration queue a nun in a blue dress and coif registered the students. Kirabo watched mothers fussing over daughters. In the car park, parents drove sleek cars and lifted out posh pieces of luggage, undermining the nuns' attempt to muffle class differences through uniform. Even things like a watch or an English accent stuck out.

Their turn came. Tom handed over the admission letter. The nun consulted a list on her desk and ticked off Kirabo's name. She got out a form and started filling it in: 'Name, please?'

'Kirabo Nnamiiro.'

'Christian name?'

Silence.

Then Tom answered, 'Kirabo.'

The nun looked up. 'Sir, there are Christian names without biblical roots, but "Kirabo" is not one of them.'

'That is all she has.'

'Baptised?'

'Yes.'

'Religion?'

'Protestant… Anglican.'

The nun stole a *No wonder* look at him.

'Family name?'

Kirabo had never heard of such a thing. Everyone had their own name. Tom's reply astounded her.

'Miiro.'

Kirabo glared: *That is a masculine name.*

'Father's name?'

'Tomusange Piitu…Miiro.'

'Mother? Is she Miiro as well?'

'Nnakku.'

Kirabo froze.

'Mother's Christian name?'

'Lovinca.'

Kirabo almost choked from holding her breath. The nun glanced at Aunt Abi. Then at her naked ring finger. Aunt Abi smiled. 'He is my brother.' The nun glanced at Tom's wedding ring. Tom glared: *Don't you start.*

Nnakku Lovinca, Lovinca Nnakku. Kirabo inhaled. *Lovinca Nnakku,* Catholic? *Nnakku Lovinca.* Her heart beat so fast she was quivering. Nnakku was of the Ffumbe clan like Nnambi. Tom must have found sweetness in Ffumbe women. Then her heart ruptured – Sio was not of her mother's clan – and she almost wiggled her bottom in glee. This was a promising start to the new school. Finding her mother had just become easier. Her mother's face even began to take form in her mind.

'Kirabo Miiro,' the nun said, smiling, 'welcome to St Theresa's. Take your luggage to Sister Mary Francis for checking.' She pointed at another nun dressed like her but European.

As they walked away Kirabo whispered, 'Won't our feminine names die away?'

'Even boys' will dwindle,' Tom said. 'Can you imagine if Father's generation was called Luutu, our generation Luutu, your generation Luutu? But that is being international for you.'

Aunt Abi was upbeat. 'On the other hand, with a masculine name, it is not immediately clear you have failed to get married.'

Kirabo smiled.

Just then a priest, white, joined the nun at the top of the queue. He was very old but sprightly. He was the first male school official Kirabo had ever seen. He held his hands as if in a posture of prayer or apology: *I am sorry I am a man, but you need a chaplain.* He whispered to the nun and she whispered back. As he left, he greeted them: 'Mulimutiya bbana bbangi?' Somehow the priest greeting and calling them his children melted the anxiety in the air.

When their turn came, the nun ticked off the items as Tom showed them to her. The hoe and knife were put aside, not allowed in the dormitories. When they were done, the nun rummaged through a box and took out a card.

'Nunciata?'

A woman rushed from under a royal palm.

'Take Kirabo to Muhumuza House, Dorm M1A.' Then to Tom she said, 'I am afraid men are not allowed in the dormitory area.'

Tom put down the trunk and glared at the nun. Her smile said *I am used to that look, young man, but you're going nowhere.*

Kirabo carried the wooden trunk containing her snacks. The trunk had belonged to Miiro when he was in college; he had sent it when he heard she was going to boarding school. Nunciata carried the foam mattress. Aunt Abi carried the cardboard suitcase. They walked down the hill. Here, the school was silent. Kirabo peered into the classrooms. The continuing students had started a week earlier. Opposite, a white double-storeyed building marked CONVENT was shrouded by a high hedge. She lugged the trunk again past a wooden barn marked CARPENTRY, past Harriet Tubman House, consisting of four blocks built around a square lawn. She rested the trunk outside Yaa Asantewaa House and blew on her aching fingers.

'Here we are,' Nunciata called from down the hill. She and Aunt Abi had arrived at Muhumuza House. Kirabo heaved the trunk by its brass handles and lugged it down the hill. She rested it outside the door. 'Your dorm: M1A.' Nunciata started to show her around the Nehanda compound. 'That building on the left is the A-level block. That one' – she pointed at a block across the quadrangle – 'has the bathrooms, toilets and laundry room. That one on the right is the O-level candidates' block.' Kirabo stared at the long building where her dorm was the first room. 'There are other new students here already,' Nunciata said, as she led them inside. 'You can start making friends.' The room was packed with bunk beds. The floor was mosaic ceramics – those tiny-tiny ones in different colours. High roof, no ceiling. Arched windows like a church. The windowsills were so wide and low you could sit on them.

'Choose any empty bed you want,' Nunciata said.

The new girls perched on the top bunks, their anxiety palpable. Only one of them spoke, the one with an American accent. Others were half-listening to her, half-watching Kirabo. Kirabo noticed a very dark girl staring at her as if they had met before. She looked away. Kirabo pointed at a bed. 'There, that one.'

'Next to a window?' Aunt Abi frowned. 'It could get draughty at night.'

'It's the one I want.'

Kirabo heaved her mattress on to the top bunk and Aunt Abi helped her make it. Afterwards, when she walked back up the hill to the car park with Aunt Abi to say goodbye to Tom, she tried to be brave. Tom kept a straight face. 'Stay well and work hard.' Aunt Abi did the emotions. 'You'll be fine,' she fussed, as she buttoned Kirabo's shirt higher. 'The first day is the hardest, but you'll soon forget us.' She patted Kirabo's collar in place. 'Handle your pocket money carefully. Keep your keys in your bag.' Then she smiled. 'You are going to like this school, I can see it.'

As he got into the car Tom called out, 'A good report is all I ask for.' But Aunt Abi promised, 'Visitors' Day is on the last Sunday of the month: we will bring home-made food.'

For the second time, Tom drove away leaving her alone to face the world. Only this time he would not be coming home in the evening.

She waved until the car drove out of the gate. Then she was so alone her hand pinched her lower lip repeatedly. Tears started to well up in her eyes.

*

A wailing siren cut through the air. Kirabo sprinted down the hill until she came to the door of her dorm.

'That is the end-of-classes hooter,' the American girl said. Before Kirabo could work it out, a buzz came, then the big girls appeared. They came down the hill shouting, 'The Bunsens are here, the Burners.' Kirabo scrambled up her bunk and by the time she settled, the girls were inside the dorm filling the aisle and spaces between the beds. They peered at the new girls' faces as if they were pieces of art on the wall.

'Which one of you is my Bunsen? I own you. You are my wally.' The voice stopped short of Kirabo's bed.

Some girls crowded around the American. 'Are you Mimi, Afrina's sister?' The girl smiled. 'Kdto,' Kirabo clicked. *That girl is full of confidence*.

'You.' Kirabo jumped. A girl stood below her bed. 'Yes, you, Dark Tan.' She was talking to her. 'Was that your brother I saw you with upstairs?' For a moment Kirabo was blank. Then she realised that 'upstairs' was up the hill at the car park.

'No, my dad.'

'Your *dad*? How dare. Your dad is a dude; what is his name?'

'Tom. I mean, Tomusange.'

'How come he is your dad?'

'I am an early one.'

'So your dad was a bad boy. Is he married?'

'Yes.'

'Look at this face, Bunsen, I said look at me. I am going to kill your mother and bang your dad until that Afro falls off his head.'

'She is not my mother.'

The dorm applauded as if Kirabo had given permission. The girl walked away punching the air: 'He is mine, mine, mine.' Kirabo wiped the tears away and stole a look at the other new girls. Apart from Mimi, who was being admired, each Bunsen sat shrunken, trying not to attract attention to herself. Kirabo started to suspect that St Theresa's was a school for girls with the original state. Nsuuta must have had a hand in this.

'Hi.' Kirabo gripped her bed. Another girl. She was petite. She had the roundest, flattest, moon face you have ever seen. 'I am Kuteesa; this is my bed.' She pointed at the bed below. 'Welcome to Muhumuza, House of Rest.' Before Kirabo nodded, the girl launched into a speech: 'We are the best house in the whole school, we win most competitions – sports, quiz, modelling, drama, music. Sister Ambrose, the headmistress, is our House Mistress. We have no Muhumuza Day.' Kirabo had no idea who Muhumuza was, but she did not ask. 'Our arch-enemy is Yaa Asantewaa House; they are thugs, always looking for a fight. Don't make friends there or you will become a traitor.' Meanwhile, she had pulled off her blouse to reveal no bra, pulled on a T-shirt, kicked off her shoes and stepped into slippers. She put the shirt on a hanger and hung it on a hook. Then she picked up a Bible that lay on top of her suitcase and took a breath. 'What is your name?'

'Kirabo.'

'Let me guess, your parents were not expecting you, or you are the firstborn.'

'Both.'

A moon smile. 'Oh, by the way, this is your locker.' She opened the wooden cupboard. 'Put all your snacks in here. Place your wooden trunk on top, then your suitcase on top. Come.' Kirabo climbed down and Kuteesa helped her heave the wooden trunk on to the locker. 'I am going to the chapel – you must join the Christian club, it is the best club in school; we host and visit Christian clubs in other Catholic schools. I think I am going to like you, even though you are not Catholic.' As she made to leave she pointed. 'You can take off your uniform. Did you bring any hangers?'

Kirabo shook her head.

'You can use one of mine. Listen, between four and five thirty o'clock is clubs, then bath time; supper is at six. Oh, useful tips: we Muhumuzans are not just queens; we are anti-colonialist, freedom fighters, Nyabingi. If anyone calls you a witch, say "We are queens, we are warriors." Girls from Nakayima House are sluts. Nakayima slept with both Muteesa I and Kabaleega.' Kirabo nodded, as if it was a fact taught in history. 'The Nzingies from Nzinga House are back-breakers – that always shuts them up. The Asantes, from Yaa Asantewaa, are militant, and if a Tubmanese gives you trouble just say '"Go get some sleep."' She glanced at her watch. 'Oh, the Nehandians from Nehanda House are the real witches. See you in one and a half hours.'

Kirabo climbed back on to her bunk; she did not take off her uniform. She did not remember the tips Kuteesa had given her. Continuing students still came, stared, commented and went.

Just then, a big girl in a straight black skirt walked in. Mimi flew to her. They whispered in their American English. She took Mimi's hand, plus one of her suitcases, and they left. Kirabo found out later that the big sister, Afrina, was a Higher – an A-level student. Though the sisters were American, their parents had sent them to Uganda to learn proper history, Luganda and their culture. Like the girls from Europe, the school van picked them up at the airport at the beginning of term and dropped them at the end of term.

Kirabo realised that time had passed when the dormitory started filling with girls again, this time in all stages of undress. No inhibitions whatsoever. Some were down to the slightest of briefs, others nude. Kuteesa rushed in. 'You had better get your bath stuff and run to the bathroom. It will soon be supper time.' Kirabo looked through the window at the sky. Kuteesa explained, 'It is five thirty.'

Kirabo fumbled with her clothes, peeling, wiggling from under the towel. By the time she finished, only the Bunsens were left in the dormitory. They walked out, huddling together like a litter of puppies. Water splashing and the smell of bath soap led them to the smallest block. The first bathroom had at least ten girls bathing in the open room. The new girls lined up at the tap to fill their basins. Instead of spreading out to all four bathrooms, they huddled at the door of the first one and waited.

'Psssss.'

They turned.

Behind them a very tall, bespectacled girl breathed, 'Excuse me, Bunsens.'

The new girls parted like the Red Sea.

The girl had not fastened her towel above her breasts like some girls, not around her waist like the amorous ones, but around her neck like a scarf. The rest of her was naked. She glided past the dazed Bunsens and breathed, 'Hi.' Her voice was deeper than Grandmother's. She had the longest straightest legs south of the Sahara. Not a suggestion of hips.

'Hi, Kana.' The elders slid their basins along the slab to make space for her. Kana put her basin down. When she hung her towel on the bathroom door, her face was level with it. Back at her station, she wetted her toilet soap and rubbed it ferociously between her palms until she made a thick lather. She stepped back to make room and lifted one leg, put a foot upon the slab and slapped the lather in her hands on to her ruins. The new girls winced and looked away. Not Kirabo.

'Kana,' an elder nudged her, 'a Bunsen is watching.'

Kana stopped washing and put down her leg. She adjusted her glasses and looked down at Kirabo. Through the thick lenses, Kana's eyes seemed very small.

'Poor girl, she has never seen her beautiful.' Then she sang, 'All things bright and beautiful, all creatures great and small...' but then she left her bath station and came to the door where the Bunsens stood. Kirabo's heart tried to jump into her mouth. She was taller than the other Bunsens. Kana scrutinised Kirabo's face like a doctor looking at a rash. 'Handicap,' she said eventually, like it was a diagnosis. 'This girl grew up in that deep, deep patriarchy which trembles in the presence of the Mighty Vagina.' The Bunsens caught their breaths at the V word, but Kana did not pause. 'A patriarchy that cannot make up its mind whether to fall on its knees in worship of the gateway into the world or to flee the crisis, the orgasmic paroxysms.'

'Watch it, Kana, that kind of mwenkanonkano is radical.'

'Any mwenkanonkano is radical. Talk about equality and men fall in epileptic fits.' As Kana walked back to her station, the new girls stole glances at Kirabo that said *You must stop attracting attention to us.* The bathroom was empty by the time Kana finished, but the new girls still cowered at the door. She towelled herself, wound the towel around her neck and walked out, her buttocks rising and falling brazenly.

The new girls rushed to place their basins on the slab. They talked at once; none listened to the others. Kirabo did not even shudder at the sting of cold water. The hooter went off again. She finished scrubbing, lifted the basin of water and flung it on top of her head. She barely covered her body as she ran out of the bathroom. A handful of elders remained in the dorm. As the last one dashed out of the dorm, she shouted, 'The warning hooter has gone. Mess doors close in ten minutes and Sister Monica is coming to lock the doors.' Kirabo pulled on a pair of knickers and flung both the towel and her inhibitions on to the bed. She oiled her skin and dressed. Thank God there was no hair to comb. She ran out of the dorm in the same direction as every running girl.

Supper was the national school cuisine – posho and beans. By the time the dishes got to the bottom of the table where the Bunsens sat, they were almost empty. There were no beans in the soup. After supper, the Teacher on Duty, a middle-aged woman with a quiet voice and a thick waist, announced that while the rest of the school would go to preps, the S.1s should go to the main hall to meet Sister Ambrose, the headmistress.

3

The main hall was long and wide. At the side entrance, the wall was folding panels. Inside were tight rows of chairs. At one end was the stage, a wooden platform with steps on either side of the apron. It was draped with a maroon velvet curtain. Above the proscenium was a huge portrait of a woman. At first Kirabo thought it was Mother Teresa of Calcutta. But as she looked at it more closely, she realised that the woman had a Ganda nose. She looked like Grandmother with spectacles. Below her image was written:

> 'If the first woman God ever made was strong enough to turn the world upside down all alone, these women together ought to be able to turn it back and get it right-side up again.'
> – Sojourner Truth (1797–1883)

At the back of the room, a huge TV sat on a shelf up the wall and out of reach. Kirabo found an empty seat. With the new girls in their own clothes, they were individuals. They spoke over each other as if someone was coming to take away their tongues. They had names like Immaculate, Specioza, Concepta, Perpetua, Scholastica, Assumpta. They came from the posh schools of Kitante, Nakasero and Buganda Road. They had achieved improbable grades by Nattetta standards – 'I got 262 marks...' 'Me, I got 280...' 'I did not do well, maths let me down...' 'I got 250...' 'I got 272...'

Kirabo's heart sank. First grade was 210 out of 300. In Nattetta, a first grade made you the talk of the villages for years. She had passed with 230 points, 85 percent in both English and General Paper but 60 percent in maths. While 60 percent in a national exam was passing with flying colours in Nattetta, at St Theresa's it was inexcusable. No one seemed to be aware that there was a world outside Kololo or Nakasero or Bugoloobi. Kirabo realised that it was not yet time to say *I come from Nattetta of Bugerere County*.

'I am Atim, which means I was born in a foreign tribe. What is yours?' Kirabo was jolted. It was the girl from her dorm who had stared. Atim was making herself comfortable next to her. She flashed a wide-open smile.

'I am Kirabo, which means—'

'You are Muganda? How?' Atim did not hide her disappointment.

'I don't know.'

'You are sure you are not Acholi or Lango, maybe Alur?'

Kirabo, enjoying Atim's heartbreak, rubbed it in. 'You should see my father, he is proper Joluo – tall, skinny, as dark as night – but we are Baganda – pure!'

Atim feigned being about to stand up and leave. 'This is a waste of time.'

Kirabo held her back. 'What did we do to you?'

'Apart from tribalism and name-calling? You are colonisers.'

'Noooo! We were good people before the British came.'

'Yeah...'

At that moment, the curtain parted and a multitude of chairs was revealed. Kirabo leaned in and whispered to Atim. 'You are too much,' and they watched as women entered from the wings of the stage and sat down. Atim leaned towards Kirabo. 'I am not enough yet: that is why I am here.' The hall was silent. The headmistress, Sister Ambrose, walked in last and went to the lectern, on the left side of the apron. She welcomed the girls and introduced the administrative staff, the teaching staff and the supporting staff of cooks and porters, medical staff and drivers – all of them women, many of them nuns. Father Anatoli was absent. For Kirabo, being surrounded by women only felt like mischief.

Sister Ambrose talked about St Theresa's history. The first woman lawyer, doctor, the first woman minister, the first woman pilot in Uganda were old girls. When she said the school would produce the first woman president of Uganda, everyone laughed, including the teachers. Atim whispered, 'That is me.' Sister Ambrose informed the girls that in terms of brains, they now belonged in the top 10 percent of the country. The privilege of it. St Theresa's was a safe space for them to develop their talents without intimidation, interference or interruption. They owed it to themselves, and to all other girls who did not have their privilege, to excel and to change the world. 'Our job is to arm the girl child with tools so she can live a meaningful life, for herself and for the nation.' The school was strict on academic performance. The wrath of the rules when broken. Indulgence in nicotine and intoxication was suicide; French leave, fatal. Which Kirabo later found out meant to jump over the fences to escape. The exuberance the girls had shown moments before evaporated. Even Atim sat frozen, awestruck.

Next, the girls were shown projected pictures of the school when it first started. A silent picture with static. Black-and-white images of white nuns and black girls walking mechanically, as if in fast forward, flickered across the projector screen. There had only been a few buildings then. Only one house called Jennie Trout House. Kirabo was surprised to hear that the school had been built as a result of Sir Apollo Kaggwa's assertion that Buganda's second hand was broken without boarding schools for girls. Sister Ambrose was keen to emphasise that while the missionaries had the expertise to start schools, it was the people of Buganda who had contributed money and animals for sale, and the poor ones who had brought bricks and labour. She said it was important to know that what were called missionary schools, especially those built during the colonial era, had been built on local effort and money, and that missionaries were engineers and teachers.

By the end of Sister Ambrose's address, Kirabo knew one thing: if her grades were consistently among the bottom five in her class at the end of term in the first two years, she would be 'discontinued'. Sister

Ambrose had explained that 'slow' girls would be weeded out of St Theresa's, so they would not be overwhelmed. That it was fair that they were sent to schools where learning was at their pace. Kirabo knew that her scores had not made the cut-off mark for St Theresa's admission, which meant she was at the bottom of all the S.1s, and vulnerable to elimination.

The following morning after breakfast, all S.1s went to the noticeboard to see which stream they had been allocated to. There were five streams, from S.1.A for students with the highest scores, to S.1.E with the lowest scores. Kirabo was in S.1.E while Atim was S.1.A. Each stream had forty-five girls. The streams were not permanent; at the end of the first and second years all the scores would be thrown into a single basket and reshuffled. The highest marks, regardless of which stream they were in now, would go into stream A, the lowest into stream E. By the end of the first two years, after the purging of the sluggish girls, each stream would have forty girls.

Kirabo had moved from studying three subjects in primary school to fifteen. There were two other language subjects, French and German, on top of English and Luganda. The day was so packed with study and, after classes, with clubs, shows, competitions, sports and scandals, that the world outside of St Theresa's rolled away. But not before Kirabo was put in her place.

It was on the second night after prep when an elder asked, 'What is your name, Dark Tan?'

'Kirabo Nnamiiro.' Kirabo could not protest her black Kiwi Shoe Polish name yet.

The elder frowned. 'I don't remember seeing a Kirabo on the admission list on the noticeboard. I checked to see what scores each one of our Bunsens got.'

'Maybe the list has Kirabo Miiro.'

The girl shook her head. 'How many points did you get?'

'230.'

A hush fell on the dorm until a girl said the obvious: 'But the cut-off mark was 240. How did you get in here?'

Kirabo looked down.

'Dad is a politician,' the elders speculated. 'Or a mafuta mingi; he offered to repair the school pump every time it breaks down. Or to paint the main hall to compensate for the lack of brains in the family gene pool.'

'But ten marks below the cut-off point? That is too much.'

'Which school did you come from?'

'Nattetta Church of Uganda Primary Sch—'

'Oh dear.'

'Where is that?'

'Up the country's arse.'

'We have a back door in our dorm? Told you Sister Ambrose is corrupt.'

After that, Kirabo settled down in her proper place, at the bottom of school society.

A month into the term, the S.1s were summoned, a stream at a time, to the Sanatorium. When Kirabo's class was called, they queued up outside the San's main entrance in alphabetical order for a medical check-up. It was the oldest building. The bricks were thick and bare, even inside. There was no plastering or paint, no pictures or ceiling. When Kirabo heard her name, she found two nurses, both nuns, in the room, and a bed. One sat at a desk with the class register, the other stood close to the bed. The one by the bed said, 'Sit down here, Miiro, and untuck your shirt.'

The bizarreness of being called Miiro instead of Nnamiiro.

'Loosen your skirt, Miiro.'

The nurse began to touch and press and listen, saying 'Breathe in, breathe out' and 'Stick your tongue out, cough'. She peeled back Kirabo's lower eyelids, knocked on her back as if Kirabo were jackfruit. When she was told to lie on the bed, the nurse pushed Kirabo's skirt lower as her hand probed her lower abdomen. The pressure increased as she prodded her stomach. 'Have you started your periods, Miiro?'

'No, I mean yes.'

'What do you mean, no or yes?'

'I have started, but they skip months.'

The nurse pressed again, as if she were kneading a mound of matooke, until Kirabo winced.

'Do you feel pain when they come on?'

'A lot.'

'Dysmenorrhoea,' the nurse called out to the other, who was jotting things down.

'What is the pain like?'

'Back pain. It radiates. Sometimes the whole pelvic area, including down there, is on fire.'

'No pain in the lower stomach?'

'Cramps.'

'How heavy is the flow?'

'Very heavy. I change like six times a day. But it lasts two days.'

'Dizziness?'

'Yes.'

'Okay, get dressed. As soon as it comes back, come and tell us.'

Later, Kirabo found out what dysmenorrhoea was, how the nurses were nice to sufferers and would give you bed rest in the San, heavy-duty pads and painkillers. Being in the San was a treat. You ate food from the convent. There were girls who were admitted to the San every time their periods came on. Like Nnakidde, whose periods made her so dizzy she could not go to class, Imma, who flowed so heavily that if she came to class, it would seep through, or Specioza, who would writhe in pain as if in childbirth. Sometimes, Specioza's father came and took her home. Sometimes he stayed with her in the San as she cried. In Nattetta, when Kirabo first told Grandmother about the pains, she said, 'Oh, that. Lie down if it is too much, but don't get into the habit. Many women get those pains, but if we all stopped when they came on, the world would grind to a halt.'

When they were done, the other nurse ticked her name on the register and told her to go to the next room, where an optician flashed a tiny torch in her eyes and told her to read letters on the wall across the room with one eye closed. Then she was sent to the next room, where a dentist treated her gums and teeth roughly, calling out numbers. After that she was told to go straight to class.

When she came out of class at lunchtime, something was in the air. Elders were staring in the direction of the car park. Kirabo went to see. A heap of luggage sat in the car park outside the San. Nunciata, the office messenger – girls called her AOD for Angel of Doom – was adding to the heap. Nunciata was the AOD because when she collected you from class or dormitory, it was expulsion, suspension or death in the family. As Kirabo arrived in her dorm, ŋŋanda, a loud elder with a droopy arse, came shouting, '1977's Bunsens have broken the record – ten pregnancies.'

Kirabo panicked. She knew she could not be pregnant, but an irrational fear gripped her. It was made worse by the elders' inhumanity – clapping, drumming and hooting as if it was something to celebrate. Meanwhile, ŋŋanda spoke into the cable of a kettle like it was a mic. 'Once again, the long arm of the patriarchy has reached deep into the nuns' womb of resistance and made off with ten chicks.' She contorted and twitched. 'The nurses are taking them back home as we speak. Let's observe a moment of silence.' She dropped her head.

'Not to worry,' another girl said. 'Ten girls on the waiting list will step into their places and life, like the Nile, will carry on.'

Kirabo's fear did not let go until she found out that the pregnant girls had been detained in the San all along. Once you were discovered to be pregnant, you would not be allowed back in the student body, not even to pack your belongings. As if pregnancy was contagious. Apparently, it was because those girls had transformed into women; the school was for girls only.

How do you go back home? How do you face your family? Kirabo imagined confronting the double loss – a childhood lost and a future squandered for early motherhood. You would think St Theresa's, with all its *Us women in this together* stance, would be sympathetic to girls in these circumstances. Especially because throwing girls out of education ensured one thing: their babies would be born into poverty. When the girls were led out of the San to get on the school bus, Kirabo pondered. The boys who had made them pregnant would carry on as before, their lives uninterrupted.

4

There was no time to see the term go by, no time to crave her mother, no moment to miss Sio. St Theresa's had no space for baggage carried from home. Besides the busy schedule, Kirabo was mesmerised by the difference between the St Theresa's she had imagined and the St Theresa's she was experiencing. Out in the world, St Theresa's was a successful matriarchy. A paradise where a lucky clever girl was moulded into a whole woman before being thrust back into the patriarchy. The perception was that without the presence of masculinity girls lived in harmony, worked hard and were thankful for the privilege. The reality was different. Despite the nuns' best efforts, some girls still went on French leave, there were rumoured abortions found wrapped in plastic bags in the filled-up latrines and a newborn found in the piggery; there was drinking and smoking after lights out and kasaawe couples who claimed to be 'trying out' lovemaking before they met men. These things went on beneath the excellent grades and glittering reputation, beyond the nuns' reach.

Some girls did not make sense at all. Like Aate Baba, who slept in Kirabo's dorm. Aate was gifted in maths, chemistry and physics – subjects considered to be masculine. Art subjects were feminine. The last time the school went to SMACK – St Mary's College Kisubi, a boys' school – for a maths competition, Aate had reduced the SMACK team to spectators, which earned her hate mail from SMACK, cartoons depicting her as an intersexual freak. Yet Aate's ambition was to get married and have children. She had no interest in further studies. Her mother had once been her father's housemaid. Aate lived in absolute squalor at her mother's house and in ridiculous opulence at her father's. She called her dad 'that man'. Apparently, she once asked him whether a housemaid could have a consenting relationship with her cabinet minister master! Yet Aate insisted that as long as men were stronger and faster, equality between the sexes was a delusion. She sneered at mwenkanonkano as women aspiring to behave as badly as men.

But the most peculiar phenomena were the flare-ups of tension in the community now and again. They came like a storm, fast, deadly and then died, leaving behind devastation. For every flare-up, at the bottom of it was the rivalry of two clubs – the Career Women and the Homemakers. If Homemakers committed suicide by drowning, Career Women would self-immolate, claiming that fire was by far the superior element. Homemakers tended to be very religious; they were the well-behaved girls, girls keen on cultivating a good reputation and a non-threatening femininity. They avoided mwenkanonkano discussions like the plague. During house sports competitions they were the girls who let their houses down because running, jumping or even throwing the ball might make them muscly. Their club was about cookery, a balanced diet, baking without sugar, knitting and childcare. Aate Baba was their vice chairperson.

The Career Women's Club, unlike the Homemakers', was exclusive. You did not saunter in there, *faa*, and register. Members were headhunted, poached from clubs like the debating, French, literature, modelling and drama clubs for girls who were pretty, articulate, assertive and confident. The whole Prefects' Council was part of it. Kana, the tall, deep-voiced mwenkanonkano extremist, was the vice chairperson. Kirabo was keen to join the Career Women, but her spoken English was still Nattetta-esque. You could not say things like *biskwit*, *clothez* or *Irie-land* and step into the Career Women's Club. There were rumours that Career Women smoked, drank and were lesbianing themselves, but Kirabo still wanted to join.

Two weeks before exams began, the atmosphere changed. Girls, now short of pocket money and snacks and besieged by the pressure of exams, had turned meaner. Fights were not uncommon. Sometimes girls were so vicious it was scary. Like that thing between Angelique from Yaa Asantewaa House and Talemwa from Nzinga. Angelique was an S.4 and a Career Woman. In St Theresa's, S.4s were allowed a day out once a year to exercise their maturity. On such days, girls did not wear school uniform. They visited boyfriends if they had one or went out to daytime discos with friends. Only nerds went home. The mad ones came back with lurid stories: 'We banged it so hard I am sore.'

A week after the S.4s' day out, a rumour started. Angelique had 'stolen' Talemwa's boyfriend. Talemwa, an S.3, was a mild-mannered girl who minded her business. Everyone in the school knew Talemwa because her boyfriend, Ssaka, was very handsome and visited her every Visiting Day. He brought her snacks and they sat on the steps of the Sanatorium, wrapped around each other. Talemwa was an orphan whose father had disappeared the way rich fathers were disappearing in Amin's regime. She lived with an aunt who did not come on Visiting Days. The whole school was in love with Talemwa and Ssaka.

Angelique, on the other hand, was one of those girls who had it all. Her grades were stellar. She was always the MC at social functions. Her family had a holiday home in France. She was a trendsetter. Always coming back from holiday with new fashions. Angelique was so pretty she could get any guy she wanted; why go after Talemwa's man?

Overnight, Angelique became a pariah. And in an intense community like St Theresa's, being a pariah was every minute of the day. The story spiralled out of control. Angelique was actually a thief, many girls had always suspected it, but she was too clever to be caught. Kleptomania ran in the family. Her father was a highway robber – 'Where do you think they get the money to go to France twice a year?' Her mother had lost her job in a bank over missing funds. Her sister in Gayaza High had also been caught with stolen stuff. Girls worked themselves into a rage.

Then a girl lured Angelique to Nzinga House. Perhaps Angelique was not aware of the extent of the hatred in the school. If she had been, why would she have agreed to go to Nzinga, which was Talemwa's house? It was well timed for Sunday afternoon, when the prefects had gone masturbating – that was what girls called the weekly tea and biscuit meetings between the prefect council and Sister Ambrose.

Once Angelique entered the dorm, *ba ppa*, the Nzingies locked the door. Heckling started. Kirabo, who had gone to borrow a copy of *Introduction to Biology*, was caught in the middle of it. When Angelique realised, a look of the condemned came into her eyes. But someone good-natured stopped the baying and suggested that Angelique be given a chance to say something for herself. Was she a man thief? 'Yeah, tell us: why do you steal people's men?' Angelique, like a goat to the slaughter, just stared.

'Slut.' A shoe flew over her head and hit the wall.

Missiles of crinkled paper, balled socks, shoes, slippers and other objects flew from all directions, never hitting her but coming close. And that was the savagery of it – the suggestion, keeping her in trepidation. Just then a gang of Asantes arrived, made up in bright tribal war paint, armed with sticks, clubs and tree branches. There were as many as twenty. Ten Asantes jumped into the dorm through the windows, opened the door and ran across the lawn to open the gate. The rest of the gang broke through the mob, grabbed Angelique and led her out. Their attitude was *If you don't know how to pleasure your men, step out of the way.* When they got outside the dorm, they stood on Nzinga's quadrangle and told the Nzingies that if they craved a beating, they could come and collect it from Yaa Asantewaa any time. By the time Nzinga House recovered, the Asantes were safely behind the walls of their house, reciting their war cry:

> Is it true the bravery of Asante is no more?
> We, the women, will.
> I shall call upon my fellow women.
> We will fight.
> We will fight till the last of us falls in the battlefields.

For the rest of that day, public opinion wavered. While most girls still despised Angelique, the Asantes had earned respect for their successful raid on Nzinga House. But then Aate declared Angelique a homewrecker, and the Homemakers, together with Nzinga House, started to hunt for Angelique. The Career Women joined the Asantes in protecting Angelique. They had managed to sneak Angelique into the Sanatorium and checked her in with a splitting headache. Kana was contemptuous: 'Which home did she wreck? Men are not objects; they cannot be stolen.' There was such anger on both sides that Kirabo wondered where the rage had come from. The Christians took Talemwa's side and advised her to read the Novena.

By the end of the nine days of Talemwa's Novena, it had come to light that Talemwa had been dumped because she was faulty down there: 'Teaspoon in a mug. Ssaka said it himself...' Apparently, Ssaka had never 'tasted' another girl until Angelique. Embarrassment for Talemwa started to seep into the community. Girls avoided looking at her, then avoided her entirely. What is the point of being a woman if you are faulty down there? For some reason, being defective became Talemwa's fault. The wind turned and clawed at her. Meanwhile, Angelique was back on the social scene as if she had never left. The Career Women treated her like a celebrity.

To compound it all, during the Variety Show at the end of term, a girl sang, begging a certain Jolene not to take her man just because she could. Angelique responded with a spectacular rendition of the Swahili love song 'Malaika' as if Ssaka were sitting right there in the main hall. It was heartbreaking because it was the Career Women who had registered both items in the show. In the end, Angelique became this carefree girl who was in charge of her emotions. Talemwa became that tasteless girl in Nzinga.

Kirabo began to see how Nsuuta's idea of kweluma operated in real life. Girls had reduced themselves to their vaginas, to objects for male consumption. They had turned on one another over a boy who visited the school once a month, a cheater at that. If they could turn on each other in a community designed for their safety and emancipation, what chances did mwenkanonkano have out there in the world? The nuns might have removed any male influence within the school gates, but by the time the girls arrived, the shrinking herb had already been sewn into their skins.

The examination season descended and the school hushed. It reminded Kirabo of what St Theresa's was all about. No cheer, no gossip, no squabbles, no clubs. Girls budgeted their time stingily – classes, bathrooms, mess, prep, sleep. Had there not been a lights-out hooter, some girls would have studied all night. It lasted the first three weeks of July. For the S.1s and S.2s, there was no break from exam papers because they did all fifteen subjects.

On the last Thursday of term, Kirabo's class lined up for report-signing. Every pupil had to be present as Sister Ambrose put her signature on their report. The girls had to account for any poor grades or negative comments by teachers on their report form. Disciplinary action was administered where necessary, promises to do better made by earnest students. Kirabo's bottom was smarting with anticipation when her turn came.

'Miiro?'

'Yes, Madam.'

'I am not Madam. I am Sister. Madam is for women who marry men. I am married to Christ.'

'Yes, Sister.'

'Sit down and tell me how you have found the school.'

'It is fine, Sister.'

'Have you made any friends yet?'

Kirabo nodded.

Sister Ambrose examined the report. 'If everything is fine, how do you explain the low mark in music?'

'I don't understand music at all.' Kirabo could not explain the tadpoles strung on a bar. For the exam, the teacher gave them symbols mounted on a staff and told them to decipher them on to sol-fa. The second part, he gave them sol-fa and told them to draw the tadpoles on a staff. When she looked up, Sister Ambrose had taken off her glasses and was staring as if she had insulted her.

'You never, *ever* say that to me again, young lady.' She pointed at Kirabo with her spectacles. '*You* have just informed *me* that *you* have no intention of improving your music.' Kirabo was beginning to protest when the nun waved her quiet. 'You realise, I hope, that you did not attain the minimum grade for this school.'

Kirabo nodded.

'Haven't you asked yourself how you came to be here?'

Kirabo hung her head, thinking of Miiro visiting his brother, Father Dewo, who must have pulled some Catholic strings.

'Well, you are a part of an experiment I am conducting. I suspect that children from rural schools who attain good grades could be better than some of the spectacular grades we get from the privileged schools. You are part of the first group. It is up to you to prove me right. So far, I am satisfied, but only satisfied. I want to be vindicated. Work harder at art and music next term. Nothing below 75 percent. Have a nice holiday.'

The moment she drove out of the school gates the following day, Kirabo was plunged back into her old life. Her rootlessness. Her motherlessness. Earlier in the term, because she now knew her mother's name, she had hoped to use the school to locate her, approaching first the girls with Ffumbe clan names and then the other Ganda girls. But she had soon chickened out. Now, knowing how the school worked when there was any announcement to make, she decided to put up posters like girls did for shows, at the mess, chapel and main hall entrances the following term.

5

Kirabo first saw Sio again during the Christmas break of 1978. She had finished her second year, and so far her DO YOU KNOW LOVINCA NNAKKU posters had revealed nothing but the incredible cruelty of girls. Some had been scribbled over with taunts: *No one wants dark tan babies* or *Abandonment issues*. Others had been torn or pulled down off the wall. But occasionally girls were supportive, asking if Kirabo had found her. Some shared their experiences of unknown fathers or a parent who had died before memories were formed. But for Kirabo, as long as more than two hundred Bunsens plus a hundred S.5s joined the school every year, there was hope. Some girls suggested Kirabo put special announcements on the radio. She decided that, if she finished her O levels before finding her, she would. She did not want to jeopardise her mother's marriage.

St Theresa's was a body of water. You dropped girls in it and they found their depth. Some sank to the bottom like stones, some floated on the top like feathers. In between, the largest group formed the middling layers, like strata.

At the end of the first year, when the mixed list of all S.1s was put up on the noticeboard, a trend became apparent. Girls who had been at the top of the admission list with 280s and 270s were gravitating downwards. Perhaps the pressure was too much. Every girl in St Theresa's was clever and competitive, but many of these girls were on their own for the first time: no mum and dad to pay for coaching now. Besides, being on top made you a target for all the girls below you. Perhaps the way you performed in three subjects at primary level was not the way you did in fifteen subjects at secondary level. Perhaps boarding school life was not for every girl. Unfortunately, the general feeling was that those girls drifting downwards had cheated in primary leaving exams, and every time results were pinned up, a new set of girls joined the disgraced. Kirabo and other girls from 'Third World Schools', as the girls referred to them, had so far proved they were worth investing in. None was in stream E any more, and none was under threat of elimination.

Kirabo was mopping the sitting-room floor when she heard Tom's new car, a Honda Accord, in the car park outside their house. She threw the mop into the basin and ran to the balcony. Tom was out of the car, hurrying towards the alleyway. She ran through the living room and the foyer, shot into the backyard and under the clothes lines, and opened the gate. Tom rushed past her. 'Abi, where are you? Abi?' Aunt Abi was in the kitchen. 'Calamity has fallen back home. Kabuye, the surgeon, was taken.'

Aunt Abi clapped and sat down on the kitchen step, then exhaled. There was something final about the word 'taken'. You did not ask why, or how or by whom. Neither Tom nor Aunt Abi noticed that Kirabo was trembling.

Tom sat on the same step and whispered, 'Apparently, a car stopped outside Ssozi's shop. Four men stepped out and asked for directions to Kabuye's house but Ssozi's heart told him not to give them the directions. Along came Father. Ssozi asked him whether he had ever heard of a surgeon called Kabuye. Father laughed, "In this dry Nattetta? Aah, you will only find peasants like us. Try going back to Bukolooto or Kayunga. That is where all the rich live." When the men had gone, Ssozi sent a boy, quick-quick, on a bicycle to Kabuye's house to warn him. But just as the boy got to the house the car arrived. Someone dumb, a child probably, had given them the right directions.'

Aunt Abi clapped and propped her chin with her hand, a mourning stance.

'Unfortunately, Kabuye was home. He has been gone since yesterday. Father and Ssozi are hiding in the bush, in case the men come for them too.'

'We have to go home.' Aunt Abi made to stand up.

'That is the thing. Father says we should stay here. They could come after us too.'

But for Kirabo, it was not Miiro living in the bush or the possibility that the men could come for Tom that was on her mind; it was Sio. Had he been at home when it happened? She could not imagine the pain of seeing your father brutalised. The prevalent disappearance and murders of fathers, often middle class and educated, was the one phenomenon boarding school protected you from. Even when your own was taken, life at St Theresa's, with all its busy-busy, distracted from the pain. You were not at home to see life disintegrate around your family. In the beginning, girls had been collected to be with their families when their fathers disappeared. But lately, Sister Ambrose had put a stop to it. When a mother came to school to say that her husband had disappeared, Sister Ambrose asked if they had a body. Or whether they were going on the run. If they were not, she told the mother to go back home. There was no need to bring pain to a girl if she was not going to bury her father. And so girls were given more time, up to the end of the term, before they discovered they had been orphaned. Sometimes, when a family went on the run, Sister Ambrose kept the girl in her house during term breaks. Then, when the family found a haven, they rang to ask the school to put her on a plane or Akamba Bus. When a girl came back from term break and whispered, 'My father disappeared,' everyone kept quiet, and some girls avoided her completely in fear because there were girls in the school related to the people in power, with dads or brothers in the army. Such girls wore flashy clothes, expensive shoes and were brought to school in huge cars with blacked-out windows or in army Jeeps. It did not matter that these girls had never threatened anyone; everyone feared them regardless. Mostly, they kept to themselves. So the only form of sympathy the orphaned girls got was in stares and girls sharing stuff with them because everyone knew they did not bring enough pocket money or snacks any more. At the end of term, the girls who came from the same village would offer them a lift home in their parents' cars. In any case, most did not return to St Theresa's after the holiday. But still no one mentioned the word *abduction*.

Kirabo had to see Sio. Because of the increased insecurity in the country, travel outside the city had become hazardous. There were many security checks, roadblocks manned by the army, where sometimes passengers were detained, but Kirabo was resolved. Unfortunately, there was a notorious roadblock outside the Namanve woods on the way to Mukono. Everyone knew Namanve was not just a dumping ground for corpses, it was killing fields. Word had it that once at that roadblock, two soldiers fought over a woman from a car they had detained, and to settle the argument they had shot her so both would lose her. In the beginning, when women were pulled from buses or taxis, the drivers would steer the vehicle a little further away from the roadblock and wait until the soldiers finished with her so she could be taken home, but then one driver was shot for saying he would wait.

Even so, Kirabo planned to see Sio. She had to console him. Can you imagine his pain? Besides, the following April, in 1979, he would be doing his A levels.

A week later was Atim's birthday. Kirabo rang her, told her about Sio's father and asked for a sleepover after her birthday party. Atim's father was a renowned gynaecologist. They lived in Summit View in Upper Kololo, an exclusive residential area. Aunt Abi let her go for the sleepover because Kirabo was making the right kind of friends. As far as Aunt Abi was concerned, going to St Theresa's was not just about getting good grades; it was about getting into the right circles as well.

Kirabo turned up early for Atim's party. At one o'clock, she changed into her school uniform, threw a jacket on top and put on a cap to conceal her face. She explained to a worried Atim, 'I'm sure Sio has moved on, but he is an only child, and losing a parent is not the same when you are an only child. He has no one to share his grief with.'

Atim did not pretend to believe a word Kirabo said. She tried to reason with her about the dangers of making such a journey, but Kirabo was firm. She planned to catch the Guy bus, praying that it was still operational. If she met anyone she knew on it, she would give them a message for her grandparents and take a taxi instead.

At the security check in the Namanve woods, all of the passengers filed out. Male passengers queued up on the left while women queued to the right of the door. Everyone held out their identity cards and opened their bags. Two soldiers got on the bus to check underneath the seats. Kirabo had stuffed her transport money into her knickers. Army men did not walk past money. Because she wore her school uniform, she was waved back on to the bus with a 'Mutoto wa shule?' Now her only worry was not finding Sio at home, something she had not thought about before she set off. She would have to look for a taxi to take her back to Nazigo and catch another taxi to Kampala. The chances would be slim of slipping out of Nazigo unseen.

When the bus drove past the churches in Nattetta, then the dispensary and the reverend's house, she ducked below the windows. Next was Widow Diba's house. A little while longer and they arrived at the junction near Miiro's. Kirabo resisted the urge to take a peek. She imagined Ssozi's shop, the *koparativu stowa*, the huge muvule tree, Nsuuta's house. When the bus began to ascend Bugiri Hill, Kirabo sat up. It felt like betrayal.

The wooden gate on Sio's home hung open, neglected and limp. The house had lost that vibrant, healthy look Kirabo had associated with Sio. When she was young, there were some houses, like Giibwa's, that were malnourished. Miiro's was just the right health. Sio's home was an upper-middle-class house which would not have looked out of place in Kololo, Nakasero or Bugoloobi. But now the swing near the hedge was rusty. How she had longed to swing on it! As she got to the house, she prayed that all the mourners and soothers had gone. It had been two weeks since Dr Kabuye's abduction. People did not hang about in such cases.

No one came out to meet her.

She walked to the side of the house and peered into the back yard. There was a large aluminium water tank. A double-storeyed pen for Zungu chickens. A matooke plantation. She had imagined Kabuye's home to be too British to have such traditional structures. Somehow it took away the remnants of Sio's foreignness. Just then a woman, not Sio's mother, emerged from the side door. Sio's mother was so pale you saw the blue of her veins. This woman was dark, but she was not a villager. She smiled. 'Are you looking for someone?' She spoke Luganda.

'Sio.'

A look of *I should have known* came into her eyes. Then she saw Kirabo's school uniform. 'Which school is this?' She lifted the left flap of Kirabo's jacket to glance at the school emblem. 'St Theresa's?'

First came recognition and then respect. St Theresa's had that effect on people. You said you were at St Theresa's and people presumed you were clever, hard-working and rich. The woman called, 'Sio? Sio. Sio ono?' When no reply came, she said, 'Come with me. He must be in his bedroom. Go to the front door, I will open it for you.'

It was a metal and glass panel door. As Kirabo looked around, the curtains were yanked back. Sio stood there. Confusion crossed his face but was soon replaced by realisation, and eventually shock. He was skinny, taller, older, and sported a little goatee like a proper man. He took in Kirabo's school uniform – back-to-school shoes, scholars' socks, skirt and blouse – and then he looked at her face. He made a gesture with his hands of *What is this?*

Kirabo gestured back: *I heard.*

That was when he remembered to open the lock. He disappeared, and the white lining of the curtains fell back. They parted again, and he opened several locks behind the door. Finally, he opened a padlock on a huge chain around the metal grilles and the double doors opened.

'Kirabo.' He stared at her, his face inscrutable.

She smiled.

He looked her up and down again, then motioned for her to show him the school emblem. She did.

'You are at St Theresa's.'

She nodded.

'St Theresa's girls are haughty.'

'SMACK boys are bean weevils.'

He laughed.

'Are you not going to invite your friend in?'

Sio looked back at the woman, then he started as if this idea had just occurred to him. He smiled shamefacedly and hurried back to the living room, picking cushions from one settee and dropping them on to another, beating the sofas as if they were dusty, arranging the coffee table. 'Come in, come in. We have not cleaned in a long time.' But the woman looked at him as if to protest: *I have been cleaning*.

The sitting room was littered with pictures of him at various stages of childhood. The ones taken in Britain were in Kodachrome, the frames posh; the ones taken in Afro Studio were black and white. The difference between the plump boy in the pictures and the skinny Sio standing before her, forgetting to greet her, was incredible.

'Did you come on that bus?' the woman asked. 'I heard it stop.'

'Yes.'

Kirabo was beginning to worry about Sio's lack of speech. Perhaps he had a new girlfriend. She said, 'I heard my father talking about what happened, so I came to check on you.'

'Oh,' the woman clapped and sat down. Just like that, tears started to flow. Sio sat down on the same settee as the woman. He leaned his head on a fist while the other hand fell to the floor and picked at the carpet. Still he said nothing. Finally, the woman lifted her head and blew her nose into a handkerchief. She savaged her nose, dried the tears with a flap of her busuuti and stood up. 'Thank you for coming, child, you are a good friend.' She walked out.

'I don't know what to say.' Sio stood up and came over to where Kirabo sat. He reached for both her hands and sat with her. Then he let go of one of her hands to wipe away his tears. 'I didn't know what to say when I saw you. And you were dressed in uniform, your eyes hidden. I thought you had forgotten us.'

'I don't know your address.'

'You know I am still at St Mary's.'

'I was not sure.' Then she whispered, 'Where is your mother?'

Shadows returned to his eyes. 'She is safe; she is back with her people in Dar.'

'Your mother is Tanzanian?' Then realisation: 'Is that why they came for your dad?'

Sio nodded.

'But she is so light-skinned.'

'She is Chagga. They can be pale.'

'Oh. All along, I thought she was mixed blood, that your father met her in Britain.'

'The men came for Mum, not Dad, claiming she was a Tanzanian spy. But she left when our troops invaded Kagera in Tanzania. All the Tanzanians left. Dad – stupid Dad – stayed: "I am Ugandan, they will not touch me, they need me at the hospital, there are just a handful of surgeons…"' Sio took a breath. 'They came during daytime, I swear, they came in clear daylight. They parked their car right there.' He stood up and pointed through the window. 'There, near the hedge.' Kirabo stood up and stared at the hedge as if the car was still parked there. 'Dad was washing the Minor. When he saw them, he ran into the house and locked the door. Stupid, really, he should have run outside, but in here, he was trapped. They shot through the lock, right here, see?'

Kirabo looked at the bullet holes.

'Were you at home?'

'Of course; we had our holidays two Fridays ago. Dad shouted, "Run, Sio." I told him, "You run – they never take children." He was stupid like that. We ran upstairs, and he helped me through the hole leading into the ceiling but did not come up with me. He said if they found us together, they would take us both. I begged and begged him to climb into the ceiling, but he ran out.' He twisted his lips to lock in the tears. Then he looked at her. 'Did you know we have drums?'

'No.'

He grabbed her hand. 'Come.' And they ran through the dining room to a long dark corridor and up the stairs. They burst into a study room with a table and a set of Ganda musical instruments – drums, harps, ntongoli, a xylophone, two pairs of nsaasi rattles and two drumsticks resting on the mpuunyi drum. 'Dad ran to this room and sounded the drum like they do in traditional alarm – *Gwanga mujje, gwanga mujje, gwanga mujje* – and residents emerged out of the bushes everywhere with clubs, pangas and hoes because most of them were in their gardens at the time. When the men saw the villagers, they shot in the air to shoo them away, and the villagers slipped back into the bushes.'

'Where were you then?'

In the ceiling. It was my aunt who told me. She is Dad's sister. She had come to look after us during the holidays after Mum left.'

Kirabo stared.

'The men came upstairs and grabbed Dad. They shouted, "Where is she? Where is she?" in Swahili. It was stupid Swahili; Ugandans can't speak proper Swahili. Dad speaks fluently, but it is Tanzanian Swahili, which of course sank him. He should have stuck to English. He begged, said he was just a harmless doctor, that his wife had run away, wa? They dragged him downstairs. I could hear them hitting him already. If his wife was not a spy, why had she run away? Why was he hiding? Outside, he called out to the villagers, "It is me, Kabuye the doctor, they are taking me." I heard the car boot bang. Then the car doors. They drove away.'

Now Kirabo thought of Tom and shivered.

'When they arrived in Nattetta at Ssozi's shop, they stopped. They opened the boot and people saw Dad being pulled out like a sack of potatoes, can you imagine?' Kirabo shook her head. 'Even then he called, "It is me, Dr Kabuye, they are taking me!" The men walked, casual as you like, to Ssozi's shop and his son, who was in the shop, disappeared. They picked a sisal rope, the ones he hangs on the door, and tied Dad's hands, then his legs, and he fell down in the dust as the world looked on like this' – Sio opened his eyes wide to show exactly how the world had looked on. He took a breath and turned to the window. He twisted his lips and shrugged in resignation. 'They threw him back into the boot and *ahhhhh...*' His hand made a motion of driving away. He stared through the window.

After a stretched silence Kirabo sighed, 'My grandfather has been sleeping in the bush ever since, because when the men first came looking for your father, he and Ssozi gave them the wrong directions.'

'I heard. Have you been to your grandfather's?'

Kirabo shook her head and explained how she had avoided being seen in Nattetta.

'You cannot go back to Kampala now; curfew will start in an hour.'

Before Kirabo could discuss it, Sio called his aunt. He told her how Kirabo had left home under false pretences, how it was too late to return to the city. He talked to her as if she was not a grown-up and unreasonable.

'Of course she can sleep here tonight.' The aunt smiled.

That evening, after Kirabo rang Atim to tell her she was spending the night in Nattetta, she and Sio could not stop talking about the past two years. They talked as if they had always talked easily, as if her visiting him and spending the night at his house was right, as if Nattetta had had no right to tongue-tie them in the first place. Before supper, Sio took her to the bathroom, gave her a towel and lent her a pair of jeans and a T-shirt. He prepared for her to sleep in one of the spare bedrooms upstairs. However, after supper, as Kirabo got into bed, Sio's aunt came to her bedroom. She was wearing that scandalised, angry expression of grown-ups that said *If you children think you are going to have sex in this house while I sleep, think again.*

'You' – she pointed at Kirabo – 'you are sleeping in my bedroom. Come.'

Kirabo jumped out of bed and the woman escorted her to the other end of the corridor. Kirabo was dying to see the look on Sio's face, but with all the sucking of teeth and muttering his aunt was doing, she dared not look back. In the woman's bedroom, Kirabo slid on to the mattress laid out on the floor below the woman's bed and hid her face under the blanket. Sex had not even crossed her mind.

'Are you catching the earliest bus back home?' the woman asked. Her tone, however, said *You* are *catching the earliest bus home.*

'Yes.'

'I will wake you up.'

When Sio's aunt roused Kirabo the following morning, breakfast was ready. They ate together, smiling and friendly again, as if she had not suspected them of lust. Kirabo gave Sio her home phone number and the one of her school's public phone. The woman and Sio waited with her at the roadside until she caught the Guy bus at seven in the morning.

6

There is nothing like love lost and found. It is unreasonable; it is reckless; it is hungry.

Kirabo's visit to Sio's was a lit match thrown on thatch. The fire caught fast; it burned with more intensity than before. All this time, Kirabo's feelings for Sio had been buried, the way Grandmother buried embers so deep in the hearth overnight you thought the fire was dead. But poke deep into the ash the following morning and the embers glowed with life once more. Cradle those embers in a sheaf of hay, blow on it, and before you know it the blaze is out of control.

Sio was new. He was so much more than Kabuye's son. Kirabo loved him the way she could not love her mother. He belonged to her the way Tom no longer did. Sio too must have found in Kirabo a distraction from his father's abduction, from the dark emptiness of his home. The way he came to see her during those Christmas holidays when it was dangerous to travel, the way he wore khaki shorts – so awkward on his hairy legs – and a school shirt with a badge; the way Kirabo walked long distances to Jinja Road to meet him; the way she risked Aunt Abi catching her at it, meant theirs was not a matter of hearts, it was blood. The Ganda had it right. Love is blood choosing blood. Nothing to do with the heart. The heart speaks, you can reason with it. But blood? Blood is inexorable. Once it has decided, it has decided.

Because now Kirabo had a language, she was bold. Because her tongue was untied, she revealed herself. Besides, what was unsaid was in her eyes. She was much more than Miiro's tomboy granddaughter.

She had ideas, attitudes, opinions and a world view. Sio was so nat-ural with her she found herself opening every part of herself to him. There was so much to discover and explore about each other. Even the limitations of Nattetta became nostalgic. Kirabo started making fun of her pain: 'I am the sad product of games children should not play.' When Sio sighed, 'My parents were plain lazy; they could have given me a sibling or two,' Kirabo was sceptical: 'I have siblings on both sides, Mum's and Dad's, but they belong more to my parents than I do.'

Then the surprise. Like the fact that the chicken pens Kirabo had seen behind Sio's house were not his parents' but his own. 'I am going to start a farm.' Which teenage boy says that? 'I will do Agriculture at university.' Only students who had failed to get the grades for Medicine did Agriculture. 'My father has a lot of land, I might as well farm it.' While every boy and girl in Nattetta with any respectable ambition was escaping to the city, Sio asked, 'Have you ever thought of becoming a vet?'

'Me?' Kirabo was flabbergasted.

If Sio was not already flowing in her blood, this was the moment she would have stepped back and said *What am I doing with this boy?* But she found herself thinking that cow dung, mucking out chicken pens and spending the day sweating in the shambas together in Nattetta would not be such a bad future for her. That gulf – London-born and gasping rich – which had lain between them as children had closed. They studied in 'First World' schools, spoke the same boarding school language, listened to the same music, danced the same, watched the same UTV programmes.

Sio lent Kirabo her first Bob Marley cassette and got her hooked on 'Stir It Up'. He said the intro was *foreplay just*. While Sio swore that Grace Jones was the epitome of black beauty, Kirabo declared she was ready to marry Bob Marley any time.

Sio came twice, sometimes three times a week to see her. Mulago Hospital had given him his father's salary, told him to keep picking it up until Dr Kabuye was certified dead. Then it would be replaced by his father's pensions. It was for his school fees, but he used some of it to travel to see her. They met outside Christ the King church and strolled up to the International Hotel and lay in the grounds of Jubilee Park. Mostly, when one of them had money, they went to the Neeta Cinema and watched old Bollywood films. Not that they saw the films at all. While the Indians sang and danced their love, Kirabo and Sio sat at the back of the empty auditorium, their hands exploring parts of each other they would not dare touch in daylight. It was there that Kirabo discovered what she was capable of.

At the end of January 1979, on Sio's last visit before the new term began, a sense of uncertainty hung over them. They lay on their stomachs under a tree in the city square, contemplating not seeing each other for so long. Sio's mother was fretting. She had told him real war was coming. Apparently, the multitudes of Ugandans who had fled into exile over the years had regrouped in Tanzania and were coming home. She wanted Sio to join her in Dar, but crossing into Kenya through Malaba was too dangerous. Amin's spies could be watching him. On that visit there was a lot of silence and sighing as they contemplated being torn from each other again. Yes, people wanted to get rid of Amin because 'the country was not functioning', as the grown-ups put it, but to Kirabo things were no longer clear-cut. She had just found Sio again and now the stupid war was coming. She was staring at the impossibility of life without him when Sio said, 'I have never seen a woman's wokoto.'

Kirabo was shocked. 'Wokoto? Is that what you boys call it? And what do you call yours?'

'Ssebukuule.'

'Hail, ssebukuule. I bow down in awe. Meanwhile, wokoto says *ugly*.'

'I am sorry.'

'I take it you have never seen *Penthouse*.'

'What?'

'The blue magazine. Girls bring them to school. Those women put everything, and I mean *everything*, out there in the sun – like a goat's tail.'

Sio sat up. 'I will show you mine too.'

'Oh, so you want to see mine?'

Sio dropped his head.

'Why didn't you say so? We shall go to a toilet and I will show you my flower.'

Sio looked at her sharply.

'That is what we call it – the flower.'

He grinned.

'Don't worry. We have a saying at St Theresa's…'

'That?'

'…sharing out what does not deplete makes you lavish.'

Sio looked down, embarrassment burning his face.

'I will lavish you,' Kirabo said. 'After all, all you want is to see.'

'Yes.'

'Name the day, the time, the place and I will unfold my flower for you.'

Sio picked up a stick and lashed the ground. Then he looked up. 'But not in a toilet. We cannot go to the same toilet. We need a room.'

'You don't want to see, you want to do.'

'No, God no, Kirabo. I would not. Trust in God.' Being so light-skinned, his skin was transparent. His embarrassment was painfully visible. 'You could get pregnant.' He paused. 'Okay, perhaps I will touch a little.'

'We *have* been touching.'

He poked the ground with the stick. 'It is not the same.'

'Okay, Sio. I will show you in a room. In fact, on a bed, lying on my back.'

He whacked the ground.

'Now what?' Kirabo asked. 'I have agreed to show you my flower.'

He looked at her, unable to say his hurt, but the silence was brutally honest.

'Relax, Sio,' Kirabo responded. 'I have not had sex with anyone – yet. I have not had a boyfriend since, I am not in the habit of showing boys my flower, and no other boy has touched me there – yet.'

'I did not say you did those things.'

'You did not have to. It was in your eyes. Tsk' – Kirabo sucked her teeth – 'you boys are confused. You ask a girl for sex but expect her to perform shock: *Do you call me a slut?* Me, I have no time for that. Now, do you still want to see my flower or are you frightened it might swallow you?'

'Tsk.' Sio picked up the stick, whacked the ground decisively and turned to her. 'Stop talking to me like that.' Then he relented. 'But you must accept, you have changed. That school has changed you. You are so… I don't know.'

'I am so what?'

But he had gone back to poking the ground, his head down. Kirabo had to bend low to look up in his face. 'I am not shy any more: that is the problem.'

Sio threw the stick in a huff. 'That is it. I'm four years older than you. You need to start trusting me. You think I don't know what I'm doing? That grandmother of yours would castrate me if I made you pregnant.'

'Grandmother?' Kirabo went along with his change of subject.

'Every time she sees me, she glares.'

'Like how?'

'Like *Touch her and I will cut off your aubergines.* Even after you left.'
Kirabo fell back and laughed. 'So she knew?'

'Of course she knew.'

'But she never said a word. No one did, not even Widow Diba.'

'Maybe they trusted me?'

'No, but *I* trust you.' She wove her hand into his. 'I do.' She dropped her head on to his shoulder. 'You know how those old women say all men are after one thing, that men will sleep with anything? You are not like that. Some men are, I am not going to lie, but not everyone. However, to take off my knickers, lie back on a bed and peel my legs apart so you can peek is foolhardy. We both – not just you, but me as well – could do something we might regret.'

Sio gripped her in such a strangling hug she had to push him off to breathe.

'Sometimes, Kirabo, you are so mature I don't even know. Women all over the world believe all men are pigs. In the end we gave up denying it.' Then he looked at her. 'I promise, nothing will happen.'

The following Monday, they went back to school. Kirabo did not even get the chance to see Giibwa. Sio kept forgetting to go to Giibwa's parents to ask where she lived in the city. In the end, he grew a little irritated. He said he did not risk coming to the city only to waste the few moments they had together looking for Giibwa. Kirabo thought that if Sio could get the address, she would look for her on the days he did not come, but Sio said it would be best for them to go together.

When rumours about the war coming from Tanzania started to arrive at St Theresa's, they sounded so mythical that they were dismissed out of hand. They were about the Saba-Saba bomb which the Tanzanians had dropped on Masaka Town. Apparently, the town had been flattened. When the bomb was dropped it cause such devastation that a woman picked up a nearby puppy instead of her child, threw it on her back and ran. But when the girls from Masaka were told they could not travel home for the holidays, the war became real.

Then war crept towards St Theresa's and paralysed the school. The postman stopped coming, so Kirabo no longer had letters from Sio to look forward to. Then the phone in the students' booth went down and all communication between Kirabo and Sio ended. Not long after that, the electricity was cut off and there was no prep at night. To save fuel, the school generator was used only to pump water from the well. Girls could not go down to the river to fetch water because army men were rumoured to lurk in the forest below the school.

Aate started to cry. 'I hope Dad' – he was no longer 'that man' – 'has left the country. He has tribal marks. People think all northerners are bad people.'

Mimi and other girls from abroad had stopped coming soon after Amin invaded Kagera. Then things got so bad that teachers who did not live in the staff quarters stopped coming. Nuns in retirement came out and started to teach. An English teacher turned up for chemistry. The threat of rape hung over the local village, and St Theresa's started to allow women and children to sleep in the classrooms at night. But then some men in Zigoti Town were killed and houses became deathtraps at night. For the first time, St Theresa's allowed men beyond the administration block. The main hall and the chapel were made available to all villagers at night. The button for the hooter was changed to a switch and Sister Ambrose announced, 'If anyone sees an army man lurking about, run and switch on the hooter. You hear the non-stop hooter, run to assembly.' No parents had come to fetch their girls because nowhere was safer for them than boarding schools. Even Amin's men would never attack a school.

The last time Kirabo was at home, before Christmas, she had slept on the roof with Aunt Abi and her next-door neighbours, because across the road the family who lived in the house with a green roof had been massacred.

It was the only bungalow on Rashid Khamis Road, the only house with an iron roof painted green. The front of the house was a large shop with living quarters at the back. That night, the shooting started early. Unlike the usual gunshots, known as popcorn, these bullets sounded like they were inside the house. Aunt Abi had pushed Kirabo on to the floor and they crawled out of the house. In the back yard, they climbed on to the roof of the kitchen and hid behind the water tank. They only went back inside at six in the morning.

At around seven, they heard noises below. Kirabo opened the front door and looked over the balcony. Across the road, a crowd surrounded the bungalow with a green roof. Kirabo ran out of the house to check it out. The first thing she saw was the child, no older than two, lying on her back on the steps with a bullet hole above her left ear. She clutched a half-eaten piece of sweet potato in her hand, her face turned away towards the wall as if she had fallen asleep while eating. The entry point of the bullet was so small it looked harmless. Kirabo stepped inside. On the left, a door opened into the living room. On the floor, corpses surrounded a mound of matooke. Bean stew had been served on a plate in front of each corpse. The corpses had fallen either forward or backward as if in morbid worship of the matooke. Someone in the crowd murmured that one of them was a visitor. She had missed the last Ganda bus home and had come to spend the night. 'It is the visitor who brought death with her.' But someone else, who knew the history of the bungalow, said, 'Wapi? This house cuts down tenants like you cut down reeds. This is not the first family to die in this house.'

Apparently, when its Asian owners were expelled from the country, the husband told his wife and children to get in the car that they were driving to Nairobi. They took nothing with them, not even money. The new owners found it all in the till. When the Asian family got to the Owen Falls dam, the father drove the car over the bridge. Ever since then, no one had found peace in that bungalow. For the first time, Kirabo wondered about the expelled Asians who had owned Aunt Abi's flat, whether their curse would only affect the landlord, or if it would fall on everyone who benefited from their pain.

When Zigoti villagers could no longer go back to their homes even during daytime, lunch was eliminated. Breakfast was at midday. Supper was at five. Luckily, maize flour larvae were white. Not so visible in posho, but porridge was so thin larvae floated on top. Bean stew was half weevils, half grains. Grown weevils floated on the gravy with their wings open, accompanied by their black-headed larvae. You did not eat with eyes open.

Then relief arrived in long articulated lorries with the Red Cross and Red Crescent symbols. The lorries were escorted by Amin's army. Though girls were told to stay in their dorms as the lorries were unloaded, the sight of life from outside the school brought some excitement into the school. Now even teachers came to the school kitchen for rations. First, Yankee sardines were served with a curious kind of rice. The grains were short, fat and yellow, flavourless and tasteless. However, mix it with the sardines and wow – *God bless*

America. Sardines were too good to last long, especially as there were villagers to feed as well. The nuns unveiled corned beef. The first time each girl got a tin to herself, it was a marvel. Those tins, with an attached key and wrapped in an American flag. But the salt was so much it bruised your tongue. Even on its own, corned beef kept hunger away. When beef ran out, tinned chicken was distributed. It came in big, tall, round tins, again wrapped in the Stars and Stripes. One tin between four girls. 'Spring chicken', the girls called it. Bones as soft as the flesh. The gravy tasted metallic, but the flesh tasted fine and the levels of salt were sane. Two weeks after the tinned chicken ran out, tinned pork was rolled out and the Muslims cursed.

As soon as Zigoti Town was captured, the wakomboozi came to St Theresa's. The hooter went off. Even the villagers ran to assembly. The school was surrounded by soldiers. When the girls realised they were the liberators, there was screaming, jumping up and down, 'We have won the war,' as if they too had fought. 'The reign of terror is over,' they shouted, even though Kampala had not fallen.

The commander assured the school that they were a disciplined army: 'We are nothing like Amin's thugs.' The school applauded every word. Who knew army men could be educated? 'While we push on to the capital,' the commander continued, 'we shall leave soldiers behind to protect you.' He promised that his officers were aware that if any of them was found 'talking, and I mean just talking, to a girl, we shall deal with them the military way.'

Sister Ambrose was not happy. She did not hide it in assembly. Liberators or not, they were men. She insisted that the army protect the school *off* the premises. The soldiers said the country was still at war. The school grounds were so extensive they had to patrol them, even though all through the war Amin's thugs had not disrupted the school. In the end, the army pitched their tents on the field below the staff quarters where athletics took place. The grounds were declared out of bounds for students.

At first it appeared as though the liberators were too disciplined to mess with the girls. But some girls had fathers, brothers and uncles in the army. There were not enough teachers to keep them from visiting their relations. Slowly, these girls started to take friends along, and soon too many girls had relatives among the wakomboozi. They came back excited: 'They speak such beautiful Swahili; did you hear it?' They began to identify individual men: 'The handsome one is Nen.' 'Yaro has a kyeppe.' 'Did you see the stones on Tumo's fatigues?' 'Topi is a dude.' 'Ah, but Keno is dudest.'

When girls discovered that soldiers had chocolate in their food packs, boundaries between students and soldiers broke down entirely. An army officer would be patrolling, minding his own business, and would find himself accosted by a group of girls: 'Affande, thank you for liberating us. Yii, but you are very brave. Now, we were thinking, can we look at your military ration pack?' Soon, tins started to arrive in dormitories. You buckled the lid with a coin and inside was a sesame bar, an oat bar, a fruit and seed bar and three chocolate bars. Now girls flirted blatantly: 'Affande, what a big gun you have. Is it not too heavy? Can I touch it?'

Soon, some girls' gratitude became physical. Behind the art room. In the abandoned toilets. Behind the piggery. Down at the lagoon. Some girls were smuggled into the tents on the sports grounds. Bottles of Yves Saint Laurent's Opium, Cacharel's Anaïs Anaïs and Christian Dior's Diorella started to flash and *psss-psss* in the dorms. Bold girls went for hardcore treats – Marlboro and Embassy, Johnnie Walker and Napoleon brandy. It looked as though the nuns had lost control of the school, until one morning the hooter went off non-stop. Five girls had been caught in the sports grounds with army men. When they were interrogated, they sold out fifteen other girls. Each of the fifteen girls was told to write a list of five names of girls they went to see the wakomboozi with. Those who said they did not know any names were threatened with expulsion. Fifteen additional names were added with question marks. At assembly, twenty girls, who had been identified as the notorious offenders, were called. The girls stepped out and were made to stand in front of assembly. The commander said, 'I told you girls that if any of my men was found talking to a girl they would be dealt with. Now, ladies' – he pointed at the twenty girls – 'watch how we do it military style.'

Twenty soldiers had been arrested, including the handsome Yaro and Nen, and were frog-marched to assembly. Disarmed, without shoes and stripped down to trousers, they were no longer liberator celebrities, just common thugs. The commander's men flogged them. Twisted wires, torn skin, the men screaming. Sister Ambrose stopped it immediately and asked the commander to administer his idea of punishment elsewhere. The school secretary's office was converted into a holding pen for offending officers. Sanity returned to St Theresa's.

Kampala fell four weeks after Zigoti. By then, Sister Ambrose and the other nuns were haggard. Still, she put announcements out on the radio that only girls collected by parents or guardians would be allowed to go home.

That end of term was like no other. Every girl, not just the ones from Masaka or those whose parents had been in government, was worried. Many were collected by relatives rather than parents. Often you saw girls crying and you did not want any news of your own family to arrive. Some girls had to leave their luggage behind because parents' cars had been taken by the fleeing army. As for Kirabo, her mind flew to her mother, then to Sio when she learned that everyone at home was okay. For some time, she toyed with the idea of asking Tom to put announcements out on the radio, not to ask her mother to come but to confirm she had survived. In the end, she let it go. Tom would not understand. She would continue with her posters.

More than a hundred girls were not collected. They were moved to Harriet Tubman House, closest to the convent, while the nuns started to make calls. For a week, the school drivers drove girls to their homes to find out what had happened to their parents. Many were brought back to school. During Amin's regime, Sister Ambrose had tried to protect the girls whose fathers had disappeared; during the war she had protected everyone from the savagery of conflict, but even she had her limits. She could not protect girls from the realities of a changed regime. National revenge was instantaneous. Daughters of the former politicians and army officers descended into poverty. Aate, who had been due to sit her O levels in November, did not come back to St Theresa's. Girls said she worked in a market with her mother; her father's house had been taken over by an army general. Some of these girls joined cheaper schools and changed their names. Some went into exile. Many found men and drifted on nature's tide into motherhood. People said it was poetic justice; after all, some of the girls who had been orphaned by the regime had also drifted into motherhood. Now another kind of girl was brought to school in the large cars with smoked windows. They typically came from the south, and their ethnicity became the new object of national envy and hate. But Sister Ambrose remained the same, working towards a bright future for the girl child and towards that elusive first woman president of Uganda.

7

The day Kirabo saw Giibwa again was the day she showed Sio what a woman really looked like down there. It was just before Christmas 1979. Sio had passed his exams and had been accepted into the University of Dar es Salaam. Because of the war, he had sat his A levels in July. The results had come out in November. Since Tanzania had brought the war to Uganda, the University of Dar es Salaam had made provisions for Ugandan students to join a term late with remedial classes. Sio was travelling to Dar the following day. He would spend Christmas with his mother before starting his course in the new year. Kirabo would not see him again until next April.

As promised, Sio showed her his ssebukuule first.

They were in a lodge, the one on Clement Hill Road where men escaped to with pinched wives, where good girls lost their virginity. Such an air of depravity hung in the room that Kirabo could not help but feel a sense of guilt about all of the women in her life who had worked so hard to keep her safe from men. She thought of Grandmother and all the women in Nattetta, especially Widow Diba, Nsuuta, Aunt Abi, Aunt YA and Sister Ambrose. They had no idea she was in a disreputable lodge with Kabuye's son.

Sio sat her on the bed, and then proceeded to peel off his clothes as if it was an art form. At first, Kirabo held her mouth in shock, giggling, unable to believe how much Sio enjoyed his own nakedness. You know that superb male bird of paradise doing a courtship dance? That was Sio.

Now that he was naked, save for his Caterpillar boots, he performed a military parade, whistling the police band tunes. From the wall across the room, *quick march*, *quick march*, to the end of the room, *abouuuut turn*. Then he came back doing the goose-step, singing, 'Okello, talina mpale…' At the wall he stopped, stomped and swivelled on his heel. He saluted, put an imaginary baton under his arm and started the slow march. Kirabo fell back on the bed, ribs aching with laughter. When she sat up, Sio was kneeling at the side of the bed.

'Your turn.'

For some reason Kirabo's confidence deserted her. Forget Aunt Abi's assertion that the vagina was a flower bud unfolding, forget all the pride St Theresa's had given her in her body. At school, she was just another girl. She could walk about naked. In this room, Sio's pale body reminded her that her breasts were not supposed to be charcoally, that her vagina was foul. If it was a flower, why did nature tuck it out of sight?

'I am not taking my clothes off to model boobs and bums.'

'Come on.'

'Hmm, hmm.'

'You promised…'

'To show you my flower.'

'But the flower does not come in isolation.'

'That is what you asked for.'

'Okay.' Sio gave in unhappily. 'Take off your knickers.'

She pulled them off and lay back on the bed but kept her knees closed.

'You know what?' Sio pulled the pillow from under her head. 'Cover your face if you are nervous.'

Kirabo held the pillow over her face.

'Lift your legs, bend them at the knees.' He sighed, like a man in charge of a delicate operation. He prised her knees apart. A brief silence. Then, 'Whwo, ho.'

She snapped her knees closed. 'What, is it disgusting?'

'No, it is floral glory… Lie back, I need to see more.'

Kirabo lay back and opened her legs properly.

'You elongated your labia?'

'Of course. Why?'

'Nothing; lie back.'

This time, Sio touched something and Kirabo screamed. Sio backed away, laughing. He put a finger to his lips. 'Shhhhh, you screamed.'

'What was that?'

He pulled a feather from behind his back. 'One of my hens gave it to me this morning. She said, *I understand Kirabo is going to unfold herself for you. Why not try one of my feathers to help her along?* I can do it again, but don't scream.'

Kirabo lay back. This time someone banged on the door. They fell silent. After a while, footsteps walked away. Sio whispered, 'I am going to stop. You cannot scream like that.'

'I didn't even realise. I won't, I swear.'

'Take the pillow and bite into it, because this feather is rampant.'

Next thing she knew, Sio was holding her mouth. The banging on the door did not stop this time. They held their breath. Then Sio got off the bed and pulled on his trousers, his Bob Marley belt buckle chinking. He opened the door a crack and a middle-aged woman said, 'Stop that noise.' She tried to peer past him into the room but Sio kept moving his head, blocking her view.

'What kind of children are you?'

'*Give me back my fucking money and we'll fucking leave your fucking room.*' Sio spoke British English when he wanted to intimidate.

'But, son, that girl is a child.'

'Did you birth me?' Kirabo called from the bed.

'Wangi? What did you say, child?'

Kirabo did not repeat it.

'Kdto.' The woman turned away. 'Children of today, misege, misegula,' she clapped as she went.

Sio closed the door and they laughed soundlessly. Then he picked Kirabo's knickers off the floor and tossed them to her. 'Get dressed.'

'Why? You paid for the entire day.'

'Get dressed.'

Kirabo grabbed her knickers. 'So you know, Sio, I cannot get pregnant from a feather.'

He finished getting dressed and stared at her. Kirabo, realising that playing with feathers was over, got off the bed and slipped into her knickers. As she brushed her hair in the mirror on the wall, Sio said, 'Did you know there is a belief that when a man finds himself alone with a woman he is not related to, he is obliged to say a word to her?'

'A word?'

'Yes, to seduce her, to show he is a real man.'

Kirabo shot Sio a sharp look. 'Now what kind of stupidity is that?'

'Apparently, women expect it. If you don't, they lose respect for you.'

'That is not stupidity, Sio, it has no name.'

'And since all girls are supposed to say no, it is okay. After all, a girl can tell when a boy is serious.'

Kirabo deflated. 'Sio, are you trying to tell me something?'

'No,' he sighed, 'it is just…it puts pressure on us.'

Kirabo shrugged.

'Apparently, some girls, if you don't say a word, they feel insulted, that they are ugly. Then they go around telling people that you are not a man, that you are dead in the pants. That is why boys hiss at any girl, often without interest.'

Kirabo sat down on the bed next to him. 'Tell you what, Sio. Throughout time, men have created all sorts of myths about women. In the past, the belief was that if you looked deep down there, as you did mine, you would go blind. Some cultures even believed there were teeth down there which could bite your ssebukuule off. The idea that girls expect a word from a man to make them feel good about themselves is another myth, perhaps to justify men's bad behaviour.'

Thinking she had answered his question, Kirabo suggested they go to find Giibwa. It was only midday, but they had nothing else to do.

Sio stood up irritably, went to the door, opened it then closed it and came back. 'Don't take this the wrong way, Kirabo, but that thing, that…erm, elongation, is wrong. It is genital mutilation.'

'Genital what? Tsk, of all boys in the world I fell for a Zungu. Sio, we Africans do it. Mutilation is when they scoop out the bean then cut the inner labia out and when it is just a shell they sew everything like shut up. Bruhu.' She shuddered. 'On the contrary, we enhance.'

'Same thing. And not all Africans do it.'

'Okay, Bantu Africans.'

'Not all Bantu.'

'Okay, Bantu Ugandans; what is your problem?'

'Not all of them. It does not contribute to pleasure.'

'Not yours, mine. Tsk! You men imagine that everything we do is for you. We elongate because some men do not know how to get a woman ready. Wait for your groom session, your uncles will teach you.'

'But that does not mean you disfigure your body.'

'Sometimes, Sio, you are so Zungu I don't even know. Not all men borrow feathers from their chickens. Chances of marrying one of those are very high. Don't worry, one day I will show you what to do with them.'

'As long as you don't tell my daughters to…no one is going to tell my daughters to do that.'

Her *hmm* was cynical because she knew there would be no one to tell his daughters about this kind of thing. Fathers' sisters prepared their nieces for sex. Sio had no one.

'As I said before,' Sio was saying, 'I believe in mwenkanonkano. It is wrong to disfigure your genitals.'

The first time Sio had said he believed in mwenkanonkano, he had used the English word *feminist*. Kirabo ignored it because as far as she knew, feminism was for women in developed countries with first-world problems. But this time he had used the Luganda word, mwenkanonkano. She asked, 'What makes you say you believe in our mwenkanonkano?'

'I know women have suffered throughout time. I would not want my daughter to go through that. I think it is time we stopped it, I try not to contribute to women's suffering. Dad does too. He said I should treat women the way I would want to be treated. But Mum is too Christian. Apparently, God created Adam from earth, but Eve was made from Adam's rib. To her how can a rib be equal to a whole person?'

'Wow, you don't realise how dangerous those myths are until you meet someone who believes them.'

'But what Mum does not realise is that mwenkanonkano would set us men free too.'

'Set men free, free from what – superiority?'

'Scoff all you like, but I want things to change. We pay too high a price for something superficial. And why? Just so women can kneel before us? Do you know how expensive dating is? On top of paying bills, girls expect you to give them your money, just like that, because you fancy them. And their entitlement is unbelievable. If you don't give them money, they tell people *He has glue in his hands…*'

Kirabo was dying of hilarity. Since they had started dating, they were both always so broke they asked each other, 'How much do you have?' on the phone before deciding to meet up. Often, Sio only had enough money to pay for one way. When Kirabo got money out of her father or aunt, she rang him to say, 'Come, I have enough for your return journey.'

'What is so funny?'

'You tried to date another girl, didn't you?'

'No, but I have seen it. A guy takes a girl out, spends his transport money on her and walks miles and miles back home. Then, after all of that, she dumps him. You know what some guys believe?' Kirabo shook her head. 'That women pretend, that some perform inferiority to give us a false sense of superiority.'

'Sometimes it is safe for us to pretend to be inferior. Some men love it. They hate clever women. We have learnt to make it pay for us. Perks of being inferior. Look, sometimes a man, instead of saying *I fancy you*, just gives you money. If you take it, it means yes; you don't take it, it means no. But of course, some girls take it and say no anyway. Poor seduction skills are costly.'

'Then don't complain when men treat you like property. You cannot have it both ways. If men invest money while dating, dress you, feed you, pay your rent, transport you, and then pay dowry on top, then after the wedding husbands are still called upon, time after time, to take care of financial problems in your families, then men own you the way you cannot own them. We can have affairs; we can throw you out of our houses, because we bought you.'

'But it is what you men want. Ganda men feel insulted when you attempt to split the bill.'

'We pretend to want it because we are expected to.' He opened the door. 'Come on, let's go and find Giibwa.'

Kirabo followed him out. She could not believe her luck. Where in Uganda do you find a man who believes in mwenkanonkano? She did not know what she had done to deserve Sio. If she had held anything of herself back from loving him up until then, she had now passed the point of no return. She reached for his hands, then wrapped her arms around him and kissed his ear and neck. She rubbed her nose on his cheek as she said, 'I think you are intelligent about our mwenkanonkano.'

'It is just common sense.'

At the reception desk in the lobby sat the woman who had banged on the door, her eyes waiting to tell them off. But then she smiled as Sio handed her the key. When she saw Kirabo, she dry-spat on the side, but Kirabo was too happy to feel the insult. She had been transported on the lightness of a feather to a place beyond shame. She looked at the woman and felt sorry for her. *She has no idea what she is missing. Her man would probably have a fit at the thought of mwenkanonkano.* Reaching for Sio's hand, she swung on it and skipped down the steps into the sunny courtyard. Sio stole a guilty glance at the woman and shook his head at Kirabo's giddiness. All the way to Nakawa Market, where Giibwa's aunt's friend worked, Kirabo was giddy. Sio kept calming her down.

'Don't hold my hand, Kirabo, people are frowning.'

'Where? I don't see them.'

'They look at me like I am a hyena that snatched a chick.'

'Ignore them.' She turned and walked backwards facing him. 'They are backward. You are only slightly taller.'

Giibwa's aunt's friend directed them to Kyadondo Road in Nakasero, and they walked back through the Lugogo swamp. The rugby pitch had flooded. Their route took them past the rows of huge, ancient mango trees, across the Lugogo bypass and over to Lugogo Indoor Arena. Soon they were in Lower Kololo. Once they crossed the golf course and Kitante Road, Kyadondo Road was just above the Fairway Hotel. Giibwa's home was easy to find; there were plot numbers on the gates. A tarmacked driveway, then a paved walkway led to a side door. Kirabo knocked on the door, wondering how Giibwa had adjusted to the incredible wealth around her.

The door opened. Giibwa stood there. A Giibwa with a posture like she had grown up in that house and the demeanour of someone newly arrived from Switzerland. This Giibwa knew she was beautiful, Kirabo realised. It was there in her eyes. That entitlement that light-skinned girls had to beauty, to being the centre of attention. Kirabo reached for Sio's hand. How had Giibwa got even more light-skinned? Her hair was enormous and dark. She had lost weight and stretched at the waist. This was no longer the innocent beauty of childhood; this was sharp and malignant. You saw it for the first time, you looked away. Then you stole small, secret glances until you got used to it. It was the kind of beauty that made you hate a girl who had done nothing to you.

'Giibwa, happy to see you.'

Giibwa should have been the first to greet them, open her arms and hug Kirabo, but she had not. She did not respond to Kirabo's greeting, so Kirabo said the next thing that came to mind.

'You have lost weight but you are looking so well. Being small suits you.'

Giibwa's eyes were a cave.

Kirabo feared that Giibwa had seen her envy. But whatever she had felt was gone. She was glad to see her again. It was almost three years since she had last seen her. Kirabo was sixteen and a half now and Giibwa was already seventeen, but she was still Kirabo's first best friend.

'Can you imagine, we walked first from Shimon to Nakawa, and then your aunt's friend directed us here and we plodded all the way from Nakawa to here.' In that inventory lay Kirabo's appeal to Giibwa: *Measure how long we have walked and gauge how much I love you.* Then she walked up the steps and went to hug Giibwa. Giibwa was a tree. In the past, no matter how viciously they fought, Giibwa never tied anger around her heart. Kirabo would come back or Giibwa would come to Kirabo's home and they would carry on as though they had not fought. This unsmiling Giibwa, the one looking at her with disdain, was new.

Kirabo pulled away and Giibwa smiled a bit. 'Hello, Kirabo.' She spoke English. '*Nice to see you.*' But there was no sparkle in her eyes, just irritation, as if Kirabo was a smitten puppy.

Kirabo had imagined their first meeting as a succession of breathless hugs, girly exclamations, high-pitched nothings like *Bannange ki kati*, gesturing, exaggerating the greatness of the moment, like girls did.

When Giibwa turned to lead them inside the house, Kirabo thought *Kdto, some girls can be slender and curvaceous at the same time*. She decided to try again. After all, this was Giibwa. She had to let her know she was still the Kirabo she knew, Kirabo of Nattetta.

'Eh,' she started breezily. 'I have been pushing this Sio' – she punched Sio in the arm – 'to find you, but he has been giving me excuses. Today I said, "Lazima, we must find Giibwa no matter what."'

Giibwa stole a glance at Sio. Sio smiled at Kirabo.

Kirabo noticed and looked down. She blinked and blinked but then shook the suspicion out of her head. It was her fault; she had to reassure Giibwa that she was not jealous of her looks. She gave it a moment then tried again. 'Remember our promise, Giibwa?'

'What promise?'

'All of us together again, bringing our Nattetta to Kampala?'

'Yeah.'

'Well, here we are.'

Giibwa did not respond.

They walked through the kitchen. The house belonged to a Zungu; the smells were not Ugandan. Neither were the utensils. The living room's sparse furnishing confirmed it – Ugandans choked their living rooms with furniture. The curtains were kikoy prints – no Ugandan would do that. Instead of a carpet, the floor was covered with a traditional straw and banana-fibre kirago. There were African carvings, masks and Maasai art. Ugandans could not have enough European art.

Giibwa looked at Sio. 'Would you like something to drink?'

'No, thank you.'

Kirabo did not answer. She wanted to make sure she had been included in that invitation. When Giibwa did not ask her, Kirabo began to well up. Yes, she had felt insecure and held Sio's hand possessively, but Giibwa treating her like this, after she had trekked across the city to find her, was too much. For a while she looked away, holding back the tears. Then she began to resent the ease with which Giibwa spoke to Sio. She looked up and asked, 'Giibwa, you are so much lighter-skinned; are you bleaching?'

Sio caught his breath.

Giibwa looked at Sio: *Do you see how nasty she is?*

Sio looked down.

Kirabo could tell natural from bleached skin, but it did not matter. Giibwa was in love with Sio.

'Giibwa is lighter because she is indoors most of the time.' Sio shook Kirabo by the shoulders, imploring her to lighten up.

Kirabo did not look at him. 'By the way, what happened to Wafula?'

Giibwa shot her a *Shut up* look.

'Wafula is at Nabumali High,' Sio explained. 'Sometimes he comes home for holidays, but most times he stays in Mbale with his grandparents.'

'Yeah, but hasn't Giibwa heard from him?'

'There was nothing between me and Wafula.'

'Oh really?'

There is no pain like seeing a best friend, and a best friend whose beauty eclipses your own at that, as she itches for your man. Bugs ran through Kirabo's veins, *chroo, chroo, chroo*, making her twitchy and impulsive. But she knew she had to act unconcerned. Giibwa and Sio kept talking. He spoke Luganda, she English. Sio must have sensed Kirabo's turmoil because he put his hand on her knee, his thumb caressing it. Giibwa glanced at it then looked away.

As their conversation deepened, Giibwa's grasp on English grammar started to slip. She had no sense of the past participle. Irregular verbs eluded her. Kirabo's eyes lit up. What did Giibwa think, that living in a Zungu's house was enough? You still need those dry and brittle grammar classes. If Sio had not been in the room, she would have corrected Giibwa's verbs ruthlessly. But if you wanted to see Sio's anger, laugh at 'broken' English. *Colonial snobbery*, he called it.

Kirabo stood up and stretched as if she and Sio were still in the lodge. 'I am tired,' she announced, looking at Sio intently. She spoke Luganda. She spoke Luganda as if she was above English, the language of desperate social climbers. 'I am leaving.' She walked across the room. She had got to the door when Giibwa asked, 'Has your mother come to find you?'

Kirabo stopped, then recovered, 'My mother? God, I had forgotten about her.' She looked at Sio. 'It is your fault, Sio. You have made me forget.' She looked back at Giibwa. 'No, she has not come. But I have been told she finished her education and has got a job. She is married and has two children. We are waiting until she tells her husband about me. Thank you for asking.' She smiled, and walked out.

Sio must have said goodbye immediately because he caught up with her before she got to the gate. Kirabo exploded. 'Who does she think she is? How can she be like that? Because she has acquired a handful of English words? Because she is a housemaid for a Zungu? I bet he is old and bald, I bet she is prostituting herself with him. That is what maids for Zungu men do. No wonder she looks so mature. Older than you, even. Perhaps she hopes to hook him. Otherwise, where did those airs come from?'

'You are being cruel, Kirabo.'

'Me? What about her? And I am telling you, Sio, that is what happens when you rise suddenly from dung-rolling to sleeping with your employer.'

'I cannot believe you just said that, Kirabo. Giibwa is not a maid. She lives with her aunt; her aunt is the maid. Giibwa is studying tailoring or baking or both at YMCA. I saw how she treated you and I didn't like it, but people can be awkward for all sorts of reasons. Maybe she had felt downtrodden all along in Nattetta, but now she feels emancipated and does not know how to handle it.'

'How do you know all that?'

'Back home everyone knows. When Giibwa visits her parents, she is haughty, dresses crazy, speaks English everywhere, at everyone. People shake their heads. That is why I was not so keen to find her.'

'Sewing and baking: that is what she is studying? Typical: pretty girl, empty head.'

'What is wrong with you, Kirabo? When Giibwa was "dung-rolling", as you call it, you loved her. Now she is getting educated you are being nasty.'

'Why are you defending her? She is the one who hates me.' Kirabo stopped and suspicion came into her eyes. 'You are in love with her, aren't you? Have you slept with her?'

'Ha.' Sio stopped, speechless. Then he stormed past her. After a while of marching ahead he stopped and spoke English. *'For your information, Giibwa came to Nattetta and I asked her where she lived because you wanted to see her. She said they were moving to a new house but did not know where. She said I could go to that lady in Nakawa to find out where. Perhaps she didn't want you to visit her. Have you considered that? You were the one who wanted to visit her.'*

Kirabo swept past him. She walked fast ahead so he would not overtake her.

He did.

Kirabo broke into a run and sped past him.

Sio fell back. He did not attempt to walk past her this time. As they came to Buganda Road Primary, Sio caught up with her. He grabbed her hand like *I am going to hold your hand whether you like it or not.* She did not shake him off. People giving them disapproving glances did not matter. They walked briskly but quietly. Kirabo's feet were sore but it did not matter; Giibwa had hurt her worse. By the time they got to Rashid Khamis Road it was almost six o'clock. Kirabo crossed the road, but Sio hesitated. He remained on the other side near the house with a green roof. He waved once and turned away. The stale taste in Kirabo's mouth became bitter, but she kept walking.

On her own that night, mortification ate at her. *I should have... I should not have...* Then she remembered Sio was travelling to Dar the following night. And you cannot hold anger against someone going on a long journey. Besides, it was not Sio's fault Giibwa was being silly. After all, plenty of boys were attracted to Kirabo; it did not mean she would pay them any attention in return. Why would Sio listen to Giibwa? As soon as Aunt Abi left the house the following morning, she rang him. He was relieved. He told her to stay away from Giibwa and promised to call as soon as he got to Dar. Long after they had run out of things to say, they stayed on the phone, their silence interrupted only by the occasional sighs. But when Kirabo put the phone down, she could no longer lie to herself. She was relieved Sio was going to be far away from Giibwa. It was not that she did not trust him, it was just that Giibwa was the kind of girl a boy cheated with and the world sympathised with him – that he could not help himself – and then blamed you for asking him to find her.

8

In January 1981, Nsuuta was admitted to Mulago Hospital with yellow fever. Tom asked Kirabo, who had just finished her O-level exams, to give Nsuuta hospital care. The country had not started to recover from Idi Amin's regime or the war that had ousted him. Hospitals were so understaffed, so overwhelmed, you had to bribe staff to be given a proper examination. At first, Kirabo refused: she would not undermine Grandmother so publicly. But asking Nnambi was out of the question, and Aunt Abi had a job. Besides, she was too loyal to Grandmother. Kirabo eventually agreed, but only after Tom promised to explain to Grandmother that he had told Kirabo to look after Nsuuta.

How do you care for a woman who had warned you against hurting your fellow women while she was sneaking around with your grandmother's husband at the same time? What would she say to Nsuuta about the original state? During her final year of O levels, the study of Elechi Amadi's *The Concubine* had resurrected Nsuuta's idea of women having originally been seen as aquatic. For some time as she read the novel, Kirabo had been excited that maybe Nsuuta was on to something universal. But during class discussion, when she suggested that maybe the human subconscious located women in the sea and men on land, both the teacher and other students had looked at her like she was crazy. They did not see persecution in the presentation of Ihuoma as a sea goddess and femme fatale. When the teacher said she was reading too much into nothing she gave up. Gradually, Kirabo's mind had converted Nsuuta into a radical mwenkanonkano activist. Kirabo was in awe of Nsuuta's bold philosophy and was grateful to her for trying to allay her fears about flying and finding her mother. But the fact remained; Nsuuta had been sneaking around with Grandfather.

When Kirabo arrived at the hospital, Nsuuta was so ill and frail that Kirabo's unease fled. She was yellow. Because she could not keep anything down, she was put on a drip. When she grew stronger and the drip was removed, Nsuuta did not say much. She seemed locked inside herself. Kirabo tried to pry her out by telling her about the nuns at St Theresa's and their attempt to create a paradise for girls, how she had thought St Theresa's was a collection of girls with the original state. But Nsuuta only batted her eyelids in return. Most of the time Kirabo sat and watched her, wondering if the fiery Nsuuta would ever come back.

Even when the women from Nattetta started to arrive with food and gossip, Nsuuta remained silent. Widow Diba came alone. Despite her swollen legs she said, 'Take a rest, Kirabo. I will take care of Nsuuta today.' When she finished the chores she sat down, stretched her legs and sighed the pain of old women. When Kirabo joined her, she laughed. 'Your grandmother will pull down the heavens when she finds out you are looking after Nsuuta. Me, I did not tell her I was coming.'

Before Kirabo could respond, nurses and a doctor arrived to examine Nsuuta. Kirabo and Widow Diba withdrew to the foyer. Diba sat on the floor and leaned against the wall. Kirabo sighed, 'But Widow Diba, what is it between Grandmother and Nsuuta?'

'Child, those two are beyond us all.'

'I know Grandfather is grazing in Nsuuta's paddock.'

'You do?'

'And I am thinking, Nsuuta knows better than to make a fellow woman miserable. But then I hear that Grandmother pinched Grandfather from Nsuuta in the first place, and I'm lost. The only person left to blame is Grandfather.'

'But what you do not know is that, as children, Alikisa and Nsuuta were like this' – she crossed her fore and middle fingers – 'so close, they would split a mite to share it. But I always said a man would be the death of that friendship.'

Kirabo looked away.

'Miiro loved Nsuuta first, and he loved her hard. You know, those wealthy people married wealthy people in our day. So, for Miiro, it was just right for Luutu's son, educated and lugogofu-handsome, to marry the Muluka's beautiful and educated daughter. Luutu had a car, but years earlier Nsuuta's grandfather was the first to ride a pikipiki.'

'You mean there were motorcycles in those days?'

'Of course. They were wooden.'

'Get out, Widow Diba. How can a pikipiki be wooden?'

'I saw it with my own eyes. Apart from the tyres, the pouch for fuel, wires and tubes, maybe the seat had a cushion, but everything else was smooth wood – beautiful. In fact, the day Nsuuta's grandfather died, his wives – there were only seven left then – pounced on that pikipiki with axes, and by the time his sons came to rescue it, most of it was in the hearth cooking food for his funeral. Apparently, the pikipiki noise drove the wives mad.'

'That is madness.'

'Forget the wives' madness; Miiro and Nsuuta brought new ways to courting. In our days, parents arranged marriages. Not for Miiro and Nsuuta. They made their decision. Miiro would collect Nsuuta from her home and they would walk down that road discussing their love while the world watched. We were waiting for their parents to set the wedding processes in motion when what did we hear?'

'What?'

'Nsuuta was off to Gayaza High for further studies. I said, "Which further studies? What model of madness is this?" It was a perfect marriage proposal. But Nsuuta wanted to do nursing. Some said she had raised herself so high she wanted to complete all the studying in Uganda and go to Bungeleza to become a doctor like men. In the 1930s a girl aiming to be a doctor was a girl intending to climb into the world of men and shit on their heads. In any case, by the time you finished all that studying you were past marrying age: who would want you? So Miiro pleads, "Nsuuta, my one, stop this nursing nonsense and let's get married." Miiro had a good plan. Nsuuta would start having children while he finished his diploma at Bukalasa. Then he would come home and they would carry on with their life. That plan made sense to us ordinary people, but not to Nsuuta.'

'So?'

'Miiro, maybe in anger, maybe because Alikisa was the next best thing, asked her to marry him.'

'Yii, just like that?'

'You joke with men, one moment he is dying for you, the next he is marrying your best friend.'

Kirabo clapped.

'Truth is that when Miiro turned to Alikisa I was the first to say, "Akale, if Nsuuta's head is sailing in the clouds, what is a young man to do?" After all, Miiro's father built churches and Alikisa's father was reverending them. "Maybe it was meant to be," we said. When Alikisa's parents heard Miiro had turned his eyes on their daughter, did they blink?'

'No?'

'Would you? Suddenly your daughter, not so beautiful, scoops a smart young man who comes from a solid education and whose family has so much land they don't know what to do with; do you doze?'

'No.'

'By the time Nsuuta came home from Gayaza for Christmas holidays, Alikisa was married and pregnant. Luutu named their eldest child Yagala Akuliko.'

'I have always wondered why Aunt YA had such a name.'

'Luutu was saying to Miiro, *Love the one you are with*.'

'But as soon as Nsuuta was available he danced back to her.'

'What can I say? Men. Nsuuta devoured Miiro's heart like no other woman.'

'Yet Grandmother and Nsuuta got on very well in the beginning?'

'They did. But here is the thing; Nsuuta did not return to Nattetta until '46. At first, she worked in Mmengo Hospital and we heard stories that she was with foreigners. At the time, men came from all over Africa to study at Makerere. We heard that Nsuuta was with a Munnaigeria. And people said when it came to love, those Nigerian men took our girls to the moon. They had money and knew how to spend it, driving our girls crazy. For a while, we thought Nsuuta was lost. But, suddenly, she got a job at the new dispensary.'

'Our dispensary at Nattetta?'

'Luutu had recently built it next to the church.'

'Why return?'

'The Munnaigeria left her on the moon and went home. Nsuuta had to find her own way back to earth. But as I said, she and Miiro were deep in each other's blood. And, perhaps, her eyes had started to die. Whatever her reason, what do we see next?'

'What?'

'Nsuuta and Miiro are throbbing. Not only that, Alikisa and Nsuuta are happily sharing him. *Ehhuu*, we heaved a sigh of relief. By then, Alikisa had had the two girls, YA and Abi. She was expecting Tom. Nsuuta too was pregnant. In our time, two women sharing a man happily was common. In my family, our Maama Mukulu used to find brides for my father. She would go home to her people for a break from marriage, as women do, and when she returned, she would say to him, "I found someone I think you will love; why not have a look and see?" And my father would marry her. All my life I never, ever saw strife among our mothers, and there were five of them. Often, we did not know who was whose mother; it did not matter because they loved us equally. But with this Christianity, all that is gone. I remember looking at Miiro and thinking *What stupid man makes his two women pregnant at the same time?* But then suddenly, I don't know where trouble came from—'

'What trouble?'

'Aah, my child; I have finished.'

'Grandmother assaulted Nsuuta and she lost her child?'

'I don't know, child. I just heard.'

'What did you hear?'

'That afterwards, Miiro sat the two women down and told Alikisa she would hand her child over to Nsuuta after the birth.'

'How did Grandmother take it?'

'How else would she take it? The owner of the child has spoken, what do you do? At least Alikisa could have another one. Nsuuta could not.'

'Poor Grandmother.'

'My child, nature is cruel. The child turned out to be a boy. He looked exactly like Muka Miiro. I looked at the situation and thought *Real trouble has arrived.*'

'Grandmother handed over Tom willingly?'

'Straight. After the first six months she only breastfed him during daytime when Nsuuta was at work, and Nsuuta took him home in the night. For fourteen years, all was well but then… I don't know where trouble came from.'

The doctors walked out of Nsuuta's cubicle and Kirabo ran to get their instructions. It was the usual. Nsuuta was to drink a lot and take the medicine as prescribed. Kirabo went into the cubicle to check on Nsuuta. She lay on her back. Kirabo returned to the foyer and told Diba, 'She is asleep.'

'Good.'

'Widow Diba, I have a little question.'

'Go on.'

'Is Giibwa not Ganda?'

Diba sighed. 'She is. Mwesigwa, her father, was Ganda until he married that Ssoga woman. Mwesigwa's father and grandfather were Ganda. However, I understand that his grandfather thrice over came from Busoga. When Muka Mwesigwa found out he had roots in Busoga, she pushed him to become Ssoga again. I said, how does one revert after years and years? Then she started stirring up things everyone had forgotten, filling her daughter's head with hate.'

Kirabo wanted to hear more, but Widow Diba was getting uncomfortable. 'That is it,' she said. 'I have said enough. What you do not know you should not know, that is my motto.'

'So it is true we raided and sold them?'

'Child, at the time everybody raided and sold everybody; they were dark times. Let's leave it at that.'

Widow Diba left for Nattetta before Nsuuta woke up.

Nsuuta had not lost her lumanyo entirely. She sensed Grandmother first and sat up in bed. Kirabo, who had not seen Grandmother yet, hurried to Nsuuta asking if something was wrong. Then she saw Grandmother standing at the door and screamed and ran to her, jumping up and down. 'You have come. Oh, Jjajja, you have come.'

'What will people say?'

'That you care so much.' Nsuuta spent the rest of her energy on sarcasm.

Kirabo laughed, hugging her grandmother. Grandmother glanced at Nsuuta, asked for a chair and sat by the door. 'How is the sick one?'

'I am fine, Alikisa, you can talk to me.'

'If she is fine, what am I doing here?'

'Stay awhile, Jjajja, have lunch with us and I will tell you about school. Do you know, Nsuuta has not sat up in bed at all until now, but look, you have made her.'

'Let's hope that sitting up is good for her.'

'She is improving.'

After greeting and asking about the villages and the residents, the farming and the weather, Kirabo picked up the stacked aluminium containers from the locker.

'Nsuuta, I am going to the restaurant to buy lunch.'

'I will be fine.'

'Jjajja, are you coming with me?'

'Back down those stairs? I don't love food *that* much.'

'But if I leave you here with Nsuuta you might upset her.'

Grandmother threw her head back and laughed. She laughed like Kirabo had never seen her laugh. A deep raspy laugh so contagious Kirabo joined in. 'Upset her? Oh-oh. This child is going to kill me with laughter.'

'Thank God you came, Alikisa.' Nsuuta could not help herself. 'Where would you laugh like that?'

'Jjajja, if Nsuuta gets worse tonight the villagers will point fingers at you.'

'Fingers are pointed already, child. Why do you think I came? Go and get your lunch. If I wanted to hurt Nsuuta I would have done it long before you were born.' She looked at Nsuuta, laughter still in her eyes and said, 'She is actually protecting *you* from *me*,' and they both laughed. As she walked away, Kirabo kept glancing back like she had no idea who those women were.

On Kirabo's return, Grandmother looked away from the cubicle, her chin propped in her right palm. Nsuuta still sat up in bed. They were silent but there was no tension in the air. As Kirabo served the food, Grandmother remarked, 'I was telling your friend here that she had done a good job of stealing love from my family.'

Kirabo stiffened. She finished serving. When she took Grandmother's plate to her, she said, 'No one can steal my love for you, Jjajja. Yours is yours only.'

'How many times have you seen Tom drive his car, rush-rush, to collect me from the village the way he collected her?'

'How many times have you been dying, Jjajja?'

'So he is waiting until I am dying?'

'I will tell him to come and take you for a drive.'

Grandmother laughed again because Kirabo had fallen for her trick. Kirabo stole a glance; was Grandmother loosening up? She had laughed, real laughter, twice in a brief time. But she was poking her food with a fork the way rural women do to matooke cooked in the city. 'Unfortunately, I could not bring proper food in case your friend gets worse in the night. The world would say *You mean Nsuuta waited to relapse until she ate Muka Miiro's food?*' Nsuuta and Grandmother laughed. Grandmother pushed the plate away, as if she had no appetite to waste on tasteless food. 'Tell your friend to get well soon. I am leaving.' She pulled the handles of her handbag up her shoulder and stood up. Nsuuta's eyes looked above Grandmother's head because her sense of direction in hospital was a bit off. Then she started to turn to lie on her right. Kirabo went to help her. Grandmother frowned but did not step in to help. Instead, she instructed Kirabo where to hold Nsuuta to turn her. Nsuuta could neither lie on her left nor her right. In the end, she settled on her back again. Kirabo pulled up the covers and whispered, 'For some reason, she never lies on her sides.'

'I am fine,' Nsuuta snapped. 'Thank you for checking on us, Alikisa. See the residents for me.'

'I will. Stay well.'

Kirabo waited a few moments and whispered, 'I think we have tired her out.' She took hold of Grandmother's hand. 'Let's go. I will walk you down to the taxi rank.'

They had come to the stairs when Grandmother said, 'Take me to the doctors.'

'What?'

'Where are the medical staff?'

'Why?'

'Take me where they are.'

Kirabo led her through a maze of screened-off beds, women carers sitting on the floor talking, eating, ironing, until they got to the nurses' desk. Grandmother stepped forward and said to a nurse, 'Musawo, I am a relative of the patient in Room 32. This is my granddaughter looking after her.'

'Oh, patient Nsuuta at the end of the corridor?'

'Yes.' Grandmother flashed half a smile. 'Look, Musawo, as you can see, I am an ignorant old woman from the rural and did not read enough books, but sometimes we old people can see.' Kirabo looked at the nurse, her eyes beseeching her to be patient with her grandmother. 'I know she has told you about the yellow fever and you have treated it well, but there is something else. Yellow fever is not alone.'

'Wait, let me get her file.' The nurse reached for a pile on top of the desk and filed through it until she found the right one. 'Vivian Balungi Nsuuta?'

'Those are her names.'

The nurse looked at the notes. 'There is nothing else here.'

'That is why I have come to you. Nsuuta was a nurse. She can hide illness. Something is wrong with her left breast. Check her and see. If I am wrong, we shall all be happy.'

'I will make a note for the doctor.' The nurse scribbled something.

Grandmother thanked her for the excellent job they were doing, but when they got to the stairs she sucked her teeth. 'This hospital is staffed by goats – goats only.'

'I thought you hated Nsuuta.'

'It does not mean I want her dead. These useless doctors. Which medicine did they study? You sit for one moment with Nsuuta and realise she has more than yellow fever. What kind of examination did they do?'

Kirabo kept quiet.

They came down to Casualty and walked out of the hospital through the back entrance. As they reached the car park where dead ambulances were rotting, Grandmother stopped. 'Kirabo,' she began, looking past her. 'Lately, you have grown not bad-looking.' She started to walk. 'I remarked on it to your friend, but she sneered, "You mean you are just realising?" You would think that woman has more sight than all of us combined.' Kirabo started to walk too, but then Grandmother stopped and wagged a finger in Kirabo's face. 'Do not go mistaking beauty for something physical.'

For a moment Kirabo felt the urge to lean against Grandmother, close her eyes and feel her. That is how she said *I love you too*. Instead, she walked behind her, looking at her back. Grandmother was intact, exactly the way she had left her. She was the kind of skinny woman who devoured years without consequence. She was the same age as Nsuuta and Widow Diba, but they were worn out and threadbare in comparison. Then she was overcome by guilt and said, 'Jjajja, I wanted to come and spend this holiday with you, but Aunt Abi has got me a temporary job in the Ministry of Finance, to get some work experience.'

'Very good. You will come when there is time. Your grandfather and I are not going anywhere.'

That night when Nsuuta woke up they talked a little. Kirabo did not tell her what Grandmother had said to the nurses but remarked, 'Grandmother is different these days.'

'Different how?'

'She laughs.'

'Years have gone by. Age gets you to a place where you think *What makes me happiest?* And you focus on that. I think for her you are one of those things.' Nsuuta paused. Then she raised herself to sit up. Kirabo propped her up with pillows. 'But you too, Kirabo, have changed.'

'Me?'

'Yes.'

'How?'

'You are tame. You are no longer Miiro's wild grandchild.' Was that regret in Nsuuta's voice? But before Kirabo could speak, Nsuuta added, 'By the way, your friend Giibwa left Nattetta.'

Kirabo caught her breath.

'But you already knew that.'

'She told me she would leave when Tom came for me.'

'Recently, she has been coming home to visit, and people say she whistles English like she invented the language.'

'Which English?' Kirabo could not keep the contempt out of her voice.

'Everyone is beneath her now.'

Kirabo laughed.

'Just a warning. In case you think she is still the same.'

'Hmm.' Kirabo had no intention of letting Nsuuta know about her fight with Giibwa.

'That whistling of English is not innocent,' Nsuuta sighed.

'Isn't it?' Kirabo feigned ignorance.

'But if you are going to allow Kabuye's son between your legs, take the pill first.'

'Nsuuta!'

'Don't you dare lie to me when I am ill, Kirabo.' She slipped down the pillows so that even her head was covered.

Kirabo took a long time to recover. Then she fought back. That word *tame*, coming from Nsuuta, had stung. 'Nsuuta, would you rather I married with a hymen so they would bring a goat to the family?' Nsuuta's face remained covered under the sheet. 'Because I would not want my hymen to be flaunted all over the villages, moral aunts brandishing it over young girls as the ultimate feminine virtue: *Even that Kirabo, Miiro's wild grandchild, fetched a goat.*' Kirabo took a breath. 'And about being tame. Being rebellious is something I cannot afford. There was no way I was going to give Aunt Abi trouble when none of my parents would have me.'

Nsuuta sat up. 'I did not say walk into marriage blind. I would say don't marry at all, but if you are going to have sex, come to me and I will take you to a clinic where they will give you the right pills.'

'I will, Nsuuta. But at the moment there are ways of playing with fire without getting burnt.' When Nsuuta slipped back under the sheets without a retort, Kirabo knew she had scored.

When Tom came to visit the following morning, he was taken aside by a nurse who whispered hurriedly at him, glancing occasionally over to Nsuuta. When he came back, he told Kirabo to go to the foyer because the grown-ups wanted to talk. Afterwards, Tom came back and said, 'Keep an eye on Maama Muto. If you see any changes in her, however little, tell the doctors.'

'Is she getting worse?'

'You know old people; they can be children sometimes.'

After the morning check-up, Nsuuta was wheeled away. She was brought back at lunchtime. At around three in the afternoon she was taken away again, this time for an X-ray. When Tom arrived, Nsuuta still had not been brought back. He went to talk to the doctors and came back frowning. Kirabo asked what was going on.

'The doctors suspect there might be something else going on. But they are still checking.'

That night, Tom waited until Nsuuta was wheeled back. He asked Kirabo to step out of the room while they whispered. When he left, he was angry. Nsuuta had covered her head.

Nsuuta was discharged two weeks later, but she remained an outpatient. Tom took her to his house. Even Aunt Abi was apprehensive about Nsuuta convalescing at Tom's house, but Tom insisted and took two weeks off work. Apparently, he had told Nnambi that if she could not bear Nsuuta's presence in the house, she could go and visit her parents, but she had opted to stay. It was not until Kirabo returned home that Aunt Abi told her cancer had eaten one of Nsuuta's breasts.

9

Throughout the four months of her holidays after her O-levels, Kirabo did not attempt to find her mother. She had abandoned the idea of putting special announcements on the radio, and she could not be bothered to put up more posters. It had dawned on her some time the previous year, when the new students were about to arrive, that she just did not care any more. That year, it was Atim who had put up the new DO YOU KNOW LOVINCA NNAKKU? posters. Since Nnakku had not come looking for her after the war, either she was dead or she was not interested. Either way, it was time to move on.

Kirabo worked at the Ministry of Finance as a clerical officer, which was a euphemism for legworker – filing away documents in cabinets, locating and taking files from office to office, including love notes, tea and lunch for officers. Sometimes she took files between ministries.

It was her last day at work. The following Monday, she was returning to St Theresa's to start her A levels. She had not collected her salary in the four months she had worked at the ministry. The amount was not worth the long queues outside the cashier's office on payday. In any case, Tom gave her pocket money every week and Aunt Abi dropped her at work in the morning. After work, Old Kampala was a forty-minute walk. But this being her last day, she was paid all of her four months' salary. She planned to get Aunt Abi a bottle of perfume and the rest was to be saved for a trip to Dar es Salaam. Sio had one and a half years to finish his degree. He had promised to show her

TZ, as he referred to Tanzania, especially the Serengeti National Park, Dodoma and Dar es Salaam.

It was one of those things that happen and people ask, *You mean you didn't see it coming?* and look at you as if you are lying to yourself. But for you, it is not until it happens that you see its inevitability.

When Kirabo arrived home, Sio was sitting on the front steps, the ones no one used. She frowned. Sio never waited for her at home. For the past two weeks, ever since he had returned from TZ, he had rung her at work to say he was coming. Normally, he was waiting at the kiosk outside the treasury building when she finished work and they went to a restaurant or he walked her home. All this whizzed through her mind as she hurried towards him. When he saw her, Sio stood up and wiped his trousers where he had been sitting. Kirabo saw the shadows in his eyes and her mind flew to his father. Had they located Kabuye's remains? She gave him a brief hug, and then said, 'Wait here, I will drop these bags in the house. I have been paid. I will take you for chai and chapatti at the restaurant down the road.' She was not going to ask him what was wrong until they sat down somewhere. But as she walked towards the alleyway, she heard him coming. She stopped, saw how miserable he looked and thought he might as well come in.

'You know what, Sio, come to the house. Aunt Abi will not be home until six.'

Sio sped up. Yet by the time they got to the alleyway he was lagging behind again, as if he was coming but not coming. Before they got to the little gate, he stopped. It was there, under the mango tree that leaned in from the former Gurdwara Temple, now a mosque, that he dropped the boulder on Kirabo's head.

'Giibwa is pregnant.'

It was like eating too soon after a dentist has drilled your tooth. One half of your mouth is dead, the other half feels so swollen it is hard to move food around your mouth. Kirabo knew Sio was responsible, but her responses – speech, pain, anger – were delayed. She asked, 'What has Giibwa's pregnancy got to do with me?'

'So you don't hear it in rumours.'

'I don't care how I hear it.'

Sio kept quiet. He stood still. Finally, Kirabo asked, 'Whose is it?'

'Apparently it is mine.'

Only Kirabo's legs reacted; they started to itch. She used a shopping bag to scratch at them, but it just slid over the itch ineffectively. She looked at Sio's tears and thought *How Zungu. You go and hurt someone, and then when it comes to apologising you help yourself to crying as well.* She had seen it in films. Man cheats, man confesses to woman, man cries, and the betrayed woman is robbed of her right to tears.

'I just found out and thought I should tell you first. I have not even told Mum. I thought I should tell you when you were at home, so you did not travel afterwards.'

Kirabo was still a spectator.

'I only asked her in jest.' Sio started towards her. Kirabo flinched. He stopped. 'That Ntaate was spreading rumours that I am not…because I had never slept with any girl in the village. But then Giibwa said yes and I did not know what to do. I would have lost face. Giibwa would have confirmed Ntaate's rumour. I wish I had a better explanation.'

Still Kirabo did not respond.

'Say something, Kirabo. Say you are mad, hit me for heaven's sake.'

Kirabo stared.

'I know you will not believe me, but I don't love her. It happened when I took a message to her from her parents. Oh God, this is a nightmare.' He covered his face with both hands. 'I cannot believe I did it.'

Kirabo wanted to ask *Had Giibwa not got pregnant, would you have felt so much pain? Would you have felt any regret?* But she just turned around and marched through the gate.

He did not come after her.

When she returned, Sio stood where she had left him. He saw her coming with a pail of water but like a Zungu chicken, he did not run. She stopped a few metres away. 'I showed you my flower. You touched me there. Even after you touched her. You said men cheat because they spend money on us' – she splashed him like a car being washed – 'but how much have you spent on me?'

He caught his breath. Then as he wiped the water out of his face he replied, 'Don't say that, Kirabo. I was weak and stupid and I don't even love her.'

Kirabo walked back to the house. Jumping over the shopping bags she had dropped on the kitchen floor, she went to the sink and filled the pail again.

Sio still stood on the same spot. As if he had come all the way to Old Kampala to commit suicide. Kirabo threw the water at him. Maddened at his lack of reaction, she ran back to the sink. She filled the pail and returned. As she soaked him in water yet again, Aunt Abi turned into the alleyway and saw her. She hurried over and took the empty pail from her.

'What are you doing?'

'He made Giibwa pregnant!' Kirabo shrieked, as if Aunt Abi had already met Sio.

Aunt Abi looked at him, then cocked her head as if to retrieve a memory. Sio, dripping, his shirt clinging to his skin so you could see his pale skin through the white shirt, turned slightly towards the tree. '*I am sorry, ma'am.*' He spoke English.

'Are you not Kabuye's son?'

Sio nodded.

'Kabuye the feminist!'

'Yii yii.' Aunt Abi threw a look at Kirabo which said *What are you doing washing silk in dirty water?* 'My child,' she said smiling at Sio, 'do you think you will manage our girl? The way she treats visitors. Now I know why her friends in Nattetta call her Mohammed Alice.' She laughed at her own humour.

'Didn't you hear what I said, Aunt Abi? He made Giibwa pregnant.'

'You mean this Giibwa, the daughter of Mwesigwa, *our* labourer?'

'And he came to tell me, so I clap. I bet Nattetta is marvelling: *Oh, that Sio, he does not just shoot, he scores too.* I bet Ntaate pumped your hand.'

'Kirabo, you twist things. I came to apologise. I came to tell you what I had done. I did not want you to think I love her.'

Have you ever seen a cockerel caught in the rain? That is what Sio looked like in that moment. Way skinnier; an embarrassed skinny.

'Listen to me, Kirabo,' he implored. 'Listen. You said once that not all men cheat. That meant a lot to me. I don't deserve you, but please don't…just don't lose your trust in men because of me.'

'Gods, oh my good ancestors protect me from this guy. Did you hear him? Did you hear the sweetness of his words? He hits you, *whack*, across the cheek, and then begs *Please, please, don't feel the pain.*'

'But you know me, Kirabo; you know I am not like that. All this time I have treated you with respect. But now—'

'I know you? Me? Since when? I have no idea who you are. I doubt you know yourself.'

'I know I am a coward but please, I am begging you—'

Aunt Abi stepped in. 'But that girl, Giibwa; me, I saw it in her all along. The way she hung about you, Kirabo. Just to see what she could get out of you.'

'He is the one who made her pregnant. And then he claims to be one of us, believes in mwenkanonkano.'

'We are not perfect: we make mistakes,' he protested. Then he began to shiver.

'Come out of the cold, child,' Aunt Abi said. 'I have some clothes you can change into while you iron your clothes.' Aunt Abi held Sio's hand and led him towards the house. She turned to Kirabo. 'You wait there.' She led Sio through the tiny gate, under the clothes lines. She pulled a dry towel off the line and wrapped it around his shoulders. When they got to the foyer, she said, 'Wait here a minute. Let me talk to Kirabo.' When she got back to where Kirabo stood she whispered, 'Listen, Kirabo. All my life, I have never seen a man come to you before you find out that he has cheated and say *I am sorry I have erred.*'

'So?'

'Which clouds are you sailing on?'

'Giibwa is still pregnant, is she not?' Kirabo started to walk away.

'Stop. You don't walk away when I am talking to you.' Now she softened her voice. 'Let me handle this; anger has blinded you. Besides, this boy has suffered a lot because of his father.'

'That is no excuse.'

'Listen, I will not let a tiny little thing like a boy having a child in his impetuous youth rob us of a potentially fantastic opportunity with a fine young man from an excellent stalk. You are throwing him right back into the arms of that dung-roller – why? Because she is cheap? Let me handle this. One day you might thank me.'

'Aunt Abi, he *made* Giibwa pregnant.' The tears had started to flow.

'I know, I know. The girl is a slut. But do you know the courage it took him to come here to confess?'

'How could he sleep with her? He has never slept with me.'

'Child, that is why; it makes perfect sense, don't you see it?' Aunt Abi pulled away and looked in Kirabo's eyes. 'He slept with Giibwa for relief. You are decent. He respects you. That is what respecting men do. They go with the cheap girls while they wait for the right girl to get ready.' She rummaged through her handbag and retrieved a hankie and gave it to Kirabo.

Kirabo's mind was too congested to process the implications of Sio using Giibwa for sexual relief. Or to see that Aunt Abi was demonstrating a form of kweluma by diminishing Sio's cheating while escalating Giibwa's role. Kirabo was focused on the fact that if Giibwa had the baby, she would be inextricably related to Sio forever. The problem was that when it came to Sio, Kirabo had ignored the age-old wisdom that a woman never gives away her whole self to a man. To think she had lied to Aunt Abi and her father that part of the A-level study would be a trip to the Serengeti National Park and they had promised to pay for her trip. To think that she had taken Sio's suggestion and elected to do physics, chemistry and biology at A level in the hope of doing veterinary medicine at university so they could farm together. She was the most guileless woman who had ever lived.

That night in bed Kirabo clawed the flesh off her bones. *You knew he would do it; you knew. Telling him you trusted him, tsk, a naked plea if there ever was one.* Then images and smells and sounds of him reeled through her mind – the chink of the Bob Marley buckle on his belt, the Brut scent of him, the way his T-shirt always seemed tucked in at the front but hung out at the back. Him smelling her hair, neck, shoulders, eyes half-closed, then frenzied, greedily, demanding 'Touch me' while he tugged at the elastic of her knickers because there was hardly any space to snake his hand through, she keeping her knees tight just to hear his frustration – 'Touch me, Makula, please touch me.' That Sio, the Sio who had made her so lose herself she did not realise she had parted her knees, the Sio who had made her tug at his Bob Marley buckle to touch him, that Sio had not only touched Giibwa with those same hands, he had inserted himself so deep into her he had made her pregnant.

As a child, when she hurt a finger or a toe, she ran to her grandfather crying and he took it and blew on it until the pain ebbed. But this pain she did not know what to do with.

WHEN THE VILLAGES
WERE YOUNG

1

June 1934

Alikisa and Nsuuta thought they were eleven when they made a pact to marry the same man. Probably, they were ten.

It was at school, during break time. The pupils of Nattetta Native School had just finished eating porridge and were out in the grounds, playing. Big boys kicked a banana fibre ball below the slopes. Smaller ones slid whooping down the steep hillside at the edge of the church grounds, playing gogolo. Besides Nsuuta and Alikisa, two girls whose turn it was to wash mugs and pans were behind the old church with the cooks. Four others were on the verandah of the new church, weaving fibre ropes for skipping before break time ended. There were only eight girls in the school because despite Sir Apollo Kaggwa's campaigns, there was still no boarding for girls in rural schools. Yet no parent would let a girl walk long distances to go to study. Thus, unlike the numerous boys who came from Eastern Buganda, Busoga, Bukedi, Bugisu up to Teso, girl pupils at Nattetta Native came from nearby villages only. But then again, it did not matter. Girls came to school for one thing only: baptism, in case they got married in church. Christianity was steadily siphoning rituals of birth, marriage and death away from traditional practitioners, but to access its services, first you had to be baptised.

Alikisa and Nsuuta sat close to the old church under the mugavu tree playing seven stones. They sat facing each other, stone kabaka anjagala seeds between them. Alikisa, whose turn it was to play, held another seed. She had managed the one-stone, two-stones and three-stones levels easily. She tossed the one in her hand in the air but as she scrambled to pick up the four, Nsuuta exclaimed, 'Do you know?'

Alikisa ignored her and caught the tossed stone coolly. She showed Nsuuta the four stones in her hands plus the one she had tossed in the air and put them back on the heap. 'Know what?' she asked as she separated the five stones for the next level.

'We should marry the same man.'

Alikisa dropped the stones. 'I have had the same thought before, but—'

'It has just occurred to me, now-now.' Nsuuta was excited. 'If we marry the same man we will be friends forever.'

'Yes, but—'

'But what?'

'Your man will not marry me.'

'Why not?'

'Because…'

Nsuuta knew what Alikisa's *because* meant, but she did not know how to address it. For a moment, awkwardness sat between them. But then Nsuuta recovered. 'Then I will marry your man.'

'How? My father will find me some *kacatechist*. You know how poor they are. Your father would never let you embarrass him by marrying a poor man. Besides, catechists do not marry second wives.'

Nsuuta ran out of ideas. Sometimes being wealthy was a problem. Sometimes even beauty was a burden. She found out what it meant to be beautiful before she knew the darker implications of being a girl. She did not see it in a mirror; it was all around her – surprise in a stranger's eyes, envy in a girl's stare, sometimes hostility, hesitation before chastising, the sting taken out of a reprimand. Besides, people complimented her parents: 'Eh, Maama, your little girl is not ugly at all,' and her mother would beam, 'She just turned out that way; we don't know why.' Before long, Nsuuta had learnt to use her beauty to see what else it would fetch.

Thus, to Nsuuta, a rich, handsome husband was a given. Handsome, because you cannot risk having ugly children. Rich, because if marriage was as bad as women lament then it should at least have some comforts. Besides, nothing aged a woman like dropping children coupled with working like a slave. 'I want my own maidservant sitting by my side, asking, *Maama Nsuuta, what do you crave to eat today?* And I say, *Mpozzi, what did I eat yesterday?* She says, *Groundnuts with dry mushroom.* And I think it over: *Okay, today I will have goat meat cooked in luwombo.* When I crave liver, I want my husband to snap his fingers: *Do that cow; my lovely feels like eating liver today.* I want my maidservant to remind me, *Maama Nsuuta, your bathwater is warmed; would you care to take a bath?*'

Alikisa would interrupt, sucking her teeth, because Nsuuta was spoilt beyond redemption. Alikisa came from a humble background and the world had already told her that her looks were less than engaging. In Nattetta she was either Nsuuta's gruff friend or the catechist's daughter. Thus, she managed her life's expectations severely. A rich and handsome husband was out of the question. She was intense. She had few words, but they were invested with feeling. She loved quietly but deeply. She loved Nsuuta like she loved no one else, but sometimes Nsuuta's words were butterflies.

'You are not ugly yourself.' Nsuuta finally addressed Alikisa's *because*. 'It is just that you don't smile properly. And you are so brusque people don't see your beauty. You should start smiling a bit so that when my husband comes along, he will see you are not ugly.'

Alikisa looked down and plucked the grass around the stones. She plucked and plucked, letting the blades fall and attacking more. She desperately wanted to believe Nsuuta, but it would hurt if she found out that these were some of Nsuuta's fluttering words.

She never meant to be gloomy or brusque. It started when she left Timiina, her hometown, and came to live in Nattetta. She contemplated the implication of marrying Nsuuta's man. A large homestead. Their husband's house, with the modern four angles and an iron roof, would be the centrepiece. Nsuuta, as the favourite wife, would have the house on the right. Hers would be on the left. She would be the quiet, unassuming but hard-working wife, Nsuuta the spoilt favourite. Their children would play from her house into their father's into Nsuuta's, knowing they had twice the mothers, twice the love. She and Nsuuta would run a perfect home, free from conflict, growing food and crops, keeping animals and fowl. They would cook, clean and bring up their children as one, so the children could never tell whose mother was whose.

'Don't worry.' Nsuuta interrupted Alikisa's thoughts. 'If my man refuses to marry you, I will run away. Where will he find another beautiful wife who is clever and can read and write?' Nsuuta inspected Alikisa's face to see that the beauty she had told her about was indeed there. 'You have the best neck I have ever seen.'

Disbelief twitched Alikisa's nose.

'On my grandmother's truth. People even say that the deepness of your voice is rare. And that gap in your teeth? I wish I had one too. But then your teeth are so regular and so white, if only you smiled.' Seeing Alikisa's unconvinced face, Nsuuta added, 'If you don't believe me, let us make a pact. Bring your tiny finger.'

Alikisa stuck out her little finger on the left, Nsuuta the little one on the right. They entwined them.

'You spit first.'

Alikisa spat on the entwined fingers.

Then Nsuuta spat and said, 'I swear to marry the same husband as you, Alikisa.'

'I swear to marry the same husband as you, Nsuuta.' Alikisa had to hold back the emotion at this promise from Nsuuta.

'Now we wait until the saliva dries.' Nsuuta said. 'Once it dries, that is it, the pact is sealed. You cannot break it. So, if you feel you cannot marry my husband, say so right now.' In her voice was the hint that if the pact was to be broken it would be by Alikisa.

Alikisa was so stung by Nsuuta's doubt she exploded – 'I won't!' – and their hands shook, but the little fingers held.

'Hmm hmm,' Nsuuta accepted, 'because the first person to break the pact dies.'

'I know. Or if you don't die, the person you love most dies.'

There was nothing to add. The girls watched the little bubbles pop and pop as the spittle shrank. When it dried, they untangled their fingers. That was when they realised what they had done. It was kutta mukago, a men's ritual when friends became siblings by chewing coffee beans coated with each other's blood, making their families related. For a long time, the girls were silent until the drum sounded for the end of break time and they started down the slope. The gradient of the escarpment was so steep it was impossible to walk down. It so hastened Nsuuta's descent that, out of control, she almost fell into the trenches of the new school block being built. Alikisa squatted and, holding the ground with one hand, negotiated where she put her feet, one by one, until she got to the bottom. They headed towards the shade of the tree beneath which their class was held.

2

At the time, Alikisa and Nsuuta thought they were eleven years old because of faulty counting. Their parents were not counting, because 'Does counting the years make you live longer? When your time comes, it has come, counting or not.' The Ganda did not celebrate birthdays – 'What nonsense. Children do absolutely nothing on their arrival that warrants presents every year. If anything, they should give presents to their mothers, who come close to death.'

The first time the girls considered their age was in 1931, when they had to produce their dates of birth before baptism. Alikisa's mother thought her daughter was born two years before the British forced Sir Apollo Kaggwa to resign as Katikkiro of Buganda, which was in 1926. That meant Alikisa was probably born in 1924. But which month? To the best of her mother's memory, it felt like Alikisa was born in the later months of the year. She counted the European months – Sebutemba, Okitoba, Novemba. It could not be Desemba because by the time they ate Ssekukkulu that year, Alikisa could sit – or was she crawling? Whichever way she looked at it, Alikisa was at least three months old by the time they ate Christmas. She counted back from December and landed on September. She decided that Alikisa was born in September 1924. The day was easy; she picked randomly – *What is the difference? It is the same month*. She picked the eighth. Wondering why the church was so hung up on the exactness of numbers, she gave 08/09/24 as Alikisa's date of birth. But she was the catechist's wife; she had to show that she was a proper Christian. The date was entered into the church records.

Because Alikisa's mother had an exact date, Nsuuta ran home to get hers. Her mother, who had twelve children at the time and had never heard of the European calendar, sucked her teeth. 'Do I look like I have nothing better to do?' Nsuuta tried her father. He was perplexed. 'Was I there when you were being born? Tsk, children of nowadays.'

If Nsuuta told her parents that she could not be baptised without a date of birth, her mother would huff *Was I baptised: don't I eat, don't I sleep?* and threaten to withdraw her from school: *That kachurch is beginning to own our lives.* Thus, by the time Nsuuta arrived at school the following morning, she was the same age as Alikisa. After all, they were in the same class and the same size. But because she was slightly taller, she had to be older. The date of 2 January 1924 was presented to the church. This was the earliest she could have been born without raising Alikisa's suspicions.

Nsuuta was baptised Bibiyana, while Alikisa was named Lozi in Christ.

In 1931, when the girls first counted their age, they counted their year of birth as well. Thus, they were both eight. Recently, with both hands folded into fists, Nsuuta had counted again by unfolding a finger at a time and touching it on her chin. Once again, she counted the birth year – '1924, 1925, 26, 27, 28, 29, 30, 31, 32, 33…' She ran out of fingers. She turned to her feet and stuck out the male toe on the right. 'We are in 1934?' she asked Alikisa.

'Yes.'

'I am already eleven, walking my twelfth year because I was born in Janwari. But you will have to wait until Sebutemba.' Seeing Alikisa's fallen face Nsuuta added, 'Don't worry, this is Juuni,' and counted on her fingers: 'Juuni, Julaayi, Agusto, Sebutemba: four months and you will be walking your twelfth too.'

'Kdto,' Alikisa clicked. She was fed up of being behind Nsuuta in everything.

For eleven-year-old girls, marriage was three, four years away if you were pretty and wealthy people were watching you for their sons. Everywhere, girls of the same age group had begun to discuss marriage, since, as soon as your moon arrived, time started to run against your market value. Once your breasts leaned on your chest, you were ready. One, two years of bleeding and you were married. Three, four years if you were not attractive and your parents had to negotiate with prospective husbands. Five years of bleeding in your parents' home? Kdto. You were pawned to poor or old or disabled men to save face. At your wedding people danced more out of relief than joy. Fathers and their sisters sourced suitors, vetting for diseases, conditions, behavioural issues or any potential blood relationships. When they were satisfied, the suitor paid a viewing visit. Nsuuta had seen it happen to her sisters. A month before a suitor visited, her sister would stop doing chores, was kept away from the sun, then pampered with herbal baths and ointments and then fed sumptuously to put some flesh on her bones. It was done on the sly in case the plan fell through. You did not want the world to know that three, four viewings had come to nothing. Then the suitor arrived, and you peered feverishly to catch a glimpse of him. Then you were called to the diiro full of aunts and uncles and told, *This is the person we told you about. Look at him carefully.*

Some girls came out excited: 'He has won me: he is the very one.' Some breathed fire: 'He will have to bring a rope to drag me to his house…' 'Did you see how wild his teeth are…' 'I am not breeding that nose…' Some were unsure: 'If grown-ups say he is the one, then he is the one.' Thus, if Alikisa and Nsuuta were going to step into the terrible rest-of-their-lives called marriage, taking a best friend along was a good strategy.

3

After school, the girls ran across the PE field and joined the deeply rutted track that ran through the villages to walk home. Two months ago, the track had been made wider because there was increased use by lumber trucks, carrying ndodo logs from Busoga and of course Nsuuta's grandfather's motorcycle. The frequency of lumber trucks was attracting other locomotive traffic travelling east. There was a sense that the region was awakening from national obscurity.

As they passed the master's house, the wind blew and Alikisa glanced at the sky. Rain was coming but the clouds were still far off. They carried on walking unhurriedly. From the look of the sky, Nsuuta would get home before the rain started. Then Alikisa noticed drips of black oil on the grassy island in the middle of the track.

'Watch your legs, Nsuuta; there is oil on the grass.'

Nsuuta stepped away: oil was hard to wash off. She frowned at the fresh-looking oil. 'I did not see this truck go down the road. Did you?'

'No; could be your grandfather's pikipiki.'

'No, he has not travelled. Might have been a truck that went down in the night.'

The girls did not see rain clouds gather. By the time the wind intensified, Nsuuta, who lived in Kamuli, would not be able to outrun the rain. She decided to take shelter at Alikisa's home until the rain stopped. As they turned into the walkway leading to Alikisa's home, Nsuuta caught a sound and grabbed her friend's hand. They stopped and listened. Beneath the wind was a faint groan. The girls looked at each other, then screamed, 'It is coming; the ndodo truck is coming!' Despite the threat of rain, they ran back to the road and as soon the head of the truck appeared, they jumped up and down, singing, 'Gyamera gyene, tema butemi, gyamera gyene, tema butemi.' The truck was so slow the boys ran alongside, also shrieking, 'Gyamera gyene, tema butemi.' The incline on Nattetta Hill was long and steep. It became a killer as you got closer to the top. Sometimes a lumber truck failed and died. One time, a truck failed like that and came down backwards without brakes. It overturned across the road and it took a whole week for the breakdown service to come and turn it over.

The truck agonised, getting slower and louder. When the girls could see the whole truck, they turned and shook their bottoms at it: 'Gyamera gyene, tema butemi, gyamera gyene, tema butemi.' When it got so close they could see the men in the cabin, the girls started to hurl English insults:

'*No senzi yu, no senzi atol.*' Nsuuta pointed to her head.

'*Yeahshi, yeahshi,*' Alikisa agreed, '*no komonisenzi atol.*'

'*Sile baaga yu.*'

'*Taaf.*'

They had no idea what the words meant, but who cared?

'*Taafru yu.*'

'*Fakini.*'

'*Fakineelo.*'

'*Bastade.*'

'*Bulade.*'

'*Bulade bastadde.*'

'*Fuul.*'

'*Buladefuul.*'

'*Booyi, booyi.*'

By the time they ran out of colonial insults, the truck was upon them. Three huge ndodo logs were fastened at the back. They could make out rings and rings of tree age, like waves, where the wood had been cut. Two lumberjacks sitting on the logs smiled and waved. The girls waved back, happy to have got a response. Soon the thick smoke from the exhaust pipe shrouded the view. More oil on the grassy island. When the truck reached the hilltop, the noise paused for a heartbeat. Then the engine made an explosion and a plume of black smoke blew into the air. The girls cheered and clapped. As if its agony was gone, the truck sped down the other side of the hill with barely a sound.

Nsuuta turned to Alikisa as they skipped towards the house. 'Do you know where the chant "Gyamera gyene" comes from?'

'No.'

'It is from Busoga. After we Gandas had sold all our old trees to Europeans for timber, we went to Busoga. At the time, the Soga had no idea you could make money out of selling trees. Ganda men would spy old trees – mivule, mituba and even nnongo – and approach the Soga who lived on the land: *Sir, do you need that tree? No*, the Soga would reply. *Can we cut it down then?* The Soga would wave them on with a *Gyamera gyene, tema butemi*, meaning the trees grew by themselves, just cut them down.'

'What?'

'For years Ganda men have paid the Soga for their old trees with laughter. But they have wised up. Now they call us thieves, Ebiganda biibi. By the way, never laugh at the Soga in my home.'

'Why?'

'Can you keep a secret?' Now that they were siblings, Nsuuta felt she could trust Alikisa with a bit of her innermost secret. But the wind had got so loud they had to shout.

'Come.' Alikisa grabbed her hand and they ran.

Alikisa's home was quiet. Nsuuta looked around at the emptiness, marvelling at the silence. Such quiet would never happen at her home. Not with three mothers and so many siblings it felt like school. Then there were the regionals who camped in the courtyard for weeks, waiting for their turn to consult with her father.

'I think Mother and the boys have gone to the Mothers' Union,' Alikisa explained, noticing Nsuuta's surprise at the silence. 'Father is helping the master to teach the big boys.'

The rain started. The girls stood by the door watching it. Nsuuta began, 'It happened a long time ago, before my father was born, when this entire region was wilderness. My grandfather was a warrior then.'

'That Ssaza chief with a pikipiki?'

'Yes, he and his bambowa used to carry out raids in Busoga. They raided animals and – please never tell – women.'

'What?' To Alikisa, only foreigners raided humans. Even then they belonged in scary folk tales. She did not know what to say.

'Whenever they returned from their raids, Grandfather would take his pick first, of animals, skins, tusks and women he fancied. You know those wives he has?'

Alikisa nodded.

'There were a lot more many, many years ago.'

'More than that?'

'That is nothing. Father says that in his young days, Grandfather had a harem. Most women were Basoga. In fact, most of my uncles and aunts have Ssoga blood.'

'You mean some of your grandmothers were loot?'

'Most of them have died. Only seven remain.'

Alikisa clasped her mouth like a grown-up. To her, Nsuuta's grandfather was like those brown tenna balls. Small and tight. He would bounce if you dropped him. The kind of man to sprout mushrooms on his back before he succumbed to senescence. By her reckoning, he was eighty but rode his motorcycle as if half his age.

'But most were sold.'

'Don't say that, Nsuuta.' Alikisa was horrified.

'Arabs took them to Buwarab. They preferred women and children slaves to men because they did not give them trouble. If you were beautiful and my grandfather or other warriors picked you then you were lucky. But if you became troublesome and tried to escape, you were sold.'

'Did Arabs marry the women they took?'

'I have heard that some were taken as wife-slaves, but most were work-slaves.' Now she looked around to make sure no one was about. 'Do you know what Arabs did to the boys?'

'No.' Alikisa clenched against the horror she knew was coming.

'They cut off their garden eggs, so they would not make children with their women when they grew up.'

Alikisa wanted to say *Nsuuta, you lie too much: we Ganda would never do that to a fellow human*. But a small voice in her head reminded her that Nsuuta was the daughter of a Muluka chief and the grandchild of the Ssaza chief. She was privy to this kind of information. Still, she was not going to believe any Ganda had sold a human being. It was only the Nyoro, the worst humans in the world, who sold fellow humans.

'But you said your grandmothers tell stories: how can they when they are living in abduction?'

'Maybe storytelling kills the pain, maybe they got tired of being in pain. They know things. If you are lucky and you catch them in the mood for talking, they will tell you things. They know all about humans, how we started to own the world, how women became property, how children came to belong to fathers even though they grow in our stomachs.'

Alikisa glanced at Nsuuta, at her impossible beauty, and felt the familiar envy rise within her. Even in the worst moments of inhumanity, Nsuuta's beauty would save her from savagery. Nsuuta would marry her abductor or her slaver and find refuge in her children. Alikisa, on the other hand, would be sold to the Arab animals. She stole another glance at Nsuuta. Was Nsuuta aware that her beauty had been plundered from somewhere? A gust of wind blew the rain where they stood and an idea occurred to her. 'Let's shower in the rain.'

'Oh yes.' The idea dispelled Nsuuta's gloom.

'Wait here.' Alikisa ran to the bedrooms and came back with a tablet of blue Dimi lya Ngombe soap. She pulled off her clothes, flung them on the floor and stepped out on the verandah. Reaching into the rain, she wetted the soap and rubbed some in her hair, and into her loofah sponge. She scrubbed her body until it was covered in soapsuds. Meanwhile, Nsuuta had stripped, folded her clothes and put them away on a chair. In a crowded home like hers, if you threw your clothes anywhere it was impossible to find them again. The girls shared Alikisa's loofah sponge. When Nsuuta was done scrubbing her skin, Alikisa called, 'Ready?'

Nsuuta's 'ready' was feverish.

'Are you scared?'

'No.' Nsuuta had never seen Alikisa's eyes shine so.

'I will count to three and we will jump.'

Nsuuta still shrieked in agony, but the rain was too heavy for the shock to last. They ran around the compound squealing and yelping, soap from their hair running into their eyes, stinging and making them red. They sang and clapped, danced and skipped. Nsuuta had never known the sheer joy and freedom of running naked, singing and dancing while rain washed her body under the open sky. When the rain eased, they ran back into the house.

The cold was waiting. It said *Now you are mine* and held so deep in their bones they squatted, hands clasped, teeth chattering, goose pimples everywhere. Alikisa got one of her mother's barkcloth sheets and they wrapped themselves, but the cold would not let go. In the end, they pulled on their school dresses and ran to the kitchen to rekindle the fire. As they warmed up, Alikisa asked, 'Have you heard about Muka Kuuku?'

'Which Kuuku?'

'Ssa Alibati Kuuku' – that was the only way a Ganda tongue could say 'Sir Albert Cook' – 'the missionary at Mmengo Hospital. You have heard of him?'

Nsuuta hesitated. She did not know any European missionaries. In their relationship, there were two areas where Alikisa was better than her – Bible knowledge and information about Baminsani, as the Christian missionaries were called.

'Of course I know Ssa Alibati Kuuku.'

'His wife, Muka Kuuku, is going to start training us Ganda girls to become Indian ward maids at Mmengo Hospital. Can you imagine a hospital with Ganda Indian nurses?'

'Do you mean we can be Indian nurses as well?' Nsuuta's eyes shone.

'Apparently.'

While Alikisa marvelled at the luxury of finally being attended to by Ganda nurses, as Indian nurses were notoriously nasty and Ganda men who worked as hospital assistants were worse, Nsuuta was marvelling at becoming one. 'Can you imagine being an Indian nurse and making grown-ups lift their clothes, so you prick their buttocks? I wonder how many buttocks you would see in a day?'

'Nsuuta' – Alikisa shook her head disapprovingly – 'you are rotten.'

4

Alikisa and Nsuuta were in lower primary now. They had stayed in school this long after baptism because of their fathers. Alikisa's father, being a catechist, had led by example. How do you preach education when your children are not in school themselves? Nsuuta's father wanted to fit in with chiefs in the capital who sent their daughters to sinagoogi, as schools were known at the time. The girls' mothers were happy about their Christian names, and after all, a bit of reading and writing would raise the girls' value on the marriage market.

When they first started school, Alikisa was presumed to be the kind of pupil they called a kiwutta – the kind of cassava that stays hard and tasteless no matter how long it is cooked. Alikisa, who had just arrived from Timiina, was fearful, but the master did not realise. Normally, a kiwutta pupil was abandoned at the back of the class to play with dust, but the catechist's daughter could not be treated like that. After two weeks, Alikisa was sat next to Nsuuta, whose brain was sharper than the master had ever known. He hoped this would rub off on Alikisa.

Nsuuta liked Alikisa instantly. For one thing, Alikisa did not hide her awe of Nsuuta's beauty. She stared as if she had never seen anything like it. And there was an earnestness about Alikisa's stare that was irresistible. For another, Alikisa attended school regularly, unlike the other girls from the village. In the past, Nnaaba had sat next to Nsuuta. Nnaaba who lived in Kamuli too was Nsuuta's best friend. But Nnaaba had no interest in studying at all. Her head was filled with dreams of becoming a woman, marrying and having children. It was easy to replace her with Alikisa. The first day they sat together, Nsuuta broke her writing stick in half and gave one half to Alikisa. She told her to move over to create writing space on the ground. First, she levelled the dust, then she drew a page covered in neat lines. She showed Alikisa how to write *a*.

'First, you draw a circle like this. Then give it a tiny tail at the front, like this, see?'

Alikisa nodded.

'Now you try.'

Alikisa, her hand shaking, both lips clenched between her teeth, drew a circle so focused she held her breath. When she finished, she exhaled.

Nsuuta smiled. 'That is it. Now fill the whole line.'

Later, Nsuuta confided that out of the five vowels, she liked *e* most. It was quiet and unassuming. *i* was loud. *a* was haughty. But *e* made a beautiful pattern: *eeeee*. Letters *o* and *u* were dumb. *o* did not even make patterns at all. *u* disappeared into waves if you tried to make a pattern with it: *uuuuuu*.

Alikisa nodded; vowels having personalities made perfect sense.

'Wait till they become capital letters; you will see how arrogant vowels get. See *A*? See how it spreads out its legs like Luutu sitting in church? Luutu thinks he is too educated. That is why his children – that Dewo, that Miiro, Levi, but especially Nsangi' (Nsuuta leaned in and whispered, 'She is not even beautiful') 'are haughty.'

When Alikisa started to write numbers, Nsuuta told her she could trust 2, 5 and 8 because they were female.

'Mother is 8, while 5 is a girl. Little 2 is a toddler. Grandmother is 88. As for 4 and 6, they are female and male at the same time, but I don't know why. They are proud because they have both male and female sides. And 1 and 3 are boys. However, 7 and 9, ho. Bullies. All the other numbers are frightened of them.'

In no time at all, Alikisa had learnt the Luganda alphabet and numbers. Her handwriting was a work of art. When the master noticed her improvement he said, 'Eh-eh, she is loosening up,' as if Alikisa's particular brand of ineptitude needed soaking before it slackened.

After her successful intervention in Alikisa's learning, Nsuuta was made the musigire of her class, a kind of pupil-teacher to monitor the class and help slower pupils. When the master was not there, she would sit at the top of the class with a long stick and make the pupils chant the times tables: 2×2, 2×3, 2×4.

Sometimes it was making syllables: '*M* and *a* make?'

'*Ma.*'

'*Ma* and *ma* make?'

'*Maama.*'

Nsuuta was an impatient teacher. She sucked her teeth a lot, pointing her stick at the boys who were too slow for her. 'Tsk, listen to this goat, nti 1×1 is 2. Why don't you just stay at home and herd your father's cows instead of wasting our time?'

Often, when the class failed at a sum, the master would say, 'Wamma Nsuuta, help us.' The fear of failing in moments like this – the boys would be vicious – made her work hard at her studies.

The day their class was given slates and chalk, Nsuuta ran home to show her father. She had written his name and her village in her own hand on the slate; she had graduated from scratching in the dust to writing on her own little blackboard. Her father was so impressed he said to the regionals, who were waiting for consultation, 'Imagine if she was a boy.'

'Next, I will be writing in a real book with a pencil.'

What came first was the promotion of her class to upper primary at the start of 1937. The girls were entering Primary Four at the time. There was a sense of achievement when the class moved into the newly completed brick block where the floor was cement and the blackboard was painted on the wall rather than a mobile one mounted on an easel. This achievement was marked by three changes. First, pupils sat in pairs on benches attached to desks. The desks had a shelf where you kept your fruit or crunchies like roast corn and nuts to nibble on when you were peckish. Secondly, the master distributed exercise books and pencils. A big pencil sharpener was mounted on the master's desk. The whole class grew feverish with excitement. Pages so smooth, so clean you hungered to write. The girls promised each other not to mess up, to get everything correct so their exercise books would be covered in nothing but ticks. But the biggest change was that all lessons were to be taught in English. No jabbering Luganda. The teacher put up a big sign at the back of the class: **No speaking Vernacular**. Studying had become serious.

Now that they looked up the wall at the blackboard, Nsuuta sat at the front of the class. Boys accused her of cosying up to the master to protect her teacher-pupil position, but Nsuuta said she had problems with the master's handwriting. The letters *c*, *e* and *o* looked the same. Sometimes the letters slanted forward like they would fall, sometimes they blinked on the blackboard. When she talked about it, Alikisa laughed, because it was just like Nsuuta to see letters and numbers dance.

Because the girls had started to bleed that year Alikisa brought up the question of children. Nsuuta's response was, 'I am not going to breed like a rabbit.'

'Then we shall have ten children only.'

'Ten?'

'Five each.'

Nsuuta shook her head. 'I want one.' At the horror on Alikisa's face, Nsuuta relented: 'Okay, two, no more. My mother has fifteen now. Father has I-don't-know-how-many. We are so crowded in Mother's house we sleep on top of each other. Recently, I asked Mother, "When will you stop?" She said, "Stop, how? If children are still in there, they will come out." I said, "Ah."'

'But only two? That means I will have to have eight. My mother has had three so far. Her womb is the kind that has to be begged. But we are dying of silence in that house. I will not do that to my children. Maybe I will have my five and then I will help you. But we shall have to marry a modern man who does not want too many children. Otherwise he will have to marry other wives.'

'Let's have eight. I will have two, you six. If our husband wants more children, let him marry other wives. That is the only thing I like about Luutu – he is richer than rich but has only four children.'

'Have you been to his house?'

Nsuuta shook her head.

'His family rattles about in that huge house of theirs like four peas in a pan, especially now that Dewo and Miiro are studying in Mmengo.'

Because of the way the girls discussed their future, because of the way Nsuuta helped her through lessons, but mostly because of the pact, Alikisa presumed that Nsuuta would always be there to walk with her through life.

5

After six years of living in Nattetta, Alikisa's hometown, Timiina, still came to her in sharp darts of loss. The feelings were less frequent, but the sting had not mellowed. Mostly, she missed her grandmother.

For two and a half years, while her father worked with Luutu to set up Nattetta Native Parish, Alikisa stayed in Timiina. She had grown so attached to her grandmother that when the time came to join her parents, she refused. At the time, Luutu had just revolted against the Catholic Church. The Protestants, who had been pumping him to rebel, quickly gave him the mandate to build a parish and sent him a catechist to work with. Alikisa's father and mother left Timiina and came to Nattetta to help set up the Native Church, as the Protestant Church was called at the time. For two and a half years, Alikisa did not see her parents at all. In the end, Alikisa's grandmother came along and stayed in Nattetta for two months while Alikisa got used to her parents again.

But every time Alikisa talked about her grandmother and how she missed her, Nsuuta would sulk as if Alikisa were showing off. Nsuuta never talked about her own grandmother, just those grandmothers. For a while Alikisa presumed it was forbidden in Nsuuta's home to single out real grandmothers from not-real ones. Then she wondered whether Nsuuta's real grandmother had died. Finally, she asked, 'Which one of those grandmothers is your real one?'

'None.'

'Oh, she died?'

Nsuuta shrugged. 'We don't know.'

'Oh?'

'After she had my father, she dumped him there, no breastfeeding, no nothing, and disappeared. It was the other women who rescued him.'

'Some women have no hearts.'

'She was Ssoga.'

'Then Ssoga women are most heartless.'

'She was raided.'

'Ha.' Alikisa caught her breath, then burst out, 'Forgive me, Nsuuta, I did not realise.'

'Even though he is old, my father is still in pain. He still dreams that one day she will come back to see him. Grandfather refuses to talk about it. Once, when Father pestered him, Grandfather said, "What is it that you are looking for that I have not given you? Why do you cry for a woman who never suckled you?" but Father will not listen. He has been to Busoga to look for her. He left messages everywhere, but nothing. When he returned, he renamed the villages – Kamuli, then Bugiri – after places in Busoga where people said she might have been abducted from. At the time, the villages were too young to resist. If it was not for Luutu, he would have renamed Nattetta too.' Nsuuta paused. 'Her name was Naigaga. That is why, for my father, each wife's eldest daughter is named Naigaga. We swear upon her name' – she shrugged – 'hoping that one day she might hear us. If Naigaga came today, Father would kill her with love. But all those grandmothers who were abducted are our real grandmothers because they loved our father.'

'Hmm.'

'Sometimes, in my mind, I see my grandmother put my father down to sneak out of the house in the middle of the night. She makes a hole in the fence, looks around, then runs and disappears into the bushes. She makes it back to her home and vows never to leave her house again. But other times I see my grandfather's men catch her as she tries to escape, and later sell her. She is somewhere in the Arab world dying, having had Arab children.'

'No she is not, Nsuuta. Your grandmother made it to safety, lived a quiet life and died in peace.'

'You know Kisoga, the village where Luutu keeps his servants and cattle?'

'Yes?'

'That is where all the loot from Busoga – animals, humans, skins and tusks – used to arrive. First, my grandfather took his pick, then his men; the rest was sold.'

Alikisa clicked.

'My father says he will never inherit anything from Grandfather. His wealth is soaked with the blood and tears and sweat of other people. My father is making his own, but I think it is impossible. Once you are born in it, it is in you. Everything terrible my grandfather did is already in our blood. But I am lucky to be a girl; I will not inherit anything.'

'Did Luutu's clan also raid in Busoga?'

'Luutu came from Ssingo. His wealth is new. It comes from being close to Christianity. But then again,' she sighed, 'with well-off people, you never know where their privilege first came from. Often someone bled, someone sweated, someone cried or died to make them rich. That is what my father says.'

Alikisa looked around her. They were standing on a plain picking bweyeyeyo to make straw brooms for school. Suddenly, Nattetta, with its wilderness and its sparse population, looked like a place where nefarious acts like abduction were condoned. She had heard that Nsuuta's grandfather was one of the earliest settlers in Bugerere. He came from the Ssese Islands in the 1870s. For a long time, he and his men reigned over lower Bugerere with no one to curb their excesses. She had heard they sold tusks, not humans, to Arabs – that was how Nsuuta's great-uncle, Nkuggwa, died. Elephant charging. The monster did not even blink when it was hit by a bullet and trampled him like a leaf. But no one had mentioned the sale of humans.

Compared to Timiina, where villages stretched for miles, Nattetta, Bugiri and Kamuli were jungle, surrounded by stretches of verdant bush. It was days before you heard human noises outside your family.

You could go for days without hearing a single voice other than those of your immediate family. Alikisa's family was lucky; they ran a church and a school. Even in holidays when the school was dead, travellers stopped at the church for a night, a week, to catch their breaths. By the road, on the musambya tree near the walkway to their house, her mother hung ripe ndiizi bananas for both schoolchildren and travellers. Every house did this. In Timiina it was only done at the edges of the village to alert travellers that they were entering wilderness and should carry as many bananas as possible. This isolation made homes in Nattetta self-contained – your own well, your own swamp for njulu and nsansa to craft mats, baskets and carpets, and your own forest to collect firewood and poles for construction. If something happened to your family, only gwanga mujje drums could raise the alert. Alikisa was a tough girl, she was slow to cry, but the thought of Nsuuta's grandmother's abduction made tears gather. She wished her father had never been sent to Nattetta. She was sure no such thing had happened in her Timiina. The Ganda never sold humans. Nsuuta's grandfather must have been a criminal.

It was surprising what a bit of history did to a place, how it coloured it. Before she came here, all Alikisa knew was that Bugerere was Buganda's paradise of sweet bananas and fruit. Most birds in the world migrated to Bugerere. As a child, whenever she saw the mpa abaana, the long-beaked ibis, flying past in pairs she would sing, 'Give me the children, give me the children / I am going to Bugerere to eat sweet bananas,' and she would imagine a shimmering Bugerere.

True to the song, all kinds of banana species and fruit thrived in Bugerere. When Alikisa first arrived she was surprised to find that even matooke ripened in plantations everywhere. But that was because there was hardly anyone to eat it. Alikisa's parents said that Bugerere was demographically challenged because of that lubwa fly. They told her that since the beginning of time, the lubwa had infested areas from Mabira Forest through Bugerere across the Nile to Busoga, millions and millions of the tiny flies that flew into your ears and nose. You yawned carelessly, you swallowed a mouthful. And, despite its miniature size, the lubwa had a mean bite. To survive, you covered every inch of your skin and surrounded yourself with smoke. Thus, by the 1870s, when Nsuuta's grandfather arrived, Bugerere was as fertile as a sow. Herds of elephants, antelope, buffalo, wild hogs, lions and leopards. But then in 1900 Chwa's regents teamed with the colonial government and sprayed the lubwa fly out of existence. From then, Kabaka Chwa launched a campaign to populate Bugerere. He sent educated envoys like Luutu, gave them a lot of land and told them to start missions and sinagoogi to encourage Ganda immigration into the region. In the 1920s Chwa often travelled in his car, an Albion, to hunt buffalo or antelope with Luutu. Alikisa's parents had seen it with their own eyes. Subjects came from all over Buganda to feast and see Chwa's car. But few settled in Bugerere, except criminals running from the law. Cynics scoffed that Chwa's campaign to populate Bugerere was a drive against the Ruuli and Nyara people in the northern parts of Bugerere who had resisted Ganda colonisation.

Despite this, Chwa's campaign would continue even after his death. By the 1950s, Bugerere would be carved up among the landed Ganda gentry. But now in 1937, brazen wild hogs looked at Alikisa as if to say *This is our wilderness; what are you doing here?* Bugerere seemed like the place which would turn humans into savages.

6

Nsuuta's mother was getting restless. The value education brought to a girl on the marriage market depleted with age. Nsuuta had been bleeding for two years; she was on the verge of overstaying in school. But Nsuuta's father was too soft. Instead of telling her firmly that a suitor had approached them and that he wanted her to seriously consider him, he would ask, 'Nsuuta, someone is interested in you; do you want to meet him?'

Nsuuta would screw up her face: 'But I have said I want to take my studies further. Masters say I have potential. I could be Kamuli's first nurse or teacher.' And her father would let the chance slip by. Her mother, having no say in what a man does with his children, would huff but keep quiet.

The real reason Nsuuta had stayed so long in school was her father's growing hatred of Luutu. The master who came to ask for Nsuuta to be put up for a Gayaza High scholarship knew the story of the hostility between the two men all too well, and had exploited it. He argued that Nsuuta would put Kamuli on the map in Bugerere. Two years earlier, Luutu's daughter, Nsangi, who was weaker in studies than Nsuuta, had been awarded the same scholarship. 'When you mention Bugerere County, the village that sounds is Nattetta because of Luutu Omusomi and his children's education,' the master told Nsuuta's father. 'Nsuuta is Kamuli's chance. Let's send a daughter to Gayaza and give hope to our children. And who else but you, the Muluka Chief, to lead the way?'

The Muluka was also worried about the growing power Christianity gave to Luutu. Luutu's roles of building churches, of starting schools, of being a liaison with the British administration, were cannibalising traditional structures and institutions. When Luutu asked for masters and catechists to come and teach in his schools, they were sent. When the Muluka asked for a tractor to clear roads and attract more locomotives into the region he was told that the task fell on residents to repair their roads – tractors were for the Kyadondo region only. It all came down to Luutu's ability to speak English, the Muluka knew. These days, Luutu's name sounded louder than the Ssaza Chief who had once hunted buffalo with Kabaka Muteesa Mukaabya, then briefly with Kabaka Mwanga. Now, because Chwa's regents had sold the Buganda Kingdom to the British, when Chwa visited Bugerere he slept at Luutu's house. Where the Ssaza used to talk of the prestige of hosting Kabaka Muteesa, Luutu boasted of Winston Churchill opening Mmengo High – what stupidity was that? Luutu had parroted Churchill's words in English when he opened Nattetta Native School – '*We yal in darkaness, bati schools like zis one are a bikon*' – even though no one understood a word he said. Often, Luutu told church congregations and schoolchildren with fawning pride how Churchill had described Uganda as '*za paal of Afirika*'. But what was a pearl? Who had ever seen one? What did it do? As if Buganda had been waiting for Churchill to come from Bungeleza and tell us what a wonder Buganda was. And yet all of that added up to giving Luutu weight wherever he went.

For a long time, the Muluka had harboured a deep contempt for Luutu and how he championed someone else's culture, but now seeing how Luutu was devouring all sorts of powers, the Muluka decided that if his sons wanted to be in the race for the next Muluka or Ssaza, they had all better speak English. He gave the master permission to put Nsuuta up for the scholarship. Then he took all his younger children and poured them into Nattetta Native.

★

Because Nsuuta was still in school, the catechist was reluctant to withdraw Alikisa. When he asked her, 'Is it not time you started thinking about marriage?' Alikisa would shake her head. Once, when he seemed to waver because a promising catechist had come along, Alikisa argued, 'But Nsuuta is carrying on with her studies even though her family does not know the value of education,' at which her father sighed at the suitor, 'Times are changing. Who rushes a daughter into marriage any more? Luutu's Nsangi, who is way older than my Alikisa, is still at Gayaza. Muluka's Nsuuta is also still in school. Everywhere in Entebbe and Kampala, girls are being educated. It is we in the rural areas who are being left behind.'

The truth was that Alikisa was waiting to see who Nsuuta would marry before making a decision. She was not curious about the world; she was not ambitious. For her, a single door opened into the future: marriage. Inside marriage were two doors. One opened into the kitchen, the other into motherhood – her realms. She had two dreams. One was having a European wedding – church, ring, tiara and white gown. But now that she was going to marry Nsuuta's man, she would pass on that. The other dream was to deliver her children in a proper hospital rather than that backward, traditional way that women did, with midwives shouting *Hold on to the kitooke tight, now push.*

It was about this time that the girls became aware of the differences in their dreams for the future. In reality, these differences had been there all along. When they were younger, Alikisa always suggested they play mothers, cooking, cleaning, breastfeeding while telling off her children – *Stop playing in the dust… But why is this child so clingy?* – and tucking them into bed. Nsuuta always suggested they play nurses. She had started when Luutu brought three Indian nurses to their school to immunise pupils. That day even children who did not study came to school to be immunised. Later, a mobile clinic started to come on Wednesdays and Fridays and camped in the church compound. After classes, Alikisa and Nsuuta would go over and watch. Nsuuta stared at the important airs on the nurses' faces as they taught women things and a Ganda man interpreted. She wanted those airs. She wanted the white-and-red uniform of Mmengo Hospital, and the cap that looked to her like a wedding crown. Thus at play, when they had tucked their children in to sleep, Nsuuta would roll the long leaves of elephant grass into a halo for a nurse's cap, cover it with cotton and put it on her head, transforming herself into an Indian nurse, while Alikisa would become a Ganda mother, fretting, 'Musawo, my child is dying.'

'Calm down, calm down: how am I supposed to work in these conditions?' Nsuuta, the Indian nurse, would rebuke. 'Is your child a boy or girl?'

'Girl.'

Nsuuta would check the baby everywhere. 'Does she eat properly, has she vomited, does her stomach run?'

And if Alikisa shook her head at all of that, Nsuuta would deploy her killer question, 'Did you immunise your child?'

'But, Musawo, I have heard that children die after immunisation. Me, I am not putting my child's life in danger: did Buganda not thrive before immunisation came?'

Nsuuta would lose her patience. 'But these people, when will you come out of your backwardness? You are killing your own children.' Shaking her head, she would inject the baby in the arm with a thorn and then on the buttocks. She would then squeeze drops from a red berry into the baby's mouth, before getting the white seeds off a dry maize cob, counting out thirty and rolling them in a leaf. 'Break each tablet into a half. Crush it on a teaspoon until it is powder, add a bit of water, hold the baby's cheeks like this so she opens her mouth and pour down the medicine as far as possible. Give her one half, do you hear me?' She would raise her voice: 'One half *only*. Not whole. One half in the morning, one half in the night.' Then she would write an invisible ½ × 2 on the leaf and hand over the tablets. As Alikisa walked away, Nsuuta would call with authority, 'And even when your child seems to be getting better, don't stop. Keep giving her the medicine until she has finished the *fuulu doozi*.'

'Yes, Musawo. Thank you, Musawo.'

'And don't go sharing that medicine with your neighbours who have sick children just because *Eh, Musawo gave me a lot of tablets, eh, why walk all the long way to hospital when we can share?*' At that point the girls would collapse into laughter, forgetting they were a professional Indian nurse and a stupid backward Ganda mother.

For a long time, the girls synchronised their play of mothers and nurses so well that they did not notice the difference in their aspirations. And because Nsuuta had not expected to stay long in school, she never brought up her nursing dreams. But now, in primary five, with one year to go, the idea of becoming a nurse had become a possibility.

When she told Alikisa about it though, Alikisa was perplexed. 'Study nursing? And do what with nursing?'

'Can you imagine wearing that uniform? We would be smart, working in the city; we would be high up there.'

'High up where? You are already high up there. Your father is a Muluka, your grandfather is a Ssaza, what more height do you want?'

'But those are not my heights. You don't understand; if your father is something it does not mean you are too. Besides, this time we will be high up there together, me and you. We will heal people, everyone crying for our help – *Musawo, I don't understand my health, check me* – and we will feel important.' Now Nsuuta whispered, 'We will make grown-ups lift their tunics, showing us their buttocks, and we will prick them.'

'And what if it is your father's buttocks?'

'Then you ask someone else to prick him.'

'And listen to all that pain that goes on in hospitals – children burnt by porridge, men with broken legs, women giving birth, people dying and their relatives howling – because of a nursing cap and peeking at buttocks?'

'But we shall get away from here, see the world, heal the sick, and people will give us respect. Can you imagine travelling in the mobile clinic every day to some new place? Everyone will know us. They will tell our parents, *Eh, I know your daughter – she is nursing people's health very well.*'

'And when do we get married? We shall soon become leftovers.'

'I don't mind being a leftover nurse in Mmengo or Entebbe.'

Alikisa did not take this seriously because Nsuuta was still around. As long as she was around, she would come up with a way.

7

1940 was knocking on the door, but most Ugandans were unaware. Somnolent villages in far-flung regions, many miles from the capital, were yet to give this European idea of time more space to control their lives. Most were oblivious to the European markers of time anyway. Those who were aware thought that if they ignored the European calendar, it would go away. In schools, children were taught to forget the equal times of day and night in their reality and imagine the improbable notion of day starting at midnight. The children laughed. It was impossible to ignore the consistent rhythms of day and night around them. They were also taught about the equator, a natural line that passed through Uganda. 'Yes, it passes through Masaka,' the master said, 'but no, you cannot see it.' In school exams Nsuuta and Alikisa told the time as they were taught, but at home the day still started with dawn and night with dusk.

However, the Ganda week had been disrupted. The British had reduced the weekend from three days to two, forcing people selling cash crops and pupils going to school to wake up early on Balaza, which they now called Monday. For a while, children born on Balaza were named Mande to mark the disruption. When a person wished for the impossible, people would encourage them: *Don't lose hope. With these Europeans coming to our world now, the sun could rise at midnight.* Ganda months, which had been transient, coming and going depending on the moods of the seasons, were being replaced by the static European calendar. There was no waiting for the moon or the season to come any more. Months could no longer be late or early, brief or outstay their welcome.

But not everyone decried this disruption of Ganda time. Rich people became even more powerful. They were the ones who could afford to buy time and fasten it on their wrists after the British took the natural clock out of the sky and chopped the day into twenty-four segments. Children were now seen running up and down the road to go to the rich and ask for the time. Even when the Ganda eventually accepted the hour as a marker of time, they counted from one hour with daybreak and started again when night fell. Twelve hours of day, twelve hours of night. However, the Ganda totally rejected the idea of 'keeping time'. They carried on with their lives as if there was no hour, no minute. After all, the world would be around the following day.

The girls had finished primary school. Nsuuta's letter of admission to Gayaza High was in the hands of the Muluka. Alikisa was in limbo. She had had enough of studying. Her breasts had settled on her chest and her mother fretted, 'Stop playing with time, Alikisa. Time hates women.' Sometimes, when she allowed herself, Alikisa regretted the pact. She knew she would sooner make the river Kiyira flow backwards than marry the rich, handsome husband who Nsuuta could return to when she finished at Gayaza. Everything seemed in jeopardy when Miiro, Luutu's second son, stated his intentions towards Nsuuta. Alikisa's hopes rose. Nsuuta would not go to Gayaza High if Miiro proposed. Now Alikisa would marry the next catechist to come along and then plan when to run away from him.

Miiro did not ask his father to approach Nsuuta's father like normal people. He approached Nsuuta himself. People who were getting European education in the city often came home with mad ideas, just to be contrary – still, this was wild contrariness. Yet there was something about Miiro talking to Nsuuta himself that both girls liked. It put Nsuuta in control of their future rather than some old aunt.

It was after service at church. The girls were outside enjoying the cool air on the hilltop. Alikisa's parents were talking to parishioners when Nsuuta felt someone poke her arm. She turned. A boy pointed to under the mugavu tree and said, 'He wants to talk to you.'

Nsuuta frowned. Miiro, dressed in a white shirt and long white trousers, leaned against the tree. He waved.

'But only you,' the boy said.

Nsuuta stared wide-eyed at Alikisa.

The boy insisted, 'He told me not to leave until you go.'

'Aahh.' Alikisa clapped dramatically. 'I am not surprised.' But her smile said she was shocked. She was as excited as if Miiro had asked to see her.

Nsuuta hesitated, overcome by self-consciousness.

'Go, go.' Alikisa shoved her. 'Go get us a man.'

As she walked towards Miiro, Nsuuta tried to conceal her self-consciousness. She looked back; Alikisa was awash with anticipation. But as she approached Miiro, Nsuuta became alert to the fact that she was doing the walking. Miiro, who wanted to talk, should have come over to see her. *Does a monkey summon the forest?* she asked herself. *This is how he starts to rule you from the beginning.* By the time she reached the mugavu where Miiro stood, she wore a severe face. 'You are calling me?'

He smiled at her direct manner. Yes, he sent the boy because it would look wrong if he walked up to her and said he wanted to talk.

'Oh.'

He asked about her people. Then he explained that he had been watching her for some time now and was satisfied that she was a good girl. He had also heard that she worked hard in school to better herself.

'Can I talk to you?'

'You *are* talking to me.'

'Not like this.'

'Like how?'

'You know what I mean.'

Silence.

'I have been thinking about you. Very seriously. I think you are the girl I deserve. I would like to know you better.' He paused and looked at her. 'Would you like to know me and see if we can…maybe start a love on which to build a home?'

Nsuuta raised her eyebrows but Miiro continued, 'I did not ask my father to talk to your father because I want us to make our own decision. I don't want to take home a stranger and then later discover this or that. Not so?'

'Okay.' Nsuuta tried to maintain a severe face, one that said she was not the kind of girl who was easily won over even by common-sense words.

'How have you heard my words?'

'I have heard them.'

'Are they good? Will you think about them?'

'I will think about them,' she said. She walked away, but her legs were not fast enough. When she got to Alikisa she clapped, 'Ha,' and rolled her eyes. 'He says I have devoured his heart, ha!' She threw back her head. 'Tells me I should think about it, ha! "See if we can build a love," ha!'

'Oh, this is it.' Alikisa was animated. 'Oh, he is the one, I swear; the very one. Miiro is the man I want for you.'

Nsuuta was still breathless from the shock of it.

'He is more than I had dreamt of for you, Nsuuta. You will marry into wealth just. From privilege to privilege. Do you know Miiro's baptism name is Toofa? Kristoofa? Next time you see him, say *Aallo Toofa*, in English. And he should reply *Aallo Bibiyana*. Oh,' Alikisa gasped. 'Ask for a European wedding – kadaali crown, church, choir singing as you walk in swaying, ring and everything. Luutu will do it.'

For a while, the girls celebrated their luck. Then Nsuuta remembered. 'Alikisa, what about the pact?'

'What about it?'

'It is Luutu's son; the *I am so civilised I marry only one wife* Luutu. The *Where I sit my wife sits* Luutu, the *Where I go my wife goes* Luutu. How can his son sit between two wives in church?'

'But who says his son is like him? Marry him and when we have him in our hands, we will think of a new plan.'

'I am worried a bit. It may not work and then you will say I broke the pact.'

'No, I will not think that. I will run away from my...' Alikisa hesitated and whispered, 'catechist.'

However, the girls were no longer ten years old. Running away from a husband to be with Miiro would involve not only her family but Luutu's and Nsuuta's. Alikisa refused to think about the implications, or the possibility that Miiro might not have her; Nsuuta would take care of it.

Nsuuta kept quiet. She too was thinking about a childhood moment of rashness returning to kill her future.

'Don't worry.' Alikisa had confidence. 'We shall do it somehow. Which Ganda man does not want two wives?'

'Kdto, your fa—'

'Father and Luutu don't count,' Alikisa interrupted. 'Christianity killed them a long time ago.'

At first, when Nsuuta's father got wind of Miiro's interest in his daughter, he felt slighted. Typical of Luutu's family to throw away age-old ways of securing marriage and copy Europeans. It was only when Nsuuta explained that Miiro had not told his father either that he relented. However, in a county meeting of Miluka chiefs which Luutu attended as a British representative, Nsuuta's father remarked casually, 'Have you heard about the children?'

'Kdto, don't mention it. Apparently, they do not want us meddling.'

'I said to myself, "Fine, let's see how far you will go without us."'

'Children are children; today they like this one, tomorrow they are not sure.'

'Exactly what I thought.'

Nsuuta's father walked away, satisfied that he had not looked desperate, while Luutu wore the confidence of a father whose son could get any girl he wished.

From that moment, right through the first three weeks of December 1939, Miiro collected Nsuuta from her home to go for walks. The couple were followed at a distance by an uncomfortable-looking aunt. Chaperoning a niece was not part of her traditional role and courtship walkabouts were not Ganda tradition. However, Nsuuta had been indulged since the aunt would make Miiro pay for her inconvenience. She expected nothing less than that new fashion, a boodingi, and might even ask for a goat. Nsuuta's mother, fretting as if she was already mother of the bride, would tell her to get ready earlier. Miiro would arrive dressed in white and lead Nsuuta away. Everyone smiled upon them the way people smile at young love. Youths marvelled at the novel courtship. Girls envied Nsuuta openly, the way they had coveted her beauty all along. 'Maama, this is a new phenomenon,' they marvelled, because this new kind of courtship ushered in by Miiro and Nsuuta was the future. Old folks, sensing that the young were moving in to elbow them out of the marriage-securing processes, snorted, 'What if Miiro changes his mind after parading her so publicly? Will Nsuuta not be stigmatised as a cursed bride? Will she not lose value? The early processes of finding a spouse are discreet for a reason.' But rash residents were already rubbing their hands together. A wedding between the Muluka and Luutu houses meant feasting for days. They would try to outdo each other on the pre-wedding celebrations.

Everyone saw Miiro – hands held behind his back as they walked down the road, a polite distance between him and Nsuuta, smiling at her like a flower just bloomed. The villages marvelled: 'Maama, don't they match just – she beautiful and he handsome, she light-skinned, he dark-skinned? Kiyitirivu, she will bring the much-needed light skin to the children... Are they not the perfect age – he much much older, she just ripe?' And the way Nsuuta bloomed under Miiro's gaze, the way she was shy but proud. When the two walked down that rutted track between the villages, clearly dying of love, people agreed that Nsuuta and Miiro were inevitable: 'You cannot suppress love: look how it hauled Miiro to Kamuli despite all the city women.' Young girls daydreamed.

*

On that first walk, Miiro started with, 'I hope your family is well.'

'They are.'

'I guess by now everyone from Kamuli to Nazigo knows you have eaten my heart.'

'Nazigo? Say Bukolooto. You know how words travel.'

'How do your parents feel about it?'

'They have allowed me to walk with you.'

'I can see. I am happy they understand.'

Silence.

'You know I am studying farming.'

'Yes, but I did not know you need to go to school for that.'

Miiro laughed, because a lot of people said that. 'We study modern farming, where you make decisions according to the type of crops you want and the type of soil on your land. I am not talking about swampy, gravelly or poor soils. It is more complicated than that. It is science. We also study how to use pesticides and weedkillers instead of manual labour. They teach us how to use a very small piece of land for maximum yield.'

'Oh.'

'Do you think we should farm both cash crops and animals? My father's ranch is katogo – this, that and everything. Whatever he sees he brings to the farm, but I think it is best to specialise.'

'What does your heart say?'

'Coffee and cotton for cash crops. Then exotic cattle, and chickens for eggs.'

'I agree, best to start small.'

'I am going to borrow money from the growers' cooperative. There is one in Mukono. My father will be my guarantor. If more farmers start to do modern farming in these villages, we should start our own growers' cooperative. It gives farmers more powers. You borrow money, improve your farm and pay back slowly.' He paused. 'I was thinking, if we agree to come together, we should not build our house close to my parents.'

'Yes, let's go further away.'

Miiro frowned. 'But you are agreeing with everything I say. I heard you were talkative, that you knew your own mind.'

Nsuuta grinned. Even a chatterbox would be tongue-tied during walkabouts with Miiro, who was much older and more knowledgeable. 'It is because I am not used to you.'

'I am a bit quiet.' Miiro said, 'I would like to marry someone talkative. So our house does not fill with silence.'

'I will talk.'

'Then next time, I shall take you to see the land where we could build our house.'

One day on one of their walkabouts, because she had been encouraged to speak her mind, Nsuuta asked, 'Would you marry a second wife?'

Miiro stopped, then laughed. He glanced back at Nsuuta's aunt, who had stopped too. 'No, of course not. We Christians don't do that.' He was even indignant that Nsuuta, whose father had three wives, whose grandfather's harem was biblical, would ask him that.

'Even when Luutu is no longer with us?'

'Let me tell you about us men. We only marry a second wife when the first one is struggling, when she is good at this but hopeless at that. But look at you, what could a second wife bring to our marriage?'

'Hmm.'

Miiro misunderstood Nsuuta's 'hmm' and stopped walking again. 'You don't believe me?'

'I do, I am not worried about it.' Nsuuta glanced at her aunt. 'I am just thinking that…what if I became a nurse?'

Miiro frowned. He had not made the connection between him getting a second wife and Nsuuta becoming a nurse.

'Why would you do that?'

'I got the scholarship to Gayaza.'

'But girls go to Gayaza to become homemakers. You already have a marriage proposal.'

'I would like to become a nurse.'

'For that you will have to do more studying after Gayaza.'

'I know. But what if I said I would like to do more studying like you and become a nurse for myself and then return and open a dispensary at the parish? On top of the mobile clinic, the villages will have a resident nurse.'

'Then when will we marry, hmm? When will you have our children? Time is edging past you. You women are not like us men. We can have children even after our brains are mouldy with age, but not women. Let's say you become a nurse and we marry, then who will look after our home and children while you work? Only Europeans and Indians use servants to bring up their children. Look, you have never stepped outside these villages, but let me tell you: there is a reason why most Ganda nurses are men. When women go out in public to work, stupid men imagine that it is because they have failed to secure a marriage, and they make passes at them as they please.' Now he pleaded. 'Nsuuta, you are beautiful. You deserve a man to look after you while you preside over your home. You deserve to be given the respect of a married woman. Besides, only ugly girls carry on to become nurses and teachers.'

Nsuuta sighed. She did not doubt what Miiro had said. She had been told over and over that with her beauty, she did not need education. Education was for ugly girls – to give them value. Further studies were also a shield to hide behind. You said to a girl, *But you, what are you waiting for? Time is going*, and she replied, *I am still studying*, kumbe wapi, it is because she cannot find a man.

Because December was coming to an end, the walkabouts were interrupted by Ssekukkulu, the Christian day when Luutu made a feast for all the villages and then another one, Lusooka, to mark the beginning of the European year. The residents knew that Luutu made feasts on these days to impose the Christian calendar, but they made merry with him and then promptly forgot about the European year afterwards. Miiro planned that after New Year's Day, their parents would take over the marriage processes. Discussions between their families would start while he was at college. However, the ritual – kukyala, the first secret visit to Nsuuta's aunt to request her to inform Nsuuta's parents that Luutu's family wished to unite with their families through marriage – would be done in April during his holidays. And if they liked the message, Nsuuta's family would research Miiro's ancestry. Hopefully no problem would arise, and they would give Luutu's family a date to come to kwajula. Meanwhile Nsuuta would start her kufumbirwa, learning about marriage, being groomed. The kwanjula – when Miiro, his brothers and cousins would take presents to her family and ask officially to marry her – would be done in August when Miiro was home. The church wedding would be in December. Thus, when they parted before Ssekukkulu, Nsuuta promised to have her answer when they met in the New Year.

8

While the villages were oblivious to European time, Nsuuta watched 1940 arrive. Right away, it was an impatient year. The day to go to Gayaza High was coming at full speed. And Miiro needed an answer to get the marriage rites rolling. Nsuuta looked at the two options facing her, Gayaza High School and marrying Miiro, and wished she could split herself into two and have both. There was no doubt Miiro was the man for her. So much older, but not too old, he was the perfect age, since women were rendered threadbare after child-birth. She even saw a happy marriage with him. He was the kind of man who came by once in a girl's lifetime. But Gayaza was also a once-in-a-lifetime opportunity. Secretly, she suspected there would be more men like Miiro out in the city. You never know what her beauty plus education would fetch in the big wide world. Besides, in the city, she felt that she would not be bound by the pact. But as things stood, she did not see room for Alikisa in this marriage with Miiro.

The solution occurred to her one night. The following day, she hurried to Alikisa and told her, 'I am going to pass Miiro on: it is up to you to grab him.'

'Why would you pass him on? And how do I grab him?'

'He said he would not marry two wives.'

'But you cannot, Nsuuta; do you see how he is dying to have you?'

'Yes. That is why I am passing him on. I know he will always love me no matter what.'

'Then let us be patient. Marry him and enjoy it while it lasts. No matter how much a man loves you in the beginning, it grows old. I have heard women discussing it in the Mother's Union. He will get used to you and when he does, he will marry me.'

'By then you will already be married.'

'I have talked to my father; I am going to do midwifery. You don't need secondary education to do midwifery. You marry Miiro now. By the time I finish studying in two years and come back, I will be a city girl, full of airs and English, and Miiro will be attracted.'

'Yii, Alikisa.' Nsuuta was perturbed. 'I am the one who chose nursing. You chose marriage. You hate hospitals. If I pass Miiro over, he might come to you. Look around these villages; which other girl is educated enough for him? But if I marry him first, you will not have a chance, even with nursing plus English. But if Miiro marries you first, I can wiggle myself into your marriage.'

Alikisa kept quiet. Nsuuta had just told her that even with the added value of education, Miiro would never find her attractive. She kept quite still for a while. Then she exploded. 'What if you come back after he has married me and he does not want you because you are overeducated and old?'

'Then I have lost him,' Nsuuta said flatly. 'But I am not getting married yet.'

Alikisa realised then that Nsuuta was determined to go to Gayaza no matter what. But instead of saying so, she was pretending that she was giving up Miiro for her, because of their pact. She did not know how to counter this. Instead she said, 'Forgive me for saying this, Nsuuta. But you know that too much reading is killing your eyes. You said yourself that sometimes you don't see properly when you look in your books.'

'It is not the reading which causes that.'

'What will you do when the shadows in your sight come back, or words on the blackboard disappear, and I am not there to read them for you?'

'That happened a long time ago. I will read less.'

'Read less in Gayaza?' Alikisa snorted. 'I guess you would speak less Lungeleza in Bungeleza.'

When Nsuuta told Miiro that she had decided to explore studying at Gayaza High first, he was dumbfounded. He did not understand why she had not said so from the start and had instead led him on while he made a fool of himself across the villages. He decided Nsuuta was playing hard to get.

'Nsuuta, don't make me beg just because you are beautiful and it makes you feel big. There are girls who would marry me before I even asked.'

'Go on then, pick one of them. After all, you can pick good women off a tree like guavas.'

'I did not say that.'

'But if you are still studying to be a farmer, why should I not study to be a nurse?'

'Because you are the woman; you don't need more education. I do. Because a home does not need both husband and wife to work.'

'But your sister Nsangi, who is older than me, is still at Gayaza.'

'Am I asking my sister to marry me?'

'Then you have refused to understand.' Nsuuta stormed off.

The aunt was stunned. But instead of hurrying after her niece, she rushed to Miiro. 'What is happening, son? I thought everything was moving very well.'

'Ask your niece. I asked for her final decision and she gave me Gayaza.'

'Gayaza? Gayaza nabaki? Leave her to me.' She made to hurry after Nsuuta, then stopped and laughed nervously. 'She is only joking; don't you know girls? They do that to test your love.'

Nsuuta told her father that it was not that she did not want to get married – 'I would like to put marriage on hold and go into nursing. When I finish, I will be able to help people in this region. That is also good.' Her father was disappointed, but times were changing.

A daughter studying at Gayaza, maybe even going on to become a nurse, was becoming as prestigious as having a daughter married into money. Besides, all that cleverness, all the learning Nsuuta had acquired, going to waste in Miiro's kitchen while his sister was still at Gayaza, was not fair. Three of the boys Nsuuta used to help in class were about to join Mmengo High. Moreover, with Nsuuta's beauty, there would always be a man dying to marry her. The Muluka indulged his daughter once again.

But not her mother. When she found out, Nsuuta's mother let off an ear-shattering cry. 'Nfudde nze! What is this you have done to us?' She oscillated between the ideas that someone jealous, probably a co-wife, was standing in the way of her daughter's marriage, and the possibility of Nsuuta being mad. Whichever it was it could have only been achieved by sorcery. 'How will I show my face in public again? The villages are laughing. We are thoroughly humiliated. Why are you doing this to us? Listen, child, men are scarce; rich men are rare, good rich men are a miracle. We women are as abundant as tomatoes at harvest. Most of us are beautiful and well groomed. But once on the market – groomed or not, beautiful or not – time is against us.'

'Then I will be a second or third wife.'

'Now listen to this child. Someone help me make her see sense! Why eat yesterday's matooke, hardened and tasteless, when you can have fresh and soft hot matooke every day?'

Nsuuta kept quiet. In her mind, there was a third option. She would be a mistress and a nurse. Best of both worlds.

News that Nsuuta had turned Miiro down gripped the villages. First, there was disbelief: 'It is not true; these villages are full of lies!' Then denial: 'It is Miiro who changed his mind. Which girl walks away from such a marriage proposal?' Then derision: 'She has chosen Gayaza over marriage? He heee, let me laugh, tsk. That is what comes out of educating girls. What a waste of brains!' Eventually, public opinion blamed Nsuuta's looks. 'She thinks she is too beautiful. Her parents indulged her; who did not see it? Now look what has happened. Kdto, Miiro has escaped: beautiful women make terrible wives.'

Overnight, Nsuuta became the fabled pretty but haughty girl in the folk tale whose beauty so went to her head she turned down all sensible suitors until a stranger, implausibly handsome, fantastically rich and charming to the end of the earth, came along. Even though he had come out of nowhere, the girl was determined to marry him. *He is the one*, she said. *He is what I have been waiting for.* She shrugged all caution to wait until research into the stranger's background had been done. Guess what happened? He took her far, far away. On the way, he started to change. First the legs, then the torso, and within a month he had transformed into an ogre. When they got home to the small dark cave he called home, he began to eat her, piece by piece, until only the head was left. If it had not been for her aunt, who came to check on the state of their marriage, the girl would have been fully consumed.

Everywhere in the villages, at story time, this was the story told. Little girls, especially pretty ones, were given sharp looks.

Old folks, now vindicated, were quick to boast:

'What did I tell you? Nothing good comes out of such public displays of courtship. Love is private, between two people: why show us?'

'It is kopa this kopa that – do they see Europeans copying anything from us?'

Now the late Kabaka Chwa's caution about the growing trend, especially among educated Ganda, of looking down on their culture in favour of Zungucisation, resonated in the villages. When Chwa had launched his campaign of plays, songs and poetry decrying the stupidity of looking down on one's culture, young and rural villages like Nazigo, Nattetta, Bugiri and Kamuli had laughed. That caution was for immoral places like Entebbe and Kampala, which had no anchor in culture. But lo and behold, Zungucisation was spreading from Luutu's house into the villages. Luckily, by the time the rumour intensified, Nsuuta had started at Gayaza High and Miiro was back at Bukalasa.

9

Gayaza High School
P.O. Box 7029
Kampala
31st Janwari 1940

Dear Alikisa,

How are you? Me, I am fine. I have been here two weeks trying to get used. This Gayaza High is so strange I don't even know. There are all sorts of girls from all kinds of tribes you have never heard of. But firstly, tell me, how are the villages blazing with gossip about me? I even fear to come home for holidays.

Alikisa, I have never known such hunger. They give us such small portions of food we are all starving. You go to bed hungry. Girls say they want to skinny us. But how can they when we are sticks already? Apparently, in the beginning, girls used to sneak to a woman who sells cassava, but now she comes to the fence. For just one waafu she gives you so much. We sit in the dark and feast. I said, yii, this cassava we feed to the pigs at home is now the best food in the world? Then in the morning, they make us run around the field and skip rope to make us wiry and ropy – ayi. Girls complain, Who will marry us? Who has ever heard of running around in the morning? Girls say we shall get used but I doubt. I have never known this amount of hunger. My stomach has caved in.

We cannot leave the school compound unless accompanied by Metu. Metu is the matron, an old turkey who acts like our mother. Think of the worst gossip among our servants. Now give her power over us. That is Metu. We are herded like cattle, fencing around the school and a gate like on a kraal. There is only one entrance to the school. The guard writes down the names of those entering and leaving. Just the other day I went for a walk, just to see the area, but they stopped me at the gate and a teacher was called. I said, for taking a little walk? But they said I was escaping. You don't know Europeans; they take simple issues seriously and serious issues simply. They don't understand us, we don't understand them, let us agree on that. We go to bed by sunset. No lights in the dorm because girls would write bad letters to boys. If you are slow to wake up in the morning, you are locked in. No breakfast. You must wait until a teacher comes to punish you. Every little thing, punish, punish, punish. But I tell you, girls in this school are so proud.

This is a whisper, Alikisa, please guard it. Some nights I don't sleep well because of Miiro. My heart beats at me – *You gave up Miiro for this hunger?* And I have nothing to say because I also want nursing. I tell my heart *Keep quiet, it is too late*. Did you see him before he left? Was he still angry? Sometimes I feel shame. Sometimes I want to write to his college but then I say, tsk, you have caused enough pain.

I am going to stop here because the bell for supper is about to go and the paper has run out and I have only one sheet. Oh, the teachers call me by my Bibiyana name, Vivian, your Lozi is Rose. So I sign off with,

Yours starvingly,
Vivian Balungi Nsuuta.

Gayaza High School
P.O. Box 7029
Kampala
24th Febwari 1940

Dear Alixa,

How come you have not replied me? Maybe the letter got lost in the Posta. I wrote two letters, one to Mmengo Hospital and one to the parish. I think if you had joined the midwifery you would have written to me by now. I believe you are still in Nattetta.

You remember when we learnt how to make envelopes in class? Go to the para tree, get its sap for gum to make envelopes. Give the letters to the people travelling from the parish to Mukono or to Kampala. They just have to take the letter to Posta with a waafu. Did you see how I wrote your name? That is how you make it exotic. I am studying a lot of subjects: Home Nursing, Dome (that is what we call Domestic Science), Dressmaking, English and Maths, Geography and Agriculture. So many tests – intelligence test, oral English, written English, arithmetic, eh.

What do I tell you? Nsangi walks past me without a glance. At first, I thought it was because of Miiro, but then I realised she only talks to girls from high families: princesses, Kakungulu's daughters, Kulubya's, Zikusooka and Sir Apollo's granddaughters. Girls here thought she also grew up in Entebbe or in Kampala, but I told them she comes from deep, deep Bugerere, where fowls scratch in reverse. I told them I turned down her brother's proposal.

We have two orphan babies. I am not lying. Real breathing human babies, donated to the school by Ssanyu Babies' Home, to learn how to look after babies – winding and bathing them, tying nappies, and diet. I said, but these Europeans know how to waste time. Who taught our mothers how to bring up children? Let me stop here about mad Gayaza for now. I will not write another letter until you reply me.

Yours studyingly,
Nsuuta.

Nsuuta Bannange,

You wrote. A whole letter. And as I got used to the first one another one arrived. You should have seen me. People said, *Eh Alikisa, we did not know you had happiness.* I read the letters again and again. Then I took them to my class to teach letter posting. We cut and glued envelopes. I showed my class where to put the stamp, the address. I showed them the date you wrote, the date on the stamp and the date they arrived. Now look at me telling you about my class, before explaining.

Don't ask what is happening. Ask what is not happening; it will be easier to write that. First, Father cancelled my midwifery. He said, *Stay here and help us with teaching at the school.* He said I don't need training to teach elementary. Now I walk in class and the children stand up to say, *Good morning, Mistress Nnanono,* and I say, *Good morning, class, sit down,* in English.

Nsuuta, Luutu has changed towards me. When he sees me, he stops and greets me with respect. He calls me *Old Woman.* If he was not a good Christian, I would have had bad thoughts. His wife is the same. Mother is very proud to be friends with high people. She is always smiling at me as if overnight I became beautiful. Then two weeks ago, Luutu bought me two sheets of cloth shining like *mya.* I said to myself, why would Luutu buy me cloth? But I kept quiet because Father and Mother were very happy. We were still admiring the garments when he came for them and sent them to Kampala to make me a gomesi, like your Gayaza boodingi uniform. That was when I realised Luutu is beautifying me for Miiro. Don't you see? What else could it be? I think he and his wife have decided who Miiro will marry. It cannot be Dewo – Catholic priests don't marry. It cannot be Levi; he is just 4 years older than me. Finally, I asked Mother what was going on; she said she did not know but the happiness on her face was of one roasting plantains. If it is true, our dream may come true. The only problem is that it is Luutu pushing it, not Miiro. Miiro might come home and say no. But how lucky will I be if it is true? I am trying to be pleasant, I smile a lot. The good thing is that Luutu has control of Miiro. When he told Miiro to give up going to Buddo for his farming studies, he did not argue. If we marry, I want to reassure you that I will be true to our pact. I am only keeping your place warm. So, forget Alixa, it might be Muka Miiro one day. I am sure these are the news you want to hear. I will write more as soon as things happen.

Me, your very own,

Alikisa ~~Lozi~~ Rose Nnanono.

Eh, I had forgotten, I am sorry you are so hungry. Next time take some roasted groundnuts, roast dry maize and coffee beans to chew on when you are hungry.

Dear Nsuuta,

I hope your studies are fine. Did you get my letter? I wrote it in the middle of last month. I know letters take a long time in the Posta, but I could not wait.

Let me say I have never met anyone cleverer than you. You said it would happen, but I did not believe you. I thought you had made a mistake, but maama, you were right. It looks like Luutu prevailed. Miiro came to visit two weeks ago after Paska, on Easter Monday. We cooked for his family. Mother was all over the place with happiness. He smiled a bit and my heart spread out. But Luutu is not allowing us to do walkabouts. It is all very secret. Afterwards his family went home but Miiro was told to stay and talk to me.

My parents left us to talk to each other in the living room, but Miiro was very quiet. He asked how teaching was going; I said, fine. He asked if I had heard from you. I lied, no. He said, *How will your friend feel about you and me together?* I said Nsuuta chose Gayaza: maybe she will not mind. Then he left. I think he likes me a little but not very much like you. Mother says if a man likes you then it is a good sign. Love comes later. He visited three times before he went back to study, but we did not have much to say. He did not stay very long. Wait till the villages find out; words will fly. He went back to Bukalasa yesterday, but I am shaking inside.

What do I tell you? Our friend Nnaaba married Diba, sickly Diba. The wedding was in Maachi. You should have seen the groom. Like a mosquito. He looked about to drop dead. But Nnaaba was proud. I think she married for marriage's sake. Serves her right. Remember how she laughed at us for staying long in school? Now she is the one who has married a small man.

Can you believe Luutu told my father that girls come out of Gayaza half-European? Apparently, Miiro should not marry a too-educated wife – they make hopeless wives for farmers because they cannot handle rural life. In my heart I thought, that means Nsangi will marry a chief. Then I realised that is why Father refused me to do midwifery. Oh, the drum for after-lunch lessons has sounded. I have to prepare tomorrow's classes.

It is me, your sister forever,

Alikisa Rose Nnanono.

Dear Alikisa,

How you have given me the best news. You don't know what your letter has done to me. I thought I had lost him, but this gives me hope. I will sleep well. Just make sure you don't lose him. The villages don't know you are being prepared for Miiro because when I came for holidays no one talked about it.

We did not even see each other. Yii bannange. I spent most of the time in the house. I dared not show my face, especially in church. Those who came to the house told me that people assumed I have Gayaza airs and don't want to associate with villagers any more. I said, yii, but what about the things they have been saying about me? Mother was dying of heartache. When I returned home, she could not even look at me. She was not even proud of my white boodingi uniform. I slept in Maama Muto's house. When Father found out, he told me to sleep in his house. I sent you messages, but you never came. I said, yii, even Alikisa has turned against me. But now I understand the Miiro thing had started and your parents would not let you associate with me.

I am used to the school now. I like netball. I wish I could bring it to Nattetta Native. Girls here are either going to do nursing or teaching. But some want to go to Buddo for higher study and they are not ugly at all. But for me, three years here in Gayaza is enough, then I will study nursing in Mmengo and then I will be back in Nattetta treating illnesses and marrying my Miiro.

Ha, but Nnaaba has embarrassed us too much; how could she marry that little man of mosquito? She could have got a better man. Her parents must have panicked her. However, had it been one of us who had married that Diba, you would have heard Nnaaba – she would be still laughing. Now who is going to do gossip justice?

Your older sister,

Vivian Balungi Nsuuta.

Dear Nsuuta,

These news are so burning it is a surprise the paper is not on fire. I will start with the small news. Look on top right hand of this letter. We got our own P.O. Box. We are lords now. Nazigo has a Posta with boxes. Luutu got his own, your father got his own, the Ssaza got his own, the two churches and the schools each.

You will not believe this: the banns for our wedding were announced in church, I am not lying you. *Kristoofa Miiro, son of Bulasio Luutu of Nattetta, plans to marry Alikisa Lozi Nnanono, daughter of Eliyafazi Lubowa...* Ayi. The church roof almost flew off with shock. Even I was stunned. Church caught fire. Father said, *Quiet, quiet,* but people kept talking until Luutu himself stood up and raised his voice. People stared at me. No one told me they would be announced. When we stepped outside church, everyone wanted to shake my hand. People said, *At least you have common sense.* Then your mother came and called me a thief. She said, *We thought you were our friend, but now we know who you are.* My mother heard and came. She told your mother her name is not Ekyagaza Omubi for nothing. I knew my mother's name was Kyagaza, but I did not know it is the short form of a saying. Apparently, Ekyagaza Omubi means that whatever makes a plain wife beloved, the pretty ones never realise.

I do not know why the banns were rushed. Miiro has not visited my aunt yet. We have not done the introduction rites. Maybe Luutu cannot keep it a secret any more and used the church to make the announcement. I hope they are not rushing Miiro. Meanwhile Luutu, his wife, Father and Mother are planning the introduction rites for Agusto and the wedding for Desemba. Me, all I do is go to school and teach.

Lastly, Luutu bought a car. Maama nyabo, it glows like embers. The first day he drove it to church, all villages came out to see: the church was overflowing. Father said it was a sign God was blessing the parish. The only problem now is Nsangi's pride – how can I avoid her when I am marrying her brother?

Now let me greet you in English. *How are you smoking the atmospheric pressure over there at Gayaza? Our Nattetta is still the same. Hunters are hunting. Farmers are farming. Father is preaching. Muka Luutu is retiring from leading the Mothers' Union. Mother is taking over. Father is studying to become a reverend. I am to become Muka Miiro very soon. How do you like my English?*

Me, your very sister and bride-to-be,

Alikisa.

Oh, I had forgotten, Diba made Nnaaba pregnant. People asked how he did not collapse dead on top of her. Even my father said, *Aha, but man is only skinny across the river; but let him close.* Maybe he saves all his energy for the night.

This is real goodbye now.

Yii Alikisa,

Do you realise I cannot come to your marriage rites? When we planned it I did not realise how things would happen. It is good that Miiro likes you. Ignore my mother, she loves wealth too much. Luutu's car must be killing her. I wish I could tell her you are only keeping Miiro for me, but she would not understand.

You will not believe this. My eyes need galibindi. That is why I had problems all along. The teachers insisted I should not read with my finger. Sit up straight, Vivian, they would say. I gave up reading aloud in class, tears were falling, my eyes could not follow the line from margin to margin without a finger to guide them. Finally, Miss Corby took me to Mmengo Hospital.

You should have seen the nurses – smart, clever and efficient. Some were white, some Indian, some Baganda. I said I was right, this is where I belong. Let me experience this nursing before I bury myself in marriage. Then the eye doctor checked my eyes. He told me I needed to wear galibindi. I almost danced, but he looked grave and there was sorrow in Miss Corby's eyes. Unfortunately, he sent me back to school without them. First, they measure your eyes, then they cut the glasses according to your measurements. Now I am waiting. Next time you see me I will look clever just. Oh, I forgot; how are the preparations for your marriage rites? We have Posta? We are on the world map. Next letter tell me my father's P.O. Box so I can surprise him with a letter. Luutu bought a car? Ha. But you are marrying rich, Alikisa. Take care of my Miiro for me.

Your older sister,
     Nsuuta.

Dear Alikisa,

I am sure you have not received my last letter, but I cannot wait. My galibindi are on my eyes right now. The world is beautiful like you have never seen. When I started to see properly, I marvelled and marvelled.

It was hard at first. I thought I was going mad because the world seemed to fall on me. When I walked, I lifted my feet too high. Sometimes my feet touched the ground too soon. Objects seemed far but when I reached for them they were close. I felt veins in my eyes stretching. But when I talked to the other girls who wear galibindi, they said that they felt the same when they first got theirs, that I should be patient. Two days later I woke up and wore them and the world transformed. Girls say I am proud to wear galibindi, but I was just ogling the world. Outlines of objects became sharp. Edges so sharp they could cut. Alikisa, you have never seen such clarity. The only problem is that when I take the galibindi off, the world seems worse than it was before. I am worried that the galibindi are killing my natural sight.

Look at me talking about myself. How are you? Tell me everything happening with my Miiro. Alikisa, I am telling you as my sister, so don't take it badly. Sometimes I hear what is happening between you and Miiro and I regret a bit. But then I say to myself, how can you think like that? Alikisa is your younger sister. Trust her. And I trust you.

Your older sister,

      Nsuuta.

Dear Alikisa,

I could not wait until I go back to Gayaza to write this letter because anger is killing me. I am writing this letter right here in my father's house. Since I cannot talk to you directly, I will use this paper.

I cannot believe what happened today. Did your mother think I was attacking you? The way she pulled you away from me. I stood there looking like a jealous woman when all I wanted was to talk to you. For the first time, I wanted to shout to the whole church that I passed Miiro on and I can take him back if I want. I expected you to say something, but you just kept quiet. Truth is bitter, but I wonder whether we are still friends, let alone sisters.

Nnaaba walked home with me from church dripping with concern because you stole my man. Eh, how are you holding out? she said as if I was dying of heartbreak. Bannange, these friends we call our sisters. Who would have known that plain Alikisa would uproot you? I said, Alikisa did not uproot me, I walked away from Miiro, but she would not believe me, especially when everyone now thinks I was trying to attack you today. I think we should protect each other. When people talk about me badly, you should tell them I don't hate you. I did not foresee that we would have to hate each other in public. Had I known, I would have married Miiro myself.

Now let me put anger aside; I saw how everyone looks at you with envy. Now people say you are beautiful. Maama, you looked so good in your gomesi. Like you are already married. Then I saw Miiro coming out of the church and I ran. Did you like my galibindi?

Eh, you have not told me about the introduction rites. I hear Miiro brought a lot of presents even though your father did not ask for dowry. My mother is still gnawing herself with envy. She counted to me the presents Miiro brought for your family as if she was there. I said, Mother, Luutu was showing off to make you jealous, but she said it worked. Alikisa, I am ashamed my mother did not come to your rituals. That she did not join your family in preparations. I said, Mother, try and hide your jealousy, but she said it was too much to hide. Apologise to your mother for me.

But how were the rituals for you? Why are you not writing to tell me? What is going on? Please write soon. I feel left out. Now let me stop here. I am waiting for your next letter.

Yours waitingly,

      Nsuuta.

Nattetta Parish
P.O. Box 004
Nazigo
Bugerere
2nd Febwari 1941

Dear Nsuuta,

Forgive me for not writing since last year. You must think I am a bad sister, but I am telling you, too much was going on, I could not steal a moment away to write. However, things have settled down now.

After the introduction rites, everything ran too fast. Firstly, I stopped teaching. Then my parents sent me to Timiina to be prepared to be a bride, also so people in the villages do not see me for a while. Otherwise, I would not make a surprising bride on the wedding day. In Timiina, they have never heard of Posta.

That time when my mother pulled me away from you, I had not seen you coming. I was not even aware you had come to church. When she pulled me, I jumped. After that, things went from bad to worse. I think it was because your mother had said those horrible things. Mother presumed you would be worse.

That woman Nnaaba is a chameleon. She said to me, *Beauty does not a marriage make*, meaning you. And then she comes to you saying I stole Miiro? I agree we should stop listening to what people say and listen to ourselves only.

About the introduction rites, yes, Luutu's family brought a lot of presents. They came in their car like lords. But me, I was not seeing, I was not feeling, I was not even smelling in the moment. I don't remember how the food tasted, all my senses were dead. I was thinking, this is too much, it is not supposed to happen to you. He is not your man, don't enjoy it too much.

Soon after the introduction rites, I went to Timiina, where they fed me, trying to put some flesh on my bones. My aunt said, *Men don't like holding skinny women: it feels like holding a little girl*. Women taught me about marriage. They gave me presents for my home – mats, baskets, knives, cloth, pans, plates.

Ha, my aunt taught me how to kuloola. On the wedding day, I had to kill the glare in my eyes like I had just woken up to look sexy. My aunt said, *Alikisa, there is too much glare in your eyes: kill it*. Men don't like it. Apparently, it is like looking in the eyes of a fellow man. So I killed it. At the wedding, she kept narrowing her eyes and I would make bedroom eyes. She said that when Miiro comes to me in the night I should look at him like that. You know me, I have no patience with such pretences, but I said, if I don't do these things and we lose our Miiro, Nsuuta will not forgive me.

Can you imagine I had to decide whether to be a weeping bride or not? Women said I was an eager bride because there were no tears in my eyes. Some women were threatening to pinch me, so I cried a bit. Thankfully someone said that only girls who have been bleeding for one or two years cry on their wedding day. I was too old. But then my aunt took me to my bedroom and showed me my bed. They had broken it and pulled the stands out of the floor. She told me they were going to use it for firewood in case I imagined running away from marriage and going back home. Father then told me I now belonged to Miiro and his family, including my dead body when I die. That was when I remembered the real truth about marriage and cried. All the worry about not marrying, then the beautiful rituals can mask the truth and you forget that you are crossing into another clan, into another world and you don't own yourself. And then Luutu's car came to take me to Jinja where the Indian would dress me in European 'bridal sweet' and I felt pride to wear kadaali.

My pre-wedding was held in Timiina because most people in Nazigo, Nattetta, Bugiri and Kamuli would go to Miiro's anyway. My father wanted his people to have a celebration of their own in our home village where we come from. Then two weeks before the wedding, my father's clan, my mother's clan, trekked to Nattetta. You can imagine their backwardness when they saw Luutu's car. I was dying of embarrassment. They told Luutu how they have more daughters for his other sons, can you imagine?

I don't know where to start telling you about the wedding. I need a whole exercise book to write about it. So much happened on that day that sometimes I feel like I was not there. So let us put that aside. When you come home, Nattetta will tell you all about it. All I can say is that it happened, Miiro is in my hands. If you want the details, ask Nnaaba, I mean Muka Diba, she will tell you everything. Me, I was not seeing because all eyes were on me.

You know how aunts prepare you in the bridal sessions? Nothing can prepare you. Luckily, I married Miiro who I like very much, but imagine marrying someone you don't know and you have seen your moon for a year or two. By the time my aunt came to take me out of the honeymoon bedroom, it was time for Miiro to go back to Bukalasa. My aunt will stay with me while Miiro is away until I get used to being on my own. Can you imagine I miss him? Up to now people call me Mugole Miiro. But I say, how long will I be called Bride? They say, until I have a baby, then they will call me Nnakawele.

You are lucky; as I wrote this letter the picture man had finished washing our wedding pictures and brought them. I have slipped our wedding into the envelope to see for yourself. That is us on our wedding. I never dreamt it would be so good. Sometimes I pinch myself. If I, plain Alikisa, was such a beautiful bride, Nsuuta, you would look like a malaika. When I arrived at church, I saw excitement in Miiro's eyes for the first time. He said, *You look beautiful: what has Timiina been feeding you?*

Ha ha, I laughed, You are lying me, Toofa, and dimmed my eyes more.

Nsuuta, I like Miiro very much. I am very lucky to marry him, but he does not love me the way he loves you. So don't worry. However, it is going to be hard writing letters now that I am married. Already people say, *You are married; stay away from unmarried friends, they don't have useful counsel for you.* But I will write any time I steal a moment. Let me stop here now.

Me, your very own,

Muka Miiro.

Dear Nsuuta,

Did you get the letter I wrote in Febwari last year? Are you still angry with me for not writing? Forgive me, please, Nsuuta. Just forgive me. I know I did wrong.

Nsuuta, thank you for praying. I gave birth. A girl. She looks like Miiro himself. Luutu, Maama Luutu, even Nsangi, they will not put her down. Nsangi brought so many things (baby soap and powder and oil and clothes and playthings from the city) that I regretted saying nasty things about her. Apparently, having a girl first brings blessings to a marriage. Luutu named my child Yagala Akuliko – what kind of name is that for a girl? Is it an order for Miiro to love me? If so, then Luutu knows that Miiro still loves you. So hurry up and come back so our Miiro stops suffering. Nsangi cut the name to Y.A. I have insisted that she gets baptised Kotilida. If I get a boy, I will name him Kristoofa – I pray I get a boy next, so I can mix boy-girl, boy-girl until I have done all my six. You must come to church and see the baby at least. There is no way you will not see her. I could not write about being pregnant. It is private apparently: between you and your husband. What if it comes out after you have told everyone?

Nsuuta, I think Miiro has not forgiven you yet. Last time I said we should invite you to visit, he told me to stay away from you, said you are a bad influence. So I am glad you are still studying. Let us give him more time. He is finishing at Bukalasa in Desemba this year and we shall celebrate. Dewo still has another year in seminary. Then there will be another celebration. Levi is in Buddo. He is planning to be a doctor. I have married big. Of course, you shall also marry big when you join us.

Guess the new rumour about us; apparently, you caught me and Miiro being immoral. Apparently, you were so hurt you left Miiro. Then we found out I was pregnant and Luutu forced us to marry. When I had the baby, Muka Diba arrived with her rumours and asked why the baby was late. That perhaps your mother had done something evil to me. When I said that no such thing happened, she asked why our wedding was rushed. Why the secrecy? I am not going to lie, Nsuuta, these lies hurt me so deeply, especially when they saw my aunt receive a virgin goat. This time I told Miiro. He talked to Luutu and Luutu is going to call a meeting, call Muka Diba, your mother and ask them to explain when and where they saw us being immoral. Last Sunday, Father's sermon was about how rumour-mongers are like swordfish. Every fish they prick with their long mouths rots and dies. Eventually the whole church is poisoned because of swordfish mouths. Eh, listen to that: Y.A. has woken up. I must stop writing and put her on the breast. I tell you Nsuuta, this being a mother is too much. It will not even let me finish my letter to my sister who is also her mother. Let me pen off for now.

Goodbye,

Me, Muka Miiro.

10

By the time Nsuuta joined nursing in 1943, the surprising pain at Alikisa marrying Miiro had settled into acceptance. There are plans you make in life which then hurt when they actually happen. At first, pain came in Alikisa's updates. Then the huge silence when Alikisa did not write for months. At times she was sure Alikisa had coveted Miiro all along. Then she doubted Alikisa's proclamations of not owning Miiro, then Alikisa's letters became poisoned darts. The biggest pain was the wedding photo, a neat stab. But other times, childhood memories returned. The way they had loved each other. Then she reread Alikisa's letters and there were no barbs and she was reassured. Unfortunately, whenever she went home for holidays, she could not see Alikisa: their presumed enmity stood between them. Gradually, like married and unmarried friends, they drifted apart.

Alikisa was not without guilt. She had married a man she did not deserve. She had started to feel Nsuuta's resentment in the unreplied-to letters. However, when Maama Luutu called her Muka Mwana and Miiro called her Wife, when residents referred to her as Muka Miiro and she had two daughters who called her Mother, Alikisa forgot the guilt. To her the villages which expected them to feud were to blame. It did not help that when Nsuuta came home, she no longer came to church. For both of them, the less they wrote, the harder it became to put pen to paper, thought into words. Eventually, the letters ceased. Thus, when Nsuuta found out that she was losing her sight she did not rush home to cry to Alikisa. She presumed Alikisa would only say *I told you – reading too much was killing your eyes*.

Four years after her first pair of glasses, Nsuuta noticed the crispness of images starting to fade. She went to an optician and reported that her lenses were losing strength. The doctor said there was no such thing. It was her eyes; they were getting worse. He gave her stronger lenses but said it would only be a temporary respite. Nsuuta did not believe him.

In 1944, American eye missionaries came to Lubaga Hospital to treat river blindness. Nsuuta went for a second opinion. They diagnosed degenerative myopia. At that moment the first part of Nsuuta's life, that with sight, came to an end. A new one of blindness began, even though she could still see. That day she decided that the world existed only in sight. And to lose sight was to die. On her days off she spent hours with her eyes closed doing chores around her house to taste her future. Life was a house. One room was beauty: once she lost her sight, that door would close. How she had counted on her beauty. Another room was marriage: with beauty gone, she would never walk into that one. The door to nursing was still open, but it would close too. The only option was to collapse where she stood and die. Except that she had to work the following morning and not be found out.

She looked back on how she had chased the future, longing to write on a slate, to write with a pencil in a book, upper primary, scholarship to Gayaza, the nursing uniform, heal the sick, marry a rich handsome man, have two children. Now she who used to crave silence and solitude felt lonely and abandoned in her room.

From then on, decisions forced themselves on her. Like staying in the city until she had had all the fun Kampala had to offer – who was she saving her body for? Like working until she qualified for a pension.

She was haunted by memories of the first time she went home wearing the glasses. The world had been vivid then. Everyone looked through the lenses bringing objects close and back, close and back, marvelling at the way they changed. Some wore them and staggered. Some said they gave them a headache. No one knew then that galibindi were not a sign of cleverness but of loss. Supposing she had married him? She would have had one or two children by now. What would Miiro do with a blind wife? Now Alikisa could keep him.

That was the day she allowed Kakande to walk with her. Unlike other men, Kakande was not coy about Nsuuta's beauty. He sang it: 'Nsuuta, you are living proof that there is an artist in the sky.' Kakande was Yoruba. His name was Akande, but Ugandans called him Kakande. He brought her presents of food, household items, even magazines. He would knock on her door, put down a parcel, step back and say, 'Are you going to allow that meat to rot? Is it not a taboo in our cultures to waste food?' Nsuuta would accept the presents but insist she could only be with a husband. At which Akande said he understood. He was married too. In fact, had she accepted his advances he would have been disappointed. 'But, Nsuuta, who said eyes cannot feed too: mine feast on you.'

When Nsuuta told him about her eyes he asked, 'How much does the doctor need?' He forgot to be disappointed when Nsuuta allowed herself to have a relationship with him. Akande treated her as if she was the first beautiful woman to drop on earth. He took her everywhere an African could go in Kampala and Entebbe. He gave her everything she needed. Akande loved Nsuuta like a man about to lose the love of his life: 'Why did I not meet you earlier? I love my parents very much, but I will never forgive them.' But when he finished his course at Makerere, Akande put a lot of money into Nsuuta's post office account, packed his bags and went back to Nigeria. Although he had been honest with her, although he never pretended that he would be able to stay with her for long, Akande's departure hurt Nsuuta deeply. Then, out of the blue, she received a panicked letter from Alikisa.

Nattetta Parish
P.O. Box 004
Nazigo
Bugerere
10th Desemba 1944

Dear Nsuuta,

Forgive this hurried letter, especially when I have not written in a long time.

But Nsangi brought bad rumours about you to the villages. Apparently, you have become immoral, cavorting with foreigners. Apparently, they are rich and you are money minded. You spend every night in nightclubs, mu bidongo, with irresponsible people. Do you know what I did? I called Muka Diba. If you have a rumour to spread in the villages, give it to Muka Diba: she will see to it.

I said, Nnaaba, you know how Nsuuta and I are not friends any more? She said yes. I said, but my sister-in-law Nsangi lies a lot. She does not like Nsuuta because she embarrassed Miiro. I said you are not with foreigners because you are still pining for Miiro. I hope Nnaaba is spreading that one. But I think you should come home and clear your name. Oh, this is a whisper. I am with a package. Two months old. I hope this one is a boy so Miiro can have his heir. I hope I have not jinxed it by disclosing. Y.A. is a big girl. Abisaagi has started walking. They spend most of their time with their grand-parents in their car. Maama, they are spoiling the children so much I am worried. I even think Nsangi will make a good aunt for our girls when the time comes.

But, Nsuuta, I am worried. I have not gained any flesh at all. Even when I am pregnant and I eat and eat, I am still skinny. Despite all the peace Miiro has given me, despite eating well – it does not show. When I give birth, two weeks and my body is back to teenage. People say *Yii, but Muka Miiro, eat and gather a body. Men don't like dry bones.* I am worried I am naturally skinny, no matter what I do. You should see Nnaaba, I mean Muka Diba, maama she is so big she reaches those ends. As if her husband is rich. The way she walks down the road, waddling and her mosquito of a husband prouding himself, kdto. Maama, let me stop here. But please come and let us bring this rumour to a stop.

Goodbye for now,

      Me, Muka Miiro.

11

Nsuuta did not reply. To her the villages, their gossip, were now too far away to matter. So what if Miiro despised her? She was glad she had not told Alikisa about her sight problems. Look at the judgemental tone of her letter. As if being a foreigner was immoral, when actually it was the Ganda who were most immoral in Kampala and Entebbe. She put the letter away.

Three months later, as she was on the ward, she saw Luutu's car in the car park. She asked a friend to find out what was going on. The friend told her that Luutu had brought a daughter-in-law, a miscarriage. Nsuuta's first instinct was to run to Alikisa, but she stopped. Luutu would be nosy – *We have heard about the Munnaigeria. When are you bringing him home so we meet him?…What do I tell your parents when I return home?* She could already picture the gloating on his face when she said there was no wedding on the horizon with the Nigerian man. And what would she say to Alikisa about the letters she had not answered? She swapped wards with another nurse and told all nurses to say that she was on leave. Because Alikisa was to be kept in hospital for a few days, Nsuuta took two days of leave. When Alikisa was discharged she left a letter behind for Nsuuta.

Dear Nsuuta,

You will not believe where I am writing this letter. On a bed in your hospital. Don't worry, I am better. Let me start from the beginning.

How are you, how is nursing? Nsuuta, who knew your nursing and my marrying would separate us like this? I have written some letters, but I think they got lost in Posta. Please come and say hello so we are reassured. I have two daughters but, mazima, they don't even know you, their other mother.

When we arrived here, I thought I would see you, but nurses said you were on leave. I realised maybe you found a man for yourself and are planning to marry him and you go to him on leave. You city people are different from us rural folks. Are we still friends? My heart hurts that I offended you. I thought about the stupid pact as I lay here on the bed and I shook my head that being young is stupid. Why would you come back to a farmer when, with all your beauty and education, you can marry a doctor who can give you servants and drive you in a car?

Maama, I lost that pregnancy I wrote to you about. I was washing clothes when blood poured down my legs. Luutu rushed me in his car with Miiro. Maama Luutu stayed at home with Y.A. and Abi. It was a boy. I cried a bit when I was on my own because you don't cry for a pregnancy. I will not lie, losing a pregnancy leaves you very lonely and empty even with crowds around you because you are the only one who felt it inside you. Then you wonder who he was, what would he look like, but there is nothing to show for your loss.

This morning the doctor sat me and Miiro down and said I should rest my womb. He asked, *How many children do you want?* Miiro said five. I held my mouth. You and Miiro would have been perfect for each other. The doctor told us to rest since we already have two children and we are still young. I thought which being young when I have had two children and a miscarriage? From now on, he told us, we are to unite only in the first five days after my moon and the last five days before I start. To be safe, Miiro should not finish inside me. So, we are going to do this for two or three years and then have children again. But I was worried. I have had only girls so far. I said, Miiro, you need an heir. He said that in his clan they have more boys than girls, that we are lucky to have two girls already and I laughed, Haa, but you, Miiro, you know how to make me feel good. But he said that a boy will come soon, let us wait. I said to myself, Alikisa, you are so lucky with your Miiro.

Lastly, thank Nurse Nnannozi for me. She has looked after me very much. She gave me this paper and pen as well. I wish you were here. You would have nursed me even better. Now let me go home.

Me, your very own,
                    Muka Miiro.

Bannange Alikisa,

Nga kitalo. And for it to happen when I was away. I have thanked Nurse Nnannozi for us because she did my job. The doctor was right. Rest your womb otherwise it will learn to miscarry every time. How are our children? Truth? I should be mothering them. I have heard you are prospering very much. I saw how modern your house is. Everybody says you are a very good wife. That is why your home is prospering. Well done.

I too laugh about the pact. We were stupid. And when you come out here in Kampala and meet new people and discover the wide world and Bugerere becomes narrow, you ask yourself, What in life do I want? You think of your grandmother's escaping from abduction and being sold in slavery, then you think of your mother having fifteen children until she has lost her urine brakes, then you ask, Do I want to get wet between the legs every time I cough, laugh or sneeze? Then you realise that life is much shorter for you than other people, and marriage, a husband and children are a small part of life and you ask yourself, What should I do while I still can? And you answer yourself, Let me see life first.

The doctor was right about your age: in Nattetta a woman walking her twentieth year is aged, but here in the city you are a toddler. Women of twenty-five are unmarried and unworried. So Miiro is yours alone. I have no claim on him.

In the end, I will come back to Nattetta. I will not be able to start a dispensary myself as I thought, but Luutu can. All he should do is put up a modern building, perhaps on the slopes of the church grounds. Then ask at Mmengo Hospital to send nurses because it is a church dispensary. They will come, inspect the building and send you facilities and two nurses. I will put my name up to be considered because I am

Bugerere-born. Tell Miiro to ask his father. I will come and nurse the villages for a while.

Let me tell you, Alikisa, Kampala is not immoral; it is the people. It is not the foreigners; it is Ugandans. I am your sister because I chose you and you chose me. One day I will see our children. Let's give the villages and Miiro time to forget. Look after our children and our husband. Continue with your good ways and the villages will continue to give you respect. Don't worry about me. I will come back to Nattetta and we shall be together again bringing up our children – that I swear to you.

Me, your loving sister,
                    Nsuuta.

12

When Nsuuta wrote that letter she had no idea that in a year's time Luutu would take ill and be brought to Mmengo, that for three weeks while Miiro kept an eye on his father they would be thrown together. Whoever said that suppressed emotions are dangerous was right. Both Miiro and Nsuuta had been in relationships; all that time, they had imagined what being with each other would have been like. They now had a chance.

When Miiro saw Nsuuta, smart in her nursing uniform, he failed to turn away. Nsuuta had never looked so beautiful. He claimed he had heard about her phenomenal nursing skills and insisted she was the right person to nurse his father. And when at the end of her shift he ran after her to say thank you, and she casually pointed out to him the door to her flat in the nurses' quarters, they both knew they would be together that night. And when he managed to climb into her room like a testosterone-fuelled schoolboy, there was no time to talk. The nursing sister might catch them; Nsuuta would lose her job. Stolen sex every night while Luutu lay ill in hospital. Then the pretending during the daytime. The following week, as their desire became manageable, Miiro and Nsuuta sneaked off and went to nightclubs, to places he would never dream of taking his Alikisa. Alikisa would never know that Miiro loved to dance.

A few months later, when Luutu was dead and buried and Miiro had become the head of his family, Nsuuta, who never fully lost her entitlement to Miiro, went to Alikisa and told her the good news: she was expecting Miiro's child. Alikisa, whose heart had finally stopped swinging with guilt and settled into owning Miiro and her home, was taken by surprise. Thereafter, she hid her resentment at seeing how fired up Miiro was for Nsuuta. He had never burned so intensely for her. Worse was the shame and guilt for her envy. Had she not made a pact with Nsuuta? Had she not written to Nsuuta, after she married Miiro, that she was only keeping Nsuuta's place? Luckily, not even Nsuuta's entitlement would allow her to share their escapades in the city with Alikisa. Besides, she began to see the Nsuuta she used to love return once more. Thereafter she tried to rekindle the dream they had had as children, but everything was wrong. She had two children already. It was too late to tell them that Nsuuta was their mother too. Miiro had built a house for one wife; there was no other bedroom for another wife. But when she looked at her, the old Nsuuta was still there. And she loved her.

WHY PENNED HENS
PECK EACH OTHER

1

28 February 1983

Tom died. He died without reason, without warning, without good-byes – right in the middle of life.

That morning, he rushed as usual. He showered, got dressed – 'Where are my socks, I am late, where is my tie?' – and guzzled his tea cold. Then he ran out of the house as if he would be coming home. But in the evening, on his way to pick up the children from school – wuubi, gone. That is how Nnaki the maid told it.

At first, perhaps because of shock, people blamed his new car, the Honda Accord. But as the facts became clearer – an army Jeep had rammed into his car on that dangerous junction on Kitante Road – common sense set in. Attention turned to the usual suspect, the widow. Everyone knew Tom had wanted to finish building his house in Busega but Nnambi, keen to show they were wealthy, had nagged until Tom bought that car.

And that was not all.

Tom's love for Nnambi had died; who didn't know? Not after what she did to Kirabo. But Nnambi, ever the lukokobe, was not giving him up. Do you know what she did? She went home to her people to fix it. And you know there is no witchery like witchery from Mityana – you marry there at your own peril.

There was nothing new in Nnambi fixing things: women routinely fixed dying marriages with all sorts. But in this case, instead of a remedy, the diviner gave her evil spirits he needed to dispose of.

Ways in which Nnambi had administered what she thought was a love remedy started to circulate. Some said she dropped the potion in the driveway; Tom drove over it and right into his grave. Others swore she hung it above the threshold; Tom walked underneath and that was that. And others still claimed she put it beneath their mattress; Tom rolled over it and was finished.

'I tell you, that woman came into this marriage determined to stay, come rain, come shine.'

'And if Tom wished to extricate himself?'

'Mulago Hospital.'

'How?'

'Either through surgery, like removing a tumour, or death do us part. Guess what happened?'

'Kitalo.'

By the time Tom was buried, there was no doubt who had done it. It was the classic case of fenna tumufiirwe – *If I cannot have him, no one will.*

2

1 March 1983

News of Tom's passing arrived in Nattetta at dawn, as people made their way to their gardens to dig. At Miiro's house, everyone who heard ran wild. No one thought of holding the other until Widow Diba arrived with her common sense. First, she rounded up everyone and put them in the diiro. Then she told Miiro, who was falling apart as if he was a woman, to hold himself together. She put him into the car of Aunt YA's husband, who had driven over to break the news. She put Ssozi in the car as well. 'Your job is to fortify Miiro,' she told him, and sent them off to the city to take care of the official processes following Tom's death.

When they drove away, she sent a lad down the road to fetch Nsuuta. Unfortunately, the idiot blurted the news to Nsuuta without preparing her. Nsuuta marched to Miiro's house, refusing to be held as if she did not have cancer, as if she was not blind. When she got to the walkway she called, 'Alikisa, what have we done?'

Muka Miiro came out, stood at the threshold and put her arms on top of her head. 'I thought it was a childish pact.' Then she walked across the courtyard and stood in front of Nsuuta. 'Tell me we did not kill our child.'

Nsuuta held her by the shoulders as if they were little girls again. As she walked Muka Miiro back to the house, she whispered, 'It is nothing to do with the silly pact.'

'But we broke it.'

'Accidents happen. If you don't know how to cry, let me do it.'

At first, when residents saw Muka Miiro and Nsuuta holding each other, they were shocked. Then they sucked their teeth in cynical irritation:

'They've wasted the larger part of Tom's life strifing; now he is dead they are so close they are whispering?'

'You joke with women. You think they are this but they are that. You think they are here but they are...'

Widow Diba shut them up. 'Hold your gossip: no one can reach Muka Miiro right now apart from Nsuuta. Not even Miiro. If you have nothing good to say, keep quiet.'

Muka Miiro did not cry like a grown woman. Just tears streaming down her face. But Nsuuta performed. She punctuated her tears with stories from Tom's childhood, repeating words he used to say, telling of things he had done, jokes he had cracked, times he got in trouble, times he was angry with her. It was lucky she was dying; Tom had been the pole on which she tied the rope that kept her from blowing away.

Then Batte arrived: 'Is it true what I heard?'

'Come here, child.' Muka Miiro hugged him – dirty clothes, stale alcohol and all. He stepped out of the house and sat quietly on the verandah. All his nonsense of being hung-over during daytime, of being a recluse, fled.

At around nine o'clock, another car, a pick-up truck, came to take Muka Miiro and Nsuuta to Tom's house in Bugoloobi so that when mourners arrived, there would be familiar faces to receive them. Tom's widow could not be trusted to receive Tom's people.

Batte was the first to climb into the back of the truck. When Widow Diba ordered him to get down – 'There are useful people to transport' – he asked her, 'Have I ever bothered you before?'

Diba shook her head.

'Then leave me alone.'

Diba did not say another word to him. She filled the truck with women who Muka Miiro would need. She reminded them to take large pans, baskets, knives and work clothes – 'Who do you think is going to feed the mourners; that woman Tom married?' She gave them half an hour to harvest the food they were taking and banana leaves to cook it in.

Then Muka Miiro refused to get in the truck: 'I want my child to be brought back here, where he grew up. We shall hold his vigil here with the people who loved him.' Diba was firm: Tom had a home and a family; he would be mourned in his house. Eventually, Muka Miiro got in the truck, but she was less mournful and more peeved.

When the women arrived at Tom's house, his coffin had not arrived. The first things Muka Miiro saw were the little kuule shrubs edging the paved walkways. They had grown higher than the kerb, covering it entirely. She pounced on the shrubs and began uprooting them: 'Which woman allows kuule to grow in her compound? If I had not missed them last time I came, this would never have happened.' All the Nattetta women, apart from Nsuuta, descended on the garden like it was a murderer and uprooted all the plants lest someone else died. Tom's wife was in the sitting room crying with her sisters when the women arrived. She saw them go mad on her plants and said, 'Only the bewitched waits for those women to come in here.' She, her family and friends hurried and locked themselves in the main bedroom.

Meanwhile, Batte had jumped off the truck when it first arrived and had run to the house. He asked Nnambi whether it was true, but she just cried. He asked for a glass of water and downed it. Then another and another. In the end, Nnaki brought him a whole jug. He asked her to drop in ice cubes because he was sweating so much. He took the tray outside and sat on the porch alone, drinking water and sweating. He alone talked to Nnambi before she disappeared into her bedroom. But because he was a drunk with neither a wife nor children, he did not have a voice within Miiro's family.

For the Nattetta women, walking into Tom's house for the first time to be received by Nnaki the maid, because the widow had locked herself in her bedroom, was a positive sign. A widow, even the wickedest, would receive mourners and cry for her husband. But to not even say a word of comfort to her mother-in-law? Heads were shaken, hands were clapped, tongues clicked, 'Kdto! Wombs bring forth all sorts.' Mourners just arriving would ask, 'Where is the widow?' and the Nattetta women would click noises, like cutlery in their throats. 'Apparently, she is in her bedroom.' The new arrival would open her eyes wide. 'But why?' The women would shrug. 'Hmm, who knows? Maybe she is too good for us.' Then they would lean in: 'Truth does not conceal itself. She knows what she has done.' And the new mourner would pull her ugliest face and exclaim, 'A demon came unto us,' because Tom, who had brought the demon into the clan, had left her to them. As more women arrived, there was more whispering than crying, and they gorged themselves on anger and disbelief.

3

2 *March 1983*

Kirabo was in the biology lab. It was one of those cold morning classes when everyone worked in silence. Outside the lab, the world was soggy from non-stop drizzle. She was startled by the teacher's voice. 'Kirabo?' Everyone looked up. 'Sister Ambrose wants a word with you.' Eyes turned to Kirabo. She frowned. *Me?* Because she was not the kind of girl the HM would have a word with. Her eyes travelled to the door. The Angel of Doom stood below the steps under an umbrella. Kirabo knew right away. During Amin's regime, when girls were collected from class by the AOD it had always been the dad. Kirabo's eyes travelled back to the teacher, pleading: *You know what the presence of that woman means*. The teacher's stare said *We are waiting*. Kirabo slipped down from the stool. Her senses were so heightened that she was aware of each girl's eyes as she left the room. Some held their breath, some avoided looking at her altogether, and others stared like cows in a herd trying not to think about their turn to be someone's feast.

At the doorstep, she glared at Nunciata. 'Who died?'

'What?'

'My father has died.'

'Because I am a kisirani. You think I do not know what you girls call me?'

There was something heartening about Nunciata snapping at her. Who snaps at a bereaved girl? Still, Kirabo walked apart from her, even though she was getting wet without an umbrella, until she got to the office block. She knocked on Sister Ambrose's office and opened the door. Sister Ambrose wore a sombre mask. 'Sit down, Kirabo,' she said. When Kirabo had sat down, Sister Ambrose started, 'I am sorry, child, but news from home is not goo—'

'I know my father is dead.'

Sister Ambrose looked surprised but relieved. Kirabo looked about the room. Three filing cabinets against the wall. Folders piled on top as well – blue, mauve and green. Shelves heaving with trophies. Pictures on the walls, some black and white, recent ones in colour. The floor was red cement. Sister Ambrose's desk was very smooth. The chair Kirabo sat on did not care. The thing about objects is they don't realise how lucky they are. Sometimes life was not worth the pain.

'And your mother, did you find her?'

Kirabo looked at Sister Ambrose a little too long, then shook her head.

'Why don't you go and pack a few things? I will write your gate pass.'

'He was alive,' Kirabo exploded. 'He was not sick when I left home. People don't just die.'

'He was involved in a car accident.'

'Involved' sounded like an accusation. As if Tom had been 'involved' in an affair. 'It is that Nunciata. I told her Dad had died, but she denied it. Our parents die when she collects us from class like that.'

Aunt Abi came into the office. Kirabo ran to her. The sudden movement provoked her flow. It gushed, but she did not check her skirt. She pointed at the headmistress. 'She said that Dad is dead.'

It was not the fact that Aunt Abi did not answer, or that her eyes were red that broke Kirabo's heart; it was her busuuti. Aunt Abi hated wearing it, called it oppressive. Aunt Abi dressing traditionally meant she had given up on Tom.

'Have I not been bringing good reports?'

'I know, I know.'

'Have I not been keeping out of trouble? But still he goes and dies?'

Aunt Abi led her out of the office. They stood on the verandah of the administration block for a long time, holding each other, crying, until the hooter for break time went. The drizzle had stopped. As they took the stairs to the car park, Aunt Abi said, 'The whole family is in disarray. We have all run out of common sense. It was only last night that Widow Diba remembered you. The burial is today. This kind of calamity has never befallen our family. Tom, of all people? I never thought I would say this, but thank God for Widow Diba.'

Just then, Atim approached with a small bag packed for Kirabo. She also held a cup of water and two Aspro tablets. She placed the bag at Kirabo's feet and handed her the tablets. Kirabo popped them out of their blisters and swallowed them with water. Atim told Aunt Abi, 'I will try and take down notes for Kirabo in class.' First she hugged Aunt Abi, who said, 'Thank you child, thank you very much.' Then she hugged Kirabo and whispered in her ear, 'I have put more Aspro in the side pocket and eight more pads I have rolled in case you continue to flow tomorrow.' As she pulled away, she said, 'Your next dose is at 2.00P.M., don't forget.' Kirabo managed a thank-you smile before Atim ran off. Then she came back. 'Nga kitalo,' she said in shaky Luganda.

Perhaps Tom was not really dead; this was Tom, after all – tall, handsome, intelligent – how could he die? All the way to Kampala, Kirabo floated on disbelief. Kampala was sunny, dusty but vibrant. But Bugoloobi Town was on assisted breathing. The OMO advert had peeled in parts, the faces of the laughing family were gone. CHIBUKU had curled on to itself, but WINNERS was intact. The famous flats were slummy. When they came to the bungalows similar to Tom's, Kirabo sat up. Then she saw smoke rise above the trees and knew it was from the funereal hearth. The gate, when they got to it, was wide open. People walked in and out as if it was a market.

*

When she stepped out of the car someone cried, 'Kirabo – oh,' and women hurried over to her. Grandmother grabbed her in a hug and they swayed their pain from side to side. Then Grandfather held her as if she was fragile. But he was the fragile one. Kirabo felt him shake through his shirt. The skin on his back was loose, very soft. She had never realised how skinny he was. When he pulled away he said, 'He was in such a hurry, your father; always impatient, was he not?'

Kirabo nodded.

'But we were blind. We did not realise. Even as a child Tom rushed through chores, in school he was made to skip levels. He had you at seventeen. You wanted to say *Slow down, Tom, take your time*, but no. Such people don't last.'

Then Widow Diba gasped, 'Child, we have run out of words.' Then Jjajja Nsangi grabbed her and said, 'What Tom has done to us, Mother Hen does to her chicks. I mean, why jump into a pan to make a stew when you have young ones?'

Uncles and aunts Kirabo had forgotten appeared from nowhere. They made comforting statements: 'Does a parent die? Not when he leaves behind bits of himself like Kirabo.' When she arrived in the sitting room, Nsuuta held out her hands to Kirabo but the angle was wrong. Her voice was hoarse when she whispered, 'He was all we had, me and you.' Kirabo buried her head in Nsuuta's lap. She could not bear to look at the coffin because the tree whose timber had made it was once a seedling with tender leaves and baby branches, then it had grown, Tom unaware.

The sitting room and the dining space were unrecognisable. The drawer-shelves used as a divider had been pulled away to create one expansive room. The sofa set and couch were outside in a kidaala, a makeshift canopy. The women sat everywhere on the carpet. Their luggage, consisting of migugu tied in cotton bitambala with crocheted flowers, was strewn along the walls. Skinny legs with calloused feet stretched out. Sunburned faces. Babies – some half-dressed, some naked except for beads around waists or talismans around necks – sat without nappies on the carpet. Jjajja Nsangi sat at the head of the coffin like a matriarch. Her chest rose and swallowed her neck, cupping her chin between her breasts. Then the chest fell and her neck re-emerged like a miracle. Grandmother was dry-eyed.

Kirabo perked up. Nsuuta and Grandmother sat next to each other. She searched their faces for the feud. When had they made up? But then Aunt Abi walked in like she was the head of Tom's house. The house keys were fastened on the sash of her busuuti. Everyone who needed something went to her. Poor Uncle Ndiira had been forced out of his shell. He was at the door saying something about burial schedules. His voice was quiet and he did not look at people directly. Aunt YA walked in, saw Kirabo and wailed, 'Tom, you have not loved this child enough!' and got down on her knees and keened.

Uncle Ndiira disappeared. The women picked up Aunt YA's lament like a tidal wave. Kirabo looked around: where was Nnambi? Jjajja Nsangi sat in the widow's place. Aunt Abi and Aunt YA strutted about the house like cockerels.

'Indeed, the child of his youth he could not love.'

For some time, the women did not say why Tom did not love Kirabo enough, until Aunt Abi came back. She did not beat around the bush. 'My brother fidgeted with this child.' She wagged a finger at no one. 'This child has been tossed from here to there as if my brother had no home.' She opened the door that led to the corridor and called, 'What kind of woman drives her husband's child out of his house, hmm?' Still holding the door, she turned to the women. 'Can you imagine, Nnambi told her sister that Kirabo was dropped on her like death by accident?'

'Eh-eh, she is a real witch, that one.'

A young woman shifted irritably. 'The truth is that there is dying by car accident and then there is dying by car accident not-so-accidentally. I have said it.'

'Yes, let's talk about it. Are we going to say beautiful things like we came for a bride?'

'Her name is Nnambi, her brother is Death: what did you expect?'

'Don't say that; we do not say things like that,' said Widow Diba, but no one took her seriously. She had not challenged the insinuation that

Tom's widow had killed him; it was the sacrilege of sullying Nnambi, the mother of humanity.

The realisation hit Kirabo hard. She had forgotten that Nnambi, the mother of humanity, had a dark side – the bringer of Death, her brother – which the nation pretended did not exist. Suddenly Muka Tom's name was made appropriate. Kirabo stole a look at Nsuuta; Nsuuta's eyes were trained on her as if she had heard her thought. Kirabo was mortified. She looked at Aunt Abi beseechingly, but Aunt Abi was just getting started.

'Now what are you going to do, hmm?' Aunt Abi launched through the door. 'Tom has abandoned you. Now you need us.'

'Which us?' a woman asked. 'You mean us, the family she drove away?'

Nsuuta leaned towards Grandmother and whispered, 'Are you not going to stop the girls?' Grandmother nudged her to keep quiet. She covered her mouth and whispered something. Nsuuta glanced in Jjajja Nsangi's direction as if she could see her. Nsuuta sat back and kept quiet.

'The Coffee Marketing Board is going to evict her in how many months?' Aunt YA waved three fingers above the women. 'Three. That is all they give you.' It was clear that the sisters were stamping their authority on the house, on Nnambi and on the children.

'As long as she leaves our children behind.'

'Were you born in Switzerland,' Aunt Abi called through the door, 'where they have never heard of different mothers, hmm? And you bring that discrimination, which does not work with our families, into our clan?'

Nsuuta rose on her knees above the women. Grandmother tried to pull her down, but Nsuuta shook off her hand. She turned her head in Aunt Abi's direction and called, 'Abi, child?' Unfortunately, her eyes looked away from where Aunt Abi stood.

'Leave them, Nsuuta.' Jjajja Nsangi also got up and helped Nsuuta down with authority. 'Let the girls express themselves. This is their brother's house. They have authority to speak up when things are not right. Tom failed to control his wife. Now he has left her to us. What that woman suggested between father and daughter is unsayable. Let her know she married into a formidable family, otherwise she will shit on our heads.' Now Nsangi addressed everyone. 'In Luutu's family, our men are quiet, you can walk all over them, but not us women, hmm, hmm. Me, I watch my brother's wives with a sharp eye. I will not let a wife grow horns around my brother. I have trained my nieces on how to be women and I am glad my effort has not been wasted.'

Nsuuta stayed down. In stating that this was their brother's house, Nsangi was telling her: *This is my family, I am Great Aunt. Who are you?*

'But in this case, I also blame my wife here.' Nsangi turned on Grandmother. 'She did not assert her authority when Nnambi first arrived as a bride. A woman marries into my family, I let her know her place immediately. How does a woman start to throw her husband's child out of the family home, hmm? How? Had I known in time, Tom or no Tom, I would have come to this house and adjusted her. I am not Children's Aunt for nothing.'

'European ways don't suit our culture.' Widow Diba tried to steer attention away from Grandmother. 'They have their own, we have ours.'

Aunt Abi was not yet sated. 'Listen, Nnambi, my brother is dead and our children don't deserve this abandonment, but as for you – good riddance.'

That was when Grandfather appeared in the doorway. Silence fell over the women like a class of rowdy pupils caught by a stern teacher.

'Abisaagi,' he called softly, 'have I died and you taken over my family? Are you dictating who is and who is not a member now?'

Silence.

'Are you the only one hurting? My son is dead, my grandchildren are orphans, my wife is in agony, but you are picking a quarrel with the widow.'

Aunt Abi let go of the door to the corridor and it fell shut.

'Where is Widow Tom? Why is she not sitting here close to her husband? Did you drive her away, Abisaagi?'

'Not I, her guilt.'

'Go fetch her.' Miiro did not reproach his sister, who sat in the widow's place.

Aunt Abi, mouth so pointed it touched her nose, disappeared into the corridor. A minute later, she came back with a frightened-looking Nnambi. She too was dressed in a busuuti. She could not look at anyone.

'Come, child,' Miiro said. 'You must sit at the head of your husband in his last moments. Move, Children's Aunt,' he told Nsangi. 'Make space for *our* daughter.' He turned to Nnambi. 'Where are your sisters, child?'

Nnambi pointed towards her bedroom.

'Abisaagi, go get her sisters.' He smiled at Nnambi. 'You need your family around you. My daughters might eat you.'

All Nnambi's sisters, and there were a lot of them, looked alike – Rank Xerox, they called such siblings at St Theresa's. They sat behind Nnambi; everyone shifted to make space for them and resentment rose.

When Grandfather withdrew, Ssozi was heard exclaiming, 'Women, kdto. They are like Zungu chickens in a pen. If you don't debeak them they turn on each other and peck, *kyo-kyo, kyo-kyo, kyo-kyo.*'

Nsangi shot up like a teenager. She stepped over women's legs, shoving shoulders out of her way until she got to the door. She stood straight. 'Mr Ssozi,' she called too politely, 'I am only asking like a chicken does; why keep the Zungu chickens in confines? Why not let them out to roam and scratch and peck at insects and worms and see if they come home in the evening and peck each other? Why debeak hens for something *you* are doing wrong?'

Ssozi did not respond.

Neither did Grandfather.

Nsuuta elbowed Grandmother; Grandmother nudged her back.

Nsangi returned to her position like a victorious wrestler. 'I have finished that one.' She sat down heaving and out of breath. 'Sometimes you have to show them that you use your brain, otherwise they presume you don't have one.' That was the thing about Jjajja Nsangi. You hated her for bullying your grandmother, but then she would go and put kweluma in the most effective image. And then you wonder why someone like her – who knows that oppressed people turn on each other to vent because the oppressor is untouchable – is the worst at kweluma?

'Kirabo.' Diba broke the silence. 'Come here, child.' Diba sat on the other side of Grandmother like a maid of honour. Kirabo shuffled on her knees towards her. First, Diba checked Kirabo's face as if to make certain that she had washed it, then she dusted her uniform sweater – a silent message to Nnambi. 'It is a closed casket,' she said, 'because your father died in a car accident. But it is him in there. Miiro, his brothers, our sons and Ssozi went to Mulago Hospital to identify him. They all agree that it is our Tom: would they lie?'

Kirabo shook her head.

'Then you must let him go. Us, we have put our hands in the air and said *Tom, you win*. Because you have not seen his remains, your mind will play tricks on you. But when it starts, remember my words – it is him. Now touch the coffin.'

Kirabo hesitated.

'Touch it, because you will not wipe your father's forehead in farewell.'

A woman said, 'Are you telling Kirabo only? We all need those words.'

The lid was as smooth as Formica. Kirabo's hand slid along the edge, which reminded her of the fallboard of the grand piano in the chapel.

Later, when Nnambi had been disregarded by the women, Kirabo observed her. Nnambi was struggling. She was in extreme pain, but she could not cry out loud and let it out. When overcome, she closed her eyes, bit her lips and shook her head. Failing to hold it in, her head dropped. Her arms, placed on the floor, trembled. Then she took a long breath to swallow the tears. Wiping her eyes, she sniffed, stabilised her breathing and looked up again. Kirabo wanted to reach out and whisper condolences, *Nga kitalo*, but Nnambi only looked above people's heads. Kirabo was ashamed of her aunts' mauling of Nnambi. She wanted to think it was because this was Nnambi's home and she deserved respect and compassion. But Kirabo knew that Nsuuta's warning – that women reacted not acted, that stepmothers did not make themselves – had caught up with her.

A concerned woman – Kirabo did not recognise her – brought Mwagale and little Tommy to the sitting room. Mwagale had grown incredibly and Tommy was nothing like the baby Kirabo had last seen. The woman said to them, 'Sit with *your sister.*' Miiro might have stopped the haranguing, but women had other ways of expressing their feelings about Nnambi. Mwagale looked so like her mother Kirabo felt sorry for her. It was not the right time to look like Nnambi. Tommy looked like himself, which was safe.

'Nga kitalo, Daddy's death,' Kirabo whispered when they had sat down. The women were watching to see whether she held anger in her heart. At the merest trace of it they would step in and say *Look here, Kirabo, they did not choose their mother.*

'Kitalo,' they said.

'How did it happen?' Kirabo asked.

'Kdto,' Mwagale clicked in self-pity. 'It was on Monday, as he came to pick us up at school—'

'Yes,' Tommy interrupted, 'he collided with an army Jeep near the Golf Club.'

'You know how the army drives.'

'He died on the spot.' Tommy was echoing someone's words.

It is Wednesday, Kirabo thought. *Tom has been dead two days; that is extremely dead.*

'The school driver brought us home at night—'

'Yes.' Tommy rushed his words. 'He brought us home because the school did not know what was going on and Mummy was not picking up the phone.'

'You have Grandmother's voice, Tommy,' Kirabo said.

'Everyone says it,' Mwagale laughed. 'Wait till you grow up; you will *boom, boom* like Grandmother.'

'Yeah? I don't mind, but you? Your feet have verandahs like Aunt Abi's.'

Kirabo watched them, wondering when Mwagale had turned into the little sister who said, 'I am coming to St Theresa's too… Everyone knows my big sister is at St Theresa's… Daddy says you want to become a doctor for animals…'

'Yes, Kirabo, do animals get injections?'

Before Kirabo could respond, Mwagale whispered, 'We are going to move out of this house.'

Tommy's face fell. 'We are moving into the new house Daddy was building.'

'Because this one belongs to Coffee: you move out when your daddy dies.'

'Even though the other house is not yet finished.'

'Thank God Daddy was building a house, then,' Kirabo said.

'Will you still be at St Theresa's next year?' Mwagale asked.

'No, but apply. If you get in, I will come with you on your first day and tell my friends to look after you. And I will come on every Visitors' Sunday.'

'I like your uniform.'

'This is the A-level one. The O-level uniform is a wrapper.'

Sio might come for the burial. Unbridled anticipation surged through Kirabo. Then the shame, then disgust. She did not know where the thought came from.

'Kirabo, Jjajja Miiro is calling you.' Aunt YA's daughter stood at the door.

'Where is he?'

'Under the canopy.'

'Come, let's go,' Kirabo said to Tommy and Mwagale, to get them out of the stifling sitting room. Outside, the sun was bright, the air felt lighter.

'Yii kabejja,' Miiro said as Kirabo came down the steps, 'what kind of wife abandons her man the way you abandoned me in Nattetta?

Every time the bus stops outside our house I say to my one, surely that must be kabejja, but wa.'

Kirabo smiled.

'Look at you, I mean, just look at her. When you next come to Nattetta, I will take a walk around the villages with you on my arm and all the young men will ask, *What is that namukadde geezer doing with her?* and I will say, *Gnash your teeth, ineffective youth, she is mine.*'

Kirabo sat down next to him and they hugged again. She took him in, the whole of him. Grey hairs had won. They openly defied his Kanta efforts now. A stubble of little white pricks had grown in the folds around his jaw and down to his throat. He was very dark but you did not notice it, maybe because he was a man. He wore a blue shirt, long-sleeved. He looked vulnerable away from his home.

'My wife has been wondering what she did to you. She asks, "Why does Kirabo not visit us at all?" And all I can say to her is, "She is studying hard. She does not need the likes of me and you disturbing her."'

'How is Grandmother really?'

'Old.' Miiro shook his head. 'Look at me; am I old?'

'Not at all.'

Miiro wagged his finger in Kirabo's face, as if to say *I did not know you were a flatterer*. But they could not sustain the banter. Silence fell like a stone. Kirabo looked at Grandfather, her eyes asking *How could this happen?* Grandfather dropped his head.

4

A car, a white Datsun, drove in. A woman jumped out and ran screaming towards the house.

'Gayi!' Kirabo did not realise she had shouted.

Miiro sat up.

Kirabo ran and caught up with her before Gayi made it to the steps.
She grabbed her but they just stared at each other. Eight years stood
between them. Kirabo was overwhelmed by suppressed emotions at
seeing Gayi again, Gayi overcome by guilt, fear, hurt and who knows
what else. Before they could hug, other women caught up and clam-
oured to touch and cry. Kirabo stepped away. It was not clear whom
these tears were for – losing Gayi, finding her, or losing Tom. Gayi
was smaller, older. Wearing a busuuti, she was a real woman. The
women, anticipating the battle ahead of Gayi as she tried to reinsert
herself into the family, whispered, 'You look well... All that matters
is that you look well... No one can argue with that; just be strong.'

When the women were done with her, Gayi went over to
Grandmother, who had stood back a little, perhaps confused about
whether to be happy to see a prodigal daughter when she had just lost
a son. They held each other. Grandmother laid her cheek on Gayi's
and they rubbed as if to make sure this was really happening. She
turned the other cheek to Gayi's. When Grandmother pulled away she
looked at Gayi's face, as if to check whether all of her was still there.
Aunt Abi and Aunt YA held back, arms folded, their eyes saying *You
hurt our parents* until Grandmother intervened, disarming them with,

'Have you not seen your sister?' They embraced Gayi coolly, under Grandmother's watchful eye. Then she led Gayi to the living room to share her. Kirabo heard the volume of noise rise from the sitting room and walked away, imagining renewed crying. Then she saw the man who had come with Gayi. He stood outside his car looking lost. He had three children on his hands – two boys and a girl. In no time, the children were whisked away. From one pair of hands to another, the children were hugged and scrutinised. All this time, the man remained standing alone, bewildered. No one acknowledged him as Gayi's man or the father of Miiro's grandchildren. It was Widow Diba who asked for a chair and sat Gayi's man close to the hedge, far away from Miiro and the male clan members. Then she whispered to everyone to go and greet him.

So this is the motorcycle man who sneaked off with Gayi in the night all those years ago, Kirabo thought as she went to greet him. She felt sorry for him: he was in so much trouble. Then she saw the body art – dark and shiny dot-dots in two rows curved above his eyebrows. They made the eyebrows prominent as if lifted, forcing you to look at his eyes. Kirabo could almost hear the communal consternation: *God in heaven, he has tribal marks?* But Gayi's man was clever; when he greeted old women, he spoke proper Luganda, acknowledging their bereavement with 'Nga kitalo, Maama, yii yii.' But when Kirabo came along he spoke English: 'Don't, don't kneel at all. How are you? What is your name? Oh, I am so sorry about your dad.' And Kirabo decided she liked him. When she walked back, women were still speculating about his ethnicity – Nubian… Madi… Lugbara. They agreed on one thing: 'Gayi has no mercy – adding that darkness to the dark skin in Miiro's house? The poor children.'

Grandmother and Gayi came out of the house. They sat on the lawn away from everyone and whispered. Kirabo hovered in the middle, undecided whether to join them or go back and sit with Grandfather. In the end, she sat under the avocado tree, where she could observe both. Grandmother tugged at the grass. 'Go now, go greet your father before he reorganises his thoughts to make it hard for us.'

Gayi began to tug at the grass like her mother. Then, as if the tugging had given her strength, she stood up and walked towards Miiro. Tension rose. People watched without looking. Neither daughter nor father looked up as Gayi crossed the lawn. Miiro sat rigid and angry. Gayi walked hunched with shame. As she drew closer, Miiro squared for confrontation. Gayi bowed for reconciliation. By the time she reached him, she had gathered her busuuti around her as if to minimise the space she occupied. The compound held its breath. Gayi knelt. 'Nga kitalo, Father,' she said.

'Kitalo.' Miiro was curt. 'Bring the children.'

And when the children were brought, he fussed over them, asking, 'Have you ever heard of Jjajja Miiro of Nattetta?' He introduced himself and asked them questions he should have asked their mother: 'Where do you live? What is the name of your father?' When he asked the children their names and the little girl said she was Jannat, and the eldest boy said he was Moussa, and the last one chimed, 'Youssouff,' Gayi's disappearance suddenly made sense.

All the while Gayi knelt, hunched and silent. But as the children moved from Miiro to greet other relatives, quick tongues changed their names from Muslim into Christian variants. 'The girl is Janet,' a youngish woman said. 'The older boy is Moses, and the youngest is Joseph.' It was ingenuous. Or not at all. Perhaps Gayi and her husband, anticipating this precise moment, had selected compliant names. Then the apologists chimed in: 'Gayi's man grew up here in Buganda with us. He is matooke-eater that one. If it was not for the tribal marks—'

'Who is she?' Miiro pointed to the woman Christianising his grandchildren's Muslim names.

'I don't know.' Kirabo shrugged. 'Funerals bring all sorts.'

Miiro spoke up. 'The children can speak for themselves; why not ask them?' However, Kirabo knew that if he had wanted to stop the tongues castrating Gayi's man, he should have pronounced the children's names in their Muslim versions. Instead, he left it to the children.

Kirabo looked at Gayi hunched on the ground and shook her head. There are things you don't need to be told. You suckle them at your mother's teat. It is the lack of these things which prompts people to say *She did not get enough breast*. Running off with a Muslim man who was a northerner before you had finished school was one of them. After all, as Jjajja Nsangi would say, there had never been foreign blood in Luutu's house, *never*. For Luutu's descendants, Christianity was *in the blood*. Luutu built churches, for heaven's sake. Grandmother's father was a reverend. How do you start to bring home a Muslim? And as Jjajja Doctor would tell you, Luutu's descendants were academic: how dare you drop out of education without even O levels?

'You mean *they* can be *Muslim* as well?' Widow Diba was asking, as if being Muslim was a delinquency that only the Ganda indulged in. To Diba, if you were unfortunate enough to be non-Ganda – one could not help one's parents – at least endeavour to take on an acceptable religion. After all, religion was a cloth you wore on certain days and took off for the rest of the week. Grandmother must have heard Diba's comment, as she raised her voice: '*My son* has looked after my child well. She is happy. He is educated, and he has not forced Gayi to become Muslim.'

The silence indicated that Grandmother was alone in this conviction. With the tendency for men to want as many women as possible, it was hard to believe that a man whose religion allowed it would pass up the chance. The women gave each other knowing looks of *Let's wait and see*.

Finally, Miiro looked at Gayi and asked, 'Does *he* treat you well?'

Gayi nodded, tugging at the lawn. When the grass broke, she let it fall and went for more.

'You are very small; you are sure you are treated well?'

'Yes, Father.'

'You are sure you have enough food?'

'I grow my own food.'

'You know there is room at home if you are not happy. I don't want to hear that you are stuck in an unhappy marriage because you fear coming home. The big boys' house is vacant.'

Gayi smiled.

'Bring the children for holidays. We have nothing to do, me and your mother. And if you want to do something with yourself, a course or a trade, and the children are in the way, bring them. You know we have good schools in Nattetta.'

'I know, Father.'

'Don't bring *him*. I don't want to see *him*, ever.'

Gayi bit her lower lip.

'Is that how they marry their wives where he comes from? Do they just run off with people's daughters before they have finished school? I brought up my daughters to be self-reliant, but look at you. These days, a woman marrying rich is not enough. You need your own source of income.'

'But I grow my own food, Father.'

'On his land? What if he evicts you?'

Gayi remained silent. *Girls have run off with men since time immemorial, but Gayi was stolen*, Kirabo thought. Many such girls ended up in the city, abandoned with children and no way of survival. Yet here was a man who wanted to make everything right, but Miiro's pride, and perhaps the man's ethnicity and religion, stood in the way.

'He wants to come and apologise,' Gayi said. 'We would like to start the marriage rites so we can get married properly.'

'Nnaggayi.' Miiro leaned forward. 'My son has just died. This is neither the time nor the place to talk about something like that. Let's bury your brother first and we will see what comes after his second funeral rites.'

Gayi stood up and walked back. She had cleared the first hurdle. As soon as she sat down, Grandmother whispered, 'What did he say?'

'He does not want to see him.'

'But you mentioned that your man intends to visit and ask for marriage rites.'

'He said this is neither the time nor the place to talk about that.'

'Don't worry. Leave Miiro to me. Your man holds a respectable job as the District Administrator of Iganga, does he not?'

'He said I am small. As if only Baganda men look after their wives.'

'He is looking for an angle; he is still hurting.'

'But why do we have to beg? Why does my man need to be wealthy and educated to be acceptable? I was not stolen, Mother. I chose to run away with him. Father's quarrel should be with me, not with my man. I am the one who wasted his money in school. Father's mantra that girls must be educated to escape oppression can also be oppressive. Mother, I stayed long enough in school to know it was not for me.'

Grandmother remained silent, as if Gayi were still talking. Then she whispered, 'This quarrel has nothing to do with us women. You cannot be held responsible for your actions. It is him that is to blame—'

'But why, am I not a person?'

'Listen, Nnaggayi.' Grandmother's voice became gravelly. 'I am on your side here, but do not make me say obvious things. Now tell me; are you going to change the clan system so we start to own our children? Do women own their children where your husband comes from?'

Gayi shook her head.

'Do men pay dowry for their wives where your man comes from?'

'Yes.' Gayi's voice had shrunk.

'Then let's focus on what we can change, like your father allowing you to marry your man. Miiro knows best why he must protect you. He wants your man to know that another man cares for you. Right now, he has the upper hand, and I suggest your man indulges him.'

Despite Grandmother's traditional common sense Gayi wept afresh. 'And if he leaves me, who will suffer? Me and my children. Mother, the man is mine, the marriage is mine, the children are mine, my life is mine, but somehow my views don't count.'

'If your man ever starts looking away from you, your father will take you back and look after the children.'

'*If* he leaves me, Mother; not all men are like that.'

'Well, *if*.'

'All the same, I wish Father would let me tell him how I feel. I am happy, Mother, even though I have no degree. I am happy working in my garden and looking after my man and my children.'

At this point, women started to stream out of the sitting room. Miiro, his brothers and other men his age entered the room and closed the door. Kirabo realised that the time to strip Tom of synthetic items and wrap him in barkcloth had come. It was around two and the compound was now crowded. Tom was to be buried at four, to allow people who had worked to attend. Kirabo walked back and sat on the mat on which Grandfather had been sitting.

People who came to commiserate with Kirabo ended up marvelling. How she had grown, how well she had done to stay in school. Apparently, most of the girls she had grown up with in Nattetta were mothers and running homes. Even some boys had dropped out of school and were hustling in the city. 'Hang on to your books: the pen never lies.' Then two women, Grandmother's age, came towards her. From their bleached faces they were city girls, the kind of women people resented for refusing to return to the rural areas where old people belonged. When they sat down, the one who had permed her hair introduced herself as Solome Jjali. Kirabo had heard that name, but the memory was distant. Unfortunately, the straightening creams had burned her so badly along the hairline the blisters had formed thick crusts. She introduced the other woman as her sister. They said nga kitalo and slipped condolence money into her hands.

'You don't know us, but we know you,' Solome Jjali said. 'Someday, someone will tell you about us. Until then we shall wait before we introduce ourselves properly.'

Kirabo smiled.

'We wanted to say that your grandparents and your aunt have done a big job of bringing you up for all of us. We are happy you have turned into a real human.' She turned to her sister. 'Hasn't she?'

'Yes, she is a real human,' the younger one said, as if some children do not turn into real humans.

After they had gone, Kirabo uncrumpled the notes they had given her and added them to the growing bundle of condolence money in her pocket. When she looked up, Batte was lowering himself on to the mat. Kirabo could not hide her surprise. She had never sat so close to him. He was sober but his eyes were like curry powder, his lips charred. She knelt to greet him.

'You have grown, Kirabo.' He smiled. 'Tom has *really* been a father.' His voice was full of admiration, as if being a father was a feat Tom had not been expected to accomplish. 'I saw you the first time you were brought to the house in Kamwokya.'

'Kamwokya?'

'We were doing our Cambridge exams. I remember it clearly. Tom was like a young bird asked to look after an egg.'

'Who brought me?'

'Your mother.'

'Did you see her?'

'No, by the time I came back from school she was gone. At the time, Tom and I shared a room in Miiro's rental house while we studied at Kololo SSS. All I know is that she was thirteen.'

'So she did not bring me to Nattetta?'

'She dropped you off at the room. That very day Tom brought you to Nattetta.'

'I did not know that.'

'But then university changed him. He would come to Nattetta and complain about everything – why you did not wear the shoes or slippers he bought you, how the education in the village was substandard, how you should not play in the dust – but you just wanted to be like other village children. We shook our heads because Tom was becoming like his uncle, Dokita.' He paused again and then said softly, 'He had been bringing me clothes and shoes. Always arguing with me that I had thrown my life away into a gourd. Now he is the one who has died and left behind three children. They will need food, school fees, clothes, but I, his best friend, am useless,' he sighed. 'Poor Nnambi, she is stuck with his sisters.'

Kirabo was astounded by Batte's humanity. 'The clan will help.'

'Miiro and Abi yes, but don't count on the others. Clans are notoriously unreliable; visible on special occasions to flex their muscles, but scarce when there are responsibilities.' He smiled. 'I had better clean up fast if I am going to help.'

Kirabo smiled politely.

Tom's coffin was carried out of the house and loaded on to a pick-up truck. Jjajja Doctor stood on the porch and announced, 'It is time to take our son back home to his grandfatherhood. Those who wish to accompany him, we are setting off.' He pointed out the taxis and the fare.

Everyone stood up. Kirabo looked to where Gayi's man sat and despaired. Grandfather held out, and so did Jjajja Nsangi. However, Father Dewo and Jjajja Doctor had greeted him. They were not Miiro, but they were close. The worst possible scenario would have been Gayi dying the way Tom had and that man bringing her body back to Nattetta. The first question would be *Who gave her to you, hmm?* and the second *How come she did not die while she lived with us?* Next would be lashes. *Okulula bukulizi, like you drag a goat on a leash.* But now, because Miiro's brothers had acknowledged him, they would say *Leave him; we have met him.*

5

In the four years Kirabo had not been to Nattetta, the region had shrunk. The distance from Nazigo to Nattetta had contracted. The main road, which cut across the villages, was now tarred, but so narrow it was a wonder cars did not collide. The churches seemed compressed. But the fir and mugavu trees in the church compound looked bigger. Nattetta Modani Baara had corrected its English to Nattetta Modern Bar after a rival, New Kidandali Bar, had set up close to it. Diba's house needed a bath of paint. Grandfather's house had shrivelled; where did all those cousins sleep? The truck carrying Tom's coffin did not even glance at Miiro's house. As if Tom had not grown up there. That roof on Batte's house would one day buckle in and break his head. *Ssozi built a bigger house? He has made money from that shop.* What had happened to the *koparativu stowa*? Without it, the muvule, the tree which had protected its roof from the wind, seemed larger. Nsuuta's house was a box. It was as if the earth was swallowing it. The valley was a mere dip now. The little forest at the fringes of Bugiri Village had drawn back from the road, replaced by beans, maize and groundnuts.

Finally, the driveway to Luutu's house. Aunt Abi stopped the car as the truck carrying the casket reversed to park closer to the path leading to the family graveyard. Kirabo realised then that all this time she had nursed an irrational expectation that Tom would get up and laugh *I was only joking*.

When she stepped out of the car, she walked to the house. The mosquito netting round the stoep was gone. She went to the front

door and peered inside what used to be Luutu's reception room for
dignitaries. The floor was earth. It was still big and dark. She ignored
all the crying and fussing people were doing, as if she had merely
come to see Luutu's house. She went to the left side of the house.
The shell of Luutu's Zephyr still had a perfect skin. She used to get
into it and kick the pedals and move the gearstick and turn the thin
wheel, honking. As she turned away, she saw Sio and Wafula sitting
on the verandah at the far end. They had not seen her. She pulled her
I am over you face.

Sio saw her and looked away. Wafula hurried to her. They hugged.
In the corner of her eyes she saw Sio hesitate, then walk over. He shook
her hand and said, 'Nga kitalo.' Kirabo said, 'Kitalo,' and it was over,
and he was walking away, and she wondered whether he was back with
Giibwa. She considered their child. When the child was born, Sio had
written to say he had a daughter. Then to say he was keeping Giibwa
at his house while she nursed the baby, that Giibwa would leave as
soon as the child was old enough to be taken to Sio's mother in Dar,
since neither had the money to look after the baby. He hoped Kirabo
would understand. Kirabo did not reply. But it did not stop her from
imagining what the child looked like.

'Kiraboo.' Ntaate's voice was still the same.

Growing up is funny. No one turns out the way you expect them
to. Who knew Ntaate would stretch himself to get a bit tall? And since
when was he shy? They hugged. She asked about St Kalemba, his
school, as they walked to join the crowd at the graveside. Unfortunately,
her eyes were constantly pulled towards Sio, thinking *Let him see me
smiling at his arch-enemy* and *Where is Giibwa?* Jjajja Doctor was talking
through Tom's obituary: 'He was thirty-five years old' – the mourners
tsked – 'survived by three children' – tsks, sighs, heads shaking – 'and
a widow' – sullen silence. 'The last rites will be held in August,' said
Jjajja Doctor.

Period pain broke through and Kirabo realised she had forgotten
to take the tablets at 2.00p.m. She had not changed either. Tom was
lowered into the grave. She caught Sio's nervous glance and looked

away. August was six months away. Sio would come for Tom's last funeral rites. Pain radiated into her hip joints. She threw soil down the hole and walked away.

On the way to Miiro's house, without Sio's presence to distract her from the reality of Tom's burial, guilt set in. She had walked away from her father without a thought. She had left him alone in a dark hole. He might be claustrophobic. They came to Nsuuta's house and she noticed that the old musambya, where the original state was buried, was gone. The thick passion fruit plant that had once roped itself around the tree was gone too. Goosebumps swept over her arms and at once she was back at Tom's graveside. Too late. The men building his grave had closed it. She knelt by the hole, put her ear to the ground and listened – silence. The men added the wire meshing, then the iron sheets. When the noise stopped, she listened again – nothing. The men poured a mixture of cement, sand and pebbles on top of the wire meshing and then levelled it. In the distance, car doors opened and closed.

'Step out, Kirabo. I need to lock the car.'

She fell back into the car. The smell of heated leather seats mingled with the plastic of the dashboard seemed stronger. She dropped her head on her knees. The pain was keen. Aunt Abi rubbed her back and neck, then she held Kirabo's hand and helped her out. It was five thirty, but the sun was still burning. Kirabo looked up at the mango tree. It had lost most of its branches. She shrugged off the idea that the original state was back in her body because Nsuuta's musambya had been cut down.

She went to the car boot and opened her bag, found a pad Atim had rolled for her and stuffed it into her pocket. Then she popped two tablets out of the Aspro blister and tossed them into her mouth and swallowed them with saliva. Avoiding the diiro where women were crying the reality that Tom was not coming back, she went to the latrine to change. Afterwards, she went in search of Grandfather. She needed to lie down until the painkillers kicked in. At the back of the house, nuns helped the Mothers' Union with food as if there were no road between the Protestant and Catholic parishes in Nattetta. Catholic priests were seating mourners to start serving food. Nattetta Church Choir was washing and drying plates.

Miiro stood behind the poultry barn for the Zungu chickens, facing away from Kirabo. His head leaned against Father Dewo's shoulder. Jjajja Doctor held him by the waist. Kirabo melted away. She went to the chicken barn and pushed the door. It was dark, empty and quiet. She leaned against the wooden wall. The chicken litter on the floor had hardened. The smell, a mixture of chicken poo and floor husks, was old and thin. The sun made tiny beams through little holes in the roof, like puny spotlights.

Kirabo closed her eyes and willed herself to fly out of her body. She would lie on her back below the ceiling and count squares. Then this pain would drain to the floor. But she stayed earthbound. When she heard Miiro and his brothers walk away, she ran after Miiro and whispered that she wanted to lie down. They did not look at each other as they walked to the house. He opened the door of his bedroom. Jjajja Nsangi was asleep on his bed. He asked her to shove close to the wall. Kirabo slipped inside his bed and smelled the sheets. It felt like childhood.

6

3 March 1983

Information about Kirabo's mother strolled in on Thursday, the day after Tom's burial. It arrived with neither elation nor relief. Kirabo would have had Nnakku die a hundred deaths to have her father back. She would sooner have wished Giibwa and Sio's child into non-existence than found her mother.

Kirabo was preparing to go back to Old Kampala when she was told that Grandfather wanted to talk to her. Aunt Abi feared that their house, being unoccupied for so long, would attract thieves. Many of the mourners who had spent the night had started to leave, and their departure was starting to be felt. After burial, people had huddled around the family, creating a false sense of warmth. But now a hole was beginning to open. Fortunately, Grandmother's people would stay longest, especially the women, trickling away slowly so she would not feel their leaving. But Miiro's people, most of whom came from the city, were in a hurry. Kirabo too could not wait to go back to school, where the world outside could be imagined away. Grandfather sat outside under the mango tree with another man of the same age.

'Someone bring us a mat,' Miiro called when he saw Kirabo coming. 'Can we have Mwagale and Tomusange come too?'

Kirabo smiled at the predictability of the moment. The traditional order, which Nnambi had disrupted, was being repaired.

'Can we have a mat?' Miiro called again.

As she sat down, Mwagale and Tommy arrived. Kirabo gave them the *They are going to talk culture* look.

'Sit down, all of you. I will start with you two.' Grandfather pointed to Mwagale and Tommy. 'Do you know her?' He pointed at Kirabo.

Mwagale said, 'She is our sister.'

'Come here, Mwagale, let me hug you because you are intelligent.'

'She is my sister as well.' Tommy wanted a hug too.

'Kirabo is not just Kirabo,' Grandfather said. 'She is Baaba because she was born before you were, and we respect those who arrived before us even though we do not know why that is; not so?'

The two nodded.

'What do you call her?'

'Baaba Kirabo.'

'Good. But most important, there is no such thing as *Our mothers are different*. We don't know such things. Our mothers are very important but, in the clan, we put them aside and focus on father, grandfather and all those grandfathers that came before. If your father is the same, you are brother and sister. If your fathers are brothers, you are brother and sister – no such nonsense as cousin-brother, cousin-sister.'

'Cousin-brother oh-oh,' the other man laughed. 'Where do they find these words?'

'English.' Miiro turned back to the children: 'Cousins are our aunts' children because they come from other clans and have different totems. You hear me?'

They nodded.

'Now, Kirabo, look at your siblings.' Miiro pointed. Kirabo turned to them. 'In the absence of your father, you look after them in every way you can. They don't call you Baaba for nothing. You set an example. You love them whether they love you back or not. Be easy to approach. I don't want to hear that nonsense of half-this or half-that.'

Kirabo nodded.

'You two, when you have a problem, the first person is Kirabo. She will say let's do this, or let's take that problem to Mother, or to Aunt Abi or to Uncle Ndiira or to Jjajja Miiro. You have heard me?'

They nodded.

'Now the two of you can go. Kirabo, stay behind.'

When Mwagale and Tommy had gone, Miiro turned to the other man and said, 'Your turn.'

'Now, wife.' The man leaned towards Kirabo. 'Who am I?'

Kirabo's mind went into a spin. He had called her wife, which meant he was her grandfather, but what kind of grandfather? Perhaps a son of Luutu's brother? She stated the obvious: 'You are Jjajja.'

'Of course, but which grandfather?'

'Jjajja Miiro's brother.'

Miiro laughed. The man clapped and dropped his head in shame. 'I am Ssemwaka Kaye, I am from Mityana; I am your mother's father.'

Kirabo took a while to absorb what he had said. Then she remembered that Nnambi was from Mityana. 'Oh, that mother?' She indicated to where Nnambi sat.

'Yes, that one, and the other one too.'

Kirabo looked at him. Now she remembered he had come to her baptism when she was seven. He brought her a pair of white shoes and those socks with pink diamonds on the side, the ones she buried with the original state.

'Which other one?'

'Nnakku.'

Kirabo opened her mouth, sucked in air to talk but closed it. Then she tried again: 'Is she alive?'

'Of course she is; did someone say she was not?'

'No, it is just that the war came and went and she did not...' She sighed away the rest of the sentence. 'They are sisters?' She creased her face in disgust.

'Yes.'

'How?'

'It just happened. Nnambi did not know Nnakku was your mother when she met your father. Nnakku had cut herself off from Tom. None of us knew she had a child. She and Jjali, her mother, hid it from us.'

Kirabo was jolted. She had problems listening to what the man was saying because her mind was galloping backwards. 'But Tom noticed the resemblance and insisted.' The man's voice came back into focus. 'Nnambi came to me to check. I came to see you. I said to Miiro, those eyes, the nose and lips are mine. I went to Nnakku and said, "There is a child. She looks like us. The father says you are the mother." There was no denying to me. But she told me what she had told your father; she did not want to know you. So, I, Tom the departed, and your grandparents agreed not to tell you.' By now, Kirabo's mind had not only recovered Jjali Solome with permed hair and Solome Jjali who had helped this man to abuse Nnambi's mother in the '50s, but Nnakku, who made Nnambi seem like an angel. She clicked her tongue at her utter blindness. All along, the truth had been so close she had sat on it.

'But do you see how truth will not be hidden?' Miiro was saying. 'Of all women in the world, how did Tom end up with Nnakku's sister?'

The old man paused, then he agreed grudgingly that indeed truth never goes into hiding. 'As I was saying, Kirabo, there was no reason to stop Tom from marrying Nnambi. After all, who better to bring up the abandoned child than a sister? In fact, tradition has always sacrificed a sister for one who died for the good of the children. So, in the past, if you died young in marriage and left behind very young children, our family would dispatch Mwagale to carry on with your marriage and bring up your children with your husband. Back then we did not tell children when their mothers died. Why bring pain to them when there is another mother?'

'I have heard,' Miiro said, 'that in other cultures men are even forced to marry their dead brothers' wives for the sake of the children. Can you imagine?'

'We sacrifice whatever is necessary so children can have a mother *and* a father.'

Kirabo began to think about this sacrifice, but it was much too big for her congested mind.

'Do you not want to know where your mother is?'

She looked up and noticed that the old man was waiting for a response. 'Does she want to know how I am?' Kirabo realised too late that she had snapped.

Ssemwaka Kaye sighed. 'You must understand that your mother was a child when she had you.'

'Is she still a child?'

The old man looked at Miiro, as if for help. Miiro did not move. Ssemwaka continued, 'When you look at the situation properly, I am to blame. I abandoned Nnakku to her mother. As I said, I did not know you had been born. As the father of your mothers, I am trying to make it right.'

'I don't know.' Kirabo stretched out a numb leg. 'This is a bit too much for me right now.' The numbness started to thaw, and fizziness started to *cha cha cha* in the leg. 'First, Nnambi does not want me in my father's house even though, as you said, she was my mother's sister and who was best to bring me up. Then I discover that my mother does not want me either because she was a child when she had me. And now my father has died Nnambi becomes what, my aunt?'

'We could not hold this information now that you don't have a father.'

'So where is she?'

'In Jinja. She married there. You have a sister and a brother. She works for Save the Children.'

Kirabo laughed. 'Save what children?'

'She is not a bad person, just scared. She lives on Kisinja Road, two houses after the ruins. Once you see the ruins, you have arrived. The first thing you will see is the eucalyptus tree. It stands right in the middle of her compound. Her house has black tiles on the roof. It is very easy to find.'

'Well, child,' Miiro said, holding Kirabo's shoulders, 'you don't have to find her. We are enough, are we not? If love does not come to us, we don't go chasing after it. We are enough.'

'You never know,' Ssemwaka Kaye said. 'As we Ganda say, Mother is sweet.'

Kirabo suppressed something unsavoury about the sweetness of mothers.

'But you must understand, she could not tell her husband she had a child. Being a woman is not easy. Men do not understand.' He turned to Miiro. 'We make them pregnant, but we will not marry a girl who has a child. You want to ask, did she have the child with a tree?' The man turned back to Kirabo. 'We all kept quiet to give her time. But most of all, no one wished you to feel rejected.'

'What does her husband do?'

'He works for Nile Breweries. His name is Jjumba Luninze.'

'They must be well off then.' Kirabo had hoped poverty had kept her mother away.

He scratched his head. 'Well, they are not badly off.'

'Will I not upset her happy family if I turn up?'

'Maybe, but I warned her that I would tell you now your father is gone. Hopefully she will be expecting you.'

'You mean you told Nnakku that my father had died but she still did not come to bury him?'

'Ah.' This time, words failed him.

'You know what, Jjajja Ssemwaka? I have no intention of finding her.'

'But I have been talking to Miiro. You must come to Mityana. I must introduce you to the family. You must meet the Ffumbe clan. And then if you change your mind, I will arrange for you to meet your mother.'

Kirabo smiled to herself. Was this the Franco whose wife described him as the bearer of the flag for the most contemptuous men in the world? Nothing about him suggested he was capable of such wickedness. How unlucky was Tom to have his children with two evil women from the same family?

Just in time, Aunt Abi came and asked Miiro if they had finished. A friend of hers was leaving for Kampala and would give Kirabo a lift. As Kirabo stood up, Jjajja Ssemwaka slipped a wad of money into her hands. She promised to visit him and his people, then went to the diiro to say goodbye to Grandmother. Nsuuta held her and whispered, 'Have they told you?'

'Hmm.'

'Miiro did not want you to know, but we could not protect you any longer.' She paused, then added, 'Or Nnakku...because she needed protecting too.'

'And you are going to say that even Nnambi needed protecting.'

'Her too, in a way. I disagree with her methods, but as I told you, with your mothers, their rejection of you should not be taken personally.'

'I don't care about Nnakku any more, Nsuuta. I set myself free of her a long time ago.'

'That is not true, Kirabo; you will look for her.'

Kirabo made to stand up because people who had never been rejected by a parent were incapable of understanding.

'Wait.' Nsuuta reached into the folds of the sash fastening her busuuti and retrieved a piece of paper. She folded it further, put it in Kirabo's palm and closed her hand over it. 'Proof that she is your mother. Me, the moment Tom brought you, at six months old, to Nattetta, I went in search of Nnakku. I have been tracking her since, step by step.'

Kirabo hugged Nsuuta again and whispered in her ear, 'I am lucky you are my grandmother too.' And she thrust the piece of paper into her pocket without looking at it.

'Don't worry about things, Kirabo. Concentrate on your exams.'

Kirabo forgot about the piece of paper until evening, when she counted the condolence money she had been given. When she unfolded the paper, she saw that it was discoloured with age. It had been filled out in ink: Place of Birth – MULAGO HOSPITAL. Date of Birth – 01/05/63. Sex – F. Weight – 8 LB 16 OZ. Time of Birth – 9.27A.M.

Mother – LOVINCA NNAKKU. Father – TOMUSANGE PIITU. Kirabo bit her lip at her father's name. Such small things now triggered the tears. She scrutinised the chit. *Nnakku once held this piece of paper in her hands. She once held me in her hands; how could she let me go?* What she would not give to fly back to that May morning of 1963 and look at Nnakku and Tom and her newborn self and pretend that death would never visit.

7

4 March 1983

Nsuuta was right. Kirabo had been lying to herself. She woke up late the following day and, without thinking about it, got ready and set off for the taxi rank in Kampala. The sun was wicked. A part of her said it was unwise to find Nnakku when she was about to do her A-level exams: that Tom's death was shock enough. But the other side said that it would be equally disruptive if she did not find her. Her mind would agonise over Nnakku and her family over and over. *Best to see Nnakku and get her out of my system*, she reasoned.

All Tom's siblings and some cousins were still in Nattetta to make certain that Grandfather and Grandmother would cope. There were decisions to make as well. Firstly, there was no excluding Nsuuta from the family any more; she had cancer, and everyone knew Tom's wishes. Then there was Nnambi, who had become a burden to the family. By the time Kirabo left Nattetta, rumour had it that if Nnambi wished to stay with her children they would move into Tom's unfinished house. All the money coming from Tom's job, the condolence money and his working siblings' contributions would be pooled to complete a wing of the house for them. But the money would not be given to her. Oh no. Beyond looking beautiful, Nnambi had only brains enough to cross the road without being hit by a car. What if she bought cosmetics with the money? If Nnambi was to find another man – after all, she was still young – she was welcome to leave. Of course, she would leave the children with their clan. Word had it that Aunt Abi would be the mukuza, the one to raise Tom's children. She was already bringing up Kirabo, and she and Tom had been inseparable: she knew his wishes. If Widow Tom was not happy with that arrangement, she was welcome to leave. Everyone else was to check and keep an eye on the children, taking food or money whenever they could. However, not everyone would take their voice to Tom's widow. If something was not right, Abi was to be contacted so Tom's widow would listen to only one person. Tommy and Mwagale were going to boarding school. Miiro would pay their school fees. They would spend a part of their holidays in Nattetta with their grandparents and a part with their mother. Under no cir-cumstances would Tom's widow bring her 'men' into Tom's house and flaunt them in front of his children. She could love her men out of sight until she got married and left the family. Everyone agreed on one thing: Nnambi was lucky Miiro's family was decent. Another family? With a wicked woman like Nnambi? As soon as Tom was put in the ground, *ba ppa*, they would have helped her pack her bags and shown her the way back to wherever she came from – *Lilabe, don't waste our time, kisirani*. Kirabo had heard these things being discussed among family the night after Tom's burial, but until Miiro stamped them, nothing was definite.

Kirabo arrived at the taxi rank and asked for the Jinja lane. Before she got to it, she heard a broker call, 'Jinja, Iganga awo,' and she boarded.

All the way to Jinja, she sat senseless, like a piece of luggage. Her heart refused to think about what she would do when she got there. But it did not stop her body from perspiring now and again. As the car sped through Mabira Forest and the fresh breath of the trees whipped her face, she wondered how often Nnakku travelled the same route. The forest gave way to the Kakira sugar cane plantations. The cane was as skinny as reeds. Then tea estates, perfectly trimmed, rolled up and down the hills like a green carpet. At last, they descended to Owen Falls and Kirabo felt lifted above the world. The Owen Falls Dam does that to you. The falls were far down below. She craned her neck, hoping that all the turbines were turned on. Finally, she was in Greater Jinja.

If cities ailed, Jinja had sleeping sickness. Idi Amin's sudden expulsion of whites and Asians back in 1972 had hit the city harder than anywhere else. In just over a decade, Jinja's status as the country's largest industrial city had become questionable. Buildings were crumbling. Boutiques sold bananas and fruit. Grocery stores had gossipy women twisting hair. Often, Kirabo peered inside a 'supermarket' to find someone's idea of a sitting room. She smiled to herself. Uganda was that woman who bleached just the face and imagined the rest of her body light-skinned too. Clearly, the government took care of Kampala, where foreigners stopped, and imagined away all the other towns. She walked towards a group of men wheeling bicycles with bright-coloured tasselled panniers. They saw her coming and rushed towards her – 'Boda-boda yino… Most comfortable… Take mine, I am so strong you will not dismount on a hill' – some making a racket with the bells. Kirabo had thought the boda-boda bicycles were limited to the Busia–Malaba border. But now the phenomenon had crept as far inland as Jinja. She was certain they would never make it to Kampala. No one with self-respect would take a ride on them. But as she had no idea where Kisinja Road was, she got on the first bicycle and asked to be taken there. Especially as she did not know whether the road was called Kissinger or Kisinja.

'I know everyone on Kisinja. Who are you going to see?'

'A woman working for Save the Children.'

'Oh, Muka Luninze? I know her. Have you been before?'

'No.'

'Are you her sister? You resemble.'

Kirabo hesitated. 'No, she is my aunt.'

From Main Street, they joined Busoga Avenue, then Oboja Road. After a while, the man began to sweat from pedalling. Then he was steaming. Kirabo asked how far they had to go.

'Almost there: a turn to the left and we are at her house.'

'Tell you what, why not drop me here? I will pay the full fare.'

Kirabo started walking. Kisinja Road was a bizarre place. Quiet and leafy, it had all the hallmarks of a former colonial residential area. All the houses were old European architecture with sprawling compounds. Some houses were abandoned, some were crumbling, some had been looted after the war, yet some had been renovated and were quite ostentatious. Kirabo had not decided what she would do when she got to Nnakku's house, whether to peek and walk past or knock and introduce herself.

She saw the eucalyptus tree first, and her heart raced. Then the huge ruin Jjajja Ssemwaka had described. Soon the black roof on Nnakku's house appeared on the horizon. From the little she could see, Nnakku's house had preserved the colonial facade.

Kirabo slowed down. She had found the house too easily. Maybe it was not the one. Probably, she was on the wrong street. The house came closer. Her heart was loud. A neatly trimmed hedge. A porch painted in cream. The gate. She stopped, looked around, then tiptoed to the gate and peered through the grille. A car was parked on a ramp outside the garage doors. Plastic toys in the compound. No one outside. Should she knock? She stepped away from the gate and looked to the left, then to the right again; no one was walking down the road. Maybe Nnakku was not at home. Of course she was not at home – it was Friday. She could knock, say she had been sent by her mother and look around Nnakku's house.

A sound of a car ignition. A rod being wedged out. One side of the gate started to open. The other side of the gate opened too. For a suspended moment, Nnakku's home stood wide open. Kirabo stood frozen. A car was coming, but her mind was far away. The car drove towards her. Then she realised and jumped out of the way. A woman was driving. She got to the road and stopped. She turned to look to her right and Kirabo stared into Nnambi's snake eyes. A chill spread over her arms. Without a heartbeat of hesitation, the woman looked to her left. But Kirabo had seen it all: recognition, alarm, panic. Yet there was no pause in Nnakku's looking to the right again and pulling on to the road. She turned in the direction Kirabo had come from.

Kirabo turned and watched the car drive away. It got to the junction, took a right and disappeared. Behind, she heard the gate close and the creaking of a rod being wedged in. Still she stood and stared at the empty road. Every part of her quivered. The sun beat so hard on the tarmac she smelt tar. Radiation danced off the road surface like a ghost.

When she began to walk, she stepped into the depression of the driveway and almost lost her footing. Then she was up on the pavement again. She walked alongside Nnakku's hedge, past another house and another. Her mind said *You came from the other direction, turn and walk back*, but her legs refused. So, that was it, that was her. All her life, from the first time she asked about her mother, the first night she shot into the night sky and saw that light germinate, to consulting Nsuuta, to Tom's house in Bugoloobi, to moving in with Aunt Abi, all those posters at St Theresa's, Tom dying, down to this moment, and that was her.

Just then she saw Nnakku's car coming towards her. She recognised the car – a Fiat Panda, white, UWP 939 – immediately. Nnakku must have driven in a circle. *She is coming for a second look, to make sure you have not gone into her house to disrupt her life. Look straight ahead, relax. You can even glance at her in a passing way, certainly no recognition.* But then a wave of optimism swept over her. *She did not believe her eyes before. She is going to stop and ask 'Are you Kirabo Nnamiiro?'* As the car got closer, it slowed a little. Kirabo looked up, glanced at nothing and walked on. The car went past. Kirabo heard it turn into the driveway behind her, a discreet horn. No voice calling, no footsteps running after her, just the wicked sun pounding the earth and the evil smell of hot tar. Kirabo turned the corner where the car had come from. She could see that Nnakku's car was still at the gate. Ahead of her was the boda-boda rank. But Kirabo would not get angry at the fact that the boda-boda man had taken her the longer way.

Just as she came to Bell Avenue, a car crept up behind her. Kirabo jumped. It was Nnakku's car. She sprinted across the road. When she got to the other side, she turned and looked at Nnakku in an *I know you would kill me* way. But Nnakku wore sunglasses now. Kirabo kept staring, no longer pretending not to know her. Nnakku could not pull away because cars kept coming. She kept looking left and right, left and right, her car indicating that she was turning right. Then she noticed a space and stepped too hard on the accelerator. The car pulled away, jerky and loud.

8

'Thank God for Faaza Dewo's generosity...we are so lucky to have him.'

'Not just that, thank God Catholic priests don't marry. If Faaza Dewo had had a family he would not have done all of that. For Widow Tom.'

'Forget all that. Thank God the Catholic Church is rich. If he was one of our Potostante Anglicans, ho. Their priests eat the peels off their cracking lips like us.'

That is how family talked. Since Tom's passing, his siblings, cousins and a few of the friends they grew up with in Nattetta had begun to get together on Friday evenings, normally at Aunt Abi's house, to drink and to keep an eye on each other. They talked about their childhoods, talked about Tom as if they dared not forget. They huddled together as if Tom had died because they had neglected each other. Kirabo, who by now was in her holidays after her A-level exams, learnt from their chatter that Father Dewo had not only smartened the annex of Tom's new house, he had installed electricity, ready for Nnambi and the children to move in.

After the three months' notice Nnambi had been given to vacate the Coffee Marketing Board house ended, Aunt Abi told Kirabo to go to Bugoloobi and help Nnambi with the packing.

When Kirabo arrived, the lorry Father Dewo had sent to pick up Tom's property was parked close to the porch. There was something washed-out about the house, the garden and everything. Inside, the house seemed bigger. It was dark, like a house that had lost electricity. Nnambi and her sisters were in the dining space, wrapping china in newspaper. Kirabo greeted them, but they did not look at her as they answered. As an afterthought Kirabo added, 'Nga kitalo ekya Daddy.' They glanced at each other. Perhaps they had not expected civility from her. One of them said, 'Hmm, we should say that to you, Kirabo.'

Nnambi had lost so much weight her neck was like a plucked chicken's – long and thin. Her shoulder joints protruded. Nnaki the housemaid had left. Thank God Tommy and Mwagale were in boarding school; imagine losing their comforts, the heartbreak of walking away from their home. Kirabo asked Nnambi to point out the items that needed packing.

She started packing in the bedrooms. First, she packed Mwagale's and Tommy's things, then she went to the main bedroom and began with the bed. Folded the sheets and blanket, and piled the pillows on top. She unhooked the curtains, then the nettings and folded them. For a while she was buried in the silence and coldness of the bedroom. But then she heard a car door bang outside. Moments later Kirabo heard the jingle of Tom's car keys at the back of the house, then his footsteps in the corridor. She stopped and listened: nothing. She skulked to the door and peered into the corridor: nothing. She crossed into Mwagale's room and peered through the window: there was no car parked outside. She crept back into the main bedroom, ashamed.

Before she removed Tom's clothes from the wardrobe, she asked Nnambi whether there were any she did not wish to keep. They could be taken to Batte. As Nnambi sifted through shirts and trousers, tears ran down her face. She put a pile on the bed. 'Batte can have those.' Kirabo did not bother to hide her tears either. Yet they carried on sorting Tom's clothes as if they did not hear each other's pain, as if they were not weeping for the same person. Nnambi knelt on the floor and looked under the bed. She pulled out a few pairs of shoes and blew the dust off them. 'I think they wore the same size. Take those as well.' She gave her three pairs and wiped the tears with the back of her hand. As she left the room, she glanced at Kirabo. 'Thank you for coming to help.'

'You don't need to thank me for that.' Kirabo smiled, but she remained standing in the same place long after Nnambi had gone. Nnambi's sheer loss of weight; you had to search for her beauty now. What did that mean for her future? Would she pull herself together and start working? Kirabo sighed and went back to packing. When she lifted the mattress from the bed, she saw, on the floor, a red can of Old Spice. She pushed the bed away, picked it up and shook it. It was empty. She pressed the nozzle and it sprayed air. She smelt the nozzle and it was the scent of her father as she walked behind him. She searched the room and found more Old Spice tins and bottles, some blue, some white, of deodorant, aftershave, shaving lotion, shaving powder. It was not just the scent, it was the image on the bottle of the ship sailing away. She would keep those for herself.

When everything the family owned was on the lorry, Kirabo looked at it in disbelief. Apart from the unfinished house in Busega, Tom's wealth did not amount to much. The fact that it could be packed in boxes, loaded on to a lorry and driven away was disconcerting. You would never wrap up Grandfather's wealth that way. Yet people in Nattetta who lived in houses they owned, built on their own land, who produced their own food, had envied Tom because he spoke English, drove a car, lived in the city and drank Cinzano. Kirabo's eyes began to open to the fact that poverty and wealth were constructs after all. Rural poverty was different from urban poverty. To city people, if you did not wear shoes and changed clothes twice a day, you were poor. But in the rural, that was silly. Wearing a different dress every day meant doing a lot of laundry on Saturday, which meant fetching a lot of water. Yet here was Tom's family with all the shoes and clothes, electric gadgets, expensive stuff, falling back on Grandfather, who neither had electricity in his house nor drove a car. But the way the world was going, people in the rural were beginning to see poverty from the city's perspective, while city people were starting to see poverty through Western lenses.

Kirabo and Nnambi's sisters climbed into the back of the lorry and sat on the furniture. Nnambi got into the cabin with the driver and they drove out. The gate closed and the chain clinked as if they were coming back. Kirabo looked away. The clink of the chain hurt. She did not see the bungalows, the flats or Bugoloobi Town. She could not bear to look at the Coffee Marketing Board building. The driver avoided the city and drove via the Kampala bypass, Nsambya and Queen's Way until they joined Masaka Road. In Ndeeba, plots narrowed, houses shrivelled, yet the population had tripled. Evening markets, toninyira, were laid down on the hard shoulder. They sold fresh produce and cooked foods, second-hand clothes and shoes, everything. In Nateete, the streets swarmed as if people had just poured out of a stadium. Hawkers sang their wares. The world here was squeezed.

Kirabo looked away from the road and contemplated life. Since Tom's passing, life spoke in a clear language. The imagery was brutal. Tom had been a god, like Buddha, huge and golden. Aunt Abi, Nnambi, Grandmother, Nsuuta, Mwagale and Kirabo had sat around him in worship. Occasionally they had snapped at each other, wrangled, formed enmities and built alliances around him. Now that the god had been pulled down, they were starting to see each other. Nnambi was no longer the evil stepmother but her siblings' mother. Mwagale was not Tom's brat but her sister. Nsuuta and Grandmother were two mothers who had lost a son. Even Aunt Abi was beginning to see Nnambi as a broken widow rather than a mujinni. Yet Tom had been a loving father, a caring brother, a good son, and even Nnambi could not say that he had been the worst husband. He had not made himself a god. They, the women, had.

They arrived in Busega, a mostly unbuilt area. Large plots were still bush, some were matooke plantations, cassava, sweet potato gardens. But there was a sense that the plots were being snapped up. Many of them were fenced off, some had been levelled by tractors, and some had structures going up.

The lorry turned off the main road into a rutted track. It drove past Aunt Abi's plot. She had brought Kirabo along to inspect it before she bought it, and she had used it as a teachable moment: 'No matter how much a husband loves you, Kirabo, you must buy your own land and build your own house – in case. Most women do it on the stealth, but I say let him know you are doing it, so he knows you have an alternative to his home. Until the law starts to protect us, we must find ways. And Kirabo,' she had added, 'You should only have children you can bring up on your own. Too many women are trapped in bad marriages because of children.' The foundation to Aunt Abi's house had been dug. There were heaps of sand, stones and blocks. Aunt Abi had started to build her house despite Jjajja Nsangi's caution. Apparently, Ganda men did not like marrying successful women; they emasculated them.

When they got to Tom's house, Kirabo realised how lofty Tom's dreams had been.

9

Tom's last rites were to be held in Nattetta because his new house was not only without facilities to cater for the multitudes of people expected, but, as Miiro had put it, there was no space for people to stretch their legs.

Grandmother's clan, from Timiina, was the first to arrive, two weeks early, and camped in two of the three double rooms in the big boys' block. They brought food, goats and chickens. The men started cutting down spare tree branches and shrubs for firewood to dry. They fetched water and filled hired tanks. They harvested mbidde bananas to ripen for brewing alcohol. They cut poles to build tents. They were unassuming in Miiro's house, these people from Timiina. Even Grandmother's brothers. They took on Grandmother's attitude – that of people who had married into the clan.

Nnambi's family came a week later. They arrived discreetly and took the last double rooms in the big boys' block. They all joined in the preparations, except her mother, who Grandmother and Nsuuta drew into their inner circle, and her father, who joined Miiro.

Miiro's relations arrived three days before the rituals started, when all the main preparations had been done. Even though they were few, you knew who they were instantly. They swung car keys and mixed Luganda with English, showing that they were not just the clan but the money. The women were loud and male. Apart from Aunts YA and Abi, who took supervisory roles, the other women did not do any chores at all: that was for women who had married into the family and their people. They sat under tree shades and found fault with young girls and asked to be introduced to children and the newly married wives. Jjajja Nsangi presided over their gossip, food and alcohol. The men drove in and out buying this, bringing that, only doing things that needed the muscle of money.

The main house was arranged in a way that if you still had tears to cry, you took them to the diiro and quenched yourself. After Little Tommy, Tom's heir, was installed on Saturday and his children's tears were washed off by Aunt YA, crying would become wrong.

For the five months Tom had been dead, Giibwa had not tried to find Kirabo to say *Nga kitalo about your father* at all. Yet at midday on Friday she made a shimmering entrance.

Sio arrived in the morning. He greeted Kirabo as if he did not know her and joined the men doing chores. All morning, he worked with Batte. First, they helped with the construction of the large canopy, then fetched firewood from where it had been chopped and left in the sun to dry by Grandmother's people. By the time Giibwa arrived at midday, Sio and Batte were fetching water to refill the tanks. Female residents were on the peripheries of Grandmother's matooke plantations, peeling and wrapping food into huge mounds. Women from Nnambi's family were cooking food for lunch and supper. Women from Timiina were preparing bunches of banana leaves for wrapping foods. The goats and chickens from Timiina had been slaughtered, the goats skinned and the chickens plucked. Male residents were brewing tonto. Some men were further away, preparing the cow for the main event.

Kirabo was at the back of the house drawing water from the barrels when she heard a woman whisper in distress, 'Kati, what has she come dressed like that for?'

'To poke Kirabo over Kabuye's son.'

'Poke Kirabo, whatever for?'

'You don't know? Kirabo was the first on him.'

'I thought it ended when she left.'

'Who lied you? When children are determined, they are determined. Kirabo has been carrying on with Kabuye's son where Abi's eyes don't see.'

'You lie.'

'But you know men, Kabuye's son saw Giibwa too. One little touch like this and she was pregnant. I think she heard that Kabuye's son is here doing chores, and has come to do battle.'

'Yii yii, when Giibwa and Kirabo used to run all over this village inseparable? Where has shame gone?'

'Which shame? You are the only one who knows shame.'

Kirabo threw the bowl she had been scooping water with into the barrel and marched around the house, past the women, who now gasped, into the back room, through the diiro, to the front of the house. Giibwa stood in the front yard dressed for an evening party. Stilettos, sheer body stocking, black glittery evening dress, dangly earrings, metallic eyeshadow and scarlet lipstick. Kirabo wanted to laugh *Giibwa, you are competing with sunshine right now*, but instead said, 'I think you are lost, Giibwa. We are at last funeral rites here, not partying.'

Giibwa replied in English, '*I am a villagement too. I have a right to be here.*'

Ssozi, who had been eating porridge under the mango tree, put his mug down, covered it with a saucer and came to where Giibwa stood. 'My child, why would you stick your hand into a beehive? Either go back home and dress for chores or don't come back.'

'Who put you in charge?' she asked in Luganda. Then she pointed at Kirabo, laughing. 'They were showing off, splashing their *bulove-love* all over the place as if they were the first to fall in love. Now where is it?'

Ssozi held Giibwa by the upper arm and tried to steer her away. She shook him off. People had started to gather, especially the youth looking for entertainment. Kirabo changed subject. 'The word is village-*mate*, not villag*ement*.'

'Don't waste your English on me. After all, the thing Sio is really interested in does not speak English.'

The compound gasped. Kirabo looked at Giibwa the way you look at a child who has pushed its boundaries. 'If you are not joining in doing chores, please leave; you are being disruptive.'

'You are so dumb, Kirabo, if you cannot see that he is only in love with your great-grandfather and your grandfather and your father and your education.'

'I don't know what you are talking about, Giibwa.'

'Take all that away and you are no better than me.'

At that moment, Sio turned into the walkway, lugging a jerrycan in either hand. Kirabo wanted to call *Sio, your Giibwa is here stirring up trouble*, but she would attract more attention. He disappeared behind the house. Giibwa had her back to the road and did not see him. Someone must have tipped him off. He returned hurrying, grabbed Giibwa's hand and steered her away. Somehow seeing Sio touch Giibwa catapulted Kirabo over the steps and by the time someone shouted, 'Hold that child,' she had slapped Sio's cheeks once, twice, thrice. Ssozi held the fourth slap. Sio closed his eyes and bit down on the pain. Ntaate ran behind the house, ululating: 'Wolololo, she has sizzled his cheeks, *ba cha, ba cha, ba cha.*'

Grandmother pulled Kirabo away. 'Swallow those tears,' she ordered. 'Swallow them right now. You slapped him; you don't get to cry.' She turned to Sio. 'Grandson, forgive us. Kirabo has done very wrong, I will deal with her presently. But why don't you take your woman away from here?'

Sio started to say that he, not Kirabo, was to blame, but Grandmother had turned away.

'Kdto, haa!' Ssozi clapped in wonderment. 'Me, I told you a long time ago; if you want to see how a woman beats up a man, marry into Luutu's clan.'

Grandmother, who had reached the porch with Kirabo, stopped and said, 'On my mother's truth, I will start with you, Ssozi. Then you can tell the world how I am a buffalo.'

Perhaps Aunt Abi did not hear Grandmother challenge a whole man, because while the entire world stood frozen, she came down the steps, held Sio's hand and led him past Giibwa, whispering, 'Child, hyenas will be hyenas even when you dress them in leopard skin,' and walked him to the back of the house. Meanwhile, inside the house Grandmother handed Kirabo over to Nsuuta and went back outside. Nsuuta held Kirabo's hand and said loudly, 'What did I say about hitting people?' Then she whispered, 'At least you did not hit her.' Then loudly, 'How would you feel if he hit you back?' Then she giggled. 'But did you hear what Alikisa said to Ssozi?'

Kirabo laughed despite her tears.

'Now, I can die.' Nsuuta whispered when she caught her breath.

10

Thankfully, the ten school friends Kirabo invited to the rites arrived at around four, after Giibwa had left. Had they been around, it would have been a different story.

Apart from Atim, who had supported Kirabo through her loss, the friends came not to mourn or celebrate her father but to escape their parents' watchful eyes. There was no fun like last funeral rites. They brought booze and boyfriends. For those who did not have a partner, Kirabo had promised a steady supply of young uncles – Jjajja Doctor's younger sons and Grandmother's nephews – for two unsupervised days. They also wanted to see Sio for themselves and sort out Giibwa the slut. Kirabo had asked Miiro for a large traditional tent to be made specifically for her and her friends.

It was as if boys in the villages had sensed the girls' arrival. Within no time, they started to whizz past Kirabo's tent, throwing quick glances at the girls as they strutted by, greeting Kirabo with exaggerated enthusiasm: '*Ki kati, Kirabo, long time no see,*' as if Nattetta was anglophone. As night closed in, more boys and girls descended on Miiro's compound dressed as if there was a disco on. Word went around that if you had beer, wine or Uganda Waragi and were willing to share, you gained entrance to Kirabo's tent. Within no time, it was heaving.

Ignoring Kirabo's feelings, Atim found Sio and introduced herself as Kirabo's best friend. When she brought him to the tent, she claimed to Kirabo that Sio could not resist the first woman president-to-be. Then she introduced him to the other boyfriends. Kirabo waved to him and carried on as if he was not there. Often she felt his gaze and was transported back to the time before Giibwa had become *that Giibwa*. There was so much bustle around Kirabo's tent that the tents belonging to Uncle Ndiira and Aunt Abi, who had brought a lot of unmarried friends and booze with them, looked mediocre by comparison.

By eight, when girls and boys had settled in and the chatter was flowing as freely as the alcohol, Aunt YA arrived in Kirabo's tent. She came nice and smiley to meet the *'lovely'* girls and boys who had come to Kirabo's dad's last rites. *'What wonderful friends you are!'* she exclaimed. Before long she was counting how many girls had come from Kampala and who their parents were (she chose to ignore the boys). And oh, she would sleep in the same tent because she had seen the wolves circling: *'And you know how last funeral rites notoriously slacken people's morals. And the parents of these good girls allowed them to come to our rites because they know Kirabo comes from a decent family.'*

In the silence that ensued, Kirabo could hear the death throes of her party as Aunt YA chased away all traces of revelry.

The boys started to slink out as the girls glared at Kirabo. Kirabo wanted to scream. She was nineteen, most of her friends were eighteen and about to start university where they could sleep around if they wished, but Aunt YA was carrying on as if they were thirteen-year-olds. And then people wondered why girls at university were sexually liberal after being tethered on short leashes all their lives. By the time the drums started, even the girls had slipped away. Kirabo went and sat in the tent because Aunt YA had made it obvious she was keeping an eye on her.

An hour later Atim came to Kirabo breathless. 'You did not tell me Sio has two cars.'

'They belonged to his parents.'

'Us, we are off to Kayunga to get more booze. And to see if there is a disco on.'

'Come on, Atim, you cannot leave me here on my own.'

'Then come along. Actually, I told Sio you are coming.'

'Atim—'

'It was your Aunt Mean who drove us away,' she whispered with a glance at Aunt YA. 'I will tell Sio you have been called by the elders to talk culture.'

'Atim—'

'It is okay,' Atim said, starting to walk away, 'he is safe with me.'

'I don't care about that.'

'Of course you don't.'

Midnight came and went, but Kirabo's friends had not yet returned. She and Aunt YA were in the large canopy watching traditional dancers when they were called into the house for a clan meeting to discuss Tom's successor and the distribution of his property. Kirabo was surprised. From what she had heard, women did not attend such meetings. If your father died without making a will and his children came from multiple mothers, it was for the sisters to meet to choose which of their brothers would inherit them and become their father. As for the distribution of Tom's estate, everything would go to Tommy now there was no will. Besides, Tom's only property was that unfinished house in Busega. Kirabo did not see why she needed to attend to hear little Tommy being given everything.

The family had gathered in the diiro. Only Luutu's descendants from male lineages were eligible to attend. No Grandmother, no Tom's widow, no Jjajja Doctor's wife, certainly not Ndiira's girlfriend, and no aunts' children. A high clan leader, the Mutuba Head, presided. Kirabo and Aunt YA grabbed mats and sat on the floor.

Miiro had broken protocol and brought his daughters and grand-daughters to the meeting. His sister Nsangi could not come because she was too drunk. The attendance of women was an irritation to the clan heads because they were not used to talking to women about clan issues. Besides, Miiro's brothers, the priest and the doctor, were intimidating to the peasant clan heads, who felt they were being bullied. At first, they reminded Miiro that only his brothers, sons and grandsons should attend, but Miiro argued that it was his daughter who was looking after Tom's family. It did not make sense to exclude her from making decisions. Father Dewo stepped in, explaining that their father, Luutu, never discriminated against Nsangi, their sister. She was included in all major family decisions and they were honouring that. The Mutuba Head pointed out that it was widely known that Luutu's house not only flaunted cultural etiquette but was condescending to clan leaders. He stopped short of saying that Nsangi was drunk precisely because Luutu gave her too much leeway, but it was there in the air.

'The problem with women is,' another clan head explained, 'you give them an inch, they demand an acre.'

But Miiro insisted that no meeting would start until all his daughters and granddaughters were present. In the end, the clan heads conceded: 'Bring the women, but only if they will sit down and keep quiet.'

For a moment all was well. The men – clan heads, Miiro, Father Dewo, Jjajja Doctor and his sons, Uncle Ndiira and his little boy, and Tommy – sat up on the chairs. The women – both Miiro's and Jjajja Doctor's daughters, plus Kirabo and Mwagale, sat down on the floor. But if Jjajja Nsangi had been present, she would have pulled little Tommy down from the chair and taken it herself: *You are not going to swing your legs above my head, little man.* Kirabo gnashed her teeth, wondering where Jjajja Nsangi was when she needed her to shake things up a bit.

First, Miiro introduced the clan heads, then everyone else introduced themselves. Miiro told the Mutuba Head about Tom's estate, the urban property in Busega and then the land Tom would have inherited from him. Then he elaborated on how he had distributed the properties. Tommy, being the only son and successor, would take half of the land which Tom would have inherited from Miiro. He would also inherit Tom's house when he grew up. Kirabo and Mwagale would share the other half of the land. The widow could stay in her home, the annex, if she wished. It belonged to her if she stayed in the family. The large house, when completed, would be let out to generate an income for her and the children. For as long as she lived in it, Tommy did not fully own the house, which meant he could not throw out his mother or sell it. On the other hand, she did not own it enough to sell either. As soon as she found a man, Nnambi would move out. Then even the annex would be let out.

Jjajja Doctor was uneasy. 'The wife does not inherit anything?'

'Culturally, she inherits through her children. As long as she does not sell, she can do whatever she wishes on their land, because in the end the land would come back to her children and into the clan,' a clan head explained.

Jjajja Doctor and his sons exchanged looks.

Then the Mutuba Head asked why Tommy was getting only half. Did Miiro not know that once you give land to daughters the clan loses it?

Miiro explained that he was aware, but that his father gave land to his sister Nsangi and he would follow his example. 'It is to prevent women from falling into poverty and daughters from being trapped in bad marriages,' he explained. However, Luutu had foreseen this loss and put a caveat in place. Children born to daughters would not inherit their mothers' land. 'It is passed on to their brothers' daughters, who would be their successors anyway. So the land my father gave to our sister Nsangi will not go to her children, it will come back to either mine or Levi's daughters; whoever Nsangi chooses to give it to. And then to their brothers' daughters, like that and like that, through the generations. What we do not want to see are destitute daughters in our family.'

Aunt Abi put up her hand.

Miiro gave her permission to speak. She rose to her knees and addressed the clan heads. 'I'm not telling you what to do, *Sirs*; I am only suggesting.' She turned to Miiro. 'Father, can I suggest that Tom's house is not given to Tommy but remains available, especially the rent, to all his children, but especially the girls, in case their marriages do not work out? Little Tommy here has been given a lot of land. When he grows up, he should build his own house like his father did.'

Miiro, then his brothers, then their sons agreed it was a sound idea, but clan heads shifted uncomfortably. One of them protested that since time immemorial the house had always gone to the successor, to protect the family seat, at which Jjajja Doctor pointed out that the family seat was Luutu's house. Aunt Abi, perhaps buoyed by the support her suggestion had received, carried on: 'I also propose that Kirabo, the eldest child, becomes Tom's successor.'

Ho ho! A wave of consternation spread through the room. Scandalised clan heads clapped so hard their hands almost caught fire. Ndiira gave Aunt Abi a side glance that said *You are bold*. Father Dewo grinned. Jjajja Doctor coughed into his fist. Even little Tommy, who was only walking his eighth year, shook his head. Only Miiro remained impassive. Kirabo hid her face so as not to give away how much she approved of the idea.

'Yes.' Gayi's head was hunched as if she was talking to the floor. 'Why not Kirabo?'

'What did I tell you?' a clan head started. 'Bring women to our meetings and you have brought chaos.'

'They are like children. They speak faa – whatever pops on to their tongues.'

'But what is wrong with you two?' Aunt YA turned on her sisters. 'Who does not know that men succeed men and women succeed women? How does a daughter start to succeed her father?' Kirabo wanted to scream *Stop it, Aunt YA, stop it* and remind her that since men no longer sacrificed their lives hunting for protein or fighting alone in wars to protect their nations, because women were part of armies too, there was no need to elevate them any more. Instead, she made a silent click and looked down.

The clan heads, feeling vindicated, continued. 'Abisaagi is clever,' said one. 'She is positioning herself to succeed Miiro, that one. Ndiira, watch out.'

'Yes, why is Ndiira not in charge of Tom's family?'

'Don't drag me into *your* argument,' Uncle Ndiira snapped. 'Abi's suggestion has nothing to do with me. And if my father wills that Abi is his successor, I will honour his wishes. Have some respect for our father, who is here with us. And if he goes, this is our mother's house.'

Silence fell. It was the type of hush that is brought about when someone who rarely speaks is made angry. There was a genuine sense of regret from the clan heads who had provoked him. Miiro looked proud but said nothing. However, Gayi, who could not protest outright because she was yet to wedge her man into the family fold, spoke into her armpit. 'Shaa. There is nothing to inherit from aunts apart from land on peripheries, forests and swamps. Why should I develop land that is not going to my children?'

The clan heads reignited:

'Have women started to head clans, hmm?'

'Have children started to take after their mothers' clans?'

'You cannot blame the women. It is fathers like Luutu and Miiro here who have brought this trouble for us. They pump their daughters with energy, now women are running out of control, cultural systems are crumbling, and we are lost.'

'Kdto!' Kirabo realised too late that she had clicked loudly.

'What?' a clan head barked at her.

'Nothing.' Kirabo dropped her head.

'Speak up,' the elder said sarcastically. 'After all, we came here to be scorned. Tell us if what we said is rubbish.'

'It is not rubbish, it is just that…women don't need their fathers to inject them with energy to ask for their rights.'

'You see that?' An elder pointed at Kirabo. 'Even the grandchild is pissing on our heads.'

'She is her Aunt Abisaagi, that one.'

'Kdto, do you think these girls will last in marriage?'

'Why would they? They can say to a husband, *How much was my dowry; my father will write you a cheque.*'

'Did I not tell you? Give women chairs and they will make men kneel on the floor.'

Aunt Abi could not take it any longer; she burst into tears and turned to Miiro. 'Father, in reality it is Kirabo who has inherited her siblings, not Tommy. Every day we drum it into her that as soon as she starts working, her siblings' education will come first. Chances are that if she gets a home, they will live with her. Right now, she is the one who visits them at school. She takes them to school, does the shopping and picks them up when I am busy. Tommy, being the youngest, will never look after his sisters, apart from presiding over their marriage rituals. You may not be around in the future. All this love the children are getting is now, but after the shock of Tom's passing has worn off, everyone else has the luxury of forgetting. But Kirabo here cannot forget. Why can the clan not honour the burden that has fallen on her shoulders?'

Before Miiro could even put in a word, the clan head jumped in. 'Because we inherit bloodlines, not just roles and property.'

'Don't waste time explaining our ways to her. If Abisaagi is unhappy with our culture, let her go and form her own, where women rule. But this is our world, our culture, and we shall uphold what our grandfathers have protected for time immemorial.'

'If she does not like our systems, let her go and strangle herself.'

'You do not tell my child to go and strangle herself in my house.' Miiro turned to the elder. 'In this place, she can speak her mind. What you do as a clan head is to explain or correct, but you don't insult my children.'

Aunt Abi stood up to leave.

'Sit down, Abisaagi. It is my land, it is my son who died, they are my children and my grandchildren. I will distribute my properties the way I please.'

'Then why waste our time calling us to this meeting?'

'Because I respect your offices and I would like my children to respect you when I am gone. But you must respect my views too. Now, Abisaagi' – he looked at Aunt Abi – 'Kirabo will not succeed her father, because she will marry out of the clan and leave. Even I cannot alter that.'

Kirabo rubbed her nose. She wished Nsuuta was here. Only Nsuuta would see the ancient struggle playing out in this room: men doing all they could to keep women as migrants on land. Now Kirabo understood why the Ganda considered the selling of family land an abomination. But then again, after Amin's regime, which had left the Ganda desperately impoverished, things were changing. Some 'despicable' men were selling land. And because money knows no gender, women were buying it too.

Later, when the meeting was over, when the only law of traditional inheritance that had been broken was the fact that little Tommy was getting only half the share of land and no house, Grandfather called Kirabo into his bedroom. It was approaching four o'clock in the morning. Outside, the drums were mad. Most people were drunk. Kirabo's friends and Sio were not yet back. She went to Grandfather's bedroom.

'Sit down, Kirabo,' he said. 'I have called you to explain why I did not mention that I gave you Luutu's house as well.'

'It is the family seat; they will not let you give it to me.'

'Oh no, it is not that. Today you inherited your father's estate. Luutu's house was not going to be given to Tom. I wanted to tell you I have written it down in my will. However, it would be good if you started to do something with it as soon as you finish studying. You never know how people, the clan, and even my own children might turn when I am gone. Now don't tell anyone about it yet. I will do the talking. Remember, it is your house. Even when you get married, your husband cannot co-own it or inherit it from you. It is your womanly house. Even your children, because they will belong to a different clan, cannot inherit it. This is why in the past we Ganda did not allow daughters to marry into a family poorer than their own. Imagine if YA's children were poor but I, their grandfather, had all this land which I could not give to them.' He whispered, 'I would be tempted to give them some because no matter what the clan says, YA's children are my blood too. So Luutu's house must stay in the family. Repair it and let it out if you do not want to live in it. Put a matooke plantation on the land. When the time comes, I trust you to do the right thing.'

'Thank you, Grandfather. I will use the place, but I will be buying my own land to build my own house, married or not.'

'You will? Come here, let me give you a hug because you are my own.' When he pulled away he said, 'Now I don't have to worry about you.'

The following day, during the heir installation rituals, Kirabo sat next to Nsuuta. Her friends, who had returned at six in the morning, were snoring in the tent. Grandmother sat with her Timiina family, Grandfather with his generation of family and friends. Mwagale sat with Nnambi and her family. Little Tommy was led out of the house dressed in a kanzu. The Mutuba Head introduced himself by reciting four of his forefathers. As he announced Tommy as Tom's successor and heir, he draped the barkcloth knot on top of Tommy's kanzu. Then he gave Tommy a shield and a spear ('To protect your family with') and a hoe ('To feed the family with'). Finally, he recited four names of Tommy's forefathers, including Miiro and Luutu, and told him to learn them by heart.

It was a ritual of men by men for men. For Kirabo, the idea of little Tommy inheriting her was so belittling, she leaned towards Nsuuta and whispered, 'I'm not calling Tommy Father.'

Nsuuta laughed.

Kirabo drew closer. 'Can I ask you something?'

'Go on.'

'Please don't be offended.'

'Go on.'

'Did my grandmother's possessiveness lead to the death of your unborn child?'

Nsuuta was horrified. 'Who told you that?'

'It has been pressing, Nsuuta. I know you lost a child and Grandfather gave you my father.'

'Listen, Kirabo, be careful. Some people have fangs. They don't talk, they bite. Alikisa has never raised her hand against me. Miiro did not even offer Tom to me – Alikisa did. I expected more sense from you, Kirabo. And before you ask, I fell. My house was new. It had rained. Because I knew I was going blind, I asked the doctors to stop me from getting pregnant again. There were no contraceptives back then. When Alikisa found out, she gave me Tom. She had promised to have children for me anyway. But people would not believe I could have given up my womb. So Alikisa must have attacked me, Miiro must have given me his son.'

'I am sorry, Nsuuta.'

There was silence.

'So why did she take him away?'

Nsuuta laughed. 'Alikisa is moral and she found out I am not.'

'You are not?'

Nsuuta sucked her teeth contemptuously. 'When Miiro and I got back together, Alikisa presumed I would be with him only.'

'I don't understand.'

'I had other men beside Miiro.'

'Nsuuta…'

'What? Miiro had Alikisa. What did I have?'

'Nsuuta, you are too much.'

'When Miiro's family first found out that I had his pregnancy, Dewo and Levi ganged up on him: "How could you do this so soon after Father's death? You are rolling the family name in dirt. How can you treat Alikisa like this?" Dewo would not even allow my child to be buried with Luutu. I said fine. I get to bury my child on my land.'

Kirabo clapped disbelief.

'It was a big scandal. They held family meetings – "Can you imagine what Miiro has done?" Then there were church meetings – "Where did he learn such heathen behaviour?" Miiro gave in. He stopped seeing me publicly. We started to steal moments with each other, creeping about the village in the night. But me, I was not going to sit around waiting for him to steal a moment for me once a week, once a month. *In the end*,' she said in English, '*I supplemented him*.'

'*You suppliwhat?*' Kirabo responded in English.

Nsuuta was cynical. 'You know why you are shocked, Kirabo?

Because women are brought up to treat sex as sacred while men treat it as a snack.'

'Okay.'

'Unfortunately, I did not tell Alikisa. One night a man came to spend the night. But Miiro came too.'

'Two men in one night?'

'Miiro saw the other man and ran. He must have told Alikisa when he got home. Next what do I see? Alikisa growling at my door. Apparently, the city had made me immoral; she would not have Tom watch me bring this man and that man to the house. Ahh, she took him. What could I do?' Nsuuta dropped her head to hide the pain. Then she lifted it and smiled. 'But for me that was not the problem. What brought strife between me and Alikisa was her suggestion that perhaps my child was not Miiro's. That was cruel.'

'I am sorry.'

'It was a long time ago.'

'But Miiro came back to you.'

'On my terms. Why do you think I am called a witch?'

'Ah, you make men do your bidding – ha!'

Nsuuta shushed Kirabo quiet. Kirabo looked up. Tommy now sat on a chair. On the floor sat a girl, the lubuga. In front of them was a basket. Most men had been up to congratulate him. Just a few elders and young men were left in the queue going up to introduce themselves: 'My name… I live at… My relation to you is… We share this great-great-grandparent, you don't call me uncle/grandfather any more, you call me brother/uncle. You are a father, an uncle now…' and put money in the basket to help Tommy start his new roles.

Kirabo looked at him and wondered whether he was overwhelmed. 'Poor Tommy,' she whispered to Nsuuta.

'He will get over it once he realises the immense power he has inherited. It is Nnambi you should worry about; the women trampled her.'

'But that is not the problem, Nsuuta. Nnambi invested too much in her looks. Yes, they got her a good marriage, but now it is gone. She has two children and a widowhood – what now?'

Nsuuta made a helpless gesture with her hands.

'Giibwa made the same mistake,' Kirabo added. 'She thought her looks would plant her in Kabuye's house. And when she realised that they were inadequate, she came to shout at me.'

Nsuuta burst out laughing. When she stopped, she only managed a non-committal 'Hmm', neither agreeing nor disagreeing.

11

After that first encounter with Nnakku in Jinja, thinking about her became too painful. Kirabo's mind took mercy on her and stored the memory away in the subconscious where, unfortunately, it festered. Even after her A-level exams, when she was working at the Ministry of Finance again, Nnakku did not emerge. It was not just that Nnakku had rejected her; the fact that Nnakku looked so like Nnambi made it hard to handle. There was no way she would ever look at Nnakku and not see Nnambi. However, the Monday after the last rites, when family went back to the graveyard to clear weeds, plant new flowers and commune with the ancestors, the thin skin that had grown over the rawness of her pain peeled away.

Before they started digging, Grandfather indicated each grave in turn, introducing the ancestors, 'This is Father Nsubuga, he was a singer – I hope you are resting well, Father Nsubuga. That is Father Piitu, he pinched the ndingidi harp... This one here is my aunt, Baagala, Luutu's sister. She never married. I am not slandering you, Aunt, but you were quarrelsome... That is Mother, Kirabo Nnabbanja. Father so loved her he called her "my gift", Kirabo kyange. She was very dark; that smooth-like-glass dark skin that seems to reflect light. But only Gayi and my kabejja' – he pointed at Kirabo – 'inherited it... That is Grandfather Sserwanja, the last barkcloth-maker. Until Luutu's generation, all our ancestors dressed the nation...' Miiro was not just introducing ancestors to new members of the family, he was explaining family traits, behaviour, talent and looks, the idea that no one was original.

They had been working for more than two hours when porridge was served and digging halted. Conversation found its way to Batte. Someone said, 'Haa, but Tom's death was so momentous it hauled Batte out of his slumps… He has forgotten the smell of alcohol.' Batte put down his Tumpeco mug. 'Eish,' someone added as if Batte was not there. 'He has stopped feeling sorry for himself.' But then Batte he clicked and talked back: 'I had no alternative,' he said, 'not after how you harangued Mulamu Nnambi.' Batte was the first person Kirabo had heard recognise Nnambi as an in-law. 'I said, someone needs to feed Tom's widow until she gets back on her feet.' And everyone agreed that Batte had a good heart. 'Me, I would not throw a coin at that woman if she was starving,' a woman said. 'Can you believe Batte sends maize, beans, sweet potatoes, cassava, sometimes matooke every weekend to her?'

After everyone had thanked Batte, an aunt, one of the many cousins who had grown up in Miiro's house, turned to Kirabo: 'Forgive me, Kirabo, but let me talk about that woman, your mother, Nnakku. Yii yii? What did Tom do to her, hmm?' Her tone said that if Tom's death had hauled Batte out of feeling sorry for himself, it surely should have jolted Nnakku out of her stupidity.

'It is Kirabo,' another aunt explained. 'To acknowledge that she is her mother makes Nnakku seem old.'

'Me, if Nnakku ever comes here – mbu *I have come to apologise*, mbu *thank you for bringing up Kirabo* – I swear, she will stumble on me.'

The men were silent; it was the women promising Nnakku hell and fire.

Kirabo did not contribute to the chatter: no one expected her to. Thus the women had no idea of the fire their conversation was stoking within her. Nnakku emerged from wherever she had been festering and consumed Kirabo again. But it was not the self-righteous anger or self-pity that had consumed her before; it was the different ways she would make Nnakku know what rejection felt like. Her absence, first at Tom's burial and now at his last rites, was indefensible. You cannot sleep with a man, have a child with him and not bury him when he dies. Yes, she did not want her husband to know, but all she had to do was nip in as Nnambi's sister, say hello, acknowledge that Tom had passed on and nip out.

By the time she and Aunt Abi returned to the city, Kirabo had decided that confrontation would not work; Nnakku would be prepared. Perhaps she had been preparing for as long as Kirabo had been dreaming. Kirabo found a telephone directory and looked for Nile Breweries. She found Jjumba Luninze's number and dialled. It was an old directory; she did not expect it to go through.

It did.

Before she could put it down, a woman answered, '*Mr Jjumba Luninze's office, Leeya speaking.*'

Kirabo hesitated. The thing with plotting someone's downfall is that it is impossible to envisage exactly how things will pan out. The humanity on the other end of the phone took her by surprise. She introduced herself and explained that she was a student at St Theresa's. She was doing a project on Nile Breweries: how they had survived the economic crisis of the 1970s. Could she consult with Mr Luninze? The woman asked her to hold while she checked Mr Luninze's schedule. There was whirling on the other end, probably paper rustling; it sounded like a storm. Then it went silent. In that silence Kirabo realised that her mind must have planned all of this unconsciously. It had come naturally.

'Could you make it for three o'clock tomorrow afternoon?' the voice came back. Leeya now spoke in Luganda.

'Tomorrow, Wednesday?' Kirabo was startled.

'The next appointment will be in two months.'

'I will take tomorrow.'

'Name again?'

'Mirembe, Mirembe Nnamiiro.'

She put down the phone and listened to the silence. She heard her internal organs trembling. Jjumba Luninze was real. Her mind said *You have gone too far, Kirabo*, but her heart disagreed: *You need to heal*.

★

At around midday the following day when she stepped through the tiny gate in the back yard, Sio stood under the mango tree. He stood like he had been there since she poured water over him. The time he spent with Atim at the last rites must have given him courage. The way Kirabo's heart was gyrating brought her to the sad realisation that she was one of those contemptible women whose men cheated, but who would take them back over and over again.

She tried to be severe. 'What are you doing here?'

'Seeing if I can talk to you.'

'How long have you been standing there?'

Sio shrugged like a man reconciled to his pain. 'I don't care.' As if standing there, not knowing whether Kirabo would come out or not, was nothing compared to what else he suffered.

'We cannot talk now. I have an appointment with my stepfather.' Kirabo walked past him.

'Your what?' He followed her.

'My stepdad,' Kirabo said over her shoulder. 'I am on my way to introduce myself.'

'But your mother did not come to the rites.'

'That is why I am introducing myself.'

'You found her?'

'Dad's death exposed her.'

'Will you not wreck her marriage?'

'I don't know. What I know is that I'm going to announce that I exist.'

'Can I come along?'

'To Jinja – and who will I say you are?' She stopped. 'I know, I will say, *I am fornicating with this one. Like my mother did when she was thirteen.*'

'Kirabo—'

'Come along if you don't fear the sight of blood. What I am going to do to my mother today—' She demonstrated war. 'Can you imagine – she told Dad, and her own father, that she never wants to see *me*?'

'I am sorry.'

She stopped. 'I, Kirabo Nnamiiro, refuse to be stuffed into an anthill. I have a mother. Her name is Lovinca Nnakku. I did not come out of nowhere.'

'You are very angry.'

'Really?'

'I mean, you have a temper.'

'Am I in the wrong here?'

'No, of course not. Just saying that sometimes you are a hard person.'

'Must have got it from her. Dad was easy.'

Kirabo, walking in front, stomped like a scorned woman. Sio, seeing a chance to wedge himself back into Kirabo's favour, hurried after her.

'Shouldn't you meet her first?' he asked.

'I did.' And she told him about the time she went to Jinja. 'By the way, she and my stepmother look so alike it is disgusting.'

'Really?'

'They are sisters.'

Sio gasped, then suppressed a smile. He gasped again. 'That is why.'

'Why what?'

'Your stepmother, the way you look like her.'

'I beg your pardon?'

'Maybe I exaggerate. What is going to happen to your sister and brother?'

'They are in boarding school already.'

'I heard your family wish your stepmother could find another man and go.'

'No one said that to her face, but that is the feeling. Her children, however, stay.'

'My mum could not take me with her. It was worse for her being non-Muganda, and Tanzanian. They wanted to keep me in the clan. There was a will – Mum and I were to inherit everything – but the clan refused.'

'Can they do that?'

'You are joking. Me being an only child, my grandparents and my uncles are clingy. They feared Mum would make me Tanzanian. They told her quite bluntly, "You want our son, you come back and live in your husband's house. You leave, you forfeit the son and property." The fact that Dad was killed because of her did not help. They also blamed her for having just one child. So everything was given to me, everything. That is why I went to the University of Dar es Salaam: to be with her.'

'Clans have this tight grip on everything.'

'Mum owned our home as much as Dad. Who knows which brick she bought, and which one Dad did? But then he dies and Mum's reduced to a tenant, given conditions by some random clan head.' He paused again. 'Problem was, Mum's people agreed with Dad's people; she did not fight it. But she was not coming back to this country.'

'But you are lucky: your mother would die for you.'

'That is true, but you are lucky you buried your dad.'

'Oh?'

'You have a grave and your father will always be there. Every time you come to Nattetta, anytime you miss him, you just skip down the road and dig around him, say hello and plant flowers. I would give anything for that.'

Kirabo touched his hand. 'I am sorry; sometimes I am so thoughtless.'

'I thought we could talk now that we both have no dads.'

'Who would have known all those years back – that evening we danced Wafula's kadodi – that this time now we would be fatherless?'

The taxi took a long time to fill. It was already one o'clock when they drove out of Kampala. Sio was most attentive. If Kirabo so much as winced, he fell over himself to find out why. Mourning Tom was over, but he treated her as if she was in a fragile state.

He kept asking whether she was all right, whether she wanted to talk about it.

Kirabo assured him that she was fine apart from the lingering sense of guilt. 'I have made peace with him dying; it is the burial bit I cannot seem to get over. I know this is irrational, but' – she twisted her lips – 'I should have stayed a little longer by his graveside. It is as if I threw him away, as if I did not love him. Sometimes I fear he was not totally dead and woke up too late in the grave.'

'That is because you did not see him dead. Same with me, still to this day I expect Dad to come home. I have even caught sight of him in town. Sometimes I'm sleeping and I hear the Morris Minor pull up at the gate.'

'Oh God, that is so true. One time, I heard Dad messing with the gears, reversing the car and I was sat in the back of the car and it was so real. Then I realised I was falling asleep.'

She relaxed. There was comfort in making this journey with Sio, unlike the first time she saw Nnakku, when she had needed to hide her tears on the way back. That day she did not see her journey home because she had been floating in Grandfather's house, hovering beneath the ceiling, counting squares, looking for calm. She did not fall back into the taxi until a passenger called to alight. That night, she flew up the road across Nattetta, swinging on the church steeple, then came down the road, checking on each resident. The landscape was exactly as it had been when she was twelve. Sleep found her in the Nattetta skies and took her.

They got out in Njeru. The entrance to Nile Breweries was a short walk from the road. They came upon the double gate, huge, metallic. Above it, a green lion sat in the middle of the archway which stretched over the gates. They wrote down their names and handed over their identity cards to the security man, who showed them where to find Jjumba Luninze. As they walked through the side gate, Kirabo was overwhelmed by the vastness of the complex. Massive silos, huge storage tanks, large pipes overhead disappearing into the ground, machinery grinding and humming, chimneys bellowing steam into the air, indeterminate smells, beautiful gardens and an immaculate compound. But to her, everything was Mr Jjumba Luninze – concealment, indifference, rejection.

When they reached the reception, they were directed to the end of the corridor on the first floor. A youngish woman, early thirties or late twenties, sat at a desk. She looked up and smiled. When they got closer, she frowned at Kirabo, as though she knew her. She said hello and Kirabo said, 'We have an appointment with Mr Jjumba Luninze.'

'You are a relative?'

'No, a student. I talked to his secretary on the phone yesterday.'

'Yes, I remember.' She paused. 'Are you sure you are not a relative?'

'Yes, madam,' Kirabo nodded. 'I have come to consult Mr Luninze on my school project.'

As the woman found the appointment book, Kirabo turned to Sio. His eyes pleaded with her not to do it. She leaned back and whispered, 'You are lucky: you know your mother.'

'Name, please?' the woman asked.

'Kirabo Nnamiiro.'

Her finger slid down the page. 'But I have Mirembe Nnamiiro.'

Kirabo pretended not to see Sio start. 'That is me. Mirembe is my other name.'

'Your appointment is at three.'

Kirabo glanced at the clock on the wall: it was 2.30. She shrugged by way of apology. 'We thought the journey would take longer. We have come from Kampala.' She pointed at Sio. 'This is Sio Kabuye: he is doing a similar project.' She flashed the clipboard to reinforce the image of a high-school student doing research.

The woman looked suspicious. 'You can wait there.' She motioned them to a seat. 'Mr Luninze will see you as soon as possible.' Kirabo realised too late that Sio was too old to be doing A levels.

Without looking at them again, the woman lifted the receiver off the cradle and started to dial. As she waited for the other end to answer, she twirled the receiver's coiled cord around her forefinger. Then she bent a bit and whispered something like 'Call me back.' As she put the phone down, she stole another look at Kirabo. Kirabo saw suspicion in her eyes and wondered. The phone rang and the woman said in an officious voice, '*Nile Breweries, Mr Luninze's office, Leeya sp—*' Her head fell forward, she turned to the wall and she switched to Luganda. But then the door to the main office opened. The woman put the phone down too quickly. A man who could only be Jjumba Luninze stepped out carrying some files. He wore a dark Kaunda suit. Maybe because his name implied that death was waiting, he looked quite tragic. Her was neither bald, nor did he wear a beard, as Kirabo had anticipated. He put the files on the secretary's desk and asked her to find some others, then went back to his office without noticing Kirabo or Sio. The woman went to a chrome filing cabinet across the room and pulled out a long drawer. She started to riffle through the files. The phone rang again and she was torn between answering it and continuing to search. Mr Luninze stepped out of his office with yet more files and picked up the phone. 'Hello…hello…hello…' He took the receiver off his ear and frowned at it. He put it back against his ear and said 'Hello' again, before turning to his secretary and shrugging. 'No answer.'

'Perhaps it has cut off.'

As he put the phone back on the cradle, he saw Sio and Kirabo. He stepped away from the door and walked towards them.

'Your three o'clock appointment,' the secretary said, before Mr Luninze spoke. 'They were early.'

'Why didn't you tell me?' He smiled at them. Sio was on his feet, arm outstretched. Mr Luninze liked that. He ushered them into the office. Kirabo looked back at the woman, but she was distracted by the phone ringing again. She heard her whisper, 'I don't know; I am not sure, she…' Mr Luninze closed the door.

Jjumba Luninze was deplorably ordinary – paternal and quietly spoken. At first, Kirabo was happy Tom was more youthful, more handsome. But then she remembered that Tom, who had only been thirty-five, was gone, while this old man, well into his forties, was still walking the earth.

'You are Mirembe Nnamiiro?'

'Yes.'

'And your friend?'

'Sio Ssekitto Kabuye.'

'Which Kabuye?'

'Dr Elieza Kabuye.'

He whispered, 'The surgeon?'

When Sio nodded, Mr Luninze stood up, walked around his desk and hugged him. Then he sat down and smiled at Kirabo as if he had not just hugged Sio.

'You look familiar,' he said. 'Where does your family come from?'

'Nattetta – my father and my grandfather were born there.' To distract him from asking how she and Sio were related, she added, 'We descend from Bulasio Luutu of Nattetta.'

'Oh, Luutu the reader. My parents called him Luutu Omusomi because he was well read.' But Luninze was still sceptical. 'Do you know anyone called Kaye Ssemwaka of Mityana?'

For a moment, Kirabo was suspended between fright and delight. It was an eerie sensation, and she wondered if people always felt like this before they exacted revenge. 'Kaye Ssemwaka is also my grandfather – from my mother's side.'

His eyes lit up. 'I knew it. Your eyes sold you. That family has such strong blood that any child descending from their house cannot be mistaken. Who is your mother?'

Kirabo heard Sio catch his breath, and she almost said that Nnambi was. She paused for a moment and plunged the knife.

'Lovinca Nnakku.'

'Lovinca Nnakku? But Lovinca is my wife.'

'Really?' Kirabo overdid the surprise. 'It cannot be.'

The confusion on Luninze's face made Kirabo wish she could take back the words. She realised too late that it was not just Nnakku who would be hurt by her revelation. Mr Luninze, and perhaps his children, would also suffer. 'I have never met her, though,' she said, 'but apparently she is my mother.' When there was only silence Kirabo added, 'Does your wife work for Save the Children?'

'Yes, that is my wife.' The tragic air about Luninze deepened.

'That does not matter, because she does not want to see me. But now that I'm here, can you tell her that my father died?'

'How old are you?'

'Nineteen.'

'My wife is too young to have a nineteen-year-old. And if you don't mind my saying, you are very dark. My wife is quite light-skinned. Of course, it can happen, but—'

'I don't know about that. But if her mother is Solome Jjali, then she is my mother. She was thirteen when she had me. My father's family are very dark.' And because the man had mentioned her dark skin she added, 'Apparently, she rejected me because you would not marry her if you found out about me. But that is not why I came. I came to discuss my project.'

Mr Luninze pressed a buzzer on his phone and spoke into it: 'Leeya?'

The secretary opened the door but did not come in.

'Cancel the rest of my appointments.'

The woman shot Kirabo a savage look before closing the door.

Mr Luninze lifted the headpiece, and without listening for the tone dialled in a number. The winding and unwinding of the phone circle, *krrrrr ha, krrrrr ha, krrrrr ha,* filled the room. Kirabo stole a glance at Sio. His eyes said *I told you.* Mr Luninze turned away from them. Kirabo reminded herself that she was killing the stubborn hope that one day Nnakku would love her.

Mr Luninze caught his breath. 'Lovi? It is me. Can you come to the office right away?' He listened. 'No, you have to come. Something has come up… No, I cannot discuss it over the phone… It cannot wait, you need to come… Okay, I will wait for you.' He put the phone down and turned to face Kirabo and Sio. 'She is coming,' he said, forcing a smile, then, 'She will sort this out,' as if Kirabo had made a mess on the floor and his wife was bringing a mop.

'Thank you, sir, but I did not have to see—'

'Let's wait and see what she says.'

Kirabo looked down.

'Which school do you go to?'

'St Theresa's.' Then she added, 'But next month I will join Makerere to do veterinary medicine.' Luninze had already seen through her lies.

'Oh, well done.' He was so impressed Kirabo wondered whether he would forgive Nnakku. Middle-class Ugandans loved nothing more than a teenager with middle-class aspirations.

'And you, Ssekitto?'

'I graduated in July. Agriculture.'

'You did not follow in your dad's footsteps?'

'No, I have always dreamt of being a farmer...'

Sio was discussing his farming prospects with Mr Luninze when Nnakku arrived. Sio stood up to greet her, but she walked past him. She went to her husband's desk without looking around. It was her undoing. For someone who did not know what was going on, she ignored Kirabo and Sio too stiffly.

Up close Nnakku was mid-sized, no skinny legs, average height, round-bottomed – nothing like Kirabo had seen in her childhood dreams, nothing like the woman she had constructed. She smiled to herself. Tom's chase after a certain kind of beauty had landed him on two sisters. Ganda men loved nothing like a light-skinned woman.

'You have visitors,' Luninze said.

'Have I?' But Nnakku did not turn to see the visitors. Silence held as they waited for her to react. Instead, Nnakku picked up a small paper punch from Mr Luninze's desk and pressed it between her hands. The lever arm folded and she held it down. But she let go and it sprung up. She pressed and held the lever down but she could not sustain the force and it sprung back. Silence was tight now.

Nnakku put down the punch and smiled at her husband. He looked at her in suspense, waiting for her reaction. When she picked up the stapler, Mr Luninze said, 'The girl' – he pointed at Kirabo – 'says you are her mother.' Again, Nnakku did not turn to look at Kirabo. Mr Luninze added, 'Her father died.'

'That I birthed her?' Nnakku finally asked, then shook her head. 'No.' Still she did not turn to look at Kirabo. 'Not me.'

Because Nnakku was blocking his line of sight, Mr Luninze leaned sideways to look at Kirabo. 'Who was your father, Kirabo?'

'Tom. Tomusange Piitu.'

Mr Luninze sat back and looked at Nnakku. She picked up a *Nile Special* brochure from his desk and flicked through it. She put it down. She folded her arms across her chest, lifted her head and sighed. She stared out of the window behind her husband. Kirabo pulled a *She is unbelievable* face at Sio. She had expected denial, but not this childishness.

Sio stood up and went to Nnakku. He spoke British English. '*Excuse me, ma'am, could you look at her, please? At least have the decency to look at her while you deny it.*' He pointed to Kirabo. '*Your daughter's sitting right there. She's lost her father. She needs you.*' Nnakku looked at him and then back through the window. Sio's demeanour changed. '*What kind of woman are you? Her dad is dead. For heaven's sake, be a mother.*' Nnakku did not turn. '*You know what? You're a monster, ma'am. A monster.*' Now he turned to Mr Luninze. '*I'm sorry, sir, but you're married to a monster. She doesn't deserve to be anyone's mother. Kirabo is beautiful, intelligent and hard-working.*' He pointed at Nnakku: '*You don't deserve her.*' Sio was close to tears. Nnakku just stared ahead. '*Come, Kirabo, let's get out of here; she's an animal.*' He held Kirabo's hand and led her towards the door.

But Mr Luninze stood up faster and walked past them as if he did not want to be left alone with a monster. As he picked up a raincoat that was hanging by the door, he said apologetically, 'Look, you are welcome to my house, Kirabo, if you ever want to meet…' He did not complete the sentence and turned to his wife. 'Lovi, she is obviously your daughter. Why would your father lie?'

'I said, I did not birth her.'

'I have proof.' Kirabo withdrew from her pocket the medical chit Nsuuta had given her and handed it to Mr Luninze. 'The hospital chit. She gave it to Dad the day she abandoned me.'

Mr Luninze read it and took it to his wife. Nnakku took it, looked at it and tore it into pieces.

Her husband recovered first. He opened the door and said, 'I am going to pick up the children from school.' He felt for his car keys in the jacket pocket, found them and said, 'Kirabo, as I said, you are welcome to our house if you ever want to.' He walked out of the office. Sio picked up the pieces of paper.

Now Nnakku turned to look at Kirabo. Kirabo braced herself for more spite, but instead tears streamed down Nnakku's face. As Sio led Kirabo out of the office, Leeya rushed to Nnakku's side, protesting, 'I swear I did not know it was her.' She paused. 'But I am also thinking, now he knows, you can move on with your life.'

Kirabo stopped in the corridor and stared at Nnakku through the door.

'How can a woman be so heartless?' Sio asked, as if heartlessness was a male preserve. He held Kirabo the way he used to when they were alone. At first, fighting the tears, Kirabo was rigid. But Sio did not let go. Eventually she gave in and held on to him. He repeatedly kissed her hair, her forehead, and squeezed her arms as if Kirabo was falling apart. Kirabo was aware of the people staring in the corridor but she did not care.

Leeya was aghast. 'Eh, eh. Look at these children. Eh, you, kale vva.' She clapped at them and turned to Nnakku. 'Do they think they are in New York?'

Kirabo pulled away from Sio and asked, 'Where were you when she was getting pregnant at thirteen, hmm? Do you think she drank me in juice or caught me in bathwater as she washed her flower? At least we are not hypocrites.'

'Leave them, Kirabo, let's get out of here,' said Sio, but Kirabo shrugged him off.

'Look at you, Nnakku. Why are you still alive? Why didn't you die instead of my father?'

Sio grabbed her. 'You can't say that, Kirabo.'

'Why not? It is the truth.'

Sio hurried her through the corridor, past the people who had stepped out of their offices to stare, down the stairs and out of the building. By then tears were flowing unhindered.

Later, as they made their way back to Kampala, Sio coaxed her into talking about her feelings. Kirabo insisted that if she had to choose between Nnakku alive and Nnakku dead, she would opt for a dead one: 'A dead mother gives you options. You can imagine and create and give yourself the perfect mother.'

'Look, Kirabo, parents are designed to make us feel let down at some point, especially as we get older. That way we promise ourselves to be better parents. It is evolution. You are going to be the best mother ever.'

'And how did your parents disappoint you?'

'I will not die until my children are grown. But seriously, I will never have just one child; it is not fair. I will be friendlier to residents in the villages. Maybe stop, give them a lift or wave a hello. I know residents have this sense of entitlement that drove my dad mad, but I don't want them to call me Zungu and isolate me.'

12

Kirabo had come to check on her grandparents. But when the taxi got to Miiro's house in Nattetta, she did not call to alight. The car carried her down the road up to Kamuli. It was about ten when she arrived.

Kabuye's compound was overgrown and unkempt, the hedge wild. Flower plants were indistinguishable from bush and weeds, the flower beds were gone. Even the solid ground on the driveway was soft like garden soil. The garage doors were open. Inside was Kabuye's Mercedes. The Morris Minor was parked outside, covered with a grey tarpaulin. There were signs that Sio was awakening from his father's death – drops and smudges of dark oil on the garage floor, tools, spanners and an old tyre lying about – but the state of the compound said he would take time to be himself again. Kirabo walked to the porch and knocked. It was Sunday, almost two weeks since Tom's last funeral rites, eleven days since the confrontation with Nnakku.

Sio opened the door. Before he could say anything, Kirabo pushed past him. 'You know, Sio, you are going to die of a snake bite and we will bury you. Keep growing those bushes around the house and you will see.' She spoke as if bushes and snakes were the urgent reason she had come so early on a Sunday morning. Now she stopped and frowned. 'Do you live alone?'

'Right now I am alone, but a young uncle – Dad's cousin – is normally around. He will soon be back. And Batte. He is helping me with things. Sit down.' He motioned to a chair which was not covered.

Kirabo looked at the chair but was too restless to sit down. Sio explained, 'The compound is overgrown because I decided to supervise its remodelling myself. I plan to get an old woman to look after the house, perhaps a gardener too.' He paused. 'When did you arrive, why did you not call?'

'You know me.' Kirabo looked at how most of the furniture was covered in dust sheets. 'Spur of the moment, to check on my grandparents.' Then she laughed. 'So you Zungus actually do this.' She waved her hand at everything covered with sheets.

'Do what? Don't call me Zungu.'

'Waste cloth covering furniture. I have seen it in films.'

'The furniture is more valuable than the dust sheets. Mum bought them a long time ago in Europe. They are made to protect furniture when you are not using the house.'

'You are lucky no thieves have relieved you of some of this stuff. Anyway, what did you want to talk to me about last time?'

Sio sighed as if to slow down Kirabo's manic pace. 'Sit down.' He sat down and patted the space next to him for her. 'Come on.' She sat down. 'I just wanted us to talk without anger. I wanted to tell you that I am back from TZ for good.' He looked at her. 'I should get you a cup of tea.'

'Do you have any painkillers?'

'On your period?'

'Last day.'

'Apparently, they improve when you have a child.'

'What are you saying?'

'That there is hope.'

He came back with two Panadol tablets. As Kirabo swallowed them he went to make tea. He came back without it. 'Electricity has gone, just as I put the kettle on. It will not come back until after ten tonight.' He paused. 'I'm so glad you have come.'

'No surprise there; you know how Aunt Abi is in love with you. At burial, she saw Ntaate standing next to me and later asked, "What was that kawawa fly doing around your ears?"'

'I saw him too, the leech.' Then he turned serious. 'But what about you? It is your feelings that matter.'

'Me? I'm one of those women who live in denial about their men's cheating.'

'Kdto, I'm not sure that is true, but—'

'By the way, what is your daughter's name?'

'Abla, Abla Nnakabuye. My grandfather named her after Dad, so I gave her Mum's first name.' Kirabo noted with satisfaction that Giibwa had not taken part in the naming.

'I don't even know how I feel about you. My brain says one thing, my heart says another.' She paused. 'It is silly because I'm only nineteen and you are what, twenty-three? And we will both meet new people and forget all of this.'

'I don't want to meet new people. For me, once I'm focused on something, someone, that is it.'

'Aren't you just.'

Sio smiled shamefacedly. 'The Giibwa thing was out of character.'

'You are such a Muzungu.'

'I am not!'

'Hmm.' Kirabo stood up and walked to the end of the sitting room. She lifted a dust sheet and peered underneath. 'What are you going to do with the cars? Do you drive them?'

He sighed as if he had failed to pin Kirabo down but had to play along. 'I have not decided what to do with them. I would keep them for sentimental reasons, but I would need two more garages. For the farm I will need a truck. The Minor is too old to fetch a good price. And I like it. I grew up in that car.'

Kirabo stopped short of saying *Yeah; you never walked on your two legs then.*

'I might sell the Mercedes.'

'Hmm.'

'I have simple needs, me. I dream that one day, after a small wedding, we will settle down here, you a veterinary doctor, me a farmer, and raise a small family – three, four children? Oh, and buy a Land

Rover. I love Land Rovers. We will grow old, die and get buried in the plantation at the back of the house.'

Kirabo raised her eyebrows sarcastically. Then she agreed. 'I guess it would be a good life, good for livestock in our villages, especially Grandfather's. First, though, I'm going to university to be free. Free to do things I could not do at Aunt Abi's – go out all night and dance myself dizzy, get drunk, get rid of this hymen before I get married.'

'No virgin goat for Aunt Abi?'

'Would you take home a car without a test drive?'

'Oh.' He looked down.

'Besides, marriage for us is migration.'

'Marriage is what?'

'You would never understand.' She turned away.

Sio kept quiet, like he had been patronised but was in no position to protest. When he recovered he offered, 'Can I at least hold your hand through your "being free"?'

'You can walk with me. But first, what happens to Giibwa?'

'How does Giibwa come into it? She is not part of it.'

Kirabo shook her head to say that of course Giibwa was part of it since she was the mother of his child, that no matter what happened, Giibwa would always be accorded the respect, rituals and customs of a mother in his house, but Sio was talking.

'Look, Kirabo, this is exactly what I had come to talk to you about the other day. I thought that maybe now I could apologise properly... I am sorry about Giibwa and—'

'Sio, it does not matter how many *sorrys* you say: sorry is not doing it again.'

'That is easy.' He smiled. 'It is trusting me...like you did before that I worry about.'

'Trust will come on its own; I cannot force it. I don't want to be insecure and suspicious about you because of it.'

'I know.' He kept quiet the way one does when contemplating a mountain. 'Dad left some money in the bank in England because of a property in Sheffield. I have money to start farming and sustain it before I make a profit. I am thinking of starting with an acre of toma-toes, another of Irish potatoes, three acres of pineapples, two hundred chicks. Then I can see what works and what does not. Later, once I have the paddocks right, I will get a few heifers. I would like to show you all the land. So Giibwa is not part of my plans. Mum is looking after Abla because she has the facilities in her house, but also to give Giibwa back her youth. If you and I stay together, by the time Abla comes of school age, we will have settled down and she will come back to Uganda and live with us.'

Kirabo contemplated how well thought out, how extremely grown up the things he said were, but... Sio saw her uncertainty and asked, 'What do you think?'

'It is a good plan.' She scratched the back of her neck. 'It sounds grown up, but' – she hesitated – 'to be a stepmother before I have even had my own children?'

'What are you saying, Kirabo?' He crossed the room and sat with her in earnest. 'Abla will not come to live with us immediately. Do you mean you don't want my child?'

'No. I would be the last person to do that.'

'Because you would be punishing her for my mistake.' He paused, overwhelmed by Kirabo's apparent blindness to irony.

'It is just that... Sio, would you still want me if I had a child in school?'

'That is why I never had real sex with you. And I swear, it was not easy with your flirting, but I kept my promise. The world is harsh to a girl who has had a child.'

Kirabo kept quiet because Sio, despite his mwenkanonkano sensi-bilities, was still blind.

'But for you to reject my child, Kirabo, would you not be turning into your stepmother?'

'What did you say? For your information, my father did not have a child with my mother's best friend.'

'No, just her sister.'

'Ekiki—'

'I am sorry, I am so sorry—'

'You say that again, Sio, and I will walk out of here.'

'I should not have said that. They are totally different circumstances.'

Kirabo swallowed her outrage. She was determined to be reasonable. Sio was too deep in her blood to walk away from. Perhaps too deep to see that while he had protected her from getting pregnant, Giibwa had been disposable. Perhaps all the properties at his disposal were helping to make her blind.

'I would never come between you and your child, but there is something presumptuous about you coming up with a plan involving a child, making us an instant family without talking to me.'

'But I *am* talking to you; we are discussing it. Maybe it is because you are young, maybe you are still angry. Maybe we should discuss it after you finish university.'

But both knew it had nothing to do with age. Girls younger than Kirabo, most of whom she had grown up with in Nattetta, had one, two children and were running homes.

'Ever thought that perhaps I would like to be the one to say *I am ready, let's bring Abla home*? Or *I think I will never be ready, I am leaving so you can bring Abla home*, or *I will visit her a few times in Dar and bring her to visit us a few times, a month at a time before it becomes permanent*? If you still don't see what I am saying, Sio, then I don't know.'

Sio was quiet for a moment. Then softly, 'I am sorry my actions have put you in this position, Kirabo. But I don't know how else to do it. I want to bring Abla up myself and I would love that to be with you. I don't know how to say this, but Abla did not choose to come.'

'I would put my child first too, but don't hide behind her so you don't see what I am saying.'

That was when tears overwhelmed her – him making her feel like a wicked stepmother already. 'You know, Sio.' She stood up. 'Let me talk to Giibwa first. It is her child, after all.' Instinct told her that if she did not diffuse this situation, she, Giibwa, Abla and perhaps his mother would turn Sio into a god, the way Tom had been by the women in his life, and start swiping at each other.

As she left, Sio did not stand up as he usually did. He did not say *Wait*. He did not call her back. Outside, Kirabo felt alone. As she walked to Kisoga, she pondered how her blood would not let go of Sio. She wished she had met him after she finished studying at university, after a few disastrous relationships, when a stepchild would seem trivial.

She decided to take the southern path she and Giibwa had used when they were young, the one that did not cross Nnankya the stream, to avoid being seen in Nattetta. As she turned into the trail, a sound of drums, faint, floated above her head. Her heart leaped and at once she was with Giibwa, barefoot, coming home from Wafula's kadodi, half-walking, half-running, Sio walking them. It was a speck of sound, but it hauled her back to a time when life was careless, when her deepest fear was flying out of her body. The drums bobbed again but they were not kadodi. A Muslim wedding, perhaps. They dissolved into the valleys beyond the hills.

The smell of cow urine and dung had not changed. It met her in the same place it used to and welcomed her into Kisoga. But Kisoga had changed. There was a stability about it. The labourers' huts had been replaced by permanent houses with iron roofs. Perhaps the death of cash crops, as a result of the embargoes during Amin's regime, had freed them to think beyond labouring on Miiro's shambas. Maybe the new law which made it illegal for landlords to evict squatters had given them confidence to build permanent houses and settle. But history sat everywhere, on everything, howling. The fact that only labourers lived here. The fact it was called Kisoga was suspicious. Had the Ssoga people after whom the village was named come of their own free will? Now she felt tears in the agitation of leaves, sweat in the sad bend of the bushes, blood in the silence of the hills.

When Giibwa's mother saw her, her face tightened. Kirabo ignored it because humans were like that; they turn their shame into anger. Nonetheless, she knelt and greeted her. She asked for Giibwa. Giibwa's mother led her into the house and gave her a folding chair, the one referred to as mwasa jutte because it was so hard it would burst a boil.

*

Giibwa took her time coming. When she did, she showed neither remorse nor relief. She looked Kirabo up and down as if it was Kirabo who had cheated with her man. Kirabo, desperate to establish that she had not come for confrontation, smiled. 'Hello, Giibwa.'

Giibwa mumbled something, refusing to meet her eye.

'I have come to talk. Let us talk like fellow women.'

Giibwa sat down, her eyes saying *Go on, it is your own time you are wasting*.

'Giibwa,' Kirabo started, 'we were friends long before Sio came along. I accept we fought and said horrible things to each other, but we were children and always made up. But this hate is wrong. My Grandmother and Nsuuta were once so close that what you and I were is nothing compared. But for years they feuded. Now that Tom is no more, they realise. But it is too late because even Nsuuta is on her way. I am not happy about what happened, but if I am to forgive Sio then I should forgive you too.' She paused. When Giibwa did not respond, Kirabo continued, 'I realise that when you got pregnant it was you who suffered, not Sio. I know your child has been taken from you and I think that is unfair. But I can talk to Sio and make him see sense. He says that when I and he get together, Abla will come back and live with us. But I think you should be included in making that decision. Either way, I do not want us to be enemies. It will not be good for Abla. I would like to love your child and maybe become her second mother in future. Not because Sio or culture say so, but because you and I have agreed.'

'Kirabooo, Kirabo.' Giibwa sighed exhaustion. 'Fellow woman? Me and you? How? Look, not all women are women. Some women, like you, are men. You go to school, get degrees, then get jobs and employ women like me to be women for you at home. Some women, like me, are children. I cannot even be trusted with my own child.' She looked above Kirabo's head as if someone had arrived, but then carried on. 'We are no longer children, you and I, when we pretended to be the same. You are Miiro's grandchild, I am the daughter of his labourer. You will be the wife of a big man. And I will be what, your maid? Even that Sio of yours' – she pointed to the door and Kirabo turned. Sio stood at the door. Kirabo frowned *When did you come?* at him, but Giibwa was talking – 'offered to pay my fees to finish my course so his child does not have an illiterate mother, but I refused. Perhaps even my child will grow up to be ashamed of her housemaid mother, I don't know. But what I do know is that I am tired of being helped. Nsuuta and your grandmother made up because they are the same. One was a Muluka's daughter, the other a daughter of a reverend. They both went to school. They understand each other. Me and you, our relationship is lopsided. But for how long shall it go on, for how many generations? Me, I decided to break it.'

By sleeping with my man. Kirabo suppressed the thought. 'But, Giibwa, we grew up together, I know your world, you know mine. My grandmother says, "You see these fingers"' – Kirabo held up her hand – '"they are not the same but they work together."'

'That is an interesting one coming from you, Kirabo. Especially as the four female fingers are not equal to the male one, which rules the hand. But for me the problem is not that the male finger rules the hand; it is the fact that the four female ones are not equal.'

'Come, Kirabo.' Sio reached for her hand. 'You have done your best to reconcile when we are the ones who wronged you. Giibwa is incapable of remorse.'

Kirabo took Sio's hand and stood up. Still she tried again: 'What happened to you, Giibwa, why are you like this?'

'Got tired of being the little finger; tired of you people having power over us.'

'Who has power over you?'

'She asks,' Giibwa laughed cynically. 'We live on your land; one word to your grandfather and we are evicted. The other day the herdsman showed us the cows and goats your grandfather gave you for studying hard. They all have calves and kids. By the time you finish university and he gives you even more you will have a whole herd. I said, yii, but these people: Kirabo has not started working, but wealth is piling for her? Next, you will be ordering that herdsman like he is your *booyi*.' Now Giibwa, one hand on a hip, the other waving about in a classic Kirabo posture, said, '*Why are my calves so thin, hmm?*' She turned to Sio. 'Did you know Luutu's house and land are hers too?' Sio did not look at her. Kirabo owning land and an ancient house meant nothing to him. 'So, Kirabo, thank you for trying, but we cannot talk like fellow women, you and I.'

'Okay, Giibwa, if that is how you want to be.' Kirabo walked out.

Sio hurried after her. 'Kirabo, you need to accept that Giibwa does not like you any more. Look, she even warned me against you.'

'Warned you?'

'Apparently,' Sio said, rubbing the small of her back, where her pain tended to be worst, 'you and the blind woman did witchcraft.'

'What?' Kirabo frowned. 'Giibwa, oh Giibwa. She is like Nnakku – relentless.'

'Maybe,' Sio suggested, 'you and I being together would make life less daunting. Where you don't see, I can, and where I don't understand, you help me. Slowly by slowly, we would figure out what to do with your mother and Giibwa.' He paused, waiting for Kirabo to respond. When she did not, he continued, 'I could say that maybe, eventually, when your anger has melted, you would see that Nnakku perhaps had no alternative but to deny she had a child.'

They walked for a while, silent, heading towards Nattetta. Kirabo's hand sought Sio's. On impulse she stood on her toes and kissed his cheek. 'Maybe.'

At the sight of Nnankya the stream, Kirabo skipped ahead. She felt the urge to greet the spirit. But she was not going to let Sio see her talk to a stream. She walked along the bank until she came to the part where she used to cross. The water was so murky she could not see the fish. It was higher than usual, rapid and loud. The greeting stuck in her throat. Calling streams clanswomen is how myths are validated, she told herself. But her eyes sought the stepping stones. They were submerged. She looked around for a stick to poke them out with but there was none. Kirabo sucked her teeth regretfully and walked back towards the bridge.

13

It was coming to two when Kirabo arrived at Miiro's house and Sio carried on to Kamuli. Grandfather was at the back of the house, listening to *O Mugga Wakati*, a Luganda adaptation of *The River Between* on Radio Uganda. Three children between eight and eleven years old sat around the radio with him, listening. Kirabo did not recognise them. She wondered where her grandparents had picked them up from. Probably, they had come for the last rites and not gone back home. She could hear Grandmother say to someone from Timiina, *If you are struggling, our house is empty – we have good schools close by.*

After greeting her, Grandfather told her that Nsuuta had relapsed. Grandmother had gone down the road to take her lunch and give her a bath. Kirabo asked why Nsuuta had gone back to her house when it was agreed before that she would move in with them. Miiro clicked his tongue. 'When she relapsed, Nsuuta's obstinacy came back. She hates herself. She does not want help. She wants to die in her house.' Grandmother, Grandfather, Diba, and sometimes Ssozi's wives took turns at sleeping at Nsuuta's house to make sure she slept fine in the night.

Kirabo got up to make her way to Nsuuta's. First, she crossed the road to greet Ssozi and his family. By the time she got to where the *koparativu stowa* used to be, the sky had turned dark. Wind was in haste. As she turned into Nsuuta's courtyard the clouds started to spit sparse but sturdy gobs. They hit the ground hard and dried promptly. The earth emitted that delicious but fleeting scent, the one when the

424

rain first touches it. She closed her eyes but by the time she tilted her head to suck it, the wind had whipped it away. Then rain came down as if being chased. She ran. Before she got to the door, she called, 'Abeeno?'

Grandmother's face came to the door. 'Kirabo. Come in, come in, before you get wet. When did you arrive?' She hugged her. 'Have you eaten?' The rest of her words were muted by the sudden raucousness of rain on the roof. Nsuuta and Grandmother had just finished having lunch. Or rather Grandmother had; Nsuuta had not touched hers. She lay on the mattress in the living room, close to the side wall where there was no window. She said something but Kirabo did not hear the words. Kirabo knelt by her mattress, held her hand and rubbed her cheek on Nsuuta's. Nsuuta was emaciated. It did not make sense how quickly she had deteriorated. Kirabo sat down in the place Nsuuta used to sit, and stared through the door into the road.

A gust burst forth. The branches of the guava tree near the road whipped the air. Nsuuta's goats, tethered on the fringes of the compound, stood still. The iron sheets on Nsuuta's kitchen threatened to fly off. The storm was like a straying husband who, on returning home, tends to overdo his gestures of affection. It stopped, hushed.

Nsuuta's voice came: 'Help me up,' and she felt for Kirabo's hands in the air. Kirabo sat her up. 'I want to go in the rain.'

'What?'

'Hurry up before it starts again.'

Kirabo looked at Grandmother, but she said, 'Help her undress.'

'You are not serious.' Nsuuta was so skeletal the storm would blow her away.

Another gust hit the house, sending window shutters flying back and forth. She heard the muvule, close to where the *koparativu stowa* used to be, groan. The angles of the iron sheets on Nsuuta's kitchen roof curved inwards. And then it stopped, clean, silent. Kirabo was mesmerised. Rain in Nattetta seemed so theatrical. Tiled roofs in the city muted the drama.

'Get her a towel.' Grandmother's voice was loud in the hush. 'It is hanging on the door in the back room.'

When she returned, Nsuuta's busuuti had fallen around her waist. The only thing remaining on her body was the left breast. It had swelled lumpily. The skin around the areola was punctured with tiny, tiny prick holes. The nipple had been sucked into the areola. Her chest was pale, but the breast was grey and askew, as if it grew towards the armpit. Grandmother wrapped a towel around her and ordered, 'Get her slippers.' When Kirabo brought them, Grandmother was helping Nsuuta on to her feet. The busuuti fell around her ankles. 'Take a stool outside to the back yard for her before the rain comes back.'

As Kirabo returned, the rain hit again: Grandmother used gestures to communicate. Nsuuta pushed her feet into her thong slippers. Grandmother and Kirabo held Nsuuta around the waist while she slung around their necks. They walked her from the diiro through the back room and paused at the door, watching the rain intensify. Kirabo looked at Grandmother. Nsuuta must have felt her misgivings for she said, 'Hurry up,' her hands impatient around their shoulders. Grandmother removed the towel from Nsuuta and told Kirabo to go and light a fire in the kitchen. Instead, Kirabo looked around the back yard as if anyone might be watching through Nsuuta's mpaanyi hedge in that torrent.

Grandmother led Nsuuta into the rain. At the first sting, Nsuuta swore upon her grandmother, Naigaga. Then she smiled up at Grandmother like a brave child. She felt for the stool. When she got to it, she let go of Grandmother. By the time she was settled on the stool, the upper part of Grandmother's busuuti clung to her skin. She gave Nsuuta a cake of soap. Nsuuta waved Grandmother out of the rain, but Grandmother hesitated. Nsuuta rubbed soap in her hair, on her arms, stomach and legs, then dropped the soap on the grass. Grandmother watched her for a few more seconds then stepped back on the verandah. The wind blew the rain and Nsuuta shrieked, arms in the air, like a little girl. Grandmother stepped into the back room, away from the gusts, her busuuti dripping on the floor.

'Why not change into one of Nsuuta's busuuti?' Kirabo suggested.

'I will get wet again when I go to get her,' Grandmother said, but she watched Nsuuta with such love.

Kirabo had turned her attention to Nsuuta when Grandmother stepped away from the door. She did not say *Look away Kirabo; I am undressing*, as she used to when Kirabo was young, but Kirabo was aware of her stripping her clothing layer by layer – the sash, the busuuti, the string that fastened the kikoy, the kikoy, bra, petticoat and finally, knickers. Next thing Kirabo saw was Grandmother flying past, naked as a newborn, and jumping into the rain. Nsuuta looked up and shrieked, 'Yeee,' as if she had seen her. Grandmother ran along the hedge, skipping and jumping. Kirabo looked back to where her grandmother had stripped. Her clothes lay in a heap. An intense sensation dried her mouth, as if she had caught her grandmother doing witchcraft. Nsuuta's warning about women's nakedness came, but Kirabo's sense of shame held her prisoner. This was her grandmother running naked, not some girl in St Theresa's. Grandmother skipped and danced and threw her arms in the air, yelping. Kirabo looked over the back yard again to make sure no one else had seen them, then she stepped away to go and light the fire.

By the time the fire caught and she had added bigger pieces of firewood, the grip of shame had relaxed. Logic started to return. *Grandmother has nakedness. You can look at her. Grandmother is human. She has desires, like running naked in the rain. Shame on you; Grandmother does not need a reason to strip and run naked in the rain. You are one of them. Nsuuta wasted her time talking to you.* She prayed Grandmother had not seen her shame.

When she got back to the back door, Nsuuta was standing unaided. Her head was thrown back, her mouth open. Rain fell into her mouth. She closed it, lifted her head and swallowed. Then she threw it back again and opened her mouth. Grandmother danced as she washed the soap out of her face. *This is exactly why ancients came up with a Nnamazzi from the sea*, Kirabo thought. When Grandmother saw Kirabo at the door, she stopped playing. As if she remembered that she was a grandmother. Kirabo waved and smiled, but Grandmother got a foam sponge, rubbed soap into it and started to rub Nsuuta's neck, back, arms, legs, and then, carefully, her chest. Nsuuta kept rubbing rainwater out of her face and stamping her feet. Even though the rain was still heavy, Grandmother took a basin and drew water from a barrel. She called in English, 'Ready?'

'Yes.'

Grandmother threw half the water over Nsuuta's back. Nsuuta squealed and stamped, swearing upon Naigaga as if she was a goddess.

'Turn around.'

Nsuuta turned and Grandmother threw the rest of the water over her lower front. Nsuuta stomped her feet, flailing her arms. Grandmother went back to the barrel for more. This time she poured it down Nsuuta's head slowly. Nsuuta gasped and gasped, shaking her head and trying to scream, but she had to catch her breath.

Kirabo bit back the tears.

Grandmother took a loofah sponge, rubbed in soap and scrubbed herself. She finished and scrubbed the insides of both their slippers. She helped sit Nsuuta down on the stool and scrubbed her feet with a kikongoliro, a burnt maize cob. She helped Nsuuta into her slippers. Then she unplaited the knots in her hair, rubbed soap in and lathered. But instead of pouring water on herself to rinse the soap out, she let the rain run down on her. She stretched her arms above her head and stood on her toes, as if to touch the sky. She looked at Kirabo and laughed. Grandmother's teeth were ridiculously white and neat. Then the gap in her upper front teeth, which she had never shared with her progeny. She brought her arms down and tried to touch the ground with her palms, like an athlete stretching. Then she stretched backwards. It was awkward because bending backwards was not easy. It was as if she was reaching into the past to retrieve something. That was when Kirabo began to see her grandmother's body. A woman's body, like hers in every way except age. Her skin, from the shoulders down to the legs, was younger and lighter and smoother than her arms, neck and face. A rectangular patch, the neckline of the busuuti, had formed on her chest and back. Her breasts looked twenty years younger. Her stomach, though small, shook jelly-like when she stamped. Two thin folds of skin had formed in the ribs. Funny, her pubis was not grey like her hair; it was brown, as if dyed with henna. Her legs were skinny but no longer tight. Now, her arms spread out, she twirled round, round and Kirabo feared she would trip. *That is Alikisa*, Kirabo told herself. *She was once a girl*. The Alikisa who Grandmother had stifled under the layers of grandmotherhood and motherhood and Muka Miirohood. For a moment Kirabo was tempted to strip and join Nsuuta and this Alikisa, but it did not feel right. She was not part of their past. Besides, she was on her period. She stepped away from the door and into the living room. The belief at St Theresa's was that every girl needs that girlfriend, nfa-nfe, for whom she would prise open the crack of her buttocks to check the pain up there without worrying about the ugliness. Because only a woman knows how to love a woman properly. Nsuuta brought Alikisa out of Grandmother. Kirabo was thankful for Atim. They understood each other without language, without complication. Even Nnakku had trusted her ugliest secret to Leeya. She hoped that Giibwa had found someone else.

The rain began to thin. When she heard Grandmother calling, she went to the bedroom and grabbed the towel on the bed. Grandmother led Nsuuta to the verandah and Kirabo wrapped the towel around her.

'Check in the cupboard for another towel.'

Kirabo found it and gave it to Grandmother. Then she led Nsuuta, who was now shaking from the cold, into the bedroom and rubbed her until she stopped trembling. She oiled her skin, dressed her in a nightie and sat her on the bed, wrapped in a blanket. Then she got the stool from the back yard, wiped it and took it to the kitchen. She stoked the fire and came back to the house. She helped Nsuuta to the kitchen, sat her on the stool, the cancerous breast facing the door. Kirabo asked, 'How do you feel now?'

'Life has returned.'

Kirabo poked the fire. The embers sparked. The flames were a deep yellow, smokeless. Then she sat down on the ramp to watch Nsuuta. Nsuuta opened her palms and brought them closer to the fire.

'Go get out of those damp clothes, Kirabo, or you will be buried instead of me.'

'I did not bring any. I will have to borrow from someone.'

Nsuuta smiled but did not pursue it. When Nsuuta was warm, she sat back and said, 'You have surprised me, Kirabo.'

'Me? How?'

'I thought you would fly. I thought you would break rules, upset things, laying waste to everything right and moral. I guess you really clipped your wings and buried them.'

'Nsuuta, this is the second time you are saying that.'

'Because I think you are going to marry Kabuye's son as soon as you finish your degree.'

'He believes in mwenkanonkano.'

'Clever boy.'

'And he is not afraid of the vagina.'

'How do you know?'

'I showed him.'

'So that is how he took the sting out of you.'

'No sting was taken. If we acquiesce in hiding our bodies, we allow the myths to stay.'

'But taking away the myths takes the little power some women have.'

'Nsuuta, it is dangerous keeping feminine power down there. Whether it is in myths or in mystery, we put a target on our bodies. Sooner or later, they come to raid. Unless you did not hear about the women raped during the war.'

For a long time, Nsuuta kept quiet. Then she sighed, 'I guess you are growing up.'

'Now you are worried?'

'Nothing takes the sting out of a woman like marriage. And when children arrive, the window closes. Wife, mother, age, and role model – the "respect" that comes with these roles is the water they pour on your fire.'

'Nsuuta, every woman resists. Often it is private. Most of our resistance is so everyday that women don't think twice about it. It is life. Even the worst of us, like Aunt YA, who massage the male ego with "Allow men to be men", are not really shrinking but managing their men.'

Nsuuta was silent as if digesting Kirabo's words. Then she sighed. 'I wish I could see you, Kirabo.'

'I think you do, Nsuuta.'

'I would like to see how much of Alikisa is in you.'

Kirabo laughed and whispered, 'I have her skinny legs.'

'Promise me you will pass on the story of the first woman – in whatever form you wish. It was given to me by women in captivity. They lived an awful state of migration, my grandmothers. Telling origin stories was their act of resistance. I only added on a bit here and a bit there. Stories are critical, Kirabo,' she added thoughtfully. 'The minute we fall silent, someone will fill the silence for us.'

Grandmother appeared in the doorway wearing Nsuuta's busuuti. Mischief still shone in her eyes.

'Jjajja, you look twenty years old,' Kirabo said.

'Listen to this child: I am an old woman.'

Nsuuta feigned irritation. 'Alikisa, for once take a compliment. Me, I am starving.'

'Ah ha.' Grandmother clapped as if she had found the medicine for Nsuuta's appetite. 'We have been begging you to eat all this time.'

She picked the knife stuck in one of the kitchen beams, plucked a few fingers of matooke off a bunch leaning against the wall and started to peel. 'I will boil these in tomatoes and onion leaves, maybe drop doodo on top?' Nsuuta nodded. 'Maybe a dollop of ghee?' Nsuuta shook her head.

When the food sat on the fire, Nsuuta, now warm, asked to be moved to the doorway where the cold would keep her left breast cool.

'I saw my mother, Nnakku.'

Both women looked at her.

'She just stood there, unspeaking. Then she denied. "I never birthed her"; that is her story.'

'Oh, you stop; stop right there.' Gravelly Grandmother had returned. 'You want us to feel sorry you have found out that a woman who has never sought you once in nineteen years does not want you? If that is what you are looking for you have come to the wrong place. My child, Abi, has been there for you. From the moment she heard you had arrived in Nattetta, Abi was there, loving you. Tell me what she has not done. But do you see her? No. Now that your craving has been sated, settle down and love the mother you are with.'

'True, Alikisa, but it was important for Kirabo to see this rejection for herself, otherwise the heart keeps hoping.'

Grandmother looked at Kirabo and relented. 'Okay, now you know. I don't want to hear you have gone looking for her again.' She stepped outside to pick vegetables in Nsuuta's garden.

Kirabo stood up to go. Nsuuta touched her. 'Don't feel down. That is your grandmother's love speaking. She hurts deeply, and it hurts when you are hurt, especially when she does not know how to stop it. Don't tell Abi you went looking for your mother. She is the same. They have tried to be your mother. They might feel like they have failed.'

'I won't.' Kirabo put her cheek on Nsuuta's and rubbed it, then the other. 'I will see you next weekend.'

'Greet everyone for us.'

Kirabo went to the garden and said goodbye to her grandmother, who was still picking doodo spinach.

When she got to the main road, it was empty. Nattetta was silent. That silence that falls after a thunderstorm. As if the world is still in awe. Residents were indoors – men in their bedrooms listening to radios, women weaving mats, children in kitchens roasting and munching maize and groundnuts. The air was fresh and crisp. Dust had washed away from foliage along the road. She started to walk, but her shoes were heavy. They had collected mud as she walked across Nsuuta's yard. Kirabo kicked at the tarmac on the road to shake it off, but it stuck. She picked a twig and scraped the sludge off her shoes. When she stood up, her watch said it was five o'clock.

As she walked, Kirabo's mind went back to Nsuuta, to how nature had melted her body away. Yet she felt neither pain nor regret. Even though there would always be questions she needed to ask her, even though she still wanted to look at Nsuuta, which was like looking in a mirror, to see the parts of herself that were yet to grow, she was ready to let her go. Kirabo closed her eyes to the tears because there was kindness in the way she was losing Nsuuta. Besides, she had this stubborn conviction that since the world had created Nsuuta's captive grandmothers, and had given her Nsuuta and Aunt Abi and Jjajja Nsangi and Kana, there were other women out there.

CAST OF KEY CHARACTERS

Kirabo Nnamiiro	*heroine*
Bulasio Luutu	*Kirabo's great-grandfather, Miiro's father*
Miiro	*Kirabo's grandfather*
Alikisa, Muka (Mrs) Miiro	*Kirabo's grandmother*

MIIRO'S SIBLINGS

Faaza Dewo (Deogracias)	*Miiro's oldest brother, a priest*
Jjajja Dokita (Doctor) Levi	*Miiro's youngest brother*
Jjajja Nsangi	*Miiro's only sister*

MIIRO'S CHILDREN

Aunt YA (Yagala Akuliko)	*Miiro's eldest daughter*
Aunt Abi (Abisaagi)	*Miiro's middle daughter*
Tom (Tomusange) Piitu	*Miiro's eldest son and Kirabo's father*
Uncle Ndiira	*Miiro's youngest son*
Aunt Gayi (Nnaggayi)	*Miiro's youngest daughter*

Nnambi	*Kirabo's stepmother and Tom's wife* *(shares a name with mythical figure Kintu's wife)*
Mwagale	*Kirabo's half-sister and Nnambi's daughter*
Tommy (Junior)	*Kirabo's half-brother and Nnambi's son*
Nsuuta	*village witch*
Widow Diba (Nnaaba)	*village gossip*
Naigaga	*Nsuuta's missing grandmother*

RECOMMENDED READING

Amadi, E. *The Concubine* (London: Heinemann, 1966)

Kalemera, A.M. *Gayaza High School in History, 1905–1962* (Kampala: Makerere University Press, 1975)

Ssekamwa, J.C. *History and Development of Education in Uganda* (Uganda: Fountain Publishers, 1997)

Wandira, A. *Early Missionary Education in Uganda: A Study of Purpose in Missionary Education* (Kampala: Makerere University Press, 1972)

ACKNOWLEDGEMENTS

The Windham-Campbell Prize, for the relief and exposure.

The Arts Council, for the grant (2015) to research this novel.

Cultureword/Commonword, for the open doors.

My mother, Evelyn Kyagaza Kalembe, who shared her family history and the history of her villages, which I have distorted and perverted with happy indifference.

George William Mulondo Majweega (Wabudi), for more family history and for the laughter.

Martin De Mello, whose savage reading of this book ultimately led to a better shaping of it.

Enoch Kiyaga, my Luganda dictionary and cultural reference in Manchester.

My (literary) guardian angel, Michael Schmidt, for consistently calming my insecurities about this book from way back in 2001.

Ellah Wakatama Allfrey, for listening, but particularly for that precise diagnosis and advice.

Vimbai Shire – who describes her work on this novel in terms of midwifery. I am lucky to have you as my reader and editor.

Nicole Thiara, for reading this book and insisting it is fantastic. For consistently telling me that it is all right, don't change it.

Manchester Metropolitan University MA class 2001–2003.

Kate Ezra, for introducing this novel in its rough stages to readers at Yale and for the advice on that chapter.

Cedric Ssebalamu Makumbi, my chauffeur as I did research. And for putting up with my demands.

Catherine Makumbi-Kakiiza and family, plus Sheila – for the accommodation, transport and love while I did research for this book.

To my brother, Ronald Mayombwe Makumbi – I love you.

Damian Morris, words are inadequate.

Marie Goreth Nandago, thank you.

Martha N. Ludigo-Nyenje, who first read this story in its shoddiest draft back in 1998.

Sarah Terry, for the sensitive but determined editing of this novel.

Masie Cochran, for the enthusiasm and vision for this book.

Juliet Mabey, for believing in what I do.

Danny Moran, for the beautiful photography.

James Macdonald Lockhart and Veronica Goldstein, thank you for everything.

To my children, Ssebalamu, Kiggundu, Nnansasi and Nnansubuga, we're enough.